THE
Canary
Keeper

THE
Canary Keeper

CLARE CARSON

HEAD of ZEUS

*In memory of Alan, who grew up in a house full of birdsong,
and Albert, my aunt's first African grey parrot*

UNCHARTED
IN 1855

N

Baffin Bay

Davis Strait

Back's Great Fish River

Cape Chidley
Labrador Sea

Hudson's
Bay

Fort Chimo

Hopedale

RUPERT'S LAND

LABRADOR

York Factory

CANADA
EAST

CANADA
WEST

UNITED STATES

ATLANTIC
OCEAN

0   500 miles
0   500 km

Lady Franklin's Lament

We were homeward bound one night on the deep
Swinging in my hammock I fell asleep
I dreamed a dream and I thought it true
Concerning Franklin and his gallant crew

With a hundred seamen he sailed away
To the frozen ocean in the month of May
To seek a passage around the pole
Where we poor sailors do sometimes go

Through cruel hardships they vainly strove
Their ships on mountains of ice were drove
Only the Esquimaux with his skin canoe
Was the only one that ever came through

In Baffin's Bay where the whale fish blow
The fate of Franklin no man may know
The fate of Franklin no tongue can tell
Lord Franklin alone with his sailors do dwell

And now my burden it gives me pain
For my long-lost Franklin I would cross the main
Ten thousand pounds I would freely give
To know on earth, that my Franklin do live

Prologue

London, June 1841

She still can't believe they'll hang him, even though she can see the hook is dangling from the gallows, ready for the noose. She turns her head away; she doesn't want to look. She didn't want to come at all, but Frank insisted and she's been here since the muggy dawn, jammed between her brother and the belly of a drunken stranger. And now the crowd is seething. A seller of rotten apples boos, impatient for the kill, then shoves her aside to get a better view. She stumbles, almost slips beneath the crush, steadies herself and gulps a mouthful of stale air that tastes of piss and sweat and porter.

'I'm leaving,' Birdie says.

'You'll stay,' Frank replies.

'I feel faint.'

'Don't tell me you're going to have one of your funny turns again.' He grabs her arm, twists it behind her back and digs his hard fingers into her thin flesh. 'Get a grip. Be proud of Da.'

She jerks her arm free of her brother's spiteful hand, lifts her gaze and sees a solitary magpie perched on the gibbet beam, scolding the mob below. The bird is the only creature to give her any comfort in this squalid London street.

St Sepulchre tolls the quarter hour. The crowd roars as the Debtor's door swings open and the wardens and the hangman spill out from the rotten mouth of Newgate prison. She barely recognizes the gaunt figure that shuffles behind, his limbs tethered like a beast. She can't fight back the tears. How can they hang an innocent man? She knows Da is not a murderer; the coppers are all liars. Fired with sudden desperation, Birdie strains to see Da's face and wills him to return her gaze with a reassuring grin that says he can fix this sham; he'll soon be home with them. He doesn't meet her pleading stare. He seems half-dead already up there on the platform underneath the gallows – more cadaver than man.

A corpulent gent with a walrus moustache leans from a window above her head and screams 'Hang the bastard,' his face apoplectic with exertion. Others take up his chant, heckling the gaolers, demanding Da is scragged without delay. Someone lobs a missile – half a mouldy potato – and suddenly the air is thick with wormy fruit, stones, shit and whatever else that can be scraped from the filthy cobbles of Old Bailey. The wardens duck and retreat to the shelter of the prison door. The hangman yanks a white hood over Da's head, eager to finish his business fast in case there is a riot.

'Calcraft,' Frank says in her ear. 'The best squeezer in London.'

Calcraft pulls the sacking so tight she can see Da's mouth moving, in prayer or pain she cannot say. The hangman loops the noose around Da's neck, adjusts the rope.

'Stop fuckin' around,' a bespectacled man shouts.

She curses him.

St Sepulchre strikes the toll of eight. The last chime fades. The feral pack is still. In the dreadful silence she hears the magpie flap as it deserts the gibbet beam and ascends to the top of the prison wall. She trains her eyes on its glimmering feathers so she doesn't see Da drop. She holds her breath. Her legs quake, her vision blurs. The trapdoors fall with a sickening thud. The ground shifts beneath her feet. The crack of the rope blasts like a cannon and shakes her bones. She struggles for air. An elbow whacks her in the face. She lurches and catches sight of Da twisting and twisting, neck broken, red-stained white hood. She howls. The crowd erupts with lustful glee. City gents lob their black hats upwards. The beaver-skin toppers cloud the sky before they flip and drop on the street like carrion crows descending. A pack of baying yobs rushes toward the gallows, eager to reach Da's swinging body and snatch a piece of his shirt so they can keep it as a talisman. Frank runs with the savages.

She takes her chance and throws herself against the horde. She shoves and ducks and, finally free from the jostle, hurtles along the streets, lungs aching and outgrown boots pinching as she flees south toward the Thames. Across the bridge to the Surrey side, the river sullen and grey below. At the Borough, she strikes west, risking a short cut through the dank maze of the Mint where sagging eaves touch overhead and banish any daylight. Thick smog creeps through the narrow alleys. Breathless, she dives into a dead-end courtyard, disoriented for a moment until she hears Da's canaries trilling in the distance. She lined their cages along the ledge of the open garret window before she left for Newgate that morning. On she runs, more confident of her direction now she is guided by their siren song until, at last, she reaches Blackfriars Road. Almost home. But something is wrong. She halts, disturbed by the lack of birdsong. A sudden and terrible twittering erupts. Her pulse races; she fears a cat has been let loose in the attic room.

She sprints the last few yards, grubby petticoats catching her shins, bursts through the front door and runs straight into Uncle Dennis. What's he doing there? Still, she's comforted to see someone she knows; she flings her arms around his waist and buries her face in his chest. He picks her up, sets her on the stairs and bids her wait quietly, for he has to finish speaking to a kind gentleman who is going to help their family. Her most of all. She senses a presence, eyes assessing her cheek in a way that makes her skin crawl. She looks past Uncle Dennis and glimpses the tall figure looming in the parlour doorway.

'God, she's pale,' he says.

The coldness of his voice sits oddly with his concern. She cranes to see his face, but he swings away and steps into the parlour before she can catch his features.

'Who's that?' she demands. 'What's his name?'

'It's not important.' Uncle Dennis rubs his hands and glances over his shoulder. 'Now go to your room.'

He retreats and leaves her standing in the dingy hall; the air holds a musty smell that she does not recognize or like.

The twittering of the canaries above reminds her of their alarm. She pounds the rickety stairway to the top of the house, finds the garret door open wide. The birds quieten as soon as she whistles the melody Da taught her, soothed by the familiar tune. She breathes a sigh of relief, savours the comforting scents of feathers and seeds; here among Da's canaries, this is where she will remain, tending them forever, just as he bade her the very last time they spoke. And she'll have a special care for the Little Prince, the prettiest of the lot with those two black feathers marking his golden crest. Frank had goaded her about the birds and said he'd offered them to the cat's-meat man, so he could skewer and sell them for a farthing a stick. I'll tell Da, she said. He laughed cruelly. Da's a dead man, he replied.

She's not afraid of Frank, she reassures herself as she scoops a handful of seeds from the sack. She will nurture the Little Prince, teach him new melodies, and one day he will become the Canary King, the sweetest songster in all London. Even before she completes the thought, she realizes what's wrong: the Little Prince's cage is missing. Along with Da's wooden serinette. The seeds drop from her hand and patter on the bare attic floorboards. Her eyes dart into gloomy corners as she tries to comprehend what has happened. Voices drift up the stairwell; the stranger's harsh pitch cuts through the burble of Uncle Dennis. She careers down the stairs, shrieking. The front door slams. Uncle Dennis stands in the hall, blocking her path.

'There, there. Stop the hollering. The neighbours will mistake you for a banshee.'

'What have you done with him?'

She pummels his chest with her fists. He tries to catch her wrists, but she's too fast and furious. She breaks free, opens the door and charges into the street just in time to see the rear end of a Hansom cab rattling away at speed. She returns inside, looks around for evidence of the visitor. Nothing, except for that odd, musty smell.

'He's taken the Little Prince.'

Uncle Dennis shakes his head. 'It was for the best. A small price to pay.'

'Why did you do it?'

'He's a good man. A Christian man. He's going to help you.'

He holds his hands behind his back when he says *Christian* and Birdie suspects there is something he's not telling her.

'What does he know about keeping canaries?'

The feel of the stranger's eyes on her cheek, regarding her like a slab of pork, makes her doubt he has much care for any creature.

'He'll look after your Little Prince; he said he'd teach it to sing the finest tunes. And he said he'll find you a school place. Think of it – a proper education. You'll go far with a little learning – a clever girl like you.'

She won't be mollified. 'I don't want to go to school. I want to stay here forever with Da's canaries.'

'You don't know what you're saying. He'll help us.'

'I don't want to be helped.'

She storms to the garret room, eyes wet with bitter tears. Da is dead and the Little Prince is gone. The bird will never become a Canary King. She is at the mercy of her uncle and brother and strange men who take whatever they want without asking. In a haze of grief and anger, she pushes the windows wide, holds the cages aloft one by one, opens the wire doors and tips the tiny birds into the air. At first, they plummet and she is afraid they cannot fly, then a breeze catches their wings and they seem to get the hang of it. They flutter and, as they ascend, they sing. She leans over the sill; the heavens above are blue, the streets below tainted by the city's perennial vapour. The canaries flock and circle high above the rooftops. They fill the air with joyous trills and dazzling feathers until, suddenly, they burst apart and rain on the grimy streets below like a shower of golden stars bursting from a firework. She watches until the glowing yellow specks fade to ash, then closes the garret window. At least they've avoided the fate of being skewered by the cat's-meat man.

Chapter 1

London, May 1855

Grey mist rises from the water and shrouds the hulls of anchored ships.

'Shh. I hear something,' Fedelm says.

The scrawny lad tuts. 'There's nothing.'

He thinks he's clever. He questions her knowledge of the river even though she's been dwelling here for years. There was a time when folk paid her views some heed, but these days even the filthy mudlarkers disregard her word. She should scold him for his lip, but not now when she needs to hear the warnings. She holds her tongue and listens to the slurry trickling through the sluices and the creak of rigging in the swirling vapours. Nothing untoward. And yet, some instinct keeps her standing guard awhile.

The bells of St Magnus strike four; the dead hour between dark and dawn. The leaden sky takes on a tinge of pewter. A faint rush of wings fills the air as starlings stir from bankside roosts. The first market wagon creaks across the bridge. Perhaps she was wrong about the boatman after all. She's about to turn and seek a dry corner to rest when she hears another sound: the regular splash of a vessel advancing through the water. She yanks the seat of the lad's shabby trousers, drags him to the bottom of the barge. He collapses on top of her and they flounder in a dank heap of rotting rags and slush.

'What d'you do that for?'

'Keep yourself hidden.'

Only evil souls and dark spirits travel the river at this hour and Fedelm has no intention of alerting them to their presence. She drags a sodden tarpaulin over the boy's head. He yelps.

'Quiet, you fool. Unless you're wanting us dead.'

He snorts.

The lad's a pain, for sure. Fedelm rescued him from a culvert near the Neckinger and brought him to the shelter of the barge and she's beginning to wish she'd left him where she found him. She turns her back on his cocky sneer, crouches and finds a peephole in the greening timbers. The boy squirms at her side, searching for a crack through which he too can spy. It's a pity the boy is watching; he's a gobby little sod. But she can't do anything about him now without creating a kerfuffle – the sharp prow of a vessel is already piercing the mist. And it's pointing in their direction.

The vessel sits low in the water as if it holds a heavy secret in its belly. It's long and narrow and steered by a single man with a double-headed paddle, like one of those covered canoes that arrive with the ships from America in the autumn. Their brown-skinned owners overwinter on the river, and pass the days paddling around the timber ponds of Surrey Docks in their animal skin coats. *Esquimaux Indians*, folk call them – nobody too bothered about their exact race. Aboriginals.

2

Natives. Name them what you will. Just more of the allsorts that arrive on the merchant ships from far-flung places and hang around the port, trying to scrape a living. Though this boat is not quite the same as those she's seen in Surrey Docks; those are dull – made from skin or bark it is hard to tell – and this one has a faint gleam to it, as if it's hammered from some grey metal.

'What kind of boat is that?' the lad whispers.

'Canoe.'

'An Esquimaux canoe?'

'Quiet.'

'A savage Esquimaux? They're cannibals they are, the Esquimaux. They eat their children.'

She raises a fist in threat, hoping to silence his whine. He takes no notice.

'The Esquimaux is going to eat us, like they ate that girl in Jamaica Road.'

'That's a story.'

Fedelm jams her hand over his flapping mouth, feels his chafed lips protesting against her palm, and squints at the river. Perhaps it is an Esquimaux. She's heard the stories too – there are plenty of them; noble Arctic explorers stranded in the ice floes and slaughtered by the cannibals of the frozen wastes. Tales of the Esquimaux of Surrey Docks turning into wolves and bears and preying on unsuspecting women in Rotherhithe's back alleys. Such lurid stories flood the city's streets as regularly as the sewers that overflow with each high tide. Londoners lap up the scandal. As for her, she tries to avoid wading through shit, so she pays no heed to rumour-mongers, just as she's careful where she places her shoeless feet when treading Southwark's cobbles. Savage Esquimaux and

3

cannibals roaming the darkened streets – these are figments
of the city's dirty imagination, as far as Fedelm is concerned.

But just in case, she reaches for the folded knife she keeps
hidden in her skirt pocket, prises it open and grips it tight
as the canoe eases toward their hiding place. The boatman
is too busy steering his overladen vessel to sense their
presence, thank the Heavens. Even the flap of the cormorant
returning from its fishing trip and landing on the gunwale
fails to distract him from his nefarious business. The boatman
leaps out, hauls his craft through the shallows and onto the
foreshore right below the barge. He huffs as he attempts to
remove his cargo, yanks and yanks again. The cumbersome
object snags before, finally, it slips free. He staggers back with
the sudden force of the release, wrestles for a moment to find
his balance, then flips the bundle on the mud. Now she can
see the full shape of his load, and it's exactly as she feared. A
corpse.

He grabs the body unceremoniously by the ankles, drags
and dumps it a few feet above the high tide mark. The dead
man's thick copper hair spreads behind him as if it were a
puddle of oozing blood. Fedelm shudders; the body itself is
not unnerving – the Thames is swimming with more dead
men than living fish – but usually it's the river's tides that push
corpses to the shore. And then the watermen come to search
their pockets and lug them away to claim their finders' reward
from the cops at Wapping Station. A boatman delivering a
dead body to the bank and leaving it there uncovered for all
the world to see makes no sense. Where's the profit?

There is something odd about this corpse. The boatman
squats by the dead man's head – a flash of silver betrays the
blade in his hand. For a moment, it seems as if he intends to

scalp the poor sod and remove his rusty hair. But his hand sinks lower and he slashes at the face. The lad cowering at her side farts with fear. Fedelm can hardly bear to watch, though she is scared to look away in case the rustle of her mud-caked rags attracts his attention.

The boatman finishes his butchery, replaces his knife in the sheath at his belt and drops the hunk of flesh he's gouged from the corpse's cheek in his jacket pocket. He stands and steps toward the river. And then he halts, bends and pokes the stones with the tip of his boot as if he has mislaid something precious. He grunts. Whatever object he has dropped, he cannot seem to find it. He gives up, returns to his canoe, nudges the vessel into the shallows, wades and lowers his stocky limbs through its open mouth. The mercurial light gives him the look of some strange aquatic monster slipping through the water, spume foaming around the vessel's prow as he vanishes in the mist.

Fedelm straightens, arthritic joints complaining, and leans over the barge's hull to get a better look at the corpse. A movement at her side alerts her to the boy; she knows what he is after, but she's too quick for him and grabs him by the scruff of his neck.

'Where do you think you're going?'

'Gonna empty his pockets.'

'You'll do no such thing. Go near that body and I'll shred your backside to ribbons with my bare hand.'

She thwacks him and winces with pain as the flat of her palm hits his bony arse. He howls, outraged. The tarpaulins squirm and half a dozen dozy mudlarkers appear from under the grimy folds; huge eyes blinking in hollow faces.

He protests. 'We always search the bodies the river leaves.'

'That's no tide offering.'

'So? The Esquimaux dumped him there. And now he's gone and I'm gonna see what's in his pockets.'

'Think, you little eejit. If somebody dumps a body on the mud and forgoes the finder's fee, it's for a reason.'

'You're trying to scare me off cos you want to search his pockets yourself.'

'You'll have some sense and leave that corpse alone.'

She twists away and catches sight of the body below, wrapped in the river's foggy shroud. There is more to come and none of it will be good, she fears.

And then, as if to confirm her foreboding, she sees a familiar figure descending the waterman's stairs by the bridge and heading for the river. The Quinn widow, all togged out in mourning, her pale skin pearly in the gloom. There has been many a time when Fedelm has spied on her from the shelter of the barge, and taken some pleasure from watching over the gawky young woman as she traipses along the banks. The foreshore can provide a useful daylight path through the city if you can put up with the smell. And have a knife to hand. But what in God's name is she doing walking the river at this hour? Does she believe the Quinns have no enemies? Does she think her name gives her safe passage along the darkened shore? If so, she is mistaken. Everyone and his dog knows Frank Quinn's name, and everyone who knows it is scared of him, but his sister is another matter. Fedelm has heard it said that Frank holds a grudge against his sister. The word is he finds her too wilful for his liking. He tells everyone she's delusional, thinks she's smarter than she really is – and he wouldn't mind if somebody did get rid of her, one way or another. Whatever the truth of such rumours, it is foolhardy of the woman to wander the riverbank in the unforgiving hour before the dawn. Especially when a fresh corpse has been dumped there not ten minutes earlier. Has she taken leave of her senses?

The widow hitches her skirt and treads cautiously over the slimy rocks. Fedelm considers shouting, urging her to retrace her path before it's too late, but she stays silent. The river flows where it wants to flow; it's not her place to interfere with fate.

'Fedelm,' she mutters to herself, 'the Quinn widow can fend for herself.'

'She's a Quinn?' the lad demands.

She'd forgotten the stupid boy was within earshot. 'One day your big mouth is going to land you in trouble. Under the sacking and stay there with the rest of them.'

For once the boy obeys, and hides himself with his mates under the tarpaulins, while she resumes her sentry duties.

Eye pressed against timbers, Fedelm watches the widow slip along the shore and she remembers the day of the young woman's birth. How could she forget? In all her years as a handywoman, she'd never seen anything like it before. Or since. The little thing emerged from the womb fully enclosed in her caul, the milky covering unbroken. Some folk might think that a bad omen, but not Fedelm.

'The caul's a blessing from the spirits,' Fedelm said as she threw a sly glance to the woman lying there, exhausted from her labour, and waited for her reaction. The ma smiled.

'The child will likely be a seer,' Fedelm added.

The ma was not surprised. 'It's in the family. A girl?'

Fedelm nodded; men may hold the earthly powers, but it's usually women who nurse these hidden gifts.

'Best kept quiet,' Fedelm said as she broke the membrane with her finger. 'Folk are afraid of females with unusual strengths.'

The ma agreed – she knew the score – then clapped her hands in delight when she saw the pretty lass being pulled from her spectral wrapping. Like a bird hatching from its egg, she declared. Which was why the woman named her Branna; beautiful raven.

Branna; a fitting name, Fedelm thinks, given the babby's tufts of feathery black hair and her nose, which was beaky even then. Unfortunately, it also seems that, like a raven, the widow is attracted to dead flesh; the reckless Quinn is heading straight for the body. She halts, gasps and reaches as if she intends to rummage in the dead man's pockets and pilfer his belongings. What is she playing at? She's as bad as the boy, hoping to profit from a corpse. But then she swoops and plucks some objects from the mud, examines her findings in the cup of her palm and is too engrossed in her treasures to espy the gleam penetrating the fog. Another vessel is out on the river. And with a beam that bright it can only mean one thing; a patrol boat with a bullseye lamp is searching the shore. It's a cruel fate that has drawn the widow to the body just as the coppers are approaching. The currents of the river are not flowing well for her this day.

Fedelm bites her lip. It's none of her business; she wants nothing to do with the police. The cormorant on the gunwale, though, has other ideas; it squawks. The widow straightens, alarmed by the bird's shriek, glances around and is alerted to the advancing vessel. Belatedly aware of the danger she faces, she twists, searching for an escape. The stairs by London Bridge are too far; a skirted woman is no match for a hobnail-booted copper on the scummy banks of the Thames. She swings this way and that, hoping to find a shorter, safer path, and then her eyes lock on the preening cormorant. The widow smiles, and picks her way across the stones.

The barge rocks a little. There's a rustle and rip of crepe catching on splintered wood as the woman hauls herself over the side, drops and flaps like a netted fish. She coughs with the miasma that gathers in the bottom of the barge. Fedelm helps her to her knees and their eyes meet. For a precious moment, she believes the widow remembers her after all these years. But the wrinkle of that beaky nose tells her it is disgust rather than recognition registering on the young woman's sharp features. Fedelm is too used to such reactions to take offence, though she'd be lying if she said she wasn't disappointed. Still, no time for sentimentality. She presses a finger to her lips. The widow nods, and they huddle together at the barge's side as they peer through the peepholes in the clinker.

The patrol boat emerges from the mist, its dark lamp shielded as it nears the shore, and lands at the very spot where the boatman dumped the corpse.

'The Filth,' the widow whispers.

That's what the river cops are called around these parts, for they spend half their time chasing those they claim are criminals through the river's stinking sewers. There's two of them in the boat, and Fedelm recognizes both the ugly mugs glowering beneath the peaks of their flat naval caps. The lanky one is a regular on the duty boats along this stretch of the river; Blackwood, she's heard him called. She's more surprised to see the bulk of Lynch heaving the galley on to the bank. He's the superintendent in charge of Wapping Station, and doesn't do patrol duty as a general rule, still less lets his hands get soiled with manual labour. Lynch's presence is not good news; the dead man must be somebody important enough, or dirty enough, to warrant his attendance.

Lynch barks his orders.

'Grab the head. Move it, Blackwood. It's getting light.'

It doesn't do to waste pity on a stiff, but Fedelm can't help feeling sorry for the dead man as they hump him to the water's edge and swing him into the galley as if he were a third-rate Spitalfields pig carcass. The coppers lumber aboard and row away, the swish of the oars muffled by the fog.

The Quinn widow straightens her bonnet. Her smoky grey eyes search the old woman's face. Fedelm would like to offer reassurance; but it's hard for her to find words that do not ring false.

'Well. That's over and done with then,' she tries.

The widow's mouth twitches. 'It was peculiar to see him there.'

She speaks as if she has an education, though the rougher traces of the docks and the lilting notes of Erin linger in her voice.

'Nothing peculiar about a corpse by the river.' Fedelm attempts to sound offhand.

'I met him last night.'

Fedelm has no desire to hear these details. 'I'm a little deaf, I fear.' She sticks her finger in her ear and wiggles. 'You'd better be getting home, dear, now the day is dawning.'

Fedelm waves an encouraging hand at the barge's lip over which the widow made her ungainly entrance, but she appears dazed and her eyes are unfocused in the way of those who have the gift of second sight. She is in another place, another time. Or else she is remembering past traumas, for she prattles and repeatedly strokes a gaudy yellow brooch as if it is her amulet.

'The dead man. He accosted me yesterday evening, in the Borough. He said he knew me. He said he had a message.'

Fedelm tries to quiet her. 'Shush, shush.'

Still the widow gabbles nervously. 'I had to fight him off. He was drunk. His red hair caught my eye as I walked across the bridge. That's why I went to look; I recognized him. It definitely was the same man. The hair. His freckled skin. And he had *Hold Fast* tattooed on his knuckles.'

'Hold fast? A drunken sailor then, that's all. He must have slipped when he was returning to his ship.'

'But there were marks around his neck. Maybe from a ligature. A rope. And there was something else,' the widow says, 'a piece of flesh carved from his cheek.'

'Hush yourself, you're suffering from nerves. Go home now and take a rest.'

'It's lucky I hid here in time, before the coppers arrived.'

'Indeed, and now they've departed...'

There is a pause, but the widow shows no sign of moving.

'I found these by the body,' the widow says and opens her fist and reveals two coins; these must be the objects the boatman dropped. 'They may have some worth. Please take one for your trouble.'

'There's been no trouble.'

The young woman raises one coin in the air, allows it to catch the strengthening daylight. 'How strange. It's not a queen's head.' She scrutinizes the coin more closely. 'Is that a star? Or a person... oh I see it now; it's an animal skin. A pelt.'

Fedelm wheezes, pats her chest and spits. Of all the dark things she's seen or heard this miserable dawn, this she finds the most unnerving.

'A pelt?'

The widow thrusts a coin at her. 'Look.'

Fedelm doesn't want to know. She's seen these queerly marked coins before and she can hardly bear to think of those poor girls whose lives have been ruined by their transaction. She shoves it away.

'I have no use for such things,' Fedelm says. 'Yours, my dear.'

The scrawny lad thinks otherwise. 'I'll take it,' he says as he springs from the sacking like a bloodthirsty flea.

Fedelm knocks him sideways and swipes the coin.

'Finders keepers,' she says. 'You know the rules.'

'She said I could have it. I don't care if no savage Esquimaux killed him.'

The widow gasps. 'Killed by an Esquimaux?'

'He had a knife; he gouged some flesh from his face and stuck it in his gob.'

'Enough,' Fedelm says. 'He ate no flesh.'

'But he did cut something from his cheek – the lady said she saw the hole. He stored it in his pocket to eat later when he was hungry.'

'Are you sure he was an Esquimaux?' the widow asks.

'Well, he paddled a shiny canoe.' He narrows his eyes; there is something sly about the boy. 'And he certainly looked like an Esquimaux.'

'How did he look?'

'He had a fur hat and straight black hair.' He pauses. 'And his ears were brown and stuck out. Like a bat.'

The lad lunges at Fedelm and attempts to snatch the coin from her hand, but she's ready for him. She flicks it in the air and it spins above the widow's head. The lad jumps. He is not tall enough to reach. The widow stretches and catches the coin to stop it falling over the side of the barge. More's the pity; she should have let it drop.

Fedelm has had enough now; the widow has to leave. She places a hand in the small of her back, urges her forward and holds the boy aside with a foot.

'Keep your coins. Now hurry, please. The tide is rising and you'll not want to ruin your fine skirt in the dirty water of the Thames.'

'Thank you for your kindness. I shan't forget it.'

'Don't mention it.'

Fedelm means what she says. She doesn't want the widow to speak another word about these happenings. Not to a soul.

The widow throws her a parting glance, clambers over the side of the barge and alights on the boggy foreshore, her crepe hem dragging as she picks her way to the waterman's stairs. And when she reaches the bridge, she swivels around just as the misty rays of the rising sun gleam and catch the yellow brooch she was fingering so anxiously. Fedelm sees then that it is cut in the shape of a canary singing.

Chapter 2

Birdie strokes the yellow brooch pinned to her bodice as she descends the stairs of Standing and Wolff's counting house. She finds it reassuring, and she needs reassurance at the moment; the episode the previous morning had left her with a lingering sense that the straight tracks of her life have been knocked off kilter. She can't rid her mind of the dead man's face; the flesh gouged from his cheek. She's had a sleepless night, disturbed by unsettling dreams in which the red-haired corpse arose and called her name.

She reaches for the office door; the brass handle sticky against her fingers – she should have put her gloves on but she doesn't like wearing them in the heat.

The senior clerk calls out, 'Off already?'

'I believe it's six o'clock.'

He glances up at the dial on the wall, then down at her through his pince-nez. 'Ah. The office clock must be slow.'

The bells of St Saviour's strike the hour and cut across his sniping.

'Indeed.' She pulls a tight-lipped smile.

The clerk's cavilling riles even though she's used to the ways of this counting house; the obsession with rank, the petty enmities and resentments, the underhand comments. She's worked here – six days a week, nine to six, half day on Saturday – since she left school at sixteen, when Uncle Dennis commended her to Mr Wolff. She continued working here after she married Patrick Collins, despite his insistence that he could deal with their finances. Patrick always was more concerned with appearance than reality. He wanted her to spend all her time making a haven of domestic perfection to which he could return after his day unloading cargo at the docks, even though their home was nothing more than a damp, rented room in the back streets of Bermondsey. On this score Frank had, for once, agreed with her. She can earn better money than you, he reminded his old pal. Patrick relented. Everybody relented in the face of Frank.

After Patrick's death, when she was twenty, the job had kept her from wallowing in gloomy thoughts and self-pity as well as giving her financial independence from her family. Office work might be tedious but it was far better than walking the streets. The narrow alleys of Southwark were always crammed with three-penny-uprights pushed against the smutty walls; a daily reminder of the depths to which a widow like herself could easily fall and enough to keep her mind on the ledgers. She moved quickly through the ranks – filer, copy writer, apprentice clerk, junior clerk, book-keeper – much to the chagrin of her fellow clerks, who gossiped and sniped behind her back. Mr Wolff had taken a shine to her, they said, despite her beaky nose.

It was true, Mr Wolff did take an interest in Birdie. He always made a point of greeting her on those occasions when he left the company's lavish head office in Bishopsgate and ventured across the river to visit the less grandiose counting house. He offered her encouragement and had been sympathetic when she was widowed. And while he distributed a bonus to all the clerks at Christmas, she also received small gifts; tickets to the Great Exhibition for her twenty-first birthday, a jet necklace, kid gloves, even a fur stole. The attention of one of the company's directors was flattering, of course, yet it was clear to her that Mr Wolff's interest had always been of a fatherly nature. He was an elderly man. He knew her history and he told her, in a kindly way, that she must never think she was not good enough for a well-established city company. Or that there was anything unnatural about a woman working as a clerk. Mr Wolff had seen what the senior clerk was reluctant to acknowledge: she had a gift for accounting. Numbers were, to her, like the melody of a songbird and created patterns which she found easy to understand. Mr Wolff admired these talents and made it plain he very much hoped she would go far in the company. He never drooled over her or whispered unwelcome blandishments in her ear, as other men in the office did, about the beauty of her porcelain skin, the mystery of her grey eyes or the lustre of her raven hair.

Birdie found it easy to confide in him precisely because she was certain his intentions were straightforward. When he had enquired, just the other day, whether she had ever thought of remarrying, she knew he was asking because he was concerned about her welfare. She had been able to reassure him, quite honestly, that she felt no need to find a husband. And when he had teasingly asked whether any man had taken her fancy, she was happy to tell him that there had been one, but she'd thought the relationship inappropriate. He had nodded when she explained her views and said she was very wise.

'One small matter before you go, Mrs Collins,' the senior
clerk says.

She pauses, hand still on the door. 'Yes?'

'Did you deal with the invoice from Hayes Wharf?'

'Yes.'

'Where did you put the papers?'

He asks with displeasure, as if she might have done
something wrong, which, of course, she hasn't. She swallows
her irritation.

'The papers are in the filing cabinet upstairs.'

'And you cross-referenced the payment in the banking
ledger?'

'Yes.'

She is anxious to leave, her head heavy in the stuffy office.

'Back at nine tomorrow?'

'Of course.'

She twists the door handle with the rancour she cannot
direct at the clerk; her palm crackles, her arm feels numb, her
sight clouds and her skin prickles, as if she is being stroked
by a spectre's clammy finger. The familiar tug of darkness
pulls. She tries to resist but the grubby walls of the counting
house dull and fade and in their place she glimpses the
dazzling Crystal Palace. The glimmering Great Exhibition
hall rises from the trampled grass of Hyde Park as if conjured
by sorcery. She tips her head, watches the sun play on the
shimmering panes until she feels dizzy and the sky blackens
and the golden glow of the palace becomes an orange blur of
flames that lick and twist through the arched roof and send
shards of glass exploding into the air. The Crystal Palace is
on fire, she realizes with a jolt. She blinks, and the flames
and the Great Exhibition hall have disappeared and she is

staring at the dull wood of the office door, the handle hot in her hand.

The apparition of the burning palace adds to her unease as she steps into the Borough. The evening is muggy; the vapour from the turgid river has thickened to a chalky mist and the cloud of soot that hangs above London Bridge Station has descended to the street. Everything is ashen. Teetering omnibuses, Hansom cabs and overloaded carts are making snail's progress in the smog. Anxiety grips her; it was as she was leaving the office two evenings ago that she was accosted by the man who insisted he knew her name. She'll feel better when she reaches home. A gap in the crush of vehicles opens, and she is about to make a dash across the road when a twinge stops her short. She glances over her shoulder; nothing to see except a line of clerks, white neckerchiefs yellow with grime, plodding doggedly along the pavement. She hesitates. A bare-footed boy dashes in front of her, across the road and into the path of an oncoming cart. The dray whinnies and halts. The boy scoops a pile of horse shit. She takes her chance, lifts her skirt and runs diagonally, heading for the butcher's with its line of trotter-hung pigs curtaining the shopfront on the far side of the Borough. The reek of putrid pork makes her queasy. She turns right and marches briskly along a narrow street, skirting the decrepit tenements of the Mint.

'Miss.'

The plaintive call of a rickety child crouching in the gutter slows her pace. It's hard to ignore the pleas, even when in a hurry. She digs in the pocket she wears tied around her waist, tosses the poor mite a farthing, and senses again a twitching in her neck. She turns. The mist swirls around an unlit gas lamp. A crow flutters to the ground and pecks at some lump of gristle embedded in the mud. She heads for the short cut across Crossbones Graveyard, nudges the rusty gate and enters. The unblessed ground has been used for centuries as a dump for the corpses of whores, paupers and anybody considered unclean or contagious; it would be a paradise for body-snatchers if it wasn't for the stories of plague and revenants that curse the place. Ma is buried here because she died of cholera when Birdie was five. Da brought her here regularly to lay flowers on Ma's grave, and she lost any of the fears and superstitions that had kept others away. Though it sealed her sense that the dead are ever close.

She clanks the gate behind her. Clouds of acrid fog swirl, catch the back of her throat and sting her eyes. It will be a relief to reach her small room in the grand house on West Square, one of Southwark's more salubrious addresses, but she cannot pass through the graveyard without paying her respects to Ma.

'Forgive me,' she whispers, a plea to those below rather than any God who might be in the heavens; the graveyard is such an overcrowded jumble, it is near impossible to pass from one side to the other without treading on buried bodies, many barely covered in their shallow graves. She passes wooden crosses and crooked angels and reaches the western wall, where Ma's resting place is marked by a limestone rectangle. She stoops, reads the familiar words – *Ellen Quinn, née White 1801–1835* – and regrets that she has nothing to leave on the grave. The creak of rusty metal alarms her. She straightens, pulls herself into the lee of the wall, though she fears her pounding heart is loud enough to reveal her location. Was she being followed after all?

'Birdie.'

She catches her breath. She knows that voice.

'Birdie. It's me.'

She doesn't move. His shadowed outline appears in the fog; the wiry frame and square shoulders, the unmistakable bowler, slightly askew. Solomon. A few seconds is all she has to compose herself before he solidifies. That same old black suit, a little too loose-fitting for a clerk, but far smarter than the greasy jacket of any docker. And as he nears, she can see the familiar curls tumbling around his face and the dark pools of his eyes. There is something different about his appearance, though, for which she doesn't care; his chin is bushy with thick black furze. It masks the generosity of his lips.

'You've grown a beard.'

He strokes his chin. 'You don't like it?'

'It hides your mouth.' She wishes she hadn't revealed her interest. She searches his face and notices the slightest flush on his olive skin.

'It's the fashion. All the men are growing them.'

'You never used to have much care for what other men did.'

He drops the corners of his mouth dismissively, and she can't help wondering whether there is some woman he is trying to impress with his fashionable ways.

'You look thinner,' he says.

He steps closer; she can smell the scent of coffee and cloves on his skin.

'Are you working too hard?'

'Standing and Wolff keep me busy.'

'I can see; your fingertips are all inky.'

She feels his eyes dawdling on her hands. 'I should have put my gloves on.'

'Not if you didn't want to.' He smiles a little. 'You're wearing the brooch I gave you.'

She replies too quickly. 'The yellow brightens up my mourning. And you,' she adds, 'You're still working for the Met?'

He nods and folds his arms. She catches sight of his wrists below the rumpled jacket and pulled-up cuffs of his shirt, the black hairs lying flat against his skin. She looks away.

'Why did you follow me here?' she demands.

'I wanted to warn you.'

'Warn me? About what?'

'The Thames Division have identified you as a suspect in a murder.'

She laughs; a poor excuse for seeking her out.

'I'm afraid it's not a joke.'

She gazes at him and sees his countenance is serious. 'Murder?'

'A body was found on the Thames foreshore below London Bridge. Strangled.'

She wipes her lips with her fingertips. 'I saw a body there, but I know nothing of the man. What's it to do with me?'

'Somebody told the police that you'd been seen arguing with him the night before he was killed.'

Her throat constricts; she tries to swallow but her mouth is dry. Who could have told them that? Would that peculiar old woman or the scrawny boy have reported her? It seems unlikely; the mudlarks hate and fear the coppers as much as she does. They wouldn't say anything to the Filth.

'He accosted me,' she blurts. 'He was drunk. I had no idea who he was but he said he knew my name and had a message for me. He tried to pull me to him. I had to shove him away and run. I couldn't sleep and I went for a walk in the early hours, as I often do when my mind is restless.' She flushes. 'I was walking across the bridge and I saw his corpse below. His hair was distinctive – red. I descended by the waterman's stairs to take a look.'

What on earth had possessed her? Why hadn't she pursued her path and ignored the wretched body? Her head begins to throb. Her legs feel heavy.

'Birdie.' He speaks her name firmly. 'They say you are a co-conspirator. The man who strangled him is, they say, an Esquimaux.'

'An Esquimaux?' That's what the mudlarker said too. 'I've seen their canoes on the river – everybody has – but I've never spoken to an Esquimaux in my life.'

'The Thames Division believe you are the instigator.'

'That's ridiculous. I had no reason to want the man dead nor the means to do anything about it if I did.'

She rubs her neck. She pictures Da, swinging from the rope.

'They'll take you to Wapping Police Station tomorrow morning for questioning, and charge you.'

That was where Da was taken when they accused him of pulling the trigger on a cop in St Saviour's dock. She shakes her head, the gravity of her situation now all too apparent.

'I can't go to Wapping.'

'That's why I came to warn you.'

'What should I do? I don't want to hang.'

She finds the helplessness in her own voice irritating.

'I'm doing what I can. I thought I could...'

He trails off; he still has that habit of letting his sentences drift. He told her once it was because he liked to leave the possibilities open but, at this moment, she senses he is being evasive.

'You thought you could what?'

He wipes his brow, then drops his hand to his side and straightens his shoulders. 'Is there anything you can tell me about the murdered man?'

His professional manner unsettles her.

She ponders, absorbing her predicament. What can she tell him anyway? He knows more than her, it seems. Except. She fumbles in her pocket, removes a token and hands it to Solomon. 'I found two of these by the body.'

He examines both sides of the coin and peers at the strange etching. 'What is that?'

'An animal pelt.'

'Oh I see.' He grimaces. 'Splayed legs and a tail. And those initials on the other side – H and B. Hudson's Bay Company? The fur traders?'

'I believe so.' She only noticed the letters on the flipside of the coins when she returned to her lodgings and examined them in full daylight. 'Their ships sail from Gravesend via Stromness to Rupert's Land.'

'Stromness? You know the place?'

'It's the last safe harbour this side of the Atlantic before the whaling grounds and the Arctic. Everybody in the shipping business knows that.'

He pockets the coin. 'I'd never heard of the place before I looked in an atlas and found it on a map.'

She can't help smiling with the satisfaction of knowing even a small fact that he doesn't. 'What has Stromness to do with it?'

He glances away and she senses he is hiding something.

'How did you hear about this man anyway?'

He shrugs, and his jacket flaps open to reveal a rolled-up newspaper jammed in his inside pocket.

'What's that paper?'

'It's nothing. A local rag. *The Orcadian*, that's all.'

'What are you doing with a newspaper from the Orkney Islands?'

He sighs. 'I found it among the murdered man's belongings.'

'Ha. I knew it. What else can you tell me?'

'I've already told you too much.'

She crosses her arms. 'You search me out, reveal I'm falsely accused of murder then tell me you can say nothing more.'

He removes his bowler; his hair flops forward and she catches the flash of his black eyes through the coils. She maintains a steady grey stare.

'Tell me.'

'It's against—'

'You've already broken the rules by coming here. You can't leave me in the dark.' She is almost shouting now. 'It isn't fair.'

'All right, all right.' He holds one palm up. 'I'll tell you what I know, not that it's much.'

He fiddles with his bowler as he speaks. 'The murdered man is called Tobias Skaill. We had a report yesterday morning, first thing, from a watchman at Surrey Docks. He saw a body being lowered like a sack of flour over the side of a ship; the *Snow Goose*. I was on the early shift and my boss sent me to investigate; get there before the Thames Division show up, he said. The bosun was the only man on board. He said he'd heard shouting in the forecastle and was surprised as he thought all the men were ashore. He recognized the man's voice – he had a particular accent – and said he was called Tobias Skaill. A new recruit. From Stromness, he thought. He went to the forecastle to see what was going on but found nothing, so he assumed he'd been mistaken. I asked to see the man's trunk. And when I looked inside, I found the newspaper...'

He peters out. A crow caws, its harsh call answered by another. She stares at his mouth, the bristles of his moustache; he's still keeping something from her, she's sure. He replaces his bowler.

'And so, you took the newspaper and—'

He cuts in. 'I thought it was nothing more than a drunken argument. That's common enough and I always start with the simplest explanation. But then my boss told me the Thames Division had reported finding the body of a sailor they'd identified as Tobias Skaill below the bridge, and this afternoon I heard they were working on the theory it was the work of an Esquimaux killer and his accomplice, Bridget Quinn.'

She laughs bitterly. 'You see? Always their first port of call. The Irish, and particularly the Quinns.'

'It doesn't help to say—'

'What does help, then?'

'It would help to leave. Go somewhere far away.'

A flash of anger bites her. 'Why should I flee? I've done nothing wrong. Why are the Filth after me? I'll stay and tell them what I think of their spiteful accusations.'

'Birdie, you must listen to me. They've made a mistake, nothing more.'

'A mistake?'

'The Wapping lot are all a bit...' He waves a hand in the air, as if grasping for the right word. 'Incompetent.'

She shakes her head. 'It's a vendetta against my family.'

'Their methods are old-fashioned. Believe me; I know what they're like down there.'

He glances sideways and stares into the mist as if he has heard something. She jumps – she hears it too: the hiss of gas seeps through the gritty air, a brimstone flame flickers and climbs. The lamplighter is nearby.

'Please, Birdie,' he says quietly. 'Take my advice and go. Stay away for a month or two, let them get on with their investigations. They'll discover they are wrong, eventually.'

The newspaper catches her eye again.

'This man – Tobias Skaill – you say he's from Stromness?'

'The bosun thought so. Though the newspaper isn't recent. Perhaps he was keeping it as a reminder of home.'

'Orkney. I'll go there.'

'Birdie, you can't—'

'You told me to go away. Orkney is a long way from here. I doubt the river cops will travel that far. Nobody will know me there.'

'Birdie, take my advice—'

'What makes a man murder someone anyway?'

'In my experience, it's money, usually. But Birdie, you must leave the investigating to me.'

A cat yowls, darts over her mother's grave and disappears in the fog.

'Birdie, please.'

She says nothing.

He tuts. 'Well, there's no persuading you once your mind is made up.' He digs his hand in his pocket, pulls out a small stringed pouch. 'So, take this.'

She has a sudden flicker of doubt; why is he so keen to help her? She rebuffs his outstretched hand with hers. 'I don't want your money.'

The sharpness of her response wounds him; she can see it in his eyes and part of her is glad to know she can still cause him pain.

'I'm trying to help. I can't let you...' He leaves the sentence hanging and brushes her hand almost playfully with the leather pouch. His fingers touch her fingers, and he lets them linger there. Her skin tingles, a warmth surges along her arm, and she hesitates to remove her hand. He presses the purse of coins into her palm and folds her fist around it.

'You should leave quickly. Collect what you need from your lodgings and go.'

'I have to inform Mr Wolff. I cannot simply vanish.'

'Write a note. Make an excuse – a sick relative in Ireland. Put it under the office door. Do the same with your lodgings. Leave whatever rent and excuses are necessary. Tell nobody where you're heading. You must go tonight. Don't use your real name when you're travelling.'

She glances at her mother's grave. 'I'll call myself Mrs White.'

He tips his bowler and steps back. 'Mrs White, goodbye. You must stay away until... until it's safe to return.'

'How will I know when it's safe to return?'

His hand drifts to the newspaper lodged inside his jacket. 'I saw a notice in the paper advertising a place to stay in Stromness; Flett's Hotel. If you take a bedchamber there, I can write to that address.' He adjusts the brim of his bowler so it shades his brow, steps away, and vanishes in the mist.

★

She collects a few belongings, places them in a small tin trunk, leaves a note in the hallway for her landlord and heads east to Borough. Past the shuttered butcher's, across the street to the office of Standing and Wolff where she posts another, apologetic note to her employer, as Solomon suggested. The leaden mist of the evening has darkened and the gas lamps throw pools of ghostly light among the shadows. She intends to take the last ebb-tide ferry to Gravesend, but first she has to visit Frank's office in St Saviour's Docks.

Frank is the oldest of her three surviving brothers. Aidan, the youngest, is her favourite; an able-bodied seaman on a tea clipper sailing between London and India. He returns to London with exotic gifts and fantastic stories. Donal, she tolerates. He is a mate on a ship that criss-crosses the Atlantic from the west coast of Africa to America. Frank, she doesn't care for at all; he still resents their father's favouritism of her, his only daughter. Da had been determined that Birdie should be lifted out of the docklands where, he was equally determined, Frank should remain. And although Frank inherited Da's job as foreman of the Irish dockers on the Surrey side, he still takes every opportunity to throw his weight around and claw her down to size. Which is why she tries to avoid him. But it's also why she must leave him a note to let him know she's leaving town. Better to warn him herself than have him find out from one of his pals. She assumes he won't be in his office at this late hour.

The foul smell of the Neckinger is overwhelming; the stream serves as a sewer for Bermondsey's tenements and knackers' yards. She weaves her way around pulleys, crates and piles of timber that line the quayside. Ships' lights wink in the darkness, a reminder of the deep water nearby. She hides her trunk behind a stack of barrels – she doesn't want to be unbalanced – and edges gingerly along a precarious walkway above the Neckinger's treacherous mouth. The rotten planks sway and give. She glances nervously at the churning inlet below; the water runs blood red with dye from the local tanneries. It's a relief to reach the far end and her brother's dilapidated wooden shack of an office. She stoops to post the note but, as she does so, squawking erupts inside the shed. Alarmed, she steps back and almost loses her footing. The door cracks and, to her dismay, Frank's bulk fills the gap.

'Birdie. What brings you here at this time of night?'

She brushes her skirt, trying to appear unruffled. 'I came to give you a note. I'm leaving town for a while.'

'Leaving town for a while?' He mimics her voice. Her educated accent irks Frank as much as his studied Irish brogue irritates her. 'What are you talking about, sister? Come in and explain.'

He holds the door open; she has to squeeze past his lardy stomach. Inside, she is greeted by screeching and flapping and the acidic smell of birdshit. She surveys the claustrophobic interior; a single candle throws a gleam on a wall of cages, each housing a restless parrot dancing on its perch. For a moment, Frank's office is an Aladdin's cave of jewel coloured feathers; ruby, emerald and sapphire glint in the stuttering light as a hundred birds' wings flutter. Then the parrots settle and she feels Frank's stare on her back.

'Where do the birds come from?'

She's glad to have something to talk about other than herself.

'Donal brought them back from the Ivory Coast. I'm going to take them over to the Limehouse dealer. He'll sell them to the sailors there. I'll make a few bob and share it out with the family.'

He utters the word *family* in a way she finds oppressive, a reminder of her obligations. The ties that bind. She avoids looking at him, scans the room and spots, in the corner nearest the door, a solitary cage holding a grey, bedraggled bird with no tail feathers.

'What about that poor creature?'

'Oh that. I've had it for months. The dealer didn't want it; nobody'll buy a grey parrot. I've tried to teach it a few cusses to give it some value, but it's refused to learn. I'm going to wring its neck.' He chortles.

She steps toward the bird. It glances over its hunched wing, and shrieks a strange phrase – *Skin for a skin* – in a voice so uncannily like Frank's, it makes Birdie jump and check he's still behind her. The bird cackles and it sounds like Frank's sinister laugh. Her brother is not amused by the parrot's mimicry; he grabs an empty whisky bottle from the desk and lobs it at the cage. His face burns with rage.

'So what's all this about leaving town?'

'I've been offered a position as a governess.'

His pallid eyes narrow. 'Birdie, you're looking a little strange. Are you sure your head is quite well?'

She ignores the suggestion she is delusional, Frank's regular gambit when she attempts to say or do anything of which he does not approve.

'It's a temporary situation with a very respectable family in Tonbridge Wells. Da would have thought it a good idea,' she adds.

'Da's dead,' Frank says. 'Why d'you bring him into it?'

'I like to think I'm living up to his standards.'

'Birdie, Da wasn't a bloody saint. The man pleaded guilty to murder, after all. Stick to what you know,' he adds. 'Otherwise you'll give yourself a funny turn.'

The menace in his tone stops her from replying that she has no doubt Da was innocent, whatever his courtroom plea. She tries a different tack. 'The money's good enough to send some home.'

The mention of money softens his countenance. He grunts. 'But what's the rush? Why the note under the door so late?' He leans over her; his breath stinks of ale. He glares at the yellow brooch.

'This isn't something to do with that friend of yours, is it?'

'What friend?'

'That Jew you were seen with a while back.'

Her lungs constrict. She has no air. Why is he bringing Solomon up now, after all this time? What does he know? She has to stay calm; he didn't use his name. He didn't say *that copper*. He is baiting her, dragging up any old rumour.

'I've no idea what you're talking about. The offer came from a friend of Mr Wolff's.' She takes a breath; it was unwise to give him a detail he could check, but it's too late now. 'They need a governess urgently and they're leaving town tomorrow. I didn't have much time to make my decision.'

He pulls a scathing face. 'Well, it seems like a rum story to me.'

'There's nothing—'

'Skin for a skin,' the parrot shrieks again and cackles. Frank dives for the cage. Birdie is quicker.

'I'll take the bird with me to amuse the children.'

She twists on her heel, opens the door and steps lightly across the swaying jetty with the birdcage banging against her skirt before he has a chance to stop her. *Skin for a skin.* She repeats the macabre words to herself as she retrieves her trunk from behind the barrels and heads in the direction of the ferry; she has a feeling she should recognize that phrase, but its origin eludes her. And then she remembers the etched pelt on the coins she found by Tobias Skaill's body, and she shivers.

Chapter 3

Where is the wretched wind? The vast steel steamer has no sails but it is becalmed in Gravesend Reach; the unexpected May heat has smothered the last breath of life from the gaping mouth of the Thames. A skeletal forest of masts and stays fills the estuary and prevents the steamer from departing. The first-class passenger deck is motionless beneath her feet. The quayside is empty, not a porter in sight. Even the loud-mouthed seller of jellied eels has retreated to the portico of the Customs House and slumbers fitfully in the shade. Only the bluebottles stir; their persistent drone fills the baking air as they dine on the water's tidemark of dead dogs and waste.

She stares upstream at the sullen path of the Thames down which she travelled on the ebb-tide ferry the previous evening. The fog lifted as they headed east. She had expected the countryside beyond London to cheer her, but the land became flatter and bleaker the further downstream they floated. Dark wharves and tenements gave way to dreary boaters' yards, stagnant reed beds and fetid marshland. Gravesend was as sombre as its name suggested. She found a room above an inn, but it was too warm for sleep and she lay awake watching the passage of the moon across the uncurtained window. In the half-light of dawn, she purchased a ticket for a berth on the *Empress of the Arctic*, a passenger steamer that plies the towns of the east coast up to Aberdeen. The clerk at the ticket office advised her that the sailing ships could be trapped for days in the estuary, waiting for winds to blow and adverse tides to ease. He failed to mention that the same forces might delay the steamer.

The lumbering beast was supposed to depart at nine, and now it's noon. She tips her face and searches the endless sky for any sign of wind. Not a wisp of cloud in sight. The sun hangs flat and sulphurous like a rotten yolk, and leaves her brow drenched with sweat behind her black lace veil. She wipes her damp skin with a gloved hand, leans further over the rail and looks toward the northern shore. The brown river dwindles into a steaming plain of cracked mudflats, patrolled by rooks and crows. These unsheltered places make her uneasy. Perhaps it was a mistake to leave everything she knows; it might have been safer to hide in the squalid alleys of the Mint where the police are afraid to venture. She squints. A distant regiment of tall poplars quivers, leaves warping, their pale underbellies exposed. Finally, a breeze. She follows its course with her eye, urges it to strengthen; white tips of ragged hawthorns dip, bulrushes bend, cats' paws scuff the water. Her veil twitches. She removes a glove, wets her finger, twists her hand in the air, feeling for the wind.

'Ma'am.'

She straightens and finds herself looking at the peak of a navy cap above a sour face and silver buttoned uniform. It's too late. The Filth have caught her. Her stomach lurches, she sways.

'Ma'am, please do not lean over the rail. If the ship moves suddenly there could be a nasty accident.'

She takes a deep breath, looks again at the figure before her; it's the ship's purser. The blue maritime uniform of the river cops is easily confused with the real thing. She regains her composure. He assesses her widow's weeds with a frankly questioning stare. Four years she has been wearing black, and while it began as a sign of mourning it has now become a defence against unwanted attention, though it doesn't always work. In the purser's case, her garb seems to be stirring rather than deterring his curiosity. His officious gaze descends from her veil and crepe-hemmed skirt to her feet, which are clad in the sturdy docker's boots that once belonged to her husband. She decided to wear them in case she had to make a run for it. She coughs and adjusts her veil, drawing the purser's eye to her face, and surreptitiously arranges the trim of her skirt over the scuffed leather toecaps.

'I hope, Ma'am, you're not distressed.'

Perhaps he thinks she is about to leap; a hysterical widow overcome by grief.

'No, not at all. Though I was rather wishing the ship would move suddenly.'

He shades his brow with his hand and examines her face, as if the revelation of her urgent desire to leave has alerted him to something untoward going on behind the veil.

'I'm visiting my aunt in Aberdeen. She'll be worried if I'm late.' She surprises herself with her easy lies – she considers herself to be honest.

'If you've an aunt in Aberdeen...' the purser places an unnerving emphasis on the *if*, 'she'll be used to the delays in the passage of the steamer.'

The wind tweaks her veil again. She anchors it with her hand.

'Anyway, Ma'am, your wish to move might soon be satisfied if this breeze picks up.'

Even as he finishes his sentence, the estuary ripples. The breath of wind fills the barricade of stationary ships with life; whistles blast, sailors swarm the rigging, great white sails unfurl and billow like birds stretching their wings, ready for flight.

The purser waves a pudgy hand at the congestion. 'Once this lot has shifted, we can be on our way.'

Church bells peal. A cannon booms. She stoops instinctively.

'No need to duck, Ma'am. It's the signal that the Bay ships are ready to depart.'

'Hudson's Bay?'

'Those four ships there, flying the Red Ensign.' He continues, thankfully not perceiving the alarm in her voice, and gestures at a cluster of schooners in the middle of the river. She restrains her fingers from drifting nervously to the pocket which contains the remaining coin she found by Tobias Skaill's corpse, etched with the Company's initials.

'Those ships are sailing to Rupert's Land?'

'That's where Hudson's Bay is located, I believe.'

His patronizing tone rankles; she bites her lip. Another blast of cannon fire ricochets around the estuary. This time, she manages not to quail.

'Friendly word of warning,' the purser says. 'Best not be on deck when the paddlewheels get going.'

'Oh? I heard the paddles were quite a sight.'

'From the shore maybe – the boxing masks the view from the deck. But it's not the sight you want to avoid, Ma'am. It's the other senses that a fine lady like yourself mightn't find quite so pleasant.'

He touches his cap with a gesture of deference, turns his back to her and waddles off. *Fine lady.* Was he mocking her? Had he seen through her thin disguise and guessed she was an Irish docker's daughter, not quite accustomed to the ways of the first-class passenger deck?

She waits for the purser to ingratiate himself with a gentleman sporting a frock coat and top hat and leans over the rail again. The wind prods the river; rowing boats pull through its thickness, carrying pilots to guide the ships through the estuary's hidden banks and currents. Mizzens and mainsails unfurl. Above, the towering funnel of the streamer belches black smoke, staining the blueness of the sky. Surely the ship is about to depart.

Shouting from the harbour attracts her attention. She hitches her skirt a decent half inch, and crosses the beam of the deck to the starboard railing. The quay, like the river, has been revitalized by the first puff of wind. Skin-and-bone stray dogs that had been panting in the dwindling shade yap and chase their tails. Porters shout at passengers to mind their backs as they trundle luggage carts across the sweltering ground. Women and children wait to wave white hankies at departing loved ones. A ragged newspaper boy meanders barefoot through the melee.

'Read all about it. Esquimaux murderer on the loose.'

She blanches. Passengers heading for ferries turn as he passes, grabbed by the headline. Men dig into their pockets, hand over coins in return for a copy of *The Times*.

'Latest news. Esquimaux murderer and his wicked accomplice.'

Sweat dribbles down her spine. She cannot breathe. She has no air. She wills the boy not to repeat the headline.

'Read all about it. Latest news. Cannibal on the loose.'

Shut it, will you? Close that loose trap of yours. He looks up at her as if he had heard her silent command, waves a rolled-up newspaper in her direction.

'*The Times*. Murder. Esquimaux cannibal.' He has an unfortunately loud voice for such a tiny shrimp. She nods at him, waves her hand, heads toward the gangplank and descends three-quarters of the way. The gusts agitate the water; the steamer pitches and the stairs scrape back and forth across the quay. Her legs are unsteady and her stomach is lurching, but she has to have a copy of the lousy *Times*. She senses eyes on her back. She twists around. The purser. She wishes he would go to hell. She places one hand on the rope bannister to steady herself, reaches in her pocket for coins with the other and presses them in the boy's cupped palm. He passes her the rolled paper, then stretches toward her as if he has an urgent message to impart. Has he heard something about her? Does every grubby newspaper boy in the south of England know her name?

'Full story of the cannibal killer on the inside pages. Gory bits and all.'

She attempts a smile, an effort that is wasted on the boy because he cannot see past the veil.

'Thank you.'

She slips him another coin, relief making her giddy with her money.

'Thank you, Ma'am. I know how much the ladies love a murder.'

He slinks back into the bustling crowds. She watches him retreat and her eye is drawn across the mooring ropes, past the porters and the carriages, to the narrow opening between the Union Jack Inn and the Customs House. The jellied eel seller is doing brisk business. And beyond, in the distance, two men in blue are striding down the hill in the direction of the harbour, their peaked flat caps visible even from afar. The Filth. She wipes the back of her neck. A sailor trots along the quayside to the steamer's rope moorings, loosens a knot.

'Lady, are you embarking or disembarking?'

'Embarking.'

She hurriedly ascends under the unwelcome gaze of the purser. A crewman in a threadbare uniform hauls the gangplank inside. The funnel spews another trail of black smoke. She heads back to the first-class passenger deck, hangs on to the port rail with one hand, and clutches her copy of *The Times* with the other. Her heart thumps.

She's too busy willing the steamer's departure to notice the upright gentleman wearing a tall beaver bearing down on her until it's too late to move. He brandishes a copy of *The Times*.

'Madam, I see you're travelling alone.'

She nods in what she hopes is a meek but discouraging manner; she doesn't want to talk to him, yet she shouldn't appear defiant. It is a thin line she treads and, on this occasion, she's not entirely surefooted. The gentleman sidles closer and nods at the paper she is holding. 'I see you have the newspaper. There's a report of a murderer on the loose,' he says, as if he thinks she might not be able to read the headline.

'An Esquimaux at large on the Thames. A cannibal. You must make sure your cabin door is locked.'

She could do without his advice, though she is relieved his interest is in the Esquimaux murderer and not the reported accomplice.

'Thank you,' she says. 'I will.'

'Not entirely surprising, of course,' her uninvited companion continues. 'It's the price we pay for the success of the port; bound to happen when so many ships are arriving from all corners of the world. Some of their crews are little more than savages.'

She positions herself so she can peek over his shoulder to watch the advancing coppers.

'I don't always agree with Dickens, but I have to say on this point I believe he's correct. You're probably not aware of his article about Franklin and his crew.'

'In fact, Sir,' she offers, 'I did read it.' Along with all of London's coffee house gossipers who imbibe Dickens' every word with their sooty beverages. It's his biting wit they admire. And there's hardly a person in London who has not been intrigued by the fate of Sir John Franklin; the two ships searching for the North-West Passage left London in 1845, sailed toward the Polar Regions, entered Baffin Bay and were never seen again. They simply vanished. None of the many expeditions sent to find them could discover a single trace. Until last year – nearly ten years after the *Terror* and the *Erebus* set sail – when the explorer Dr Rae reported to the Admiralty that he had been given remains from the doomed, ice-trapped ships by a band of passing Esquimaux – and they had told him the starving officers had resorted to eating their dead colleagues' flesh to keep themselves alive.

Dr Rae's account was printed on the front page of *The Times* last October and caused immediate uproar. Dickens' scathing riposte was published in the December editions of *Household Words*. Debate about Englishmen and cannibals raged in London's coffee houses for weeks. The whole gruesome episode is still more talked about on the streets of the capital than the progress of the Crimean War.

'That Scot – Rae,' the gentleman says and flaps his hand. 'Repeating stories told to him by the Esquimaux without checking their veracity.'

'I did wonder whether...'

But the haughty gentleman is less interested in her views than in expounding his own.

'Yes, I have to agree with Dickens on this,' he continues. 'Sir John and his crew were civilized Englishmen, risking their lives in the name of science and exploration. Queen and country.'

She watches a cormorant flying upstream with an eel dangling from its hooked beak, and says nothing.

'Eating another man's flesh would be unthinkable to such Christian gentlemen. Dickens is undoubtedly correct to suppose the starving explorers were attacked and killed by the barbaric Esquimaux. That's the way savages behave, I'm afraid. And this terrible report of an Esquimaux murderer proves the point. Savages. Cannibals.' He points the rolled-up *Times* at the sluggish water. 'And now they're here, running amok on the Thames.'

'Everything all right, Sir?'

The purser has crept up behind them.

'Indeed. Just warning this unaccompanied lady to be careful and make sure she locks her cabin door. Too many strange men around to take chances.'

'Sound advice, Sir.'

'And where, Madam,' the gentleman asks her, 'are you heading?'

'Aberdeen.'

'So far north? Well, at least the Scots are of the Christian faith.'

'Are they, Sir?' the purser interjects. 'I've heard they're all witches up there.'

The anchor chain scrapes through the hawseholes.

'Are we about to leave?' She cannot disguise the desperation in her voice; the coppers have now passed the Union Jack public house and are making for the steamer. The purser lifts his head, scans the harbour and catches sight of the men in blue.

'It looks like there might be a delay. I wonder what they're after. Or whom.' He glances her way. Sweat makes her thighs clammy beneath her petticoats. Black dots dance like clouds of flies before her eyes. The shriek of a whistle pierces her dizziness.

'Is that us?' Her voice is faint.

The purser ignores her; he is watching the cops pushing through the throng. The larger officer raises his hand as if he is about to order the steamer to halt. He opens his mouth. Rushing and splashing drown out his command. The paddles of the vast steamer wheel rise, lifting streams of water from the depths of the Thames. A putrid odour fills the air; it's worse than Bermondsey after a spring tide when the Neckinger has flooded. A lady standing on the portside of the steamer's deck screams and buckles. The officer lowers his hand from its peremptory mid-air wave to cover his nose and mouth. His skinny companion searches his pockets frantically.

The purser retches and flaps his palm in front of his face. 'Blimey, it's bad today. Must be the ruddy heat.'

The gentleman fans his copy of *The Times* as he scurries for the companionway, without a word of farewell.

'I did warn you to go inside,' the purser tells Birdie. 'It's the city's dirt; it gets carried downstream and ends up at the bottom of the river in Gravesend. The paddle wheels dredge it up.'

He jabs his finger, directs her to the stairs. The steamer shudders, the paddlewheels rotate with urgency, the reek intensifies. She holds her breath and glances over her shoulder at the quayside as she heads for her cabin; the scrawny cop is offering his boss a handkerchief to cover his nose. He takes it, straightens and stares menacingly at the departing steamer. Too late, mate. You've missed your chance.

She closes the cabin door firmly, locks it, removes her veiled bonnet and gloves, throws herself on her tiny bunk, and assesses her surroundings. Cramped, even though she is travelling first class and all she has in the way of baggage is one small tin trunk and a caged parrot, but relatively clean with enough sunlight spilling through the porthole to dispel any lingering dinginess. She can smell how fortunate it is she had enough cash to avoid steerage. The stink of sewage is not as rank as it was on the deck, but it penetrates the hull. A berth below the water line wouldn't have been pleasant. Thank God for Solomon's purse full of sovereigns.

'Solly,' she says, then glances at the parrot, embarrassed to have revealed the pet name she used for him, even if it is only in front of a bird. Her hand rises instinctively

43

to touch the brooch pinned to her mourning dress. She's worn it every day for nearly two years. Every day, in fact, since she told Solomon she no longer wished to see him. She had been certain, at the time, it was the right thing to do, even though her feelings hadn't been straightforward. She's not sure how she feels about meeting him again now either, particularly in such strange circumstances: emerging from the shadows to warn her she was in danger then behaving shiftily, as if he had some information he could not reveal.

Solomon and his work had always been something of an enigma, she reminds herself. It was what attracted her in the first place; she'd found his mystery appealing after the cosy familiarity of Patrick. When she first met Solomon, she'd only recently been widowed. The death of her husband had left her sinking; Solomon's offer of friendship had been a life raft. She'd been surprised, though, to find herself swept away by his charms. Their secret trysts in secluded places brightened up her life and gave the grimy streets of London a dusting of enchantment. It took her a while to realize she was out of her depth and needed to return to the safety of known land. Even if she wasn't worried about Frank's reaction, she would have come to the same conclusion. But, as it was, she knew she had to act swiftly because Frank's wife had been waiting for her when she left the office one evening, and had whispered she'd been seen walking with a stranger who was dark enough to be a Greek. Or even a Jew. God only knows what Frank would have done if he'd discovered the dark stranger was a copper. She lets her hand drop from the brooch, shakes her head, reaches for *The Times* and reads the headline story.

Thames Division police investigating the murder of Tobias Skaill, a sailor from the Orkney Islands, have indicated that the ruthless killer is thought to be of the savage tribe of Esquimaux, who travelled from his native Arctic home aboard a merchant vessel. The unfortunate victim's corpse showed signs of having been attacked by a barbaric cannibal. Superintendent Lynch of the Thames Division has further indicated that there might be an accomplice, or an instigator, involved. They have grounds to believe this person is a woman of Irish descent who is known to have argued with the victim the evening before the murder took place. Superintendent Lynch said that, regrettably, women of the communities of his fellow countrymen from across the water are often of low intelligence and moral fibre, but high cunning. Unfortunately, he suspects the woman in question is likely to fit the profile, with which he is all too familiar, of criminal tendencies that are passed from generation to generation, particularly among those Irish families that settle around the docks.

She folds the paper, fans her face, an action that fails to dispel the lingering aroma of sewage. *A woman of Irish descent who is known to have argued with the victim the evening before the murder took place.* The air is stifling, she cannot breathe. She drops the paper, pulls at the collar of her dress; it's too tight.

'What am I going to do?' she asks the parrot.

The parrot doesn't answer. She regards the bird, the dull grey of its plumage, the stubby feathers at the base of its back that it has niggled and plucked. The mangy creature fluffs its wings, preens its stomach with its cracked black beak. She has to pull herself together; at least *The Times* didn't report she was a widow and neither did it mention her name. She purchased her ticket as Mrs White, which doesn't sound as Irish as Collins or, indeed, Quinn. With any luck, this will throw the river cops off her scent if they ask to see the steamer's passenger manifest.

Luck, that's something she thought she possessed – a steady job, kindly employer, comfortable lodgings; rare commodities in London which all dropped into her lap. But good fortune seems to have deserted her these last few days. Her fingers reach for her pocket and she fiddles with the coin; she wonders what it signifies. Perhaps it's an evil charm: the change in her fortunes certainly seems to coincide with the moment she spotted the two tokens and the Filth appeared. And that queer old woman with the cormorant – she refused to take one. She removes her hand from her pocket and gazes at the dowdy bird. Tears trickle down her cheeks. The parrot tuts. She wipes her eyes; she can't afford self-pity.

'I'm not going to hang,' she says.

'Skin for a skin,' the parrot replies, and cackles like her brother.

Chapter 4

Maudlin Aberdeen dwindles in the distance and her spirits lift. Six days since she left Gravesend, two spent in Aberdeen searching for a passage to Orkney; it's a relief to be on the deck of a mail packet, the *Dog Star*, heading to Stromness. At Wick, a pilot rows out to guide them through the Pentland Firth. He clambers aboard and his dinghy is towed behind. No ship dares sail this hazardous stretch of ocean without the assistance of a pilot who knows its treacherous currents and tides.

Out in open water the ship rolls and pitches. The wind carries with it flurries of terns that drift like unseasonal snow and, for a moment, it seems as if all the surrounding sea and sky is white and frozen and the ship is hemmed in by bluish ice floes that shift and crack. An Esquimaux in a skin coat stares in her direction. Birdie raises a hand to wave, and the Esquimaux waves back. A sharp gust of wind blows the image away, and the terns flit and vanish. She inhales the salt air and feels a sudden exhilaration; heading north into the unknown or, at least, the unknown to her, like some wild adventuress. The birds, the waves, the endless sky – these are her new companions. She regularly purchased supplements of

William Yarrell's *History of British Birds* as a treat on pay-
day – she's always felt an affinity with birds – and now she can
identify the species she has only encountered before on paper.
Gannets shoot the prow before they plunge at breakneck
speed into the brine. A stormy petrel skims the swell. Up
ahead an island looms – Hoy, the steward tells her. From the
ship's deck it appears as a soaring wall of red cliffs veiled by
a mist of crashing breakers. As the ship skirts the rockface
she sees the sandstone is splattered white with the guano of
nesting birds – thousands of black razorbills and guillemots
cling to narrow ledges. This rugged coast is as overcrowded
as the dismal human rookeries of Southwark. For the first
time since leaving London, she feels unexpectedly at home.

The bosun's whistle shrills and sailors flood the deck, ready
to ascend the rigging and trim the sails for the approach to
Stromness Harbour.

'The view is better from the top.' A sailor stands at her
elbow; he sounds as if he was raised in the Borough. 'Fancy
a climb?'

She tips her head. She grew up with ships always in her
sights; topmasts looming over the run-down terraces of
Bermondsey, giant prows filling the river-end of narrow
streets, sailors swarming the ratlines like ants crawling along
attic beams. But the ships and the sailors she has seen up
'til now have been in the shelter of the river. There were
stormy nights when the grey water sloshed the walls and
the violence of the waves broke mooring ropes and smashed
tugs to pieces. But nothing compared to the open sea, the
vastness of the waves, the dark blue of the depths.

'I'll leave the rigging to you, Sir.'

'Ain't so bad in this wind. It's when a storm blows up out of nowhere you have to be careful – one slip and you're a gonner.' He grins and reveals two lines of yellowing teeth. 'There's a thousand ways to die aboard a ship.'

She knows; her husband found one of them. 15th March 1851 was the day she learned he had been reported missing from a schooner heading to the Baltic; swept overboard in a gale. She was betrothed to Patrick at fifteen, and married him two years later. It was Frank's idea, and he had been insistent. Determined, in fact. He's a good man and with a beaky nose like that, he said, you'll not have a better offer. She resented Frank's interference but, truth to tell, she didn't need much persuasion. She'd known Patrick since she was a child and in some ways, he felt more like a brother to her than Frank; Patrick was kind and caring. Da would have approved of the marriage, she was sure. She wept every night for a week after she learned he had perished at sea and tried not to picture his last moments, sucked beneath the heaving waves.

'You get used to it quick enough,' the sailor adds chirpily. 'On days like this, there's nowhere better to be.'

He pivots, fairly skips to the mast and hauls himself up, hand over hand, eases himself along the yardarm, feet on dangling ropes. He waves at her and she wishes he would concentrate on gripping the beam.

'Hold fast,' she shouts.

He waves again. He couldn't have heard what she said above the crash of the breakers.

'Hold fast,' she says to the sky and she thinks of Tobias Skaill, his grip on life let go.

The bosun blasts his whistle again. The steward limps across the deck, and stands by her side; he's a sandy-haired Scot.

'I see the Bay ships are here; a grand sight, the fur fleet.'

He points at the schooners anchored ahead of them, their Red Ensigns flustered by the wind. She assesses the ships curiously; she has trailed their course north. Though there were four ships in the convoy when they departed Gravesend, and now she can count only three. Maybe the fourth is on its way.

She searches beyond the masts for sight of their destination; a curtain of misty rain hangs over the island ahead. She cannot see a town, only a straggle of drab houses, gables to the water with a decidedly unfriendly attitude. And all around low, brown, treeless hills with hardly any habitation at all. It's a desolate place. The only sign of life is a flock of sheep drifting in an aimless cloud across the slopes. She looks again for Stromness, but still cannot see a town.

'Where is Stromness?'

The steward scratches his gingerish beard, before sweeping his hand at the granite ribbon fringing the shore. 'There.'

'Is that all of it?'

'Is that no enough?'

She's afraid it isn't. 'I'd heard Stromness was the port where all the whalers and traders stopped before they set sail across the Atlantic.'

'So it is.' He tweaks his beard again. 'It's a wee town, I give you that.'

Town? There are so few houses it hardly merits being called a village let alone a town. She was hoping to make herself invisible, here in the north. This place is so small she reckons she could walk from one end to the other in fifteen minutes and everybody who lives there would know her face.

'The whaling's not what it used to be,' the steward adds. 'I used to do it meself. 1843 – that was the last year I sailed to Baffin Bay. Not that I miss it.'

He pats his lame leg; an injury, she supposes, from his days in the Arctic.

'It must be a hard life, whaling.'

'Aye. All cramped up for weeks. Nothing to eat but salt horse and scouse. Rats crawling over your feet. Frostbite. It's no fun being trapped in the ice.' He shakes his head at the memory. 'Are you resting in Stromness a wee while then?'

She nods.

The steward's watery eyes search her face. 'You'll find the folk here somewhat queer.'

'Queer?'

'I'd be careful not to cross any of the womenfolk, if I were you.' His eyes flit along the shore. 'They're known for their skills with black magic. Shapeshifters. They control the winds around these shores.'

He's the second person who has warned her of the mysterious practices of the north.

'Orkney is well known for it,' the steward says. 'There used to be so many women causing mischief, the magistrates had to do something, so they rounded them up, made them confess, and the guilty ones were strangled and burned.'

Birdie shudders; Orkney's magistrates sound more dangerous than the witches. The steward doesn't notice her discomfort.

'They thought they'd got rid of them all, but they're cunning women. Folk say their descendants carry the knowledge and still continue with their dark ways. The place is full of these giant stone rings that have been here since ancient times.' He waves his hand at the misty hills. 'Eerie places. Haunted. I've heard the stones dance in the moonlight and the witches gather there to perform their evil acts. I never venture beyond Stromness when I'm harboured here.'

She is gripped by a sudden sense of alarm; the steward appears to be a practical man who has survived the hardships of the Arctic, and yet he is scared to travel in Orkney. Perhaps there is some truth in the rumours of rampant witchcraft.

'And the waters around here,' he continues, 'are where the Finfolk live.'

'Finfolk?'

'The sorcerers of the seas. You've not heard of them?'

She shakes her head and glances at the green swell.

He narrows his eyes. 'They're like the witches but in winter they live below the waves, then in summer they come ashore and snatch wee lasses and take them away to their kingdom in their canoes.'

'Canoes?'

'Aye. They have dark skins and black hair and they wrap themselves in fur.'

Her brow knots. 'And they come from the sea?'

'From the frozen northern deeps.'

A spit of water tickles her cheek and she wonders whether it was one of these strange Finfolk that dumped the body of Tobias Skaill on the shore of the Thames, and not an Esquimaux at all. The steward extends his hand, lets the drops splash on his palm.

'Rain. There's no shortage of that in Orkney.'

She smiles weakly and looks again at Stromness, shrouded

now by dismal clouds, and she wonders what she's doing here.

The *Dog Star* anchors in the deep water of the harbour; large ships can only come alongside the piers at high tide. The steward insists she disembarks in the bosun's chair – many an incautious soul has been snatched by the waves here while transferring from ship to rowing boat. She would rather use the rope ladder. Still, it isn't worth contesting; she is concerned her gown might rip if she has to raise her arms too high as she descends. And the steward's tales of vicious Finfolk are still playing on her mind. She acquiesces. Though not without first insisting that she has to collect her birdcage from her berth. She doesn't want to leave the parrot to be rowed ashore with the luggage.

She clutches the cage against her chest as the steward helps her into the canvas seat. She has grown fond of the parrot; she feels a certain kinship with the bird. The steward secures them with a yellow flag. She tries not to look down as she is hoisted over the bulwark and finds herself level with the fulmars. She swoops with them, gliding over the sea and harbour, and her gaze lands on the quayside gathering – a huddle all swathed in dark cloth as if in mourning; women draped in black shawls, men with black jackets buttoned against the wind. Even the birds hopping at their feet look as if they are dressed for a funeral; the grey crows sport black hoods over their heads.

The gusts rock the bosun's chair alarmingly. She grips the rope with one hand and the birdcage with the other and is glad of the flag across her ribs. From the quayside, eyes in upturned faces follow the arcs of the swinging canvas chair. She sees herself through their careworn gaze; a curious circus act, all bedecked in black crepe and yellow pendants, a grey parrot in her arms. The flying widow. A tawdry spectacle dangling from a rope. She closes her eyes and tries to banish the image of her father twisting on the gallows' noose.

Hands reach up to steady her descent, grab the ropes, unknot the flag, and assist her to a bench on the rowing boat. The oarsman pushes off and the boat slips through the ranks of fishing craft with dun sails furled. The blades dip and lift. She warily surveys the approaching shoreline, with its crenellations of piers and slipways, and wonders how many of the women huddled there practise witchcraft.

She reaches for the hand the oarsman is kindly proffering, steps onto the slipway, enquires whether the waiting luggage porter can ensure her trunk is delivered to Flett's Hotel and asks him to point her in the right direction. He replies in a barely audible voice that she should turn north when she reaches the street and walk a peedie way along.

'Peedie?'

He gives her a blank stare and then says, 'A wee way along.'

The rain is pelting so hard and cold it might as well be hail. She hurries along the slipway, reaches a stack of creels and a wooden shack, notices a torn poster flapping against its timbers and slows to read it as she passes.

£20,000 REWARD WILL BE GIVEN BY HER MAJESTY'S GOVERNMENT FOR ANY PARTY OR PARTIES, OF ANY COUNTRY, WHO SHALL RENDER EFFICIENT ASSISTANCE TO THE CREWS OF THE DISCOVERY SHIPS UNDER THE COMMAND OF SIR JOHN FRANKLIN.

She thinks of Franklin and his crew, their souls lost in the frozen wastes, and conjures up the picture of his widow's haunted face, printed in all the newspapers; Lady Franklin racked by the years of torment, praying her dear husband might still be alive. And now the poor widow must feel more dismayed than ever; after all her efforts to find him, her hopes have been cruelly dashed by the report in *The Times* that the crew had starved and resorted to cannibalism. It is hard not to be moved by Lady Franklin's predicament and impressed by the strength with which she maintained her faith that Sir John still lived. Birdie compares herself to Lady Franklin – they have both been widowed by northern oceans – and can't help wondering whether she behaved with as much dutiful loyalty in the months after Patrick perished. She fears not.

She marches on, half blinded by the rain, salty water pouring off her bonnet and running down her neck. There is indeed only one street in Stromness; uncobbled, marked by rough-hewn steps and narrower than some of the back alleys of the Borough, barely wide enough for a carriage. Wide enough, though, for the flock of sheep that bleats and panics as she edges her way through the trembling wet fleeces. Shawl-wrapped women shelter in doorways, engrossed in conversation. They fall silent as she passes. A small boy shouts in a strange accent.

'What kind of bird is it you have in the cage?'

'A parrot.' She replies with relief, glad it is the bird and not her that is the subject of discussion. Exotic birds are two a penny in London. Here, the bird is an oddity. The boy skips toward her.

'Who's a pretty boy then?' the parrot shrieks.

A calloused hand shoots out, grabs the boy by the scruff

and drags him back to the safety of the doorway. The woman admonishes him in an unintelligible dialect.

'White hid noo! White hid thoo ill-answeran bairn.'

The boy answers in the same tongue and Birdie feels she's in a foreign land. Though she's used to feeling like a stranger even at home, she reminds herself; her visions have always made her feel abnormal, marked by a shameful secret she must keep hidden. You're a changeling, Frank used to say when her eyes misted and she went into one of her trances. Or a lunatic, he'd add. Sometimes she thought he might be right.

She hoiks her skirt with her free hand and trudges the muddy street, runoff rainwater cascading along its course, flashes of silver sea to one side and, to the other, stepped alleyways cutting upwards. The strengthening wind roars around the corners and tugs her skirt. In London the weather feels man-made, the thick fogs dense with soot. Here the elements seem untamed and unpredictable. The air is alive with strange, sharp smells – seaweed and salt. And there is no clanking of cranes or pounding of factory hammers; instead she hears the haunting calls of curlews and the cries of the gulls. For a moment, she thinks she is not in a street at all, but in some deep river chasm that has carved its channel through a mountain of grey rock, and she wonders whether she has indeed been spirited away to an enchanted land of witches and sea sorcerers. A hooded crow plops in front of her feet and cackles, as if to confirm her fears about the unearthly nature of this place.

She hurries along, overcome by the unfamiliar, and is comforted to see the sign above the double door of a dour stone building. Flett's Hotel; its exterior too stern, she tells herself, to be the work of some enchantment. She enters and finds a bony woman wearing a mob cap and a pinny behind a mahogany reception counter; her pleated brow and nervous glance suggest that despite her occupation she is not used to strangers. Her timid appearance hardly matches the descriptions Birdie has been given of wild witches and black magic. She says, in the quietest of voices as she eyes the cage, that there is a chamber available, though it might be better if the bird stayed in the courtyard. Birdie panics. She does not wish to be separated from her bird. The parrot comes from a hot climate, Birdie explains, and would perish in the cold. The woman assesses the parrot warily.

'Perhaps you could consult the manager,' Birdie suggests.

'I do all the managing here meself,' she snaps, and Birdie is reminded of the steward's warning not to cross the womenfolk.

'I'm sorry, I...'

'My husband has no time for the business,' the woman continues. 'He's away fishing most days.'

Birdie sees her opportunity to recover the situation, even though it involves lying.

'My husband went to sea as well. He brought the parrot back with him on his last voyage. Or, I mean, the last voyage he survived.'

At the mention of her husband's death at sea, the woman's expression changes from suspicion to sympathy. She shifts her eyes from the cage to Birdie's face. 'Does it make a noise?'

'Not at all. And he's clean.'

'Aye, very well then, thou can keep it in thy room.'

Birdie is about to go when she sees a copy of *The Orcadian* lying on the counter. The sight of it makes her uneasy; do the pages contain a report of Tobias Skaill's murder? The woman notices the direction of her gaze.

'Take it,' she offers. ''Tis old news.'

A young chambermaid guides her up the stairs. The room is airy and painted white. A walnut dressing table is neatly laid out with a comb, brush and nightcap, a jug and bowl for washing and a small mirror fixed on the wall above. A pair of slippers nestles underneath. A dim lamp glows by the narrow bed and a window overlooks the street. The chambermaid indicates the bedpan.

'The closet is on the far side of the yard.'

Birdie nods. She doesn't want to encourage further conversation. Apart from anything else, the speech of the Orcadians perturbs her; they have their own language they use with each other but even when they are speaking English it is hard to decipher what they say. It isn't so much their accent, but their murmuring voices. The men whisper so quietly, she can hardly hear them. The women twitter softly like Da's canaries.

She moves the nightcap and places the cage on the dressing table.

'Well,' she says to the bird, 'it might be cold and damp here, but I bet you're glad I brought you with me.'

The parrot lifts one claw, shrieks, 'Skin for a skin,' and cackles. She cringes; the bird's mimicry of Frank is vexing. Still, it's not the bird's fault; he's merely repeating what somebody else has said. She wishes, though, he'd stick to the less alarming phrases in his repertoire. She looks for the twist of seeds, which she managed to purchase in Aberdeen, pokes some millet through the bars of the cage; the bird clucks contentedly. She turns and spreads the copy of *The*

Orcadian on the counterpane. It is indeed old news; the paper is dated Saturday 5th May and it is now the 29th. At least there cannot be a report of Tobias Skaill's death, for he was still living at the beginning of the month. The top half of the front page is filled with a report of the war in the Crimea. She flips the pages and casts her eye over the notices, and one of them catches her attention.

Situation vacant. Book-keeper. Must write a good hand. Complete master of figures and accounts. Experience of shipping agents essential. Apply to Mrs Margaret Skaill of Albert Skaill's shipping agents. Narwhal House. Stromness. Testimonials required.

Mrs Margaret Skaill. She reads the name twice. Surely, Margaret Skaill must be related to Tobias Skaill; she doubts it's a common name. Though it seems to her this is such a small place everybody must be related to everybody else. She shivers, touches her forehead and wonders whether she has caught a chill from exposure to the cold and rain. But no, her head is cool; she is simply bothered by the sense that there is some inescapable pattern here, some force of fate drawing her together with the murdered man. She recalls their one encounter – that is to say the one with him still living – the evening before he died. He was drunk and his behaviour lewd, although initially not so very different from the behaviour of any tar out on the razz in the Borough. But he had been persistent. Usually one of her demonic stares or caustic putdowns would be enough to deter the casual gropers. Not him, though. She had given him a mouthful, told him to get lost in no uncertain terms. He hadn't desisted. He had shouted, pursued her down the street. Insisted he knew her name. Said he had a message for her. She had assumed he was pissed and rambling. Was she too hasty in her judgement? Perhaps he did have a message for her after all. She shakes her head. She doubts he did know her, but it seems they are certainly connected now; shackled together by the Thames Division, keen to pin his murder on her because she is the daughter of Gerald Quinn.

She re-reads the notice for a book-keeper. The purse of guineas from Solomon won't last forever; if she is to stay here a while she needs to earn her living. Whether it is good or bad luck that Margaret Skaill is searching for a book-keeper, she cannot tell, but she resolves to find Narwhal House first thing in the morning and enquire about the situation.

Chapter 5

Tobias lies on the foreshore, his copper hair a gleaming halo. She leans over his face and sees his coal-black eyes, his skin spangled with mud and freckles. The circle of flesh gouged from his curved cheek. Suddenly, he sits upright, opens his mouth and groans. He grabs her arm and pulls her to him. *Birdie, save us from this terror*, he implores. *Don't let them die.*

She awakens with a jolt. A man wails and for a moment she is unsure whether she is still dreaming. Her heart is pounding. Wide awake now, and reluctant to return to sleep in case Tobias comes back to haunt her, she listens to the noises from the street. The familiar sounds of harbour life are reassuring. Ribald songs of rowdy sailors, brawling men and drunkards sobbing to the gutters. Men from the Company's ships still anchored in the bay, she supposes. She stands, edges to the window, pulls aside the velvet curtain and is surprised to find the night is not black but shimmering gold and red, as if lit by a huge fire beyond the furthest hills. She briefly wonders whether it's the blaze of witches gathering around the ancient stones – flaming torches held aloft – before she realizes it's the sun, which dawdles in the summers of these northern latitudes and barely dips below the horizon. Even at this late hour, the rooks chorus as if it were dawn. She returns to bed, slumbers fitfully, and is stirred by the call of a curlew and the splatter of rain against the window.

She rises, dabs herself with a wetted flannel, gasps – the water in the jug is freezing – glances up and thinks she catches a flash of Solomon's face in the clouded mirror. She smiles to herself; the image reminds her of an icy Sunday he stood waiting for her on a Southwark street corner, his breath smoky in the cold.

'It looks like snow,' she said.

As she spoke, a white star drifted and landed on his shoulder, gleamed for a second before it melted. He held out his hand, caught another flake. Flurries filled the air. They laughed as the dirty pavements and smutty roofs were glazed white. London rarely appeared so innocent. Only the robins and sparrows kept them company in the twilit streets until the lamplighter appeared, paused to doff his cap, then continued along his way.

'I should walk you home,' Solomon said.

They strolled through deepening drifts, leaving dark footprints in their wake, their breath mingling in one frosty cloud. St George's struck the hour of five. Unexpectedly, he reached for her mittened hand and held it in his for a moment before he let it drop.

'I have to go,' he said.

She watched him walk toward the river, stamping her feet to keep warm, wondering what mysterious business called him away so suddenly. She suspected the lamplighter gave him a secret signal as he passed them in the street; Frank was forever warning her that London's lamplighters were in cahoots with the cops. It took her a moment to realize he had left something in her hand. She held it up and examined it in the glow of the street lamp – a tiny yellow brooch in the shape of a canary; a reminder of the first time they met. The glass even had a small crack on the bird's crown that resembled the two black feathers of the Little Prince, Da's precious songster.

She rouses herself with a splash of freezing water from the jug and pushes thoughts of Solomon aside as she rubs her face with the flannel. Her more pressing concern is the vacant situation at Albert Skaill's shipping agency and her less than pristine appearance. She assesses the state of her clothes. She purchased the half-mourning black bombazine, crepe-trimmed skirt and bodice from Jay's in Regent Street three years ago to replace the full mourning she had worn for well over a year. The skirt, in particular, now looks the worse for wear; the escapades of the last few days have left the trim torn and hanging loose below the hem. She could attempt to repair it or she could remove it – after all, it is perfectly acceptable for a widow to slight the mourning and detach the crepe after a year or so. She tugs at the manky black strip and finds it comes away quite easily. The skirt will be less cumbersome without it, she concludes, and will undoubtedly smell less offensive minus the Thames-dragged trim. She decides to abandon the bonnet and veil as well. She packed a black wool cape and she'll wear that, and then she'll look more like the shawled women of Stromness.

The chambermaid gives her directions to Narwhal House; south along the main street of Stromness toward the Ness. 'It's no difficult to locate,' the chambermaid adds in her sing-song voice, 'it's marked by a whalebone arch.' Birdie steps into the rainy, dank day and unexpectedly finds herself in an excited crowd. Fishermen and women in oilskin aprons surround a skinny man balanced on a crate, waving a bottle and yelling, 'Yer rheumatics cured in fifteen minutes.' He has a Cockney accent and a familiar, roguish face. She has seen him hanging around the bars of the Borough, claiming he has the cure for syphilis; she is bemused to bump into him so far north. He selects another bottle from his open case. 'Removes all toothache pain forever. Only three pennies. Cures bad breath as well.' A bevy of young men heading to the harbour stop to listen. 'Come on, lads. You knows the ladies like a man with sweet breath.' He makes no mention of syphilis; he has toned down his act for Stromness.

The innocence of the scene is reassuring, she thinks, as she weaves around the crowd; the folk of Stromness have a naïvety about them which city dwellers lack. Islanders scratching a living from the soil and the sea are purer of mind and deed, she reckons, than the inhabitants of London. No sellers of penny dreadfuls here; no lurid tales of gruesome murders being whispered on every corner. No syphilis, only toothache. She recalls then the rowdy noises of the night before and reminds herself that this is a harbour town. Sailors are sailors, in Stromness as much as Rotherhithe. People here may not behave so very differently from those further south, she decides, though the townsfolk appear more reserved than the bawdy occupants of London's rookeries.

The street is boggy; deep puddles fill ruts. Children splash, their mothers too busy listening to the quack doctor to pay any heed.

A bedraggled boy shouts as she passes, 'Where's thy parrot?'

Even without the birdcage, she is recognized. She pretends she hasn't heard and stomps along, glad of her sturdy boots, skirt raised to avoid the copious piles of sheep shit. From underneath the hood of her mantle, she assesses the premises fronting the street – butcher, grocer, tobacconist, cobbler – but can find no sign proclaiming Albert Skaill, shipping agent. The chambermaid is right, though, the whalebone arch cannot be missed; bleached white and smooth, the monumental jaw points heavenward as if bellowing one last curse against the whalers before succumbing to its painful death. She passes under the leviathan's mouth and feels like Jonah, slipping into the darkened gullet of the beast.

She finds herself in a narrow passageway flanked, on one side, by the back of a terrace and, on the other, by Mrs Skaill's premises. The alley descends to a slipway, and the rain-pocked sea licks the gable-end of the building. In stormy weather the waves must surely reach the slated roof. No wonder the houses are built from such sturdy rock; solid but not grand, stoically weathering the onslaught of wind and waves. There is a sign above the door; a painting of a whale with what looks like a unicorn's horn stuck on its nose. The narwhal, she presumes, after which the premises is named, though she is not entirely certain whether the creature depicted is real or mythical. Below the sign, double doors are painted black and on the right half there is a greening bronze ship knocker, the wood underneath dented from heavy use. She lifts the ship and raps with as much confidence as she can muster. There is no reply. She stands awhile and knocks again.

'A moment.'

Footsteps advance. The door is opened by a towering woman, her hefty frame contained in a plain dun pinafore, her face well carved with a firm wide mouth, thick, stern brows and a plait of sleek mahogany hair streaked silver wound around her head. Birdie assumes this is Margaret Skaill, not least because she suspects she sees a resemblance to Tobias in her coal-black eyes and the striking cut of her features. She is like a gracefully ageing ship, Birdie thinks, and she pictures HMS *Temeraire*, the grand naval man-of-war that fought the Battle of Trafalgar. When she was a child, she watched the fading giant being hauled upstream to the breaker's yard in Rotherhithe; Margaret Skaill carries the same air of long suffering and brave endurance. And also the same strength, Birdie reckons; she is reminded again of the steward's warning about crossing Orkney's womenfolk and silently concludes it would be a foolhardy person who took on Margaret in straight battle.

'Good morning, Ma'am.' Birdie tips back her hood.

'Good morning.' Mrs Skaill does not sound surprised to see her. Indeed, she is assessing her as if she were expected.

'You'll be the new housemaid.'

Birdie is momentarily caught on the back foot, though she is encouraged to find that Mrs Skaill does not speak in dialect.

'No. I came to enquire about the other situation.'

'Other situation?'

'The book-keeper. I saw a notice in *The Orcadian*.'

'Placed last month.'

Birdie's face drops. 'I suppose it's filled already.'

'Not yet. I'm still searching for a suitable candidate.'

Birdie smiles with relief, but Mrs Skaill's forehead furrows and her brows join in one forbidding line.

'Your husband sent you with his details?'

'I'm the one who wants to apply.'

'Yourself?'

'Yes.'

Mrs Skaill pulls the door wider. 'You're no from Stromness.'

'No.'

'And your name is?'

'Birdie White.'

'Birdie?'

'It's my nickname.'

'I see. And you can call me Margaret. I have to say, though, I had a man in mind.' She pauses. Her brow unfurrows. 'Well, I'm in charge of the business; so why should the book-keeper not be a woman too?' She steps back. 'You'd better come inside.'

The shadowed hall is quite bare apart from a coat stand and a gilt-framed blotchy mirror. A staircase ascends one wall and there are two closed doors beyond the steps. Margaret stands before the nearest entrance as if barricading it, and directs Birdie to the other.

'The office is at the back and my living quarters at the ben-end.'

The squealing of children is audible, playing behind the forbidden entrance. They sound young; she would have expected Margaret's children to be almost grown – she guesses her to be well into her forties.

The office is cavernous and gloomy. There is one salt-flecked window, which has a good view of the harbour. Or at least it would have a good view of the harbour if the curtains of rain parted. The pendulum of a wall clock swings and ticks loudly behind a tall and sloping clerk's desk, its stool tucked underneath as if it has not been used for a while – there are no papers on its ink-splattered surface, though a second, lower table is littered with letters and ledgers. Behind the table stands an open-fronted cabinet, which is also heaving but not with papers. Rather, it seems to be full of relics salvaged from a shipwreck. From where she is standing, Birdie can identify a brass spyglass, a length of knotted rope, a small bell, a compass and a pocket chronometer. She takes a step closer to the cabinet, curious to see what other objects are on the cluttered shelves.

'I can view my ships from here,' Margaret says, as if to distract Birdie's attention from the peculiar collection. 'See – the two-masted schooner anchored there, beyond the pier.'

Margaret pushes the window open; waves slap against stone and raindrops patter on the water. The smell is not too bad. It would be worse if the day were hotter.

'The sea reaches the window?'

'Not quite. Though near enough to fish for sillocks. Take a look.'

Birdie steps across, leans out and, as she does so, the rain ceases. The sun dances on the harbour. The water is transformed as if by magic from grey to blue and the drab sails of the fishing boats that crowd the shore brighten. A woman pins white sheets to a line festooning a nearby pier. She is about to comment on the prettiness of the scene when a monstrous black head appears above the water and stares at her through bottomless eyes. She gasps.

'What is that creature?'

Margaret crosses her arms. 'A selkie.'

'A selkie?' She remembers the steward's stories of strange Orcadian creatures. 'One of the Finfolk?'

'Finfolk?' There is a sudden harshness to Margaret's tone which catches Birdie by surprise.

'I heard one of the sailors—'

'You'll do well to pay no heed to the gossip of sailors.'

Birdie's heart sinks; she has stepped out of line in some way she cannot comprehend. 'I'm sorry, I didn't…'

Margaret sees her confusion and waves her apology aside with a brisk flap of her hand. 'No matter. Folk here gab; you'll learn to ignore them.' She points at the creature staring at them from the water. 'You'll maybe call that a seal.'

'Of course – a seal.'

She feels foolish. Birdie fears she has ruined her chances; a young woman who is affrighted by the sight of a common sea creature is hardly likely to impress.

'Some folk here say that if a person drowns at sea they are taken by the seals and become a selkie.'

Margaret smiles as she speaks and Birdie suspects it's not the folk tales in general that bother her, but specifically the stories about the Finfolk. She stares at the seal. The creature's mournful eyes are surprisingly human; they remind her of Patrick and she wonders whether this animal could be him.

'You've no seen a seal before?'

Birdie shakes her head; she's heard they sometimes appear in the Thames below the bridge, but she's never seen one herself, except in picture books. The seal raises a flipper, rubs its whiskered nose and disappears below the surface.

'Not long in Orkney then?'

'I arrived yesterday.'

'Which ship?'

'The *Dog Star*.'

'The mail packet from Aberdeen? But you're no from Scotland.'

'I took the steamer from Gravesend to Aberdeen.'

'London?'

The questions are tinged with suspicion and remind Birdie of the unlikeliness of her story; a young woman travelling alone from London to apply for a book-keeping position advertised in a local newspaper. Margaret is regarding her quizzically. Birdie senses her cheeks flushing, her pulse quicken. Has she read *The Times* article about the murder of Tobias Skaill? Has she put two and two together? Panic ties her tongue; she cannot answer a simple question.

Margaret thankfully fills the awkward silence. 'That's quite a journey for a young woman on her own. You are on your own, I assume?' She nods at Birdie's black attire. Birdie nods back.

'And you're here because you saw the notice in *The Orcadian*?'

Birdie has calmed herself sufficiently to find her voice. 'I was working for a shipping agents in Southwark and one of the clerks was given the paper by a sailor.' This is as close to the truth as she dares to come. 'I was hoping for an opportunity to leave London.' She hesitates. 'Since my husband's death, I've found it hard to settle.'

Margaret shifts her weight, tilts her head to one side, and Birdie senses a lessening of her wariness.

'It's a hard blow when we lose a husband.'

We. Margaret is a widow too; they have a common bond.

'I took the business on when my husband died.' Margaret pushes up her sleeves.

'Albert Skaill was your husband, then?'

'My grandfather.'

It strikes Birdie that Margaret could be Tobias's sister, and she might not even know that he is dead.

Margaret continues. 'My husband's name was Callum Fraser. He took on Grandpa's business when we married and I inherited it when Callum died. I use Skaill, my maiden name, as it's the name by which folk here know me.'

'You were born in Orkney?' Birdie ventures.

'Stromness. Though some folk doubt my ancestry. Three generations dead in the kirkyard, they say, and then you may be considered one of them.' She laughs, bitterly. 'Albert Skaill was an Orkney man, and he is buried over in Warbeth. He was a servant of the Hudson's Bay Company and he took a wife in Rupert's Land. When he returned to Orkney, he brought their bairns – Bruce, my father, and his brother Edward – so they could be schooled here. But he left his wife behind.'

Birdie knows from her own family that when men migrate they do not always take their wives, so she is not surprised by this arrangement.

Margaret continues. 'My grandmother isn't from Orkney which, in some folk's eyes, counts against me. And I did myself no favours by marrying a man from Leith.'

'Isn't Leith in Scotland?'

'Aye, but folk here think of themselves as Norse, a different race from the Scots.' She sniffs. 'Well, as far as I'm concerned they can keep their kirkyard. I'll not go there again 'til I'm dead, and then I'll be buried in the Skaill family tomb and maybe folk here'll finally accept I'm one of them.' She laughs again, dismissively this time. 'You took quite a chance setting off from London without any kith or kin. Folk here are wary of strangers.'

Birdie nods; if she had known what a small place Stromness was and how much a widow with a parrot would stand out from the crowd, she might have been less intrepid. On the other hand, if she hadn't left London immediately, she would almost certainly be locked in a basement cell in Wapping Police Station by now, listening to the ebb and flow of the Thames and wondering how many more tides she would hear before she was hanged. Birdie glances at the harbour. The seal's head surfaces, a silver fish dangling from its mouth.

'Nothing ventured, nothing gained,' she says.

'Aye.' Margaret tucks a stray strand of sleek hair behind her ear. 'The last book-keeper I employed was a local who knew too many people, and most of them, it seemed, of the wrong sort. That didn't turn out so well.' She rolls her lips inward, as if to indicate this is a subject on which she is reluctant to expand. 'I was hoping to appoint somebody from beyond Orkney this time.'

There is a pause. Birdie can sense she is being weighed; her appearance, her manner. Her story.

Eventually Margaret says, 'You worked for a shipping agent, you say?'

'Standing and Wolff.'

'The name is familiar.'

'I was employed in their Southwark counting house. The office was situated close to the home I shared with my husband.' She wonders whether she is overdoing it. 'I couldn't escape the memories.'

'Well, Birdie.' Margaret smiles sympathetically. 'Now you're here I'd better find out what you ken about the shipping business.'

Birdie is happy to answer questions about book-keeping;

they are easier to deal with than enquiries about her own history.

'Mine is a varied business. I do something of everything to make ends meet. I have a warehouse up near the north pier and I'm away most days overseeing the loading and unloading there or talking to merchants in town. I need somebody I can trust to run this office – somebody who can write a good letter, as well as oversee contracts and accounts. Have you experience in all those areas?'

'Yes.'

'Bills of lading?'

'My first post with Standing and Wolff was as a clerk's assistant, checking and recording the receipts handed over by ships' masters in exchange for the goods received.'

A vast black-backed gull lands on the windowsill and pecks at the glass. Margaret waves her arm at it. 'Off with ye, you ugly baakie.' The gull screeches and flaps away. She continues. 'I own three ships – two schooners and a barque.' She gestures again at the harbour, and her vessel anchored there. 'If a merchant intends to charter one of my ships, what clauses would you write in the contract?'

An easy test; Birdie replies without much thought.

'A charter party between you and a merchant should include clauses that define conditions for freight, lay days, demurrage and penalties – on both sides of course.'

Margaret appears pleased with the answer.

'And book-keeping?'

Birdie tries not to grin; the relief of being on firm ground.

'I took maths and accounting exams before I left school, and I was given oversight of the ledgers at Standing and Wolff.'

Margaret nods. 'At what age did you leave school?'

'Sixteen.'

'Unusual for a girl.'

'I attended a charitable school in Rotherhithe. St Edward's. I boarded there for six years. My mother died a few years after I was born.'

'I'm sorry to hear that.'

'Cholera takes its toll in London.'

'Your father too?'

'No, my father...' She doesn't want to admit he was hanged. 'My father passed away when I was ten. I was fortunate enough to be helped by a benefactor.'

'A man who knew your father?'

'He was an acquaintance of my uncle, though I never knew his name. A philanthropic gentleman who provided for many orphans like myself. I wanted to make the most of my good fortune, and I studied very hard.'

Though her determination to learn did not always please Matron, who thought young girls were better suited to worsted-work than maths and often said that Birdie's interest in numbers was unhealthy and a sign of troublesome wilfulness, for which she was regularly beaten. Birdie's pale complexion and funny turns were interpreted by Matron as further symptoms of this malady. Matron pronounced she was suffering from some form of neurasthenia and only grudgingly conceded that she should be allowed to study maths and accounting after, apparently, an intervention from her benefactor. He had firm views about the importance of education for girls, according to Matron.

'And do you have any certificates or a character?' Margaret asks.

'I have papers from the school.'

She fiddles with the drawstrings of her reticule, withdraws her folded certificates and testimonial and passes them to Margaret. Birdie holds her hands in front of her skirt so she is not tempted to twiddle her fingers nervously. The exam grades are impressive and the reference is glowing, but it is in her maiden name – Quinn. She's taking a chance: if Margaret has read the *Times* report about the Esquimaux killer and his accomplice of Irish descent, it might set an alarm bell ringing. Birdie is very much afraid Mrs Skaill will hear her heart pounding. Margaret returns the certificates without comment, but holds the testimonial to the window's light.

Birdie offers nervously, 'I could write to Mr Wolff and ask him to send a reference.'

She hopes Margaret will not think it worth the bother. Birdie keeps her smile fixed as Margaret tips the testimonial back and forth as if she is testing the quality of the paper on which it is written rather than reading its contents.

'No, no, this is fine.' She squints at the paper still. 'This shield is curious, though.'

'Shield?'

'Here.' She slants the paper. Birdie has not paid much attention to the testimonial before; this is the first time she has been required to show it to anybody. When Uncle Dennis arranged the position at Standing and Wolff, no reference other than his name was required. She examines the coats of arms to which Margaret points; one supported on either side by a lion rampant, the second with animals she does not immediately recognize.

'Those must be the crests of the school's benefactors.'

'Aye.' Margaret peers again at the paper. 'Lynx,' she adds.

'Lynx?'

'The creatures on this crest. I've seen one on the flag of a ship named the *Lynx*. Killed for their skin.'

Skin for a skin. Birdie's nervous mind slips around uncontrollably. She feels a sudden chill, goosebumps form on her arms and in the engulfing darkness she glimpses a heraldic emblem pinned on a mahogany panel; she tries to identify the creature on its crest but the light is flickering and dim. She sways, steadies herself and blinks to clear her vision – she cannot afford to allow her nerves to get the better of her now. She doesn't want Margaret to think she's feeble-minded.

Margaret doesn't seem to notice her momentary fit of faintness; she folds the testimonial and hands it back to Birdie.

'I sense I can trust you.'

Birdie tries to stop herself from blushing.

'You've taken a chance coming all this way, and I will take a chance on you.'

Birdie exhales and allows herself to smile. 'Thank you.'

'You'll need to start tomorrow, though; as you'll have seen, the Company ships are here, and I'm busy dealing with the supplies they ordered.'

'You supply the Bay's ships?' Her voice has taken on an edge of anxiety again.

'There's hardly a merchant or shop-keeper in Stromness whose business does not depend on some dealing with the Company. The jawbone outside the door was placed there by Grandpa when one trip to Baffin Bay could set a man right for life. But now the whaling is harder. We have to make our profits elsewhere these days.'

'Of course. I could start straight away.'

Margaret nods at the sprawl of papers littering the table.

'As I explained, the last book-keeper, Donald Shearer, was a local man and that didn't work out well.'

Birdie assesses the mess. 'How long have you been without an accountant?'

'Shearer left the business last autumn. He departed quite suddenly. The maid was helping me out with the odd letter here and there until she left a couple of weeks ago.' She gives Birdie a furtive look, and then glances behind at the cabinet. There is a silence that goes on too long and Birdie begins to feel uncomfortable.

'There is something I should tell you,' Margaret says eventually.

Birdie is conscious of her pulse racing, the tension in Margaret's voice makes her wonder what secret is about to be revealed.

'I have trouble reading.'

Birdie almost breathes a sigh of relief. Now she understands why Margaret regarded her testimonial in that peculiar way; she wasn't reading it at all.

'My ma died when I was seven. I stayed at home to look after the house. After that, learning to read didn't seem worth the effort.'

'There are plenty of folk who never learn to read or write. It must make running a business quite difficult, though?'

'I've always managed. I have my own way of keeping track.' She points at the clutter of objects on the shelves behind her.

'Oh?' Birdie cannot keep the scepticism from her tone.

'These top shelves here hold objects that remind me of the contracts I have to supply ships.' She picks up a goose feather.

'This tells me I supplied a dozen geese and half a dozen chickens to the *Ice Queen* – a whaler that sailed to the North Water in July. I ken the Captain well, and I trust him to pay me on his return in November.'

The look on Margaret's face is suddenly vulnerable, searching for approval.

'Well, that is a form of book-keeping,' Birdie suggests. 'You use objects and their placement on these shelves instead of figures and a ledger book.'

'Exactly.'

Birdie crosses to take a closer look at the cabinet; the shelves are a cornucopia of seashore finds and ships' paraphernalia – harpoon tips, buttons, knives, needles, scrimshaw, thimbles, shells, blue-speckled eggs, delicate birds' skulls. A puffin's beak. Her eye is caught by a small, brass volcano which she cannot immediately identify. She picks it up and holds it closer to her eye.

'Part of a sailmaker's palm,' Margaret says. She has recovered her authority. 'It holds the needles so they can be pressed into the canvas.'

Birdie tilts it to the light, and sees letters punched around the border. Sailors have a habit of marking their belongings and tools with their initials or those of their ship. She squints and deciphers HMST. Her mind springs back to the sight of the *Temeraire* being towed along the Thames.

'Did you supply HMS *Temeraire*?'

'The *Temeraire* has never anchored in Stromness. That palm is from the *Terror*.'

Birdie gasps. 'Franklin's ship?'

'A sorry tale. Stromness was her last port of call this side of the Atlantic. May 1845.'

Of course, it would have been. Still, it takes her by surprise to trip over these ghostly relics of Franklin's expedition that seem to litter the town – the reward poster, and now this melancholic reminder of all those men who set sail to the Arctic and never returned. She turns to examine the shelves again, half expecting to find a coin with a pelt etched on one face – Margaret supplies the Company's ships, after all. She is disappointed. As far as she can see, there is no Company token of any kind among Margaret's mementoes. The flaws in Margaret's system, however, are easy to spot: her cabinet of objects may give her an overview of her contracts, but the devil is in the detail. And in the shipping business, the detail is always written in a contract. Margaret's inability to read makes her dependent on her book-keeper and vulnerable to swindlers.

Margaret senses Birdie's concern. 'The business is sound. I have no problem with the sums; I do those in my head. I can make a good deal. But I need a reliable book-keeper.'

Birdie shuffles her boots. She is here, after all, to search for information on Tobias Skaill and she is uncomfortable with the extent to which Margaret is placing her trust in her after barely one hour. She feels the need to confess her own weaknesses to balance the scales. 'Well, I'm good with accounts. But I can be quite reticent with strangers.'

Margaret gives Birdie a firm gaze. 'I'm not paying you to blether. I'm paying you to manage the books. So long as you do that, we'll rub along just fine.' Margaret flashes her a conspiratorial smile. 'Anyway, you may be quiet, but I suspect you're no doormat.'

Birdie grins; Margaret's assessment is correct – she retains a stubborn streak despite the attempt of Frank and others to stamp on it. Margaret looks Birdie up and down, still appraising her, even though she's already offered her the position.

'You'll be needing lodgings?' Margaret asks.

'I have a room at Flett's Hotel for now. It's quite costly, though.'

'I could offer you board and lodging. I'd deduct the rent from your wages, of course, though I think you'll find the terms reasonable.'

Birdie opens her mouth, hesitates. The offer is both good and bad; she wants to discover more about the Skaill family, yet she mustn't reveal too much about herself. She has a feeling Margaret's offer has not been made out of simple kindness – she wants to keep an eye on her. She's beginning to suspect that Margaret's rationale for taking her on is as complex as her own reason for being here. Still, she warms to Margaret. And she has nowhere else to stay.

'Thank you. That's a very helpful offer.' Her face falls. 'I have a pet.'

Margaret chuckles. 'The talking bird?'

'Yes. A parrot.'

'I've heard it mentioned.'

Word travels fast in Stromness.

'It doesn't make much mess. I'd keep him in my room.'

'And I have two peedie bairns, so I hope you don't mind them. I'll keep them out of your way. Orphans,' Margaret adds. 'I'm caring for them.'

There is a possessiveness in her tone that deters Birdie from asking further questions.

'The parrot, where does it come from?'

She told the manager at Flett's it was her husband's; she'd better be consistent with her stories, as notes will inevitably be compared.

'It belonged to my husband. He was a sailor.'

Margaret nods sympathetically. Birdie holds her breath, hoping Margaret won't ask about Patrick; it's true he was on a ship when he died and therefore technically a sailor, but he had only joined the crew when he was accused of a trail of warehouse robberies and had to escape the police. Thankfully, Margaret is more interested in the parrot than Patrick.

'I've heard sailors are attached to these birds. Although there are not so many on the ships heading to the Nor' West.'

She steps toward the office door. Birdie follows suit.

'Ask the porter at Flett's to help with the trunk.'

As they pass through the hall, Birdie notices the second door is open a crack, and in the instant before Margaret pushes it firmly shut, she spies two identical faces, one above the other – straight hair shiny and jet black, skin the colour of cinnamon. Margaret ushers her to the front entrance. 'I'll keep them from under your feet,' she says. 'Have no fear.'

The sun burnishes the muddy puddles and lightens the gloominess of the street. She enters the reception of Flett's Hotel. The maid is waiting.

'Thou found Mrs Skaill?'

'Yes, thank you.' And she saw Margaret's bairns too.

In her room, the parrot is sulking in his cage. She searches for her twist of seeds, notes she needs to replenish her dwindling supply and realizes that, in her keenness to secure the position, she forgot to ask Margaret for the details of her remuneration. She reaches for *The Orcadian*, spreads it on the desk, intending to re-read the notice to check whether it contains any information about the salary, when a short paragraph on the front page catches her eye. Here is another mention of the doomed Franklin expedition.

While scarcely any subject however important in itself is now gaining adequate public attention besides that ill-engrossing topic, the war in Crimea – yet a tear must be shed at the recital of that tale of woe, as told by Dr Rae, of the probable end of our enterprising countryman Sir John Franklin, and his gallant companions, in discovery in the Polar Regions. We believe that another expedition is about being fitted out, and is following, as far as possible, Dr Rae's report, any additions to which, we fear, can only amount to a melancholy confirmation of the Doctor's Report.

She is interested to note that, in contrast to Dickens' article, the *Orcadian*'s reporter does not rage about cannibalism, savage Esquimaux or Dr Rae's naïvety. She reads the final line.

Dr Rae is a native of Orkney, and a son of the late John Rae Esq., who resided in Clestrain House, parish of Orphir.

Ah. Now she sees. Dr Rae is an Orkney man and a well-regarded member of this community; he would hardly be judged a gullible fool by the reporters of the islands' newspaper.

'Dr Rae is an Orkney man,' she says to the parrot. The parrot lifts a claw and picks it with his beak. 'What do you make of that?'

The parrot says nothing, but she finds herself pondering on the connections. Tobias Skaill is an Orkney man who was murdered by an Esquimaux and Dr Rae is an Orkney man who discovered, from the Esquimaux, the fate of Franklin's crew. It's a knot she cannot quite untangle, though an idea is forming in her mind; perhaps the murder of Tobias Skaill has some link to the search for Franklin. But what could the motive possibly be? Money, Solomon said, was the usual incentive for murder. She recalls the poster flapping on the fisherman's hut advertising the Admiralty's reward for information about Franklin's fate.

'Twenty thousand pounds. A fortune.'

The parrot is more interested in nibbling his claws than in listening to her theories.

And then there is Margaret Skaill. Birdie is convinced she is related to Tobias in some way and, furthermore, it appears she has two Esquimaux children in her care. She feels ashamed that she has not been honest with Margaret about the true reasons for her journey north, yet she is beginning to wonder which of them – her or Margaret – has more to hide.

Chapter 6

The parrot preens himself as she carries the cage along the street, enjoying the sly glances of passers-by. The hotel porter has delivered her trunk to Narwhal House, and the manageress has promised to hold her letters. Birdie dashes under the whalebone arch and raps on the door. Margaret welcomes her inside, nods at the parrot. 'What a queer bird.'

'He'd look better if he had his tail feathers, for sure. I don't know why he plucked them out.'

A protest, she thinks, at Frank's cruel treatment.

'Does it bite?'

'No, he's a shy creature.' Shy is not quite the right word to describe his character; he picks his moments carefully is probably more accurate. 'He doesn't speak much.'

'Keep it upstairs all the same. It'll no disturb us there. Your room is at the back, above the office.'

She follows Margaret up the narrow staircase. Hinges creak and she senses eyes on her back. As she reaches the top, she glances down and catches the door closing. A moment of silence follows and then she hears muffled giggling; children with their hands over their mouths, trying to suppress their laughter.

Her room is separated from Margaret and her charges by a long landing. It is bare – a narrow bed, a small desk, an oak press in one corner, and a mirror with a rosewood frame fixed to the wall. There is one window with a view over the harbour.

'Supper is at six in the parlour. The bairns eat earlier, in the kitchen with the cook. I'll leave you to make yourself at home.'

Margaret pulls the door shut behind her. Birdie places the birdcage on the desk and surveys the view from the window. Skiffs and dinghies scuff the shoreline. Skuas fight for fish gut on the far end of the nearest pier. There is no sign of the seal. Beyond the grey water, the dark island of Hoy rises in a steep heathery slope to the lofty sandstone cliffs. And beyond Hoy lies the heaving Atlantic. Clouds chase across the vastness of the sky. The room moves in and out of shade, but even when the sun breaks through, it's chilly. She searches for a shawl, wraps it around her cold shoulders, catches her reflection in the mirror. Could she pass as an islander? She lifts the shawl over her head and peers; her skin is paler and smoother than the weather-beaten faces of the people here, and her limbs are long and gangly while many of the women have brawny arms from lifting heavy baskets of fish. Her fine, black hair, which refuses to form ringlets no matter how many curling papers she uses, and beaky nose mark her out anywhere. She's been surprised, though, to find that many of the folk here are quite tall – like her – it must be their Norse ancestry. She'll have to take care in this small town where the moves of every stranger are the subject of doorway conversations; Stromness is remote, but she cannot make a slip with her name or her story.

She selects three hemp seeds from her twist of bird feed. Hemp is the parrot's favourite, she has discovered. Da's canaries ate hemp seeds too. Keep it as a treat, he used to say. She holds the tiny seeds to the bars of the cage. The parrot takes them one by one in his scaly claw, cracks the shells with his beak, lets the husks drop to the floor, nibbles the kernels delicately.

'Skin for a skin,' she says.

The bird ruffles his feathers. She unpacks her trunk, hangs her layers of black mourning in the press, stacks the petticoats and drawers on a shelf. The giggling of children somewhere below catches her attention. And then she hears an adult's chuckle too. It takes her a moment to realize it's Margaret – the light-hearted laughter contradicts Birdie's assessment of her somewhat severe countenance.

She waits for the sun to cross the harbour before she descends the stairs. She does not wish to intrude. There is laughter coming from the parlour. She lifts her hand, raps shyly at the door. The merriment stops abruptly.

'It's me, Birdie.'

'Come in, come in.'

She enters the plainly furnished room and catches a glimpse of two children squatting in one corner, playing with a kitten, dangling a length of string in front of its nose, teasing it and coaxing the tiny ball of tortoiseshell fluff to cavort and jump in the air. They glance up simultaneously as she enters. Four dark eyes peering out with shy curiosity below shiny, straight black fringes and prominent, round brown cheeks. They are identical; cast from the same mould. They can't be much older than eight. It's difficult to tell whether they are boys or girls with their pudding-bowl hair and their thick woollen clothes gathered around them as they crouch on the ground. Birdie is certain now, though, that they are Esquimaux children, and the supposition causes her pulse to quicken. She finds herself looking askance at Margaret. She calms herself, tries to resist leaping to conclusions. She has not discovered yet whether Margaret is related to Tobias, or even knows of him. The fact that she has two Esquimaux children in her care may be a coincidence.

Margaret positions herself between Birdie and the children, and blocks her view. There is a defensiveness to her move, as if she is afraid Birdie might attack her charges.

'Hope and Grace.' Margaret makes a vague gesture of introduction with her hand, but before Birdie has a chance to greet them she turns and orders them away.

'Upstairs. To your room.'

She shoos them with a flap of her fingers. The girls giggle and show no sign of leaving their games with the kitten. Margaret steps toward them.

'Upstairs.' Her voice is stern, a sharp contrast to the carefree laughter Birdie heard as she descended. The twins understand her tone and respond immediately this time, jumping to their feet, their movements synchronized. One of them grabs the kitten. It swipes playfully at the child's hair as she bundles it in her arms, skips across the floor and follows her sister through the door.

Margaret catches Birdie's enquiring glance. 'The tailor's cat had kittens. I needed one to catch the mice.'

Birdie wonders how much she can ask without provoking a defensive reaction. 'They are as alike as peas in a pod. Are they twins?' She tries to make the question sound like a casual enquiry.

'Aye.'

'How do you tell which is Grace and which is Hope?'

'Grace has a scar above one brow.' Margaret grimaces, plainly battling with how much she should give away. 'They're from the Nor' West. Labrador,' she adds. 'They came here on the *Harmony*. A ship that makes the journey every year to supply the Moravian mission at Hopedale, on the coast. They'd been abandoned and one of the missionaries rescued them.' She reaches for a basket of crumpled linen sitting on the table. 'I was happy to take care of them. I have no bairns of my own.' She rummages in the basket.

'They are Esquimaux children?'

Margaret brushes her hair back from her forehead, twiddles and pins the strand that has worked its way loose and mumbles something which Birdie takes as confirmation. 'They speak no English,' she adds more clearly. 'They communicate with each other in their own language.'

'They seem to understand well enough what you say,' Birdie suggests.

Margaret does not respond.

'Have you been caring for them long?'

'A while now, aye.'

Margaret selects a napkin from the linen basket, folds it neatly, and makes it plain she has no wish to discuss the origins of the orphans further.

A heavy thump on the ceiling causes Margaret to look up. She dashes for the door, concerned that one of the girls might have had an accident. Her stride is broken by a gurgle and a burst of laughter. She shakes her head, places her hands on her hips.

'They can be a handful. Thankfully the cook helps around the house, but she's getting on in years and there's too much work for her alone. The last maid left – she was offered a position in Kirkwall with the minister's family. I'm hopeful that a cousin's daughter can come to help with the household duties soon.'

'Do they attend school?'

Margaret scowls. 'School isn't the right place for them when they don't speak English. I don't want them getting the strap or bullied.'

Birdie suspects they'd learn the language very quickly if they went to school – they seem lively and bright – but she keeps her opinion to herself, not wishing to aggravate. She spies a wooden toy on the floor and stoops to pick it up; a doll-sized sledge with skilfully carved slats and beads for decoration. A toy that has been crafted with love and care.

'This belongs to the twins?'

'Ah that.' Margaret snatches the sledge from Birdie's hand and places it in the linen basket. 'Their father made some toys for them. I'll return it to them later.'

Margaret's response strikes Birdie as odd, though she cannot instantly put her finger on the problem.

'I could help you look after them,' Birdie says. 'I'm happy to play games with them, or teach them some English.' She is curious about the twins but it is a heartfelt offer, if tinged with an edge of guilt; she wishes to assist Margaret in any way she can.

'You'll be busy enough with the papers,' Margaret says, and takes the linen basket into the kitchen.

*

Birdie spends the week with Margaret, learning about the business – debts, current commitments and future plans. Its foundations are strong, even if the recent papers are in disarray. She accompanies her employer to the wooden warehouse by the north pier, where she is introduced to the two local men employed to oversee the stored merchandise and deliveries. Margaret is more at home here, organizing men and supplies, than in the office with the ledgers. Birdie watches as she ensures the provisions for the Company's convoy are all carefully packed in watertight crates and loaded onto the rowing boats that ply between shore and ships. There are still only three Bay ships anchored in the harbour; Birdie concludes the fourth that was with them at Gravesend Reach must have set sail across the Atlantic before she arrived.

Back in Narwhal House, she familiarizes herself with the office. The children – the peedie bairns as Margaret calls them – remain a ghostly presence. She hears faint laughter, and discerns whispered conversations in a language that sounds to her ear like the call of gulls or the rush of the sea; it could be their native tongue or a secret language which only they know. The girls themselves remain invisible, apart from the occasional glint of an eye or a disappearing heel. And sometimes she hears the knock, knock of the small wooden sledge as it bounces down the stairs. Or trips over a toy canoe, made by the same skilful hand as the sledge she supposes, and left in the darkened hall.

By the end of the week, Margaret has enough confidence in Birdie to leave her alone for the day and trusts her to deal appropriately with any prospective patron who might visit. She has hired a gig that will carry her and the twins to Orphir, where a producer of oilskins resides. Birdie senses that Margaret has been suffering from cabin fever, unable to leave the office unattended for too long, and now she has a book-keeper on the premises, she is determined to make the most of it. In the absence of a maid, Margaret also has many household purchases, or *messages* as she calls them, to complete. When they return to Stromness in the afternoon, she intends to do the round of the local merchants and purchase cotton smocks for the girls; they have no clothes suitable for warmer weather, if and when it arrives. Soap, flour, beremeal, butter and mutton are also on her list. If the bairns behave themselves they will buy sweeties from Mrs Robinson's shop on the corner when they return, Margaret promises them as they descend the stairs. The smiles on their faces confirm Birdie's view that the twins understand more than Margaret allows.

Birdie sits alone in the damp and dreary office. Rain batters the window and flattens the water of the harbour. Margaret's assessment was correct; there is plenty here to keep her busy. Opposite the cabinet of aide-mémoires, there is a bookshelf crammed with ledgers; the labelled spines indicate their contents. Wages, party contracts, bills of lading, provisioning, merchandise, the commission of crews and other personnel, and even the day books – the diary of what happens each day – are neatly ordered by date up until 1850. This is the year that Margaret's trusted book-keeper died, and she was forced to employ Donald Shearer. He didn't serve her well; even a cursory glance at the shelves suggests that, beyond 1850, there are missing ledgers. Piles of invoices, notices of unpaid bills and letters about various business matters have accumulated since Shearer was sent packing the previous autumn, but she can't help thinking these might be easier to deal with than the accounts to which he put his hand. Birdie can understand Margaret's delay in hiring another clerk; the records are in a mess that requires careful and tactful untangling rather than gung-ho yanking at the knot. She decides to work backwards and address the most recent letters first.

A monotonous church bell chimes. She corrects herself; a kirk bell chimes. She intends to learn the locals' vocabulary, an attempt to blend in with her surroundings. She glances at the office clock; nine – she'll have to make a bigger dent in the unsorted piles of invoices before Margaret returns if she is going to impress her employer.

A knock at the door derails her concentration. She tuts with frustration, crosses the hall, drags the front door across the flagstones and is met by a face that is the opposite of hers in almost every respect: his skin the ruddy shades of a cox's orange pippin, his hair flaxen and curly below his cap. If she is a pale crescent moon, he is an unclouded, blazing sun. He beams with an openness that is hard to resist. He wears a fusty jacket and moleskin trousers but he is, she reckons from the smoothness of his full cheeks and the unworn look of his hands, younger than her. The windswept rain pounds him from behind, though he appears entirely untroubled by the drenching.

'Please, come in out of the rain,' she says.

He steps over the threshold.

'Peter Gibson.' He removes his cap, and shakes the drips

on the hall floor. 'You'll be Mrs Skaill's new book-keeper?'

She nods.

'The lady with the parrot, if the gossips of Stromness are to be believed.'

He speaks with more confidence than his boyish face suggests he should possess.

'I do indeed have a parrot.'

'I'm sorry for your loss.'

'My loss?'

He nods at her black dress. 'You're in mourning.'

'Of course. My loss. Thank you for your sympathy.'

'Birdie White, isn't it?'

He is inquisitive, but his questions are delivered with a charm that makes him hard to resist.

'That's right. How can I help?'

'I was wondering whether Mrs Skaill has any notices she would like to place in next month's *Orcadian* – ships arriving, cargoes landing, that kind of thing.'

'You work for *The Orcadian*?' She hopes she doesn't sound alarmed.

'Indeed. A reporter. I cover Stromness and the western half of Mainland.'

She takes a step back, his chirpy manner suddenly less appealing.

'Perhaps I could leave a note for her?'

Birdie certainly doesn't care to be friendly with a reporter, but neither does she wish to arouse suspicions by behaving defensively. She invites him into the office, and attempts to hide her misgivings.

'I have some paper and a quill.' She gestures at the clerk's desk.

'Ah, thank you. I have my own pencil with me. I'll be quick and leave you in peace. I have a story to investigate.'

'A story?' Her stomach lurches.

'The editor wishes me to go to Evie to report on a chicken that was believed to be on its last legs but has been revived by a glass of whisky.'

He chuckles, and she laughs along.

'I'm afraid there's never anything very dramatic to report in Orkney.'

He says it wistfully; he's a young man with ambition that stretches beyond the confines of these small islands.

She reaches for a piece of paper. 'Here, let me make a note of your message for Mrs Skaill.'

'Of course; you must be very busy. I shan't detain you. Perhaps it would be easier if you simply informed Mrs Skaill that I dropped by to enquire about possible advertisements, if you don't mind?'

'Not at all.'

'Mrs Skaill will be aware of our terms and conditions; she's sent her housemaid to place notices with us before.'

Birdie had wondered who helped Mrs Skaill write the advertisement for a new book-keeper.

'And Mrs Skaill is, of course, a good friend of the *Orcadian*'s proprietor.'

'Is she?'

'Indeed. The proprietor is on good terms with many of the merchants here, not least because he's dependent on advertising revenue to keep the newspaper afloat. He has ambitions to publish the paper weekly instead of once a month.' Peter rubs his smooth chin. 'In point of fact, I was prevented from running with what I considered to be an interesting story in this month's edition precisely because the proprietor didn't want to upset Mrs Skaill.'

Birdie curses herself for allowing Peter to charm her with his chatter into what she suspects may be a difficult corner.

Peter continues undeterred. 'I had a mind to follow up on a report that appeared in *The Times* recently.'

Her vision blurs, she sways and sees the body of Tobias lying on the foreshore. She places one hand on the table to steady herself and feels certain that Peter has read the report of Tobias's murder. There is no restraining him, she calculates; she might as well get it over and done with as quickly as possible and find out what he knows.

'What story would that be then?'

'It was about Mrs Skaill's cousin.'

'Cousin?'

'Tobias Skaill.' He gives her a conspiratorial nod. 'Murdered.'

'Murdered?' Her stomach flutters and she is afraid it will erupt. 'That's terrible.'

'According to *The Times*, the body was found by the Thames.'

'How awful. Perhaps he got into a drunken argument.' She manages to keep the alarm from her voice. 'Such fights are common in London.'

She is relieved Peter hasn't mentioned the Esquimaux and his accomplice; he has an envious gleam in his eye, which makes her suspect he is more concerned with the scoop he has lost than the detail of the story.

'I've heard Mrs Skaill and her cousin were close,' Peter says.

'Well, she's said nothing about his murder.'

He folds his arms, leans back against the wall and muses. 'Though Mrs Skaill does know about it, I'm sure, for when I asked the editor if I could write a report on the story, he came straight over here from Kirkwall to obtain her views.'

'And what were her views?'

'Mrs Skaill made it clear to the editor that she didn't want Tobias's death talked about and the editor ordered me not to mention it. He's very strict. He doesn't like fuelling gossip.'

She smiles. 'Quite right too. Though now you've broken your word to the editor and told me about the story.'

'Indeed. But you have a trustworthy face.' He grins in a way that is more evil imp than cherub. 'And anyway, you're a stranger here so folk will be more interested in telling stories about you than listening to the tales you might have to tell.'

She attempts to ignore his needling; this is the way reporters work, she has concluded, they charm people into unwariness and then goad them into saying more than they intended.

'It's a shame, though,' Peter says. 'It would have made a good story. The name Tobias Skaill alone is enough to get folk here interested even though he hasn't set foot on the islands for ten years.'

'Why does this Tobias arouse so much interest?'

'Well, I'm afraid he had something of a dark reputation; always in trouble, getting in fights. And worse.'

'Worse?'

He glances over his shoulder. 'The rumour is, he murdered another lad, and when the bailie came to question him, he disappeared without a trace. Vanished.'

'And all this happened ten years ago?' She attempts to sound offhand.

'1845. That's a summer folk remember here, the year Franklin's convoy was anchored in the harbour.'

'Oh, I've heard about that.'

'I remember it well, though I was only a bairn. It was such a grand sight. The two ships *Erebus* and *Terror* heading for the Nor' West, the men-of-war steamers that accompanied them from Gravesend, all on display out there.' He nods at the harbour, barely visible through the curtains of rain. 'They were caught in a storm off the English coast and lost most of their livestock. They arrived in Stromness harbour on the last day of May, and there was a rush to resupply them before they had to set sail again for the Arctic.'

He pauses and gives her a sly glance. 'Some folk say that, while they were anchored here, Tobias stowed aboard one of Franklin's ships, and that was how he made his escape.'

Birdie tries to stop her gaze sliding toward Margaret's cabinet of aide-mémoires and the sailmaker's palm from the *Terror*.

'Well, that's very interesting, Peter. But I'm sure your editor's decision not to publish a story about his murder is the correct one. It sounds as if there are more than enough stories about the poor man already.'

He shrugs. 'Still. It's a shame.'

There is a pause in the conversation, filled with the tick of the clock and the beat of the rain.

'I'd better be getting on,' Birdie says awkwardly. 'I'll let Mrs Skaill know you enquired about notices.'

He grimaces as he nods, and she suspects he's not on good terms with Margaret. He probably waited until he knew she was out before he knocked on the door, hoping to win Birdie over in Margaret's absence. He replaces his cap, heads for the hall, pauses at the front door, tilts his head.

'And the twins?' he asks.

'What about them?' she retorts.

'They're well?'

'Yes.'

'Mrs Skaill hasn't spoken about their origins?'

'No. She hasn't.'

'I've heard a few stories about them too. Finfolk, that's what people say.'

Her mouth opens as the penny drops – so that was why Margaret reacted angrily when she mentioned the Finfolk tales she'd heard. 'I would have thought folk had better things to do than gossip about small children.'

She leans past Peter and hauls the front door open. Wind and rain blast in; a hooded crow flaps against the gusts.

'Well, it was very pleasant meeting you,' she says.

'Likewise. I hope we find time to talk some more.'

She smiles and says nothing as she pushes the door shut with her shoulder; she will have to be wary of Peter – his inquisitiveness and nose for a story could be dangerous. On the other hand, she has gleaned more from him than she gave away, she hopes. She has learned that Margaret and Tobias were cousins. Furthermore, Margaret is aware he was murdered, though, thankfully, she can't have read all the details in *The Times*. And Tobias had a bad reputation, though the more she hears about him, the less inclined she is to judge him harshly. Accused of murder he might have been, but as she well knows, such accusations are often false and directed at those who may be viewed as different or strange by others. She returns to the office, picks up the sailor's palm from the *Terror* and holds it to the dull window light for a moment before she replaces it on the shelf and settles herself at the desk.

The cook shouts that there's a stew on the range for supper and she's leaving for the day. The rain eases. The sky blazes crimson and gold. The leaden sea deepens to black. Birdie lights a candle so she can continue sorting papers while she awaits Margaret's return. The long twilight in these islands is eerie, it shifts the shape of things. She holds the candle high and surveys the office; the guttering flame carves grotesque shadows from the bird skulls, telescopes and chronometers jammed on the cabinet's shelves. Nothing here is quite as it first seems. The light flickers on the sailor's palm, and she wonders whether it's possible that Tobias was aboard the *Terror* when it left the safety of Stromness in the summer of 1845.

Margaret and the twins return late. The front door creaks and, through the open door, she spies the twins slip past and silently climb the stairs. When they giggle, they seem like other young girls. But they also have a quietness to them; a stealth and gracefulness of movement. Margaret's desire to keep them hidden under her wing is understandable; she can see why they may fuel other folk's curiosity.

Margaret enters the office. A knock and a giggle come from above. 'Into bed now,' Margaret shouts. There is more laughter, the patter of feet, silence and then a bump, bump, bump as some object glides down the stairs. Margaret shakes her head, retreats to the hall, returns clutching the toy sledge.

'They've been as good as gold all day.'

She places the sledge on the table, lights an oil lamp, snuffs the guttering candle. The waves of high tide break below the window. The oil lamp sways in Margaret's hand and the yellow glow slips and washes across the room, as if they are in a rocking ship, adrift upon the ocean.

'How did you fare with the papers?'

'As you said, there's a lot to do. I've made a start.'

She holds the lamp higher. 'Did anybody come by the office today?'

The tone of her voice suggests she was half expecting trouble.

'Peter Gibson.'

Margaret's mouth tightens.

'You shouldn't trust him.' She gives Birdie a reproving look and adds, 'What did he want anyway?'

'He wondered whether you had any notices for this month's *Orcadian*.'

Margaret plonks the lamp on the desk; the sledge bucks.

'Oh really?'

Birdie is alarmed by Margaret's sudden anger.

'Tell me,' she says. 'Was he bad-mouthing my family?'

Birdie can feel the heat in her cheeks; she is tongue-tied, unable to speak for fear of revealing what she herself knows about Tobias. Margaret spares her the dilemma.

'Did he blether about my cousin, Tobias?'

Birdie nods.

'Did he say he was accused of murder?'

Birdie catches her breath. 'He mentioned something of the sort.'

'I suppose he also told you that they found his body in London a couple of weeks ago. Murdered, they say.'

Margaret catches Birdie's eye. Birdie opens her mouth

and wrestles with her conscience; this is the moment to confess. She senses Margaret would sympathize if she were to explain now the events that brought her to Stromness. Margaret has also plainly suffered from the false accusation of murder against her cousin; she would have little time for the unfounded charges of London's river police. She tries to formulate the words. The clatter of the black-backed gull landing on the windowsill breaks the silence.

'I'm sorry for your cousin's death,' she says.

'You've no need to apologize.'

Birdie flushes with guilt.

'Tobias was a fine lad,' Margaret says. 'I looked after him when he was a bairn. His mother passed away young. Agnes Rouse. She was a rare beauty. He inherited her red hair. Shankie we used to call him – his hair was the same bright shade as the redshank's beak. And he was hot-headed, but then he had a lot to be angry about.' She arches a brow. 'And, I suppose, Master Gibson was also digging around for information about the orphans in my care?'

Birdie winces. Margaret thumps the desk with her fist and the lamp rocks, topples and drops on the flagstones before either of them can catch it. The glass casing splinters. A pool of oil seeps out. The wick flickers and burns in the spillage. Margaret lifts her foot and extinguishes the flame with a stamp of her boot.

'What business is it of his?' she hisses. 'Why is he prying?'

Margaret slumps in the wooden seat, reaches for the sledge and clutches it to her chest, head bowed as if in silent prayer. The rawness of Margaret's reactions flusters Birdie; she stands awkwardly for a moment, wondering what to do, then steps over and places an arm around her shoulders. And as Birdie comforts her, she notices Margaret's red-knuckled hands still grip the toy sledge as if she is afraid it might come to life and take flight. Margaret takes a deep breath, stands, waves the sledge in the air.

'I'll take this to the bairns.'

Birdie is left alone in the office. The white walls glow scarlet as the rainclouds clear and the glow of the setting sun fills the room. She remembers Margaret said the toy was carved by the father of the twins, and she has an intuition that Margaret knows more about his identity than she admits.

Chapter 7

It is nearly a week since Peter Gibson visited Narwhal House. Birdie lies on her bed in her dress, as she has done every night since she arrived in Stromness. The curtains billow in the sea breeze gusting through the open window. The town is peaceful. The Company ships have departed for Rupert's Land and there are no rowdy sailors carousing in the street. Yet she is unable to sleep. It's not the crimson glow of the sky that makes her restless; the coppery light washing the room is quite calming. Rather, it's the pressing thoughts of Tobias Skaill's murder that keep her from slumber. She fears she is as far as ever from finding answers to the questions on which her own life depends. She heaves a sigh – she hoped to have some news of the investigation from Solomon by now, but she's asked three times already at Flett's Hotel, and they've received no letter. Has he forgotten her? She tuts at the thought and tells herself she'll have to solve this without him; she's beginning to wonder how much help she can expect from Solomon anyway. He might be a good detective, but he's never going to find it easy contending with the Filth who've had their grip on the river for years.

'Solly,' she says. The parrot clucks, as fidgety as her despite the shawl she's draped over the cage to block out the light. She sighs and rolls over, but still she cannot sleep. A kirk bell clangs; there are several kirks in Stromness but only St Peter's, the Presbyterian church, has a bell. Its chime is sterner than any of the peals of London's steeples; save perhaps the grim toll of St Sepulchre that announces the hangings outside Newgate. Margaret told her she attended St Peter's every Sunday – and added Birdie was welcome to accompany her if she wished. Birdie politely declined the offer. She'd been baptized and married in the local Catholic chapel, but has not regularly attended a Sunday service of any denomination since she left school; she finds no comfort in prayer. Distance from her childhood faith is something she has in common with Solomon, she recalls; he stopped attending the synagogue when his father died.

The bell tolls again. Birdie gets up, closes the window to try and block the noise and returns to her bed. But now she is wide awake. She decides she will do what she did in London when sleep evaded her; she will walk. She wraps her cape around her shoulders, takes the heavy iron key which Margaret has given her, creeps along the landing, and carefully avoids the creaky board halfway down the stairs. The office door stands ajar; she glances at the wagging clock as she passes through the hall. Eleven. She eases the bolts on the door, inserts the key, twists, pulls, steps into the alley and locks the door behind her. Hopefully, Margaret will not awaken, and slide the bolts while she is wandering.

The jawbone of the whale looms, pale and larger than ever in the twilight. She runs beneath it, not wishing to linger in its shadow, and steps briskly south, thankful that the summer nights are indeed so light for there are no oil or gas lamps along the street. She hasn't strolled this way before – her exploration limited to the piers and warehouses to the north. The road is so narrow here, if she stretched her arms she could touch the bleak buildings on either side. Ahead, a huddle of men stand drinking outside an inn; she doesn't want to pass them in case she is recognized. The tinkling of a stream draws her attention to a steep flight of steps on her right, squeezed between forbidding granite walls. She climbs, following the tumbling water. Hunched sycamores squat in the small breaks between the stone; their leaves whisper as she passes. Even the trees notice the presence of a stranger in Stromness. The stairway leads to a rutted track, lined by a row of low, decrepit dwellings with turfed roofs sagging and puddles of midden slurry lapping at their thresholds. It's something of a shock to come across these sorry crofts, invisible from the main street; every town has its hidden, shameful rookeries, she supposes.

She follows the track south-west, up Brinkie's Brae to the pilot's look-out above the town. The ground tilts beneath her feet. A dog howls. Another answers its call. She keeps walking. Past a crumbling barn and the clinkered half-hull of a schooner, serving as a fisherman's shed. The buildings peter out and are replaced by lichen-scabbed dry stone walls. The hoot of an owl first scares and then thrills her. She quickens her pace, hitches her skirt indecently high, and runs up the hill, the wind strengthening beyond the shelter of Stromness. Her lungs ache with the exercise. At the summit, she pauses. Purple thistles, their heads as large as artichokes, dip in the breeze and the flowers of eyebright gleam like fairy dust in the twilight. Ahead, the green and brown patchwork of ridged fields falls away to the indigo sea. The moon is luminous and pink in a magenta sky. Night-time usually leaches everything of colour, but here in midsummer the landscape is drenched in rich and dreamlike shades.

She breathes deeply. A curlew calls. The wind rustles the grass and nettles. She stretches her arms, half expecting a gust to carry her away over the fields like a swallow. She tips her head back to drink in the heavens. And freezes. Her left ear catches a peculiar creaking sound; she has been followed. She pivots, heart thudding and legs heavy, and peers along the rutted track. A speckled bird runs across the path and disappears in the long grass of the verge. She thinks at first it is a quail, but when it makes its queer call again she realizes it must be a corncrake. She laughs at herself – the city dweller scared by a bird – though her sense of freedom has evaporated and she cannot conjure it again from the night air. She flaps her hand, dispersing the midges which, she now notices, are everywhere. She surveys the bleached stone walls and identifies a grey path that winds around the boundaries of the fields and descends to the sea. The track continues along the shore to a headland, where she spies the crosses and sepulchres of a walled kirkyard; it must be Warbeth where Margaret's family lie buried. In Southwark, the living and dead are packed so close, bones and skulls poke through the damp walls of Surrey-side basements. Here the dead are exiled to the very edge of the island, their past and all their secrets well and truly hidden. Beyond the lonely kirkyard, a lamp glimmers in the window of a low croft. The light arouses her curiosity; a wakeful soul, like her, unable to sleep in these long, mysterious hours. She heads in the direction of the tombstones and the lamp's inviting glow.

The fields on either side of the path are divided into strips by earthen banks and planted with potatoes and kale. The land, she assumes, belongs to some grand Laird, and farmed by the families that dwell in the meaner fringes of Stromness and struggle to make a living from their paltry furrows. The owl hoots again. She halts, glances over her shoulder. Satisfied she is alone, she continues to the coast. The whiff of rotting seaweed is almost enough to make her gag. Down below, ridges of blackened kelp scar the shingle – dried and burned here to make potash, according to Margaret. She quickens her pace, eager to escape the sulphuric odour. The track dwindles to a narrow path hugging shallow cliffs. The steady rhythm of the waves soothes her rattled nerves, though she is unable to shake the sense that somebody is following her.

The kirkyard marks the neck of the headland; the defensiveness of the wall invites her to peer over. She cannot pass by without having a look for the graves of Margaret's family: her grandfather Albert Skaill and husband, Callum Fraser. She scrabbles for a foothold in the crumbling mortar, heaves herself up, holds her weight for a moment on the toe of one boot, raises the other leg as high as she is able in her constraining petticoats, perches on top of the wall, surveys her surroundings and is surprised to detect the notes of a fiddle carried on the breeze. The music can only come from one place – the croft with the lamp. Somebody is playing 'Lady Franklin's Lament'. She listens to the familiar notes – there's something uncanny about the fiddler's choice of this particular ballad – and finds herself drawn in by the melancholic song. She pictures Lady Franklin grieving for her husband, lost in the Arctic; cold fingers stroke her cheek, icy eyes gleam in the shadows. Whispers fill her head. She tries to resist and stop her mind from slipping, but her skin prickles and her limbs go numb as the spirits of the dead surround her and the grassy headland disappears. For a moment, her vision blackens and her head feels dull, then she glances down and sees the corpse of Uncle Dennis laid out below, his watery blue eyes wide open. Frank is at her elbow; the two of them here to pay their last respects. Her gut is tight with fear, but she cannot look away; her uncle seems to be staring up so pleadingly. He tried his best for her, she thinks. Dennis always was a greedy sod, Frank mutters; fitting that he should die from a seven-course feast with his pals. Birdie leans over her uncle's body and closes his lids with a brush of her hand. They spring open again and he stares at her once more as if he is determined to convey some final message before he departs. Frank offers her some coins to weigh the lids down, but she has already turned away and the coins clatter to the floor.

The music stops abruptly. Her skin is clammy, her mind spinning, disturbed by the vision of Uncle Dennis. What was he trying to tell her? She wonders whether she should return to Stromness; her night-time visit to this kirkyard has stirred the ghosts that haunt her. She reasons with herself – she is here now, she might as well continue. And anyway, she can't escape her spectres – they accompany her wherever she walks.

She adjusts her cape so it doesn't catch, springs away from the wall and lands with a thud. She looks around. No ghosts, only headstones. She examines the nearest markers; small limestone tablets, etched with a name and short inscription.

Further away, she sees the more elaborate obelisks and draped urns of the wealthy. The Skaills are a merchant family and they will be buried among these grander tombs, even if there is a question about the ancestry of some of the family members. It doesn't take long to find their graves. Albert Skaill is buried next to his sons, Bruce and Edward. And nearby is the grave of Agnes Skaill, née Rouse. She recalls Margaret telling her that Tobias inherited his red hair from his mother, Agnes. She glares at the tombstone, as if it might reveal some clue about Tobias, but there is none.

She spies a headstone marked *Callum Fraser, beloved husband of Margaret, died 1840.* Margaret had implied she no longer visited the kirkyard, but the grave is well tended by somebody. At its head, there is a small jar containing sweet-smelling fresh flowers – roses, fuchsia and veronica. She stoops and sees that, behind the flowers, two more names are etched in the stone – Alison and Elspeth Fraser, who also died in 1840 aged four and six, beloved daughters of Callum and Margaret. She stares, almost embarrassed to have discovered Margaret's buried secret. She had two children and some accident or sickness took all three of her precious loved ones in the same year. Her eyes brim; she lets the tears drop. If the daughters had lived, they would be about the same age as she is now; this surely helps to explain Margaret's generosity to her. And the arrival of the twins on a mission ship from Labrador must have seemed like God-given compensation for the girls she lost. Yet they must also stir deep fears; Margaret is undoubtedly haunted by the deaths of her own children and worries that she will be unable to keep her charges safe. Birdie kneels awhile, head bowed, overcome with pity for Margaret and her grief.

The mew of a gull stirs her; time to return to Stromness. She stands, steps to the wall and heaves herself up as quickly as she can; she does not want to be caught by the spectres again as she crosses this boundary between life and death. She's about to dismount when she's distracted by a sound – snuffling. She twists her head, trying to locate its source. There it is again, a muffled snort, and rustling grass. A rabbit or some small nocturnal creature, she reassures herself. Another snort draws her eye along the kirkyard wall. She drops clumsily to the ground, stumbles, rights herself and follows the path. At the corner, she peers around and yelps, unable to contain her astonishment when she sees two black-haired children retreating. Her intuition was correct, she was being followed. It had not occurred to her that the silent trackers might be eight-year-old girls. Hope and Grace. They should not be wandering at this time; Margaret would be apoplectic if she discovered they were out of bed. Their sleep must have been disturbed when she descended the stairs; she guesses they climbed out the bedroom window – they are both agile enough to make it safely to the street below.

'Stop. Come back.'

They take no notice, and scamper along the wall, away from the path. She shouts again and this time they both turn in unison, hands on mouths, shoulders heaving. They are giggling. Their failure to see the seriousness of their situation frustrates her. Without pausing for thought, she does what she has witnessed Frank do many times when he wants to halt his nippers in their tracks; she curls her hands in the air like a monster and roars like a mad beast. The effect is immediate and far worse than she intended. The twins shriek and clutch one another and appear to be truly terrified. She is appalled; what was she thinking? She should have known better than to copy Frank.

'I'm sorry,' Birdie shouts as she stumbles toward them. 'Wait.'

They are too petrified to move. She crouches, opens her arms to embrace them. They flinch, but thankfully do not try to escape. She can feel their hearts beating next to hers, their breaths shallow and fast. They were brave enough to trail her in the gloom, laugh when she first caught them, and yet, suddenly, their courage has deserted them.

'I didn't mean to scare you. I was pretending to be a monster because I wanted you to stop.'

Their eyes regard her searchingly. One of them mumbles something that sounds, to her ears, like *monster*, and she supposes they have understood what she is saying, though they are still clearly alarmed by her actions. Her imitation of a monster must have hit a peculiar nerve – reminding them of some fierce creature of their homeland; a giant polar bear perhaps or some vicious sea creature. Still, this is no time to speculate; she must return them to the safety of Narwhal House.

'I'm going to take you home.'

They nod. Their synchronized movements are disarming; she finds it hard to be severe or admonish them for following her. She smiles, stands and offers them each a hand, which, to her relief, they take.

'The path,' she says and nods at the coast.

Before they have time to move, a gunshot cracks the night air. One of the twins yelps, as if she has been hit. Birdie instantly ducks, pulls the girls to the ground, and encircles them in her arms again. They are unscarred, but their eyes are round with terror. She is momentarily as petrified as the twins until a second shot is followed by a triumphant yell.

'Got the damned creature.'

The man's voice is loud and he isn't a local; a hunter of some sort, she assumes. The twins sniff and shake in her arms; they recognize the crack of gunshot.

'Shh. Shh.' She places her finger on her lips. 'Have no fear. He's not after us.'

She says it with more confidence than she feels. He might not be after them, but he is a strange man with a weapon and nobody knows they are alone with him here in the twilight. The scent of gunpowder drifts on the breeze. She listens again, hoping for more noises that will reveal the hunter's whereabouts. There is silence. She releases the girls from her grip.

'Stay there.'

She raises her palms to them, then presses a finger to her lips. They nod obediently. She crawls along the wall to the corner, hands pricked by thistles, skirts snagging on rocks, and surveys the headland. The lamp in the isolated croft has been extinguished and, as she watches, a huge black bird rises from the roof and flaps toward her. A raven. It caws, reaches the edge of the cliffs below the graveyard and plummets. The clattering of stones is followed by shouting.

'Get away, you evil beast.'

More rocks fall.

'Leave me alone. Find your own damned dinner.'

The raven is attacking the hunter, attracted by the smell of blood and eager to share the corpses he carries. Serves him right. More pebbles fall and a squat figure emerges above the rim of the cliff, scrabbles onto the coarse grass and heads in her direction. Birdie stoops and runs back along the kirkyard wall.

'We have to climb over and hide until he passes,' she says as she reaches the twins.

She doesn't want to take any chances – at the very least, if he meets a strange woman in a cape out at night with the twins, he might spread harmful tales around the bars of Stromness.

'Quickly. Let me help you.'

They stand without further explanation and reach for the top of the wall. She lifts the nearest to assist her, but the girl is nimble and does not need much help. The second child is already halfway over before she can offer her arm. Birdie is the one who flounders, hampered by her wretched mourning garb.

They crouch between two tombstones. She places her arms around them again. A surge of fierce protectiveness makes her draw them close; she knows what it's like to be an orphan. And the thought of Margaret's turmoil if anything should happen is too much to contemplate. Her musings are interrupted by footfall on the path. She tightens her grip on the twins. The steps become louder, then pass beyond the wall. A self-satisfied whistle floats on the breeze. Birdie dares to peer above the parapet. The hunter swaggers along the path, long-barrelled gun in his hand and, slung over one shoulder, the dangling corpse of a grey bird, garnet eye glinting in the rays of magenta light. A patch of ruby feathers marks its neck. A dead red-throated diver.

She bobs, brings her face level with the twins.

'We'll wait a little longer.'

CLARE CARSON

They both frown, and she is momentarily reminded of Margaret's stern expression. The phrase *family resemblance* plays on her mind and, as she observes them, she notices something odd; their hair gleams more coppery than black. Perhaps it is an illusion, a reflection of the reddish midnight sky.

'He's a hunter,' she says. 'He shoots birds.'

Grace – the white scar above her brow is more visible in this crepuscular light – points to the brooch pinned to Birdie's dress.

'It's a canary. I like birds. Do you?'

In the tail of her eye, she catches Hope nodding, a gesture which the girl abruptly curtails when Grace elbows her in the ribs. Birdie makes no comment on their silent communication, though she is certain they understand most of what she has said. And, as she glances at them again, she sees they both have amber freckles scattered across their cheeks. A picture of Tobias Skaill's face, splattered with mud and freckles, flits into her mind. Is it possible Tobias is their father? That would explain Margaret's reticence about their origins; she wouldn't wish their paternity to be known, for Tobias's reputation in Stromness is not good.

She stands and sees the hunter has disappeared. The horizon still glows crimson and gold and casts the fields in a hazy purple glow. *Grimleens*, the locals call this mysterious midnight twilight; it is more shadowy than clear though, as she looks down at the twins crouching at her feet, she realizes it reveals all kinds of secrets.

Chapter 8

She steps into the office, bright with early morning sunshine. She blinks, tired from the adventures of the previous night. A shadow blocks the sun and dims the room; the black-backed gull is on the window ledge, its white eye roving the office through the glass as if it were searching for something.

'What do you want?'

The gull opens its beak, displaying its cavernous gullet and long pink tongue, and calls *uk-uk-uk*.

Margaret appears, 'Oh the baakie. Away with you.'

The gull flaps off. Orcadians have their own names for every gull and wader. What was the name Margaret used for the redshank and her red-headed cousin Tobias? Shankie, that was it.

Margaret readies herself for a meeting with a solicitor in Kirkwall. A Stromness shipbuilder has issued a summons against her, claiming she owes him a sum of money for a schooner she ordered ten years ago but was never delivered. He's a desperate man, Margaret says. A drunkard who's frittered his family's cash in the taverns of Stromness. Kirkwall is nearly three hours' bone-rattling drive away by coach, but it's where the best solicitors are to be found. There is a carriage departing at eight from the Mason's Arms, and it will return from Kirkwall at five. It's a relief to have someone to mind the office, she says, while she runs around the place dealing with these dishonest men.

Birdie feels a twinge of guilt when Margaret praises her reliability; not that she is unreliable, but she's keeping an increasing number of events and thoughts to herself. To her own unfortunate connection with the murder of Tobias, she can add the night-time escapade with the twins and her suspicion that Tobias is their father. She can hear Hope and Grace now, laughing in the kitchen while the cook encourages them to tie their laces. The promised housemaid hasn't yet materialized, and Birdie is beginning to suspect Margaret doesn't want another person around the house, asking questions about the twins. They seem to have recovered from their fear, but she remains puzzled by their reactions; something in their past still has the power to terrify them.

'I can keep an eye on the girls while you're away,' she suggests.

'No need,' Margaret says firmly. 'The cook has kindly offered to take them over to her sister's farm for the day. The bairns seemed a little out of sorts this morning,' she adds.

Birdie holds her breath.

'Will you mind being alone for the day?' Margaret asks.

Birdie shakes her head, pleased they've not been discovered. 'I'll be fine.'

'Bring that parrot of yours downstairs if you need the company.'

The cook returns with the twins at four, feeds them a supper of clapshot – the heavy mix of neeps and tatties sufficient to make anybody drowsy – and escorts them to their bedroom. Birdie catches them peering curiously through the open office door at the birdcage as they are ushered upstairs to bed. The sky has blurred from turquoise to coral before Margaret returns, tired and irritated after her day in Kirkwall. She is surprised to find Birdie still in the office.

'I wanted to make some headway with these papers.' She nods at the diminishing piles of letters on the desk.

'And to think, when I first saw you I questioned whether a woman could be a book-keeper. These men.' Margaret waves her hand dismissively. 'Some of them think they can take advantage. You'd have thought they would have learned better by now. No visitors today?'

'Nobody.'

The town bell ringer interrupts their conversation; he shouts the day's news as he passes through the streets at nine each evening.

Margaret nods at the cage on the table. 'And the bird, has it been good?'

'He's hardly made a noise all day.'

Birdie is about to reach for the cage when the parrot stirs.

'Solly,' he says.

Birdie gasps; the imitation of her own voice is startling and completely unexpected; she's sure she hasn't said the name aloud more than a couple of times.

'Did that bird just say Solly?' Margaret asks.

Birdie nods.

'I thought it was you speaking. Goodness, what a canny bird.'

Margaret bends, bringing her face level with the parrot.

'Solly,' Margaret says.

The bird ruffles his feathers, repositions his black claws on the perch, hunches one wing coyly, tilts his head to one side.

'Solly,' the parrot repeats, and sighs.

Margaret chortles with delight. 'Weel, that's certainly cheered me after a trying day in Kirkwall.'

She straightens and catches Birdie's eye.

'And who is Solly?'

Birdie feels the heat in her cheeks.

'Solly? That's the parrot's name,' she says quickly.

'Ah. Solly.' Margaret nods and smiles. There is a spark of mischief in her black eyes. 'You're obviously fond of the bird, if its imitation of your affectionate tone is anything to go by.'

Birdie opens her mouth, about to repeat the story that it was her husband's pet, but she sees that Margaret is gently teasing. She smiles, lifts the cage and heads upstairs to her room.

She places the cage on the desk; the parrot squawks hungrily. 'Solly,' she says, but she isn't thinking about the bird; her mind is on the creature's namesake. Her hand touches her yellow brooch and she pictures their first meeting – Wednesday 1st October 1851. Her twenty-first birthday and Mr Wolff had given her the day off along with the two tickets for the Great Exhibition in Hyde Park. She was with Hugh O'Brien, one of Frank's less disreputable pals, so he claimed. Hugh could not be budged from the Colt stand, where a handsome showman with a long moustache and big-brimmed hat was demonstrating the new six-shooter revolver to the gathering throng. The American twirled the gun around his finger before loading each of the cylinder's six chambers with powder.

'The ruler of the New World,' he proclaimed. 'Six rounds without the effort of reloading. It's what you need when you're surrounded by Indians; you can shoot your way to safety.'

Birdie failed to see what shooting Indians had to do with the Exhibition's message of the peaceful benefits of free trade. She edged away, her attention drawn by the tinkling of the central Crystal Fountain. She glanced back to look for Hugh, but he'd disappeared. He could come and find her, she decided as she drifted through the crowds to the India Court, and the giant stuffed elephant at its centre.

Hugh appeared at her elbow.

'What a beast.' He nodded at the elephant's wrinkled flank.

'The poor creature...' She faltered; in the periphery of her vision she could see a line of coppers in their tall top hats advancing through the throng. 'Hugh, look over there...'

His face dropped.

'I've gotta leggit. Grab hold of this, will you? Careful, though. It's loaded and ready to go.'

He dived into the crowd, and headed for the entrance. She glanced down at the object he'd stuffed in her black silk hand muff, the grip protruding. A revolver. She hardly had time to realize he'd stolen the loaded Colt and palmed it off on her before a copper's whistle shrilled. Pandemonium erupted as the police chased Hugh. She watched helplessly as they closed in on him on the far side of the hall. Without thinking, she searched for a gap, lifted the revolver, aimed at the stuffed elephant and squeezed the trigger, her instinct to create a distraction and give Hugh a chance to escape. The kickback winded her, the cloud of smoke made her cough and the instant tinkle of breaking glass flipped her stomach; she was sure she'd misfired and hit a glass pane. The crystal walls would crack and shatter. Petrified, she waited for the roof to splinter and rain down on the crowd below. Nothing happened. Through the cloud of smoke, she noticed the swing of the beads that dangled from the golden howdah on the elephant's back – she'd clipped the decorations and hit one of the creature's legs. In the commotion, nobody had noticed the gunshot. Satisfied she wasn't observed, she dropped the revolver, gently kicked it toward the stuffed elephant, grabbed her skirt in one hand and headed to the entrance.

Outside at last, she took her bearings; the sun was listing and London's dusk was pink and smutty and full of starlings. If she could make her way south to the river she'd be fine. A shout made her turn; Hugh was being carted in her direction by a bunch of bobbies. Panicked, she bolted across the grass and over a road, dodging Hansom cabs and omnibuses. She glanced behind, certain she was being followed, but could only see vague shadows. Breathless in the autumnal heat, she took a side street, pounding past imposing terraces and hurrying through grand squares. Across the sweep of Regent Street, heading into Soho. She glanced over her shoulder again and, this time, she saw a man pursuing her; quite tall and spare, jacket flapping, a bowler hat on top of loose black curls. Who was he? What was he? Too rakish to be a clerk, too smart to be a docker. He raised his hand.

'Madam, please. Wait.'

She tried to run but couldn't pick up much speed with her stupid petticoats catching around her legs. She skipped and tripped over a kerb. A hand grabbed her arm, prevented her from falling. She twisted around, expecting a hard, accusing stare but instead found an amused and fiery glint. It took her a second longer than it should have done to detach her gaze from his olive face. She righted herself, brushed her skirt, stole another glance at her pursuer. He wasn't exactly handsome, she told herself. Though his mouth was broad and full and his eyes gleamed with dark intensity. And what was that smell? Cloves. Coffee. A spiciness that made her want to draw a little closer.

'Madam, are you hurt? You're very pale.'

'I'm always this colour.'

She dodged his searching gaze, peered over his shoulder and spotted a gaggle of prostitutes in gaudy dresses gathering in a doorway further along the street. She didn't need their help, not yet anyway. She had no idea who this stranger was, but she could handle him; he wasn't that hefty. He tightened his grip on her arm. Perhaps she had misjudged the situation.

'Madam, will you come with me?'

'I'd rather not.'

'There's a matter I need to discuss with you.'

He started walking, urging her along, edging her toward a shaded alley. She'd had enough of this now. 'Let go of me.'

'Please, try to stay calm.'

'I am calm. You're assaulting me. Now piss off or I'll call the police.'

'Madam,' he said. 'I am the police.'

She opened her mouth, no words emerged.

'Madam, I'm a policeman and I saw you fire a revolver.'

She spluttered. 'You're no policeman. Where's your uniform?'

'I don't have a uniform.'

'Well, you can't be a policeman.'

'I am.'

She perceived an edge of defensive insecurity to his tone that made her suspect he wasn't a proper policeman. Perhaps he was a guard from the India Court – his skin was dark enough to be an Indian, she reckoned.

'Who do you work for then?'

'The Met.'

She didn't believe him; he looked like no Met copper she'd ever seen, and she'd had the misfortune to see a fair few. 'You're from London?'

'Yes.' He sounded offended. 'Though my parents were from the Rhineland.'

Now she got it. 'You're Jewish?'

He shrugged.

'And they let you work for the Met?'

'Why not?'

'Well, I don't know…' It was true that Disraeli had become a Member of Parliament, but only after he'd renounced his faith and been baptized. She was about to argue, then decided to drop the subject. What did it matter? 'I didn't know the Met had any plain-clothes policemen.'

'They do. It's called the detective branch. There are ten of us. Hand-picked.' He beamed. 'Detective Sergeant Solomon Finkel.'

She couldn't see what he had to be so proud about.

'That's not fair.'

She glanced over his shoulder again; if she could catch the eye of one of those girls, she might be able to make a dash for it and take cover in the brothel.

'What's not fair?'

'Plain-clothes detectives. That's what they do in France. That's spying on people.'

She attempted to step backwards to get a clearer view of the street, but his hand still held her arm and prevented her from moving.

'How else are we supposed to keep track of Hugh O'Brien and his ilk?'

'Ilk?'

'Irish dockers on the fiddle. Men like your father, done for murder, am I right?'

'Sir, you are very wrong. My father was an innocent man. And as he is deceased, perhaps you could show a little respect.'

She had an urge to kick him.

'I'm sorry. You're right. It was wrong of me.'

His apology took her by surprise – when did policemen start admitting their faults? Though she wasn't about to back off now.

'How do you know about my father anyway? I hope you've not been spying on my family.'

'Not your family specifically, no. That's not my remit.' He flushed.

'What is your remit then? Chasing innocent women across Soho? I'll have you know, my father might have been an Irish docker, but I'm a clerk in a very respectable London shipping agency.'

She yanked herself from his loosened grasp, broke away, managed to run a few steps before he grabbed her hand again. His black-lashed lids crinkled at the corners. Was he laughing at her?

'You're a respectable clerk?'

'Yes. I work for Standing and Wolff.'

'Well, you're the first respectable clerk I've met who takes potshots with a revolver at stuffed elephants in the middle of Hyde Park.'

There was a note of admiration in his voice. And much to her irritation, it pleased her. She reddened, trying to work out how to respond, when the trilling of a bird made them both look up. A cage was sitting in the open window of the premises behind them, a canary perched inside, serenading the sunset.

'Oh. That's the best thing I've heard all day,' she said.

'A Harz Roller.'

'How do you know it's a Harz Roller?' she asked with astonishment, forgetting he was a copper.

'My father purchased a pair from a Huguenot. He kept them in his workshop; he said they reminded him of home. I'd recognize their song anywhere.'

'Da always said they were the best singers. He had a chick he named the Little Prince; it had two black feathers on its crest. He was sure it would become a Canary King and win all of London's singing competitions. He used to have a serinette.'

'A serinette? A little wooden barrel organ with a...' He mimed turning a small crank with his hand.

'Exactly so! We used it to teach the canaries to sing.'

The memories of Da made her eyes water.

'Here.' He dug in his pocket and produced a cotton handkerchief.

'Thank you, Detective Finkel.'

'My pleasure, Mrs...?'

She hesitated. What should she give as her name? Widow Quinn? Birdie? 'Mrs Bridget Collins.' She wiped her eyes, returned the handkerchief, glanced at him slyly. It was hard to dislike a man who recognized the song of a Harz Roller. Even if he was a copper.

'Well, Mrs Collins, would you be so good as to confirm that the revolver you fired was removed by O'Brien from the Colt Exhibition Stand?'

She said nothing.

'I understand. You don't want to rat on your friend—'

'He's not my friend, as such.' She flushed again. Why was she explaining herself to this man? Why did she want him to know she wasn't attached to Hugh? The canary trilled above her head and it occurred to her that the Harz Roller was a sign, a nod from Da.

'Look, this is what I suggest we do,' he said. 'You confirm to me that it wasn't you who took the revolver. I'll report I found it underneath the stuffed elephant in the Exhibition Hall. And then it's up to the officers over in Hyde Park to ask O'Brien how it got there, and we'll assume he has the sense and decency not to mention you.'

She narrowed her eyes. 'Are you sure you're a policeman?'

He arched one eyebrow.

'I didn't take the revolver from the Colt stand,' she said.

'Thank you.' He raised his bowler and his dark curls flopped over his forehead. He smiled at her in a way that made her skin tingle.

'Nice to meet you, Mrs Collins.'

He swung around, walked away and left her wondering whether it was the last she'd see of him.

The parrot squawks and reminds her he's still hungry. She reaches for the twist of seeds and drops some through the bars. He flutters and bobs as if to thank her for her efforts; he's an endearing creature in his own funny way. Solly is as good a name for him as any, she supposes, though she suspects she'll never be able to use it without thinking of Solomon. Here she is, after all, nearly four years since she first met him, waiting anxiously to see if she'll hear from him again.

Chapter 9

The day is bright, but cold gusts rattle the office window and carry the smell of tar and salt into Narwhal House. Birdie waits for Margaret to leave for the warehouse before she crosses to the memory shelves and surveys the array of objects that provide a coded key to the shipping contracts. The office is like a giant reliquary, the clutter on the shelves the ghostly remains of Atlantic crossings and lives lost to the sea. Every ship embarking on that perilous six-week voyage has to be a self-contained floating world holding everything the crew needs to stay alive and sane. Franklin, she heard, took a barrel organ for each ship on his ill-fated voyage, to provide musical accompaniment for the daily exercises of the crew.

She searches again for the sailmaker's palm, which Margaret placed there as a reminder of her contract to supply Franklin's expedition. She lifts the brass needle holder from the shelf and holds it at eye-level, regards the letters punched along one side. HMST. Her Majesty's Ship the *Terror*. Margaret Skaill supplied the *Terror* in the summer of 1845, after Franklin's ships arrived from Gravesend and found safe anchorage in Stromness harbour on the last day of May. And, according to Peter Gibson, one of the expedition's ships is rumoured to have taken aboard an extra person before they set sail again on their doomed search for the North-West Passage. Tobias Skaill.

She replaces the brass palm, spins on her boot heel, crosses to the shelves on the far side of the office, locates the day book for 1845, heaves it from the shelf by its leather spine, coughs as dust motes fill the air, and places it on the tall sloping clerk's desk. The damp pages stick; she separates and turns them with difficulty. The journal is reluctant to reveal its secrets. She reaches June, casts her eyes down the entries, all made in the neat handwriting of Margaret's trusted original book-keeper, and locates the lines for which she is searching: *4th June supplied and delivered to HMS Terror; two pigs, four sheep, 1,248 pounds of Scotch barley.* There is another entry on the line below. *In addition, supplied one bolt of appropriate weight canvas for repairs to flying jib torn in storm on first leg of journey from Gravesend.* Well, now she knows why Margaret chose a sailmaker's palm to remind her of this contract. But the prosaic note in the day book fails to reveal any further clues to the mystery of Tobias Skaill's life and death.

The clang of the kirk bell makes her jump; she has yet to do any work. She returns to the table with its piles of papers that Donald Shearer left in his wake – she is steadily working through the backlog as well as dealing with the current accounts – and takes a letter from the top of the pile; a query about contracting one of Margaret's ships. She reads the details, crosses to the clerk's desk, levers herself on the high stool, reaches for her quill and starts scratching a reply.

Giggling from the hallway breaks her concentration. She dismounts, steps across the office, opens the door a fraction, glimpses black eyes peering around the parlour door. She crosses the hall and enters the parlour. She can hear the cook bashing pans in the kitchen. The twins have retreated under the table. Hope and Grace have been wary of her ever since the night she caught them trailing her and pretended to be a monster; she still feels the need to make amends for scaring them so much.

'Would you like to see my parrot?'

They do not answer.

'My parrot talks.' She beckons.

They glance at each other, searching silently for agreement, and edge out from under the table. Grace is clutching the wooden sledge. Hope, the canoe. *Their father made some toys for them.* The oddness of Margaret's words strikes her again; Margaret told her the children were abandoned orphans, rescued by the missionaries. And yet, she knew the wooden toys were made by their father.

Birdie indicates the toys. 'Father?'

The twins stare at her, their eyes round and unblinking like a pair of owlets. Fear, incomprehension, or perhaps some pact to stay silent; it's hard to tell. She points again. 'Da? Pa? He made these?' She hesitates. 'Tobias?'

Neither of them respond, though she spots Grace's eyes flick to Hope and back as if she is looking for some confirmation of her own thoughts. It would be counter-productive to push them too much.

'I'll fetch the parrot.'

She carries the cage downstairs to the office, clears a space among the papers on the table and rests it there. The parrot hunches his shoulders. She returns to the parlour and finds the girls, still clutching their toys and nursing anxious expressions.

'Come and meet my parrot.'

They follow obediently.

'This is Solly.' She flushes as she says the name. The twins rest their toys on the floor and inch closer to the cage. She hopes the bird will co-operate.

'Look.' She crouches so her face is level with the bird. She raises her arm, creates a beak shape with her hand and snaps her fingers and thumb together in front of the bird's eyes. She watched the Limehouse birdseller perform this trick on his parrots and cockatoos. 'Settles 'em,' he said when she asked him why he did it. 'A nervy parrot don't say dicky.' Solly is unimpressed by her bird calming gestures and tilts his head sceptically. She gives up, digs a paper twist from her pocket, removes a couple of millet seeds and pokes them through the bars of the cage. He cracks them in his beak, drops the husks, turns his back on Birdie and the twins while he consumes the innards.

She straightens. 'Solly only speaks when he feels like it.'

The girls' faces register disappointment.

'He needs some encouragement to talk.'

She grins at the twins. They stare down at their feet. The black-backed gull taps on the window. The parrot flaps, clucks, shuffles around on his perch to face the window.

'Who's a pretty boy then?'

The twins laugh with glee. The parrot assesses them over his hunched wing, as if he has only just registered their presence.

'Hope. Grace.' Birdie says the names clearly and gestures at the twins.

The parrot bobs up and down. Birdie repeats the girls' names. Hope steps closer to the cage, copies Birdie's impression of a beak, snapping her stubby child's fingers and thumb together.

Solly whistles, long and loud. Grace joins her sister and peers at the cage. The parrot mimics Birdie's voice. 'Hope. Grace.'

The girls jump back with surprise, clap their hands with delight. The parrot squawks and repeats his newfound words. 'Hope. Grace.'

The twins shriek and laugh. The parrot whistles again; he's enjoying the attention.

'I'll take him to the parlour,' Birdie says. 'You can talk to him in there.'

Margaret might not approve, but she is absent for the morning, the cook is in the kitchen and she cannot afford to lose much more time entertaining the twins.

She settles herself back on the stool, dips the quill in the ink bottle and, as she does so, she catches sight of the wooden toys with which Grace and Hope were playing. She sinks to the floor and reaches for the canoe. A wooden frame covered with taut animal skin. Seal? She places it gently beside her skirt then takes and examines the sledge; an exquisite snowflake has been expertly carved in the centre of each strut. A canvas harness for pulling the sledge is attached to a slot in the front strut by means of a bone toggle. She examines the fastening; it's the type of toggle used to close a sailor's pea coat, and there are letters engraved in the bone. She squints. HMST. Her skin prickles and her arms feel numb. The room darkens and a sudden chill descends. The floor, it seems, is no longer made of wooden planks, but cracked ice. She stretches her free hand to test the surface and feels something hard beneath her fingertips. She drops her eyes and gasps when she sees what she is touching; grey skin. A human face, one eye staring up and the other an empty socket, the eyeball missing, lips drawn back as if in a snarl to reveal clamped teeth. A frozen corpse, lying partially submerged below the ice. She yanks her hand away, puts it to her mouth to cover her scream, sees the body is still fully clothed in a striped shirt and navy wool jacket which has been carefully fastened with a bone toggle. Her breath is short and shallow. She squeezes her eyes.

The kirk bell chimes. She blinks. Her head throbs. The office is awash with sunlight. The twins are laughing, repeating the parrot's words, encouraging the bird to speak. She looks around; there is no ice. No corpse. She cannot make sense of this apparition. She stands silently, walks to the office door, still clutching the sledge, leans against the frame and listens to the twins talking. *Hope. Grace.* The parrot repeats their words and then starts showing off. *Who's a pretty girl then?* he shrieks. Now the twins repeat Solly's phrase. *Who's a pretty girl then?* They speak the syllables with an ease which convinces her they are familiar with the sounds. If they don't speak English, it isn't because they cannot, but because they will not; she suspects they are afraid. Perhaps they have good reason to be scared.

The heavy rap of the door knocker interrupts her thoughts.

'Hello there.'

A man's voice.

'Wait a moment, please.'

She returns the day book for 1845 to its correct position on the ledger shelf. She takes the sledge and canoe to the parlour. The girls are so engrossed in talking to the parrot they do not notice her enter.

'Hope, Grace.'

They startle. She smiles reassuringly, places her finger to her lips.

'Hush now. I have a visitor.'

Her concern is not so much that the twins will disturb her conversation, but more that their chatter may rouse the curiosity of her visitor. She is adopting Margaret's tactics, protecting the twins from the curious eyes and loose tongues of Stromness bletherskates.

The rap-rap sounds again. She closes the parlour door, crosses the hall, heaves the front door and is met by the glowing face of Peter Gibson. He has a newspaper rolled under his arm.

'I never heard back from you about the notices.'

'Mrs Skaill had none.'

'I thought you might like to see this month's edition anyway.' He puts his foot in the door, removes the paper from under his arm and waves it like a baton. 'Hot off the press. I'm pleased to say I managed to slip some proper news in this month's edition.'

She wills herself not to flush; has *The Orcadian* published a report about Tobias's murder after all?

'Stromness has a detective,' Peter says.

'Detective?' she asks, with a mixture of relief and apprehension.

'Aye.' He unrolls the paper, points halfway down the front page. 'If I rest it on the desk, perhaps you could read it more easily.'

She recalls Margaret's warning not to trust Peter, but he's halfway inside the hall already, so there seems little point in refusing him entry to the office.

He arranges *The Orcadian* on the desk and indicates a paragraph below the heading *Law and order.*

She reads:

Crime of late has been very prevalent in Stromness, even shop-breaking. We are happy to state, however, that Mr James Thompson has been appointed Detective Officer in this district, and we are certain that he is in every respect adapted for such an office. Mr Thompson has already been very successful in cases that would do honour to anyone, even in Edinburgh or Glasgow. We hope that he will be the means of keeping down street rows etc. and every assistance and encouragement should be given him in promoting peace and quietness in the town. We also observe Detective Thompson on the look-out every morning on the steamer's arrival, in case any suspected character should arrive in town, and he has full power to bring such persons before the magistrates to give an account of themselves. If your police should so act at your end, we would have less of the riff-raff that usually frequent our affairs.

He beams. 'What do you think?'

He is fishing for compliments, and she obliges. 'It's very well written.'

'Thank you.'

'And Detective Thompson...'

'Oh, he's most impressive. The council was lucky that he agreed to take the post. Apparently, it was the birds that swayed him. He's an ornithologist in his spare time.'

'He studies birds?'

'Yes. Shoots and stuffs them.'

She recalls, with a sinking feeling, the hunter firing his gun the night the twins followed her to Warbeth kirkyard.

'Is he stout?'

'Indeed. A bulldog, in appearance and in nature, so I've heard.'

That's all she needs; a belligerent gun-swinging detective on her trail.

'Has he been here a while?'

'He arrived a few weeks ago. Have you met him?'

'I...' She scrabbles for a convincing story. 'I think I might have seen him up by the warehouse pier. He's employed to watch the harbour?'

'He investigates crimes too.'

'Ah.' Her gut feels heavy. 'Though from what you say about these islands, he might not have many of those to solve, unless they involve drunken chickens.'

'Ha, yes. His talents may indeed be somewhat wasted here. He should go to London and join the detective branch at Scotland Yard if he wants to make his name.'

Her throat is dry. 'He has a connection to the police in London?'

'Not that I know of. I was merely suggesting that London might offer more opportunities for a man of his talents.'

'Of course. Is he a plain-clothes detective?'

'Yes. Though if I'm to be honest, his plain-clothes are not very discreet; he has a patch over one eye – a hunting accident – which marks him out from the townsfolk somewhat.'

She hadn't spotted the eye patch in the gloom. Despite her anxiety, she can't help smiling at the idea of a plain-clothes detective with an eye patch. 'Indeed. Most plain-clothes officers make an effort to blend in with those they are observing.'

'You're familiar with plain-clothes detective work?'

'No. No. Not at all.' The words flit from her mouth like nervous moths. 'I know very little.'

'You sound as if you're well informed.'

He gives her a sideways glance and a hint of cunning appears in his cherubic features.

She thinks quickly of a way of distracting him and grabs at the first thing that comes to her mind. 'By the way, I was wondering about the story of Tobias Skaill stowing away on one of Franklin's ships when they left here in 1845.'

'Oh?' His eyes light up.

'Is there no report of him at all after he vanished?'

'Well, of course there are stories.'

There are always stories in Stromness it seems.

'What stories are those?'

'Well.' He leans closer. 'Some folk say Tobias remained aboard the ship after it sailed from Greenland and entered Baffin Bay. But then he came across the Finfolk, who dwell underwater in the far northern seas, and he made a bargain with them; they helped him escape the ship and reach safe land in exchange for the lives of Franklin and his crewmen.' He whispers, 'So it was Tobias and his Finfolk friends who drew all those poor men to their icy death.'

'That's not what Dr Rae reported,' she retorts more fiercely than she intended, irritated by the malicious story. 'He said Franklin's ships were trapped in the ice and the crews starved to death. He made no mention of Finfolk.' She shakes her head dismissively. 'It's nothing but tittle-tattle.'

'Quite so, but you did ask me to tell you the stories. I'm not suggesting they're true. The Skaill family,' he adds, 'have a reputation for mixing with the Finfolk. Margaret's grandfather, Albert Skaill, is rumoured to have taken a Finn bride.'

'I thought his wife came from Rupert's Land.'

'Exactly.' Peter raises an eyebrow. She opens her mouth, then closes it abruptly when she grasps the implications of what he is saying; she sees it in the sleekness of Margaret's mahogany hair and her coal-black eyes. Margaret's grandmother was a native of the Nor' West – an Indian maybe or an Esquimaux – and Margaret carries faint traces of her ancestry that would pass unremarked in London's streets. But here in these tiny islands, small shades of difference are noticed and those who do not fit in for one reason or another may be vulnerable to accusations that they are vindictive Finfolk and witches.

A cloud shadows the sun, darkens the room and she wonders whether Tobias is indeed a sea sorcerer who lured Franklin's ships to their ice-bound fate. Though if Tobias did possess such evil powers, she reminds herself, he would have found a way to escape the prosaic fate of being murdered and unceremoniously dumped on the sludge banks of the Thames in the bleak hours before a May dawn. She pictures the ligature marks on the corpse's neck and the flesh removed from his cheek; he was strangled by a length of rope, killed by a man's brute strength and butchered by human savagery. There is an earthly explanation for the disappearance of Tobias in 1845, and his murder ten years later. If only she can find it.

'Did you ever meet him?' she asks.

'Tobias? In fact, I did meet him once when I was a child. He repaired the church in Orphir – my father was the minister there. I remember seeing his red hair as he climbed over the roof; it was hard to miss.'

'He was a roofer?'

'No. A carpenter.'

She thinks of the toy sledge and her eyes widen.

'Is that surprising?'

'No. No. Not at all.'

'He was very skilled, I heard it said. The Ness boatyard has produced many Orkney men who are fine carpenters.'

The squawk of the parrot from the parlour draws Peter's attention.

'That must be the famous bird that folk are talking about?'

She nods.

'Could I…'

She glances at the clock. 'Another time. I should be working.' She gestures at the table and its piles of paper. 'I'll be out of a job if you detain me much longer.'

'Of course. My apologies.'

He makes as if he is about to leave, stalls, raises his hand to his mouth and says, 'By the way, if you're interested in stories about Tobias Skaill, Morag Firth is the woman you should visit. She's rumoured to know what happened to him after he disappeared from Orkney.'

'Morag Firth?'

'You've not heard of Morag Firth? The witch and windseller of Stromness?' he asks melodramatically.

'I've heard other people say Orkney is full of witches.'

'Well, I don't know about that.' He rubs his chin. 'I have to admit, though, Morag Firth does have some queer ways. She keeps a raven for a pet and it's hard not to think it could be her familiar.'

Birdie is curious. 'I've heard ravens are very intelligent creatures and can be taught to speak quite well.'

'Like your parrot?'

He says it with a grin, but the comparison between a witch's raven and her parrot is unnerving; the steward of the *Dog Star* told her that many Orkney women accused of witchcraft were rounded up and burned. It might have been a long time ago, but she fears the old attitudes run deep. She attempts to make light of the conversation.

'Does this Morag Firth fly on a broomstick?'

'No. But according to the local gossip, her mother was a mermaid, taken as a wife by a Finman.' He giggles, almost nervously. 'I've heard that Morag's powers of shapeshifting are well known and witnessed. Apparently, she changed herself into a man, sailed to Rupert's Land and worked as a Company voyageur for many years without a soul suspecting her true identity.'

The Hudson's Bay Company seems to be woven through every story in Stromness.

'And now, apparently, she sells winds and God knows what else to any sailor who will pay her.' He leans forward. 'Folk say she's a whore; for how else would she find the means to maintain her croft and garden so well?'

She steps back; she doesn't want Peter to think he can be so intimate.

'Morag Firth sounds like quite a character.'

'She's certainly somewhat fierce.'

'Does she live nearby?'

'She has a croft on the ness.' He waves his hand. 'Beyond Warbeth kirkyard.'

Birdie opens her mouth and closes it quickly when she sees Peter watching; Morag Firth must surely be the fiddler she heard playing 'Lady Franklin's Lament'. Birdie can half believe Peter's description of her strange powers – she's already felt the unnerving enchantment of her night-time music.

Peter adds, 'Though if she does have stories about Tobias, she's quite reluctant to tell them.'

'You've asked?'

He nods. She supposes Peter tried to question her about Tobias for his proposed article on the murder.

'Maybe she's too busy to gossip.' Her comment is sharper than she intended. Peter takes it with good humour and a smile; he needs a thick skin to be a reporter.

'And now I'll leave you to your work.'

Peter leads the way to the hall. The parlour door sits ajar. As he crosses the flagstones, the parrot shrieks. 'Who's a pretty girl then?' Hope and Grace laugh aloud.

Peter swerves, his prying blue eyes betraying the benign sunniness of his face.

'So it's true – the parrot does talk.' He says it triumphantly and she fears he may be planning a report about her bird. 'What a clever creature. And those, I assume, are Mrs Skaill's charges; I haven't met them myself, though I have heard...'

Birdie reaches for the handle and heaves the front door.

'Thank you for dropping by, Peter. I'll ask Mrs Skaill again about notices for *The Orcadian*.'

She eases him into the street, and is relieved when she can shut the door on his receding back. He's like a dog with a bone in his search for a story. And yet he is entertaining and a useful source of information. He's given her the name of Morag Firth and, more than this, he's told her something interesting about Tobias; he was a carpenter.

The door of the parlour is still open. She catches a glimpse of faces disappearing as she crosses the hall. How much of her conversation with Peter did they overhear, and how much did they understand? A slice of sunlight breaks through the cloud as she enters the office; dust from her earlier examination of the damp ledger still speckles the air and glitters in the golden rays. The papers on the table gleam white in the sudden brightness. The heading on the nearest letter attracts her attention; it's from Mr Boyd, a clerk in Ness House – the Company's office here; notification of the number of servants the Company's agent is looking to recruit this season for York Factory. Dated 5th April 1855; too late to do anything about it now, the ships set sail across the Atlantic a while ago – the beginning of June. She tries to imagine where they are heading. Factory. The word conjures up soot and furnaces, steam, smoke, red brick, shouting men and pounding hammers. York Factory cannot be like that; a trading station in the wilderness of Rupert's Land where the skins of dead animals are traded. The thought of animal pelts makes her shudder; she urges the sleeve of her dress over her goose-pimpled wrists. Her eye slips down the list of servants for which the Company's agent was searching: four tailors, fifteen canoemen, three smiths, three armourers. And three carpenters.

She leaps from the chair and tilts to the shelf of ledgers, finds and removes the volume labelled *Recruitment of personnel and crews 1840–1845*. She can't be bothered to heave it over to the desk; she drops the ledger on the floor, opens the greening and sticky leather cover, flips to the end and works backwards until she reaches May. The entry for 25th May 1845 indicates that Mr Boyd paid Albert Skaill's shipping agents thirty shillings in commission for the recruitment of six men as servants for York Factory. And below there is a list of names. Hugh Brough, tailor. John Corrigall and Martin

Halcro, canoemen. Edward Stewart, cooper. And finally, Shankie Rouse, carpenter. She sits back on her heels and laughs.

She has solved at least part of the mystery of Tobias Skaill. He did not stow away aboard one of Franklin's ships in 1845 and lead it to its icy fate; he sailed to York Factory in Rupert's Land on a Company supply ship. Margaret recommended him to the clerk at Ness House – but gave him a false name – a combination of his nickname and his mother's maiden name, which her trusted book-keeper faithfully recorded in the correct ledger. Birdie used exactly the same ruse when she purchased her ticket for the Aberdeen steamer. And now, she reckons, the tokens she found by Tobias's corpse, etched with a pelt and the initials HB, begin to make sense: he was employed as a servant of the fur trading Hudson's Bay Company.

Yet in solving one puzzle, she creates another; if Tobias Skaill did not slip aboard the *Terror* and join Franklin's expedition in 1845, where did he acquire the bone toggles etched with the initials HMST which he used to make the sledge for the twins? She momentarily recalls her apparition of the frozen corpse and wishes she hadn't conjured up an answer with quite such visceral clarity.

Chapter 10

She pauses in the gloomy hall and listens. Margaret snores softly. She can hear no other noise. She slips the bolt, lifts the door so it does not scrape the flagstones, shuts and locks it behind her and heads down the slipway to the sea, away from the whalebone arch, the street and the bedroom window of the twins. There is no wind and damp mist fills the air. The scarlet of the midnight sun, only just below the horizon, is dimmed by clouds, but still bright enough to illuminate the shore. The tide is low. An oyster catcher hops over rocks, its red beak and legs luminous in the gloaming.

She is about to step onto the shingle when she hears the thin, wheezy notes of someone whistling behind her; she has been followed. Alarmed, she crouches beside the slipway, hunched against the stones of Narwhal House. She holds her breath as a figure saunters past above her head, a long-barrelled shotgun slung over one shoulder. He reaches the shingle and stands with his burly back to her, peering this way and that along the shore. Her stomach lurches; it's the man who was hunting birds by Warbeth kirkyard. Detective Thompson. Was he watching Narwhal House? She clenches her fists; if he turns around and looks behind him he will almost certainly see her hiding in the shadows.

His gaze fixes on the rocks to the south of the slipway. He lifts his gun from his shoulder, aims at the oyster catcher dabbling in the bladderwrack. He fires. The crack echoes around the bay. She watches the white bars of the bird's wings as it escapes across the Sound. The detective heads north along the shore. To her relief, when he reaches the next slipway, he cuts back to town. She waits a few minutes before she makes her way south, keeping close to the shadows of the buildings that line the waterfront. She reaches a break in the grey stone, peers along the alley to ascertain the detective is not there, scrabbles onto the road and walks quickly toward the hill.

At the crest of the slope, she catches her breath under a sycamore. The rooks shake their wings, and send droplets flying. There is no rain, yet everything is drenched. She is surprised to see flames leaping, despite the damp air, and figures silhouetted against a fire beyond the southern edge of the town. She hears the faint notes of an accordion; gypsies. She watches their campfire gathering, catches the faint smell of smoke and finds her mind drifting; she remembers a bonfire night in London, just a month after she was first accosted by Solomon in Soho. She can picture the darkness closing in around her as she headed east along Tooley Street, the usual smog thickened by smoke and ash. In the periphery of her vision, she glimpsed Solomon Finkel crossing the street toward her, and her heart fluttered with an unaccustomed agitation. What was he doing there? She gave him an even glare as he approached.

'Mrs Collins.' He tipped his bowler. 'I thought I should walk you home. There's trouble on the streets tonight, what with Guy Fawkes and all the anti-popery mobs running riot.'

As he spoke, there was a whoosh and a glittering fountain

of silver and gold stars erupted behind his head. Somebody had ignited a Roman Candle in one of the narrow passages leading to the river. Two barefoot boys scampered from the alley and pelted toward Bermondsey.

'I think I can deal with a couple of boys, thank you, Detective Finkel,' she said. 'They're the ones that need worrying about, not me; they'll go to bed without a bite to eat. They've spent all their pennies on fireworks.'

'They'll be happy, though.' He paused. 'Sometimes it's good to follow your heart's desires.' He glanced at her and she caught the intensity in his gaze before he disappeared in the night and left her wanting more.

The rooks in the sycamore above her caw. She shakes her head; she needs to stop this pointless reminiscing and get a move on. A cloud of melancholy descends on her as she follows the track to the coast; the dank night has dampened her spirits, she tells herself. Nothing to do with the fact that she still hasn't heard from Solomon. The mist is more like drizzle now; the hood of her cape is dripping and the hem of her skirt heavy with moisture. The obelisks of the kirkyard loom, desolate in the dimness. It's a relief to see the yellow glow of a lamp in the window of Morag's croft. Though as she cuts across the ness, Birdie's stomach knots; whatever the truth of the stories about her strange powers, Peter made it clear that Morag Firth was not an easy character.

The drizzle evaporates as she reaches the stone wall marking the boundary of the croft's land. The climate is kind to Morag – her garden flourishes with abundant kale, leafy herbs, fuchsias and even a couple of apple trees. Birdie cannot help wondering whether sorcery is indeed fuelling the fertility of her garden. A path leads to the whitewashed croft, where a ragged figure sits on a bench beside the door; wild coils of black hair escape from his grey tam. Birdie is flummoxed; she had expected Morag to be alone, not guarded by a man. Perhaps it's a passing tramp or a gypsy from the campsite; he certainly has the rough appearance of someone who leads an outdoor life. She considers turning back, but it's too late to retreat; the strange man notices her loitering at the wicket, and beckons her to enter. She pushes the gate with trepidation, treads the garden path.

'Good evening, Sir.'

'It's late for visitors.'

His thick woollen jacket is threadbare, patched at the elbows with leather, his breeches baggy and held up with a rope belt, though his handsome, sharp-featured face has a mischievous cast to it.

'I'm looking for Morag Firth.'

'Why?'

His voice is soft, with a hint of amusement.

'I wish to talk to her. I was told this was where she lived.'

A raven lands at the man's feet, struts along the path.

'You're no scared to visit her at this hour? Weren't you warned she is a witch?'

Birdie's eyes flit nervously from the man to the raven and back. She has made a mistake coming here.

'I don't take much notice of gossip,' she says. 'Unless, you're telling me the stories about Morag are true?'

The man laughs, tosses his head back, sends his tam tumbling to the grass and liberates his hair which hangs halfway down his back. She gawps. The trousers, the way of sitting, the forthright manner, are all markers of a man. Yet the long tresses, the smooth chin, the slender frame, convey something different. A shapeshifter, according to the gossip of the townsfolk. Daughter of a mermaid. A witch and seller of winds.

'You shouldn't leave your mouth hanging too long. The peedie beasties will crawl inside.'

She flushes. 'You must be Morag Firth.'

'Aye. And you're Birdie White from London, lodging with Margaret Skaill. The widow with the talking parrot.'

Birdie nods. Morag might live at a distance from the town, but she knows all the news.

'You're dressed as a man.' Birdie cannot let the obvious slip by without being stated.

'I'm dressed as I want to dress,' Morag replies dismissively. She points at Birdie's feet. 'You're wearing men's boots. Why are you wearing those?'

'They belonged to my husband. They're good and sturdy.'

Morag studies Birdie's gown in a way that suggests she can see through the bombazine and read her true feelings. Birdie assesses Morag with a sideways glance; how old is this woman? Her face is brown and weathered, yet there is a vitality to her face and movements. She can't be much more than thirty.

'Birdie. Is that your real name?'

'It's a nickname.'

'What's your true name?'

'Bridget is the name given me at school.' Matron had never bothered to ask for her real name and had assumed that, because her nickname was Birdie, her full name must be Bridget.

Morag leans forward. 'But what's the name given by your mother, when you were born?'

Birdie senses an ulterior motive behind the question but is unable to think quickly enough to avoid answering honestly.

'Branna.' Few people know her birth name; revealing it makes her feel exposed.

'That's no English name.'

Birdie doesn't provide a direct response. 'It means raven.'

'Aha.' Her answer pleases Morag. 'It suits you well. And it means we have much in common; the raven is my spirit guide.'

'Spirit guide?'

'All witches have a spirit guide. A familiar.'

Birdie cannot tell whether she is being serious.

'You should be careful walking around here in the dark. Folk will think you're a witch too.'

Morag flashes her a smile and she feels a sudden kinship with this woman. Birdie has grown up feeling odd; teased by Frank and bullied by Matron because of her trances and other supposedly unnatural ways. Yet here is a woman who, she suspects, shares some of those differences and revels in them. For once, she does not feel quite so strange.

Morag stands, brushes her hands on her britches. 'Well, if you want to talk to me, we should go in-aboot.'

She doesn't wait for agreement, disappears through the door that rests ajar. Birdie follows her inside and casts her eye around the croft. Two windows; one overlooks the ness to the kirkyard, the other faces west and is filled with sea and sky, crimson now the drizzle has cleared. The peat fire glows at the far end of the room. A line of splayed herrings dangle in front of the hearth, browning like rotten teeth in the wraiths of peaty smoke. Flat bread is cooking on a griddle held over the flames by an iron arm. Flagstone cubbyholes are occupied by plump, conker-red hens. On top of their roosts, a cupboard holds pots, plates and a gigantic brindled cat, curled as if asleep but with one watchful eye visible above the curve of its tail.

'Have a seat.'

Morag gestures at an unforgiving wooden chair with a rush-woven back positioned by the hearthside. Birdie sits and arranges her skirt. The cat bounds from the cupboard and drops on a mouse scuttling to a shadowy corner where, Birdie notices, a fiddle is propped against the wall. The cat allows its tiny captive to escape and dash halfway across the floor before it pounces again and crunches the creature in its jaw.

'There must be something playing on your mind,' Morag says, 'to bring you here at this late hour.'

Birdie hesitates; she feels Morag's eyes on her face; amber and unyielding. Birdie is intimidated by the intensity of her gaze, but she can't afford to be afraid. If she wants information she must reveal some first.

'I came to ask you about Tobias Skaill.'

'Now there's a thing. You're the second person who has asked me about him these last few weeks.'

'Peter Gibson?'

'Aye. He came to tell me Tobias Skaill had been murdered in that big city of yours.' She tips her head at Birdie. 'He asked me what I knew of him and I said nothing. Poor Tobias. What a sorry end.' Sadness clouds her features before her mouth hardens again. 'And now you're here, asking too. Though I sense you have some more pressing reason to find out about Tobias Skaill than a need to fill the front page of a newspaper.'

Birdie's cheeks burn.

'Peter Gibson showed me the report about Tobias in *The Times*,' Morag continues. 'It mentioned an accomplice; an Irish woman.'

Birdie's head swims as she stares at the green flames, twisting in the hearth. She sees now why Morag was interested in her name; unlike Margaret, she's read the article in *The Times* and maybe she's already guessed Birdie might be the Irish accomplice mentioned.

'You're in trouble somewey because of Tobias Skaill?'

It seems pointless trying to deceive this woman; better to try to win Morag to her side.

'I met him only once,' she begins.

Morag nods, as if this does not surprise her. Does anything surprise Morag?

'That is to say, I met him only once when he was alive. He accosted me in the street the night before he died and I assumed he was a drunken sailor and sent him packing. And early the next morning I saw him lying dead on the shore of the Thames. I hid when the river police came to collect his body. The very next day, I learned I was a suspect in his murder.'

Birdie shuffles on the chair. Morag stands with her back to the fire, holds her hands behind her. It's as if she is confessing, and Morag is her priest.

'And there's nothing else to connect you with him?'

'Nothing else of which I know. I have to find out who murdered him,' she adds. 'Or I will be hanged for the crime myself.'

Morag tuts. 'I see your predicament. Trouble clings to Tobias Skaill like smoke from a peat fire.' She glances at Birdie. 'It seems to me you may have stepped into the reek.'

Birdie is reassured to find her version of events is not doubted.

'Does Margaret know of this?'

'The proprietor of *The Orcadian*, I believe, informed her of Tobias's death. Though I haven't told her that I met him. Or...' She lets the sentence drift. The shadow of a bird flutters by the window, an owl or a raven, she cannot tell.

'Margaret is no fool,' Morag says. 'And she is the last person to care about unfounded accusations.'

Morag bends and nudges a large rock over the hearth, half smothering the flames. 'That'll stop the smoke. The peat will burn all night. If the fire dies, and the room falls dark, it draws in the bad spirits.'

'Finfolk?'

Morag reaches over to lift the bread from the griddle pan, and as she does so, reveals a mermaid tattooed on her forearm. 'Call them what you will. Finfolk. Ghosts. Demons. Dark thoughts that keep you awake in the dead hours. We all have those.' She sets the bannock on a plate at the side of the hearth to cool. 'Tobias Skaill. He had more demons than most. Folk here think he was a bad man, but I say he was haunted.'

'By what?'

'By his past. The death of his mother. The lads who taunted him and beat him black and blue when he was a peedie bairn.'

'Why did they pick on him?'

'Because they could. Because he had no Ma to protect him. Because he wasn't like them. His grandmother – Margaret's grandmother – was Indian. Cree. All of Albert Skaill's grandchildren carry something of her appearance.'

Birdie nods.

'Tobias's hair was red but it was thick and straight, his eyes black and, in some folk's view, his skin may have freckled, but it went too brown in the sun for him to be a pure Orkneyman.'

'Margaret said her grandfather left his wife in the Nor' West.'

'A country wife they call them. Many Orkneymen have sailed from Stromness to make a living from the fur trade in Hudson's Bay. But the Company didn't like women to travel with their husbands – they didn't want the expense – so the men took local wives. Of course, they had children. Half-breeds, folk called them. Métis. The Company wasn't too happy to cover their expenses either, which forced some of the menfolk to bring their bairns back here to be educated. That's what Albert Skaill did – he took his two sons home with him and used the money he saved from his years at York Factory to start his shipping business in Stromness.'

'And folk here took against his sons, and their children too, because they were half-breeds?'

'Well, most folk here were welcoming, glad to see young lads returning to their homes, whatever the shade of their skin. Though of course, there'll always be those with small minds and mean hearts, who harbour jealousies and petty hatreds.'

'Peter told me there is a rumour that the Skaill family mixed with the Finfolk.'

Morag scoffs dismissively. 'Folk here tell many stories about those with unusual powers, who know the ways of birds and wild creatures, and can read the tides and winds.' She pauses. 'Only bitter folk use those tales against their neighbours.'

Morag folds her sinewy arms and displays, again, the tattoo of the mermaid. Birdie shivers and pulls her cape around her; the room is less cosy now the fire is dying.

'Peter also said Tobias was accused of murder.'

'Murder.' Morag shakes her head. 'There was a bar brawl and one lad pulled a knife and another was stabbed. The knifer disappeared, and Tobias had the bad luck to walk in at the wrong moment. The murderer's mates closed ranks and Tobias was blamed. He had to disappear to avoid being carted off to Aberdeen gaol.'

Morag stretches for the round slab of bread, breaks a lump and hands it to Birdie, who takes it gratefully, hungry from her walking. She bites a mouthful and splutters crumbs as she speaks, eager to continue with the conversation. 'Margaret helped Tobias find a position as a carpenter with the Company, so he could sail to the Nor' West and escape the noose.'

'Did Margaret tell you that?'

'She told me Tobias was nicknamed Shankie because of his red hair, and I found a ledger entry for Shankie Rouse who sailed with the Company in 1845.'

'Shankie Rouse.' Morag chuckles. 'The Company's agents never ask too many questions. There aren't so many men these days willing to face the risks; life in the Nor' West is harsh and wild. In winter the cold eats at flesh and bones and in summer the midges cover your skin like fur.'

'Yet you travelled to the Nor' West, or so I heard.'

Morag sighs. 'I was in love with a man named Jonathan. He joined the Company as a voyageur – paddling canoes to collect furs from inland posts. I was bereft when he sailed from Stromness. I believed I would never find another to take his place.'

Birdie finds it hard to imagine Morag pining after a man.

Morag throws Birdie a wry smile. 'I was hot-headed. I decided to follow him, and if the Company only took men, then I would become a man. I chopped my hair and borrowed some britches. Owen Muir I called meself. I visited Margaret in her office and asked if she would add me name to the list she gave the Company's agent.'

Morag picks the bannock crumbs from her trousers, drops them in her mouth.

'Margaret saw through me straight away. But she knows what it's like to lose the man you love, so she took pity on me and helped me look the part.'

Margaret, it seems, has a history of smuggling people aboard Company ships.

Morag crosses the room, fetches a bottle and two tin beakers from a stone alcove in a murky corner.

'Whisky?'

Birdie usually stays away from spirits – she has seen the effects of too much drinking slumped in the gutters of Southwark – but in the clearing night, the chill is creeping under the door and down the chimney. And, she realizes with some surprise, she wants Morag's friendship as much as information.

'I'll have a small drop, thank you.'

'A peedie dram.' Morag pours with a confident hand. 'You have to watch it doesn't become a habit.'

'The whisky?'

'Pretending to be somebody you're not. You have to be true to yourself.'

Birdie keeps her eyes on the low glow of the peat beneath the flagstone, watches the red heat that burns dull and reignites with the slightest breath of wind.

'I ended up at York Factory, at the far end of Hudson's Bay,' Morag continues. 'Jonathan was away on a journey inland, so I decided to stay as Owen and wait for him. I was given a job in the kitchen. Tobias was there when I arrived. He recognized me and we became friends.'

Morag sips her whisky; a wistful look slips across her face.

'When Jonathan came back and I revealed meself, he was furious and made it clear that he wanted nothing to do with me. He was happy with his country wife. He intended to report me to the Factor and demand I be sent back to Stromness. I didn't want to go, and Tobias talked him round.'

'Jonathan's reaction must have been a bitter blow for you.'

''Twas a lesson. I realized Jonathan had never been worthy of the risks I'd undertaken. Yet I'd found something I wasn't looking for. I sailed to the Nor' West because I was in love, but I stayed because I loved the untamed land. And the people. I remained as Owen, and became a steersman travelling with the voyageurs.'

Morag crosses to the west window, opens it, admits a gush of salt air and the distant breaking of the waves and leans over the sill.

Eventually she returns to the fireside, with a faraway gleam in her eyes and perches on a low stool.

'And Tobias?' Birdie asks, cautious about pulling Morag back to her own concerns. 'Did he enjoy his life there?'

'At first. Folk from Orkney settle well in Rupert's Land – we're used to tough conditions. Tobias was a skilled carpenter, and carpenters are always in demand at the Factory. He was a hard worker. He wanted to start afresh.' She shakes her head. 'I'm afraid, though, he still managed to land himself in trouble.'

'How so?'

'He was tasked with packing skins for shipping. The skins were pressed into bales and a clerk recorded what was in each pack before it was crated for loading. There was one particular clerk who got on everybody's nerves. He ordered Tobias to repack some bales that had come apart, but told him not to waste too much time, because it was only a consignment of castor sec.'

'Castor sec?' She's heard the term, but she doesn't remember what it means.

'Beaver pelts that have been sun dried after skinning – they're not worth much because they still need combing before they can be made into hats. The more valuable skins are the castor gras; they've been worn by the local trappers to loosen the long fur.'

'You mean the Indians?'

'The Cree, mainly around York Factory – they trap the beavers, skin them, wear the pelts then trade them with the Company's men. And the Company ships them to London, where the Committee oversees their sale.'

Morag pauses, nudges the hearth with her boot and provokes a shower of sparks. Birdie observes her rugged profile in the flickering light, intrigued by this woman who lived as a man in the wilds of the Nor' West.

'Tobias started repairing these packs,' Morag continues. 'But one of them fell apart and he saw that the bale was all castor gras below the outer layer. He checked the other bales and found they were the same – a layer of cheaper pelts covering the more valuable skins inside. Which wouldn't have been unusual – except for the fact that the clerk had indicated otherwise. Tobias told the clerk he'd recorded the consignment wrongly. The clerk said it wasn't the carpenter's job to classify the pelts. Tobias was furious. He came to see me, and I tried to calm him. He wasn't having any of it. He went to the Factor and told him he suspected the clerk was fiddling the books. Of course, the Factor didn't want to hear. He told Tobias he couldn't possibly know what the clerk was doing, because he couldn't read.'

Birdie is about to intervene and say that Margaret can't read either, then thinks better of it.

'The Factor's reply left Tobias raging,' Morag continues. 'When a member of the Company's London Committee came to visit the Factory, Tobias complained about the clerk and the Factor. And the very next day, he was given the boot.'

Morag swigs her whisky. Birdie takes a sip too, and lets the liquid warm her gullet.

'He told me he'd a mind to make a living as a free trader, dealing with the Cree or trapping furs himself. Then he left.'

'That was the last you saw of him?'

'Yes, but I heard word of him later, after I became a teacher.'

'Your disguise was discovered?'

'Rumours were starting to fly because I didn't take a country wife.' She tips her head back, cackles, then straightens herself again. 'I went to the Factor and confessed. He was astounded. Still, he was a canny man and concerned about his reputation. He offered me a post as a teacher for all the Métis bairns running around; that way he could claim he'd no been fooled by an Orkney lass. Suited me, though, because it brought me closer to the Cree. I learned a lot from those women; herbs and healing, how to predict the weather from the way the raven flies.' Morag glances at the window and smiles to herself. 'Then in the summer of 1853 – the year before I came home – the Company Governor asked whether I would travel to Ungava Bay with him and tutor his two bairns. The Company had an old trading station at Fort

Chimo which had been more or less abandoned. There were plenty of creatures in the area – silver foxes, wolverines – but the terrain was harsh.' She narrows her eyes as if she is weighing the story in her mind. 'There were rumours that the Fort was still being used, by illegal traders. The Governor wanted to see what was going on for himself. I agreed to go with him; I was feeling restless and wanted to travel the rivers again. So we headed north.'

Birdie edges her chair closer to Morag, eager not to miss a word. 'How far north is Fort Chimo? Is that where the Esquimaux live?'

'Esquimaux? That's the name white people use.' Morag's tone is scathing. 'It's not a name the people of the north use themselves. Some call themselves Inuit, though many prefer to use the name of their tribe, or the place that they were born. And yes, there are Inuit living around Ungava, and a few came to Fort Chimo while we were there, hoping to trade.' Morag gives Birdie a sideways glance. 'Why d'you ask about the Inuit?'

'I wondered whether Tobias had some connection with these people.'

Morag raises an eyebrow. 'Well, one of those who visited the Fort was a shaman who spoke good English, which he told me he'd learned from a man named Tobias who travelled and hunted in his area. He said that Tobias had married a woman from the Kilinigmyut, the people of the lacerated land, up near Cape Chidley on the Labrador coast.'

Morag drains her mug and rests it on the flagstones. 'And you think all this is connected to Tobias's murder somewey?'

Birdie takes a deep breath.

'Have you met the twins for whom Margaret cares?'

'I've seen them wandering the paths, and I've heard the gossip of course.' She snorts. 'What about them?'

'Do you think they are Esqui—'

Morag interrupts. 'Well, yes, they look as if they may be part Inuit. So?'

'Margaret told me they were rescued by a Moravian missionary and brought here on their supply ship, the *Harmony*.'

'I ken the Captain. A good Graemsay man.'

'The Moravian missions are on the Labrador coast, where you say Tobias is thought to have taken an Inuit wife.' She pauses. 'And the girls' skin is freckled.'

'Ah, now I see your point. You think Tobias may be their father.'

Birdie nods. 'I believe Tobias handed the twins to the missionaries and asked them to deliver the girls to Margaret.'

'Margaret has mentioned their father?'

'No. But they brought with them a toy sledge which Margaret said their father made for them. Tobias was a carpenter.'

'Indeed.'

'And the sledge had a bone toggle, carved with the initials HMST.'

'HMST?'

'The *Terror* – one of Franklin's ships.'

Morag shrugs. 'How can you be sure of that? It could have belonged to a sailor from any number of ships.'

'I had a...' Birdie pauses, searching for the right word. 'An apparition.'

Birdie has never spoken to anybody about her visions before, even though she's had them for as long as she can remember. Her apparitions are disturbing, but she is as much afraid of the consequences if she reveals what she sees as she is of the wraiths that haunt her. If Frank found out she saw the dead, he'd say it proved she was deranged – a victim of spectral illusions – and drag her off to be exorcised by the priest or, more likely, have her locked in the mad house. And even though she sometimes resists these visions, she feels they are part of her; presences attached to something deep inside. The thought of being cured, or forced to suppress the phantoms, makes her breathless, as if she is having her lungs constricted by overtightened stays. She reckons, though, that Morag is unlikely to condemn or dismiss her as delusional and, as her features remain unruffled, she continues. 'I saw a corpse, frozen in the ice. A sailor. He was wearing a jacket fastened with a similar toggle.'

She shudders as she speaks, and she tries to block the image of the grimacing face. Morag folds her arms, stares into the embers for a while.

The yowl of the cat breaks the silence.

Morag leans down, strokes the creature, straightens and asks, 'Do you think this revelation is of something that has happened or a premonition of events yet to pass?'

She feels Morag's eyes searching her face.

'I saw the image when I picked up the toy sledge Tobias made for his daughters, which made me think I was looking at something he had seen.'

Morag nods thoughtfully. 'Go on.'

'And when I put that together with the toggle carved with the initials of the *Terror*, I came to the conclusion that Tobias had travelled from Labrador to the place where the remains of Franklin's crew were reported to have been found. Perhaps, like Rae, he heard Inuit stories about the dead men found at this place.' She tries to remember the name; she read it in Rae's report in *The Times*. 'Back's Great Fish River?'

Morag says, 'Konajuk – the big river – is the name the Inuit give it. They have names for all the places the great explorers claim they have discovered.'

'Tobias must have journeyed there last year, and found evidence of the fate of Franklin's crew,' Birdie continues, determined to outline her theory. 'Then, this spring, he travelled to London so he could make a first-hand report to the Admiralty, and was murdered by somebody who didn't want him to claim the reward.'

Birdie sits back, and looks at Morag to assess her reaction. 'The Admiralty is offering twenty thousand pounds,' she adds.

Morag reaches for a clay pipe that is lying by the hearth, lights it and pulls on the stem. 'Weel, I suppose the reward is great enough to tempt a man to madness. Including murder. And I suppose it's possible that Tobias crossed Hudson's Bay and reached Konajuk. He was used to hardship and learned the ways of the Inuit.' She puffs grey smoke. 'But there are many gaps in this account.'

'Which is why I came to visit you.'

'I'm not sure how I can help.'

Morag sounds uncertain rather than unwilling.

'Did you learn anything of the Inuit language?' Birdie asks.

'A few words.'

'Perhaps you could teach me so I could try to gain the trust of the twins and find out what they know of Tobias? Maybe they have some information which would help me prove the case.'

'They say nothing of their father?'

'They only speak in their own tongue to each other. Margaret says they speak no English, though I suspect they understand much of what is said and stay silent because they are scared.'

The crescent moon gleams through the west window; she has stayed longer than she intended. Morag places a hand on Birdie's knee. She catches the amber of her eyes, the tattoo on her muscled forearm.

'I would like to help,' Morag says. 'I can see your need is great. But I'm wary of dragging the bairns into this, they're young and Margaret's love of them is fierce.'

'I've no wish to cause them any harm.'

'Let me think on it. Come again, and we can talk some more. Go now. Before Margaret wakes and finds you're missing.'

Morag stands and holds the door for her, bids her goodnight. Stars spangle the purple roof of the sky, the path of the Milky Way vanishing when it reaches the red-rimmed horizon. The cry of a bird makes her turn as she reaches the coast path. The croft door is ajar. Morag has vanished. Nothing moves except for a raven, flying north-west toward the sea.

Chapter 11

'Penny for your thoughts.'

Birdie stirs. She is so busy contemplating her conversation with Morag the previous evening, she has allowed herself to drift and forget the presence of Margaret, who is sitting on the floor testing the quality of some ship's biscuits she has been sent by two rival suppliers. Through the open parlour door she hears the twins conversing in their own, strange language.

'I was listening to the twins. When they speak, it makes me think of icebergs and polar bears.'

Margaret glares and crunches the dry biscuits. Birdie tries to concentrate on the invoices in front of her. The clock ticks. Rain laden clouds cast the office in shadow. Birdie is relieved when shouting from the harbour fills the awkward silence. They stand and peer through the grimy window at the source of the hullaballoo. A rowing boat is heading for the harbour; a large black and white cow occupies the prow, lowing and shifting from side to side, disturbed by the wake of the postal steamer heading for Hoy. A knot has gathered; fishermen jostle to grab the boat, guide it to a slipway, and calm the creature as its panicked movements threaten to topple beast and oarsman into choppy water. Women in their oilskin aprons pause from gutting herring to laugh at the cow's antics. Margaret shakes her head.

'Old farmer Clouston. He's bringing his livestock to market. That's the way he's always done it; one cow at a time, rowing across the bay. He thinks the steamer should give way to him, because he was rowing this stretch before steamships were even imagined.'

The clouds burst suddenly. Fat drops hit the window, flatten the harbour water and encourage the cow to leap for the shore. Birdie returns to the desk, watches rivulets pouring down the pane and calculates whether it's worth pursuing a conversation about the twins with Margaret. She clicks her tongue absentmindedly.

'You're no concentrating today.'

'I keep thinking about the twins.'

'You'd do better to think about those invoices. That's what I pay you for.'

Her words are stern, though her tone is weary, as if the burden of protecting the girls by herself is weighing heavily. Birdie decides to take a risk.

'I wonder whether they might know more English words than they say, and whether there is some other reason that is preventing them from speaking. Fear perhaps.'

Margaret stares at her shrewdly. 'They haven't had enough time to learn English yet.'

They've been here over a year, Birdie thinks. A gust of wind shakes the window frame and slams the parlour door shut.

'Do you think it's possible their father is not an Esquimaux?'

Her question falls awkwardly out of her mouth and lands with a hard clatter on the flagstones. Margaret lets it lie there silently. Rain batters the window.

Eventually Margaret speaks. 'Their father is my cousin, Tobias Skaill, as, I think, you may have supposed.'

There is accusation in Margaret's voice; she knows Birdie has been speculating about the twins. Birdie's stomach knots, but it's too late now. She is the one who prised this clam shell open, so she cannot complain if the meat inside is not as easy to digest as she might have hoped.

'It is what I supposed, yes.'

She peers over the top of the clerk's desk. Margaret is still on the floor. The light is so dim now, it is difficult for Birdie to make out Margaret's expression.

'Their mother was an Esquimaux.' Margaret pauses. 'When she died...' There is another hesitation. 'Tobias asked the Captain of the *Harmony* to take them to me.'

The wind howls around the harbour and whines in the rigging of the anchored ships and fishing boats. Margaret is skirting the truth, she senses, but she is in no place to challenge her account. She tries another tack.

'Do the girls know their father has died?'

'They're peedie bairns; I've said nothing. I don't want them upset. I'll do anything to keep them safe,' Margaret adds with sudden ferocity. 'I have two bairns buried in Warbeth and I've spent many a year wishing I was buried there instead of them, wondering why God spared me.'

Birdie pictures the tombstone of Alison and Elspeth, Margaret's daughters who died so young, and searches for the right words of comfort. 'I'm sorry for your loss.'

Margaret shakes her head. 'I failed to save me own bairns. But I will make sure these two are safe, as they have been delivered into my care.'

Margaret's dark eyes find her in the gloom. 'I want no talk of Tobias's death in this town. I don't want folk telling more poisonous tales about my cousin or his bairns.'

'I'll say nothing. I have no friends to tell anyway.'

'Morag Firth.'

'I've visited her once.'

'I know. I'm warning you what folk are saying. I have no issue with Morag Firth. She's a canny lass and was always good to Tobias. But I'm telling you, be careful when you go visiting her in the late hours. Folk will gab and they'll turn their tales against me and the bairns.'

The rain drenches the last of the light; its incessant beating drowns out Margaret's warnings. She understands Margaret's concerns, but she reckons the best defence against malicious tongues is to uncover the truth about Tobias's murder.

Birdie leaves the subject a while, lifts her quill and scratches numbers and dates in ledger columns. The rain persists, though the drumming is now interspersed with howls of wind.

She tries again. 'Perhaps Hope and Grace learned some words of English from their father.'

'Perhaps.'

'If they could be persuaded to speak, they might be able to tell you more about the fate of Tobias.'

'I have no desire to know more about the fate of Tobias.' She reaches for a candle, strikes a match and lights the wick; it splutters then catches, bends and casts wild shadows against the wall. 'Tobias is dead. I want to keep his bairns alive.'

For the first time, Birdie hears fear in Margaret's voice.

★

The summer is nearly over, Birdie thinks as she lights a candle and peers at the list of Inuit words that Morag has given her, but at least the clouds have cleared. It rained on St Swithin's Day and it seemed as if there would indeed be another forty days of miserable weather; the last half of July slipped away in a blur of downpours, drizzle and mist. Then, that morning – the first Sunday of August – the rain had relented abruptly. Birdie took advantage of the dry spell to visit Morag a second time. She begged Morag again to teach her a few words of the language spoken by the twins. Birdie explained she was only interested in using the words to encourage the girls to converse in English, and if she could do that, it might keep them safe as well as help her. The more the twins spoke, the less reason people would have to whisper they were Finfolk bairns. In the end, Morag acquiesced. Not that she had much to offer, she said. There wasn't one common tongue for all the people of the far north. The shaman taught her a few words of his language but, she added as she dropped some bannock crumbs for the raven, she was more interested in learning other skills from him – shapeshifting, communicating with the spirits of the animal world. Controlling the winds.

It suits Morag, Birdie thinks, as she stares at the strange words written on the paper, to have the townsfolk a little fearful of her. The unsteady candle flame makes the ink lines dance. She holds the page closer to her eyes, as if that might help her pronounce the words. She always found it easy to pick up phrases from the sailors of different nations who thronged the streets of London. Russian. Spanish. Greek.

She's even acquired a smattering of Hindi. The language of these people of the frozen north is a more taxing proposition. *Qujannamiik.* Thank you. *Qamutik* – sledge. *Angeko* – shaman. *Kaiak* – canoe. *Tukisiviit?* – do you understand? She says the words aloud. They sound wrong. Morag gave the words a guttural edge which Birdie cannot replicate. The parrot tuts as if to suggest he does not think much of her efforts.

'Well, you do better then,' she says 'Qamutik. Caw-moo-tick.'

'Solly,' the parrot says.

Solomon – she's still not heard from him. What's he up to? She shakes her head – and catches sight of the pouch of sovereigns he gave her. She reaches for the purse, weighs it in her hand. Solomon's finances, like much else about him, were something of a mystery. He always had cash and never hesitated to spend it on entertaining her even though, she knew, he wasn't well paid by the Met. Afraid he might be taking backhanders, she'd once asked him where he got his money from. He'd laughed and told her he'd got a tidy sum from selling his late father's garment business. Why on earth did he join the Met, she persisted, if he had plenty of cash? Well, he still needed to earn a living, he'd replied, and anyway he wanted to try something different. He hadn't thought he'd stick it long because he hated the uniform and the rules, and had been on the point of quitting when he was asked to join the Met's new detective branch; the Commander wanted a German speaker to keep an eye on revolutionary refugees from the Continent and then, later, tasked him with watching the docklands. Which was how he'd ended up as a detective on the turf of the Filth, and how his path had crossed with Birdie's. The job had its good moments, he'd added with a reassuring smile that made her forget the niggling doubts.

The purse sits heavily in her palm – she's hardly spent any of the sovereigns; she'll return the coins when she sees him again. If she ever sees him again. She tuts and wonders whether the manager of Flett's will be irritated if she drops by tomorrow to check for mail.

The second week of August, and it's raining again – the dry spell lasted all of two days. The dampness seeps into the walls and her bones and makes her despondent; time is slipping away and she has got no further with her enquiries about Tobias. Margaret is meeting the solicitor in Kirkwall again and has left Birdie keeping half an eye on Hope and Grace until she returns. Birdie fetches Solly's cage and places it on the parlour table. The twins glance up from the game they are playing with the toy sledge and canoe.

'I've been teaching Solly to speak your language.' The girls' expressions remain blank. She has another go. She points at the sledge in Hope's hand.

'Qamutik.'

The parrot shouts, 'Who's a pretty girl then?' He bobs on his perch. The girls laugh with delight.

'Perhaps you can teach Solly some words?'

They exchange glances and approach the cage. Hope raises the sledge.

'Qamutik.'

Birdie is gratified to hear her pronunciation is not too inaccurate. Grace joins in the lesson. 'Qamutik.'

Solly bobs and preens, though shows no inclination whatsoever to utter anything other than his well-worn phrases. 'Who's a pretty girl then? Who's a pretty boy then?'

She rebukes the bird. 'You're supposed to be copying Hope and Grace.'

The parrot is affronted, ruffles his feathers and shrieks, 'Skin for a skin.'

The twins jump like startled rabbits. They glance at each other with terrified eyes, retreat from the cage, grab the sledge and canoe, scuttle for the parlour door, clatter up the stairs and slam their bedroom door. Alarmed by their reaction, Birdie races after them to the hall.

'Hope. Grace. Please, come down.'

There is no response. Birdie hesitates by the parlour door, perturbed. The parrot's imitation of Frank was sinister yet hardly sufficient, she feels, to cause such a reaction. The parrot shuffles to the far end of his perch and turns his grey back on Birdie, as if he realizes he is the cause of the commotion and is ashamed by his own behaviour.

She climbs the stairs and, at the top, turns left to the front of the house – the ben-end, Margaret calls it. She has not visited this part of the premises before. She knocks on the first door along the landing. Silence. She panics, fearing they may have scrambled out the window and run away. She twists the handle, leans her shoulder against the door and almost tumbles over the threshold. A musty smell fills the room. A wooden boxbed occupies one wall, its heavy red curtain drawn.

'Grace. Hope. It's me. Birdie.'

Snuffling comes from behind the curtain. Thank the Lord they have not disappeared.

'Will you come out?'

No reaction.

She assesses the room. A wooden press holds piles of neatly folded smocks, socks, blankets and gloves. The sight of what looks like a heap of dead animal skins on the floor disconcerts her, until she realizes they are the girls' deerskin parkas – the source of the cloying smell she assumes. The sledge and canoe rest in front of the boxbed where they have been dropped by the girls in their haste to hide themselves behind the curtain.

'Please don't be scared.'

Silence.

'What scared you? Was it Solly?' she persists, certain they comprehend at least some of what she says. 'Solly didn't mean to upset you.'

A low murmur comes from behind the curtain; Hope and Grace conferring. She waits. Outside, men shout. Sheep bleat. A dog barks. Barrels clank as they are rolled along the street. Beyond the slate roofs opposite, through the spears of rain, the canopy of sycamore is visible, rooks flapping, circling and landing.

'Please tell me what scared you.'

The curtain twitches and two faces appear side by side, black eyes unblinking. She finds it easier to tell them apart these days. Hope's hair is straight as a poker. Grace's hair has the slightest wave and she has more freckles. Hope is taller by a whisker. Their temperaments are different too; Hope is bolder, the leader. Grace hangs back and is more considered. And now it's Hope who sits up first, swings her stockinged feet over the side of the bed and grips the wooden frame with her hands. Still, she says nothing.

'Was it the words? Skin for a skin?' Birdie repeats the phrase as softly as she can. Even so, Hope emits a startled cry.

She tries to imagine why the phrase might scare them and conjures up her own childhood terrors: dead men hanging, the miasma of the river, the eels with their razor-sharp teeth which inhabited the Neckinger and could, Frank insisted, rip your foot from your ankle if you slipped and fell on its muddy banks. And then she remembers the girls' reaction when she pretended to be a monster that night at Warbeth.

'Did Solly's words make you think of a monster?'

Grace says nothing.

'Not monster,' Hope says. 'The mast—'

'No,' Grace shouts. She is usually so quiet. They stare at each other; silent messages pass between them. Grace shakes her head almost imperceptibly. Birdie watches, trying to intercept their psychic conversation without much luck.

Hope turns to look at her and says, 'Monster.'

Birdie is not sure she has heard correctly. She leans forward and repeats the word. 'Monster?'

Hope and Grace flinch in unison.

'Have you ever seen this monster?'

They shake their heads.

She sinks to the floor, her black skirt fanning like a raven's tail around her knees, her face now level with the girls' eyes. 'Did Tobias tell you about this monster?'

Hope nods. Birdie nearly gasps, surprised at having her suspicions confirmed, then nods back reassuringly.

Birdie picks the wooden sledge from the floor and twists it in her hands. 'Tobias told you a story about a monster?'

Hope nods again and glances over her shoulder at Grace. They murmur something to each other. Grace shuffles and perches next to Hope; they tremble like two nervous swallows balancing on a fence.

'The monster skins people and eats them,' Hope says.

Grace clutches her sister's arm. Birdie shudders and tries to block Frank's voice from her mind. *Skin for a skin. Skin for a skin.*

'A polar bear?' Birdie suggests.

The girls shoot each other sideways glances.

'Not an animal,' Hope says.

'A person?'

'Kabloona,' Grace says quite suddenly.

'Pardon?'

'Kabloona.'

Birdie attempts the word. 'Kabloona? Is that the monster's name?'

Grace nods and hugs Hope. They gape, their eyes round with terror.

Birdie edges closer to the bed. 'Please. Don't be scared. There is no monster here.'

Still, they are petrified.

'Solly is very fond of both of you.' This is true; the bird revels in their attention. 'He is upset that he scared you.'

Finally Hope shifts her gaze and Grace relaxes her grip on her sister.

'Do you want to come downstairs again and see if we can get any further with his lesson? Tukisiviit?'

The twins do not respond; perhaps she has misremembered the word. 'Tukisiviit? Do you understand?'

This time Hope grins, and corrects her pronunciation. 'Too-kee-see-veet.'

Birdie repeats, 'Too-kee-see-veet?'

Grace replies, 'We understand.'

'Good. Let's find Solly.' The parrot's utterance might have terrified them, but it has also prompted them to communicate with her.

The kirk bell tolls, marking the end of the evening service. Margaret has returned from Kirkwall and retired to her bedchamber. The rain has stopped. Birdie slips from Narwhal House, under the whalebone arch. She takes a deep breath of fresh night air; it's a relief to be outside after so many days cooped up inside. Two schooners have anchored in the harbour and the main street is alive with drunken sailors belting out ribald songs. Head down, the hood of her cape shading her face, she wills herself invisible as she marches along the street. She is about to take the muddy track up Brinkie's Brae when a hand grabs her arm. She twists around and finds herself looking at an eye patch. Her stomach sinks. It's the detective. The broken veins on his cheeks burn angrily. He reeks of liquor.

'Not a good night for a walk. There's a storm coming; the ships are sheltering in the harbour.'

'Another storm?' She tries to sound unflustered. 'There's been nothing but rain this past month.'

'You'd better be heading home.'

'I'm not going far.'

'You're going to visit Morag Firth.'

Her pulse races; how much does he know about her?

'Sir, please let me go, you're hurting me.'

He drops her arm and jabs his finger at her face. 'Morag Firth does the devil's work.'

His face is distorted with vitriol; it would be foolhardy to argue with him, but she is determined not to let him deter her from her course. She is doing nothing wrong.

'Thank you for your warnings, but I wish to take a breath of fresh air while it's dry.' She strides away before he has a chance to say any more.

A wet blast hits her cheek as she crests the hill. Behind the cliffs of Hoy, the sky is filthy yellow. To the west, black clouds tower. Seething waves pound the shore. The detective is right about one thing: a storm is coming. She has never seen anything like it. In London, nature is poisoned by the city; choking fogs mix with factory smoke and force gas lights on in mid-afternoon, winds are broken by the grimy walls of factories and warehouses. Here the wild darkness is like a beast unleashed and it fuels her fear of the darker forces on this island.

She reaches the kirkyard and pauses for breath. Blue lightning flashes above the waves and turns the black gloom crimson. She looks to the horizon as a white fork cracks and blazes and, in the moment of illumination, she sees the tortured face of a woman etched in the storm clouds, her features twisted with pain, her mouth gasping for air among the smoke and flames that engulf her blistering flesh. Birdie cries out. An explosion of thunder rocks the ground, and the sky is obliterated by the downpour. Birdie is momentarily winded by the fleeting vision of the woman, burning at the stake. It feels like a warning, a reminder of her own peril. She lifts her arms and shouts in rage at the heavens. The rain lashes her face and drenches her cape. She has to run. She sets off across the headland, the mud squelching beneath her boots.

'Are ye mad?' Morag holds the door open for her.

'I need to talk to you.'

'Could it no have waited for the morning?' Morag ushers her inside.

Wind howls down the chimney, blows smoke into the room and sets the line of splayed fish clattering.

Morag reaches for the kettle.

'Tea?'

She nods. She needs something soothing; the detective and the vision of the burning woman have disturbed her. Morag hangs the kettle on a hook above the hearth. The thunder blasts overhead and rattles pots and pans. Rain cascades down the windows.

'The first storm of the season.' Morag says it with glee. 'The ships returning from the Nor' West will be setting sail soon.' She leans, warms her hands in front of the flames. Her damp clothes steam.

'Tell me then, what could be so important you risk the storm to see me?'

'The twins.'

Morag twists around sharply. 'What's happened?'

'They're safe at home with Margaret. I was left alone with them this afternoon and I managed to persuade them to speak a little. The words you taught me helped.'

'I'm glad to hear it.'

'It was the parrot, though, that set them off.'

'Ah. The famous parrot. You must introduce me to the bird some time. What did he say?'

'Skin for a skin.'

Morag seems perplexed.

'It's a peculiar phrase he picked up from his previous owner.' Birdie is too ashamed to admit the previous owner was her brother; she doesn't want to tell Morag about Frank. 'The bird's words terrified the twins.'

Spears of rain fizzle in the hearth.

'When they'd calmed down, I managed to ascertain that Tobias told them a story about a monster that skinned and ate people. Hearing the parrot reminded them of the tale and scared them witless.'

The croft flashes blue with lightning.

'Does the story mean anything to you?'

Morag perches on the low stool by the fireside, the sharpness of her features exaggerated by the gleam and shadows of the leaping flames.

'I've heard similar stories told in the Nor' West. The Cree tell a tale about a monster that stalks their villages at night and takes folk back to its lair, skins them alive and devours them limb by limb.'

Vapour puffs from the kettle's spout. Morag covers her hand with a rag, lifts the kettle from its hook, pours the water into a teapot.

'But why would Tobias be telling them a story from the Cree when he was married to an Inuit woman?'

'You forget, he started off at York Factory which is in Cree territory. He had a country wife there. He would have heard her stories. But as I said, there are many such tales in the Nor' West.' Morag passes a mug to Birdie. 'Nettle tea. Clears the lungs.'

She feels deflated by Morag's explanation.

'The twins were scared witless. I can't help thinking it was more than a fireside tale that frightened them.'

Morag scowls. 'You misunderstand me. These are stories folk tell about the things they fear most.'

Birdie sips the nettle tea.

'Starvation stalks the people of the Nor' West. In a bad winter, hunger drives people insane. People fear that madness will force them to extremes of behaviour, make them eat their neighbour, or even one of their own family.'

Rain batters the flagstone roof. The raven's disgruntled caw echoes down the chimney.

'People face that fear by giving it a monster's form and telling tales about it. The Cree give the monster a name – they call it Wendigo.'

A gust of wind catches the hearth's flames and makes the red tongues leap. 'Then, it cannot be a Cree tale that Tobias told them, because Grace said the monster was called Kabloona.'

'Kabloona?' Morag sounds surprised.

The croft blazes cobalt, then plunges into darkness again.

'You know that name?'

'Kabloona? Aye.' Morag pokes the peat with the tip of her boot. Smoke and flying embers fill the room. 'It's not a name. It's a word some Inuit use for a white person.'

A bolt of lightning strikes the ground beyond the croft; the crack reverberates around the walls. Birdie leaps to her feet, paces to and fro across the floor.

'Well, that makes sense of the story. It's what I thought; it confirms what I saw when I picked up the sledge with the toggle from the *Terror*. Tobias told the twins a story about Franklin's starving crew.'

Morag shakes her head. 'Sit down, will ye?'

Birdie ignores her, stands in front of the hearth, waving her hands emphatically. 'Tobias told the twins a story about the white cannibals. When Franklin's crew were caught in the ice floes, they starved and resorted to cannibalism.'

'Aye. That is what the Inuit told Dr Rae. I read his report.' Morag rocks on her stool and gazes at the flames. 'Though I'm still not...'

Birdie refuses to be deterred by Morag's doubts; she wants to spell out her version of events.

'Dr Rae reported that Franklin's crew had starved and resorted to cannibalism, but he wasn't believed because he relied on the testimony of the Esquimaux. If a white man could say he'd seen the bodies with his own eyes, and could produce some evidence to show he'd been there, then the Admiralty would have to believe him. Tobias must have left Labrador and journeyed north. He saw the cannibalized bodies of Franklin's crew, then set off for London with his evidence. But if there were another man who was also after the reward...'

'There are still a lot of *ifs* in your account.'

'It all adds up. It was reported that the killer was an Esquimaux. Perhaps he also had evidence to give, but knew that Tobias was more likely to be believed than him.'

Morag stands, as agitated as Birdie now, and jabs her finger as she speaks. 'I can see that the Admiralty would be more likely to believe a white man than an Inuit, but you say an Esquimaux killed Tobias? Now that part of your story doesn't ring true to me. I read about the supposed Esquimaux killer in the *Times* report Peter Gibson showed me. I assumed this was another made-up tale about savages that English people like to tell.'

Morag spits at the fire, her saliva sparking green in the embers.

'I didn't mean to suggest that the Esquimaux are savage and murder people.'

'A less savage race of people would be harder to find.'

'There could be bad individuals among the good,' Birdie persists. 'Orkneymen are a gentle race of people, and yet these islands also produce a few who are malicious, and spread false rumours, as you yourself have said.'

'May I remind you, it was also reported in *The Times* that you were the accomplice of the Esquimaux, and you tell me that's not true. It seems quite likely that if one part of the story is concocted, then so is the other.' She glares at Birdie. 'Kabloona also means a person who jumps to conclusions.'

Birdie looks away, angered and upset by Morag's judgement. She stares out the window; Venus glimmers below the bank of clearing cloud and Birdie thinks of the tortured woman's face she saw there earlier.

'I have to come to quick conclusions. I don't want to hang.'

'Well, flailing around is hardly going to stop the noose from tightening, Branna.'

Morag crosses to the door and opens it wide. Lightning forks and dances over the Pentland Firth; the storm is slipping away to the south. She steps outside and leaves Birdie alone, fuming.

Birdie glares around the croft and a glint catches her eye; Morag's fiddle rests against the wall. There is something peculiar about the instrument but she can't think what. She walks over to investigate and takes the fiddle by its neck. Close up, its oddness is obvious; it's made of dull metal, not wood.

'Do you play?'

Morag's silent reappearance startles Birdie, though her tone is conciliatory.

'No. I was curious. Is it made from tin?'

'Aye. The gypsies made it for me before I set sail for the Nor' West. Margaret warned me she'd heard many reports of wooden fiddles crushed in the storms of the Atlantic, and I could no bear to be without an instrument.'

Birdie turns the fiddle; it gleams in the last glow of the daylight. 'The canoe that brought Tobias's body ashore and dumped his corpse on the Thames; I heard it was shiny.'

'Who told you that?'

'A mudlarker. A poor boy who lives on the Thames and saw the boat and body. I wonder whether the canoe could have been made from tin?'

'A tin canoe.' Morag ponders. 'I suppose it would float well enough, if it was lined. Though I've never seen such a thing.' She takes a deep breath, then continues. 'But I can tell you this: the Inuit make their vessels from wood and skin. Not tin.'

Morag reaches for her pipe. She lights and puffs and the smell of tobacco marries with the sour peat and damp ground. Rain patters on the roof and thunder rumbles in the distance. The raven caws from the rooftop.

'I'm sorry if I was sharp, Birdie.'

'I'm sorry too.'

'I want to help. I know you've been wrongly accused, but I canna see how you'll advance your cause by responding with more false accusations and sorry stories about savage Esquimaux.'

Birdie regards the tin fiddle in her hands.

'You're trembling,' Morag says. 'You must be tired.'

Birdie rests the instrument on the ground, though she knows it's not her damp and aching limbs that are causing her to shake; it's her fear that Morag is correct. And her sense that she's further than ever from discovering the truth about Tobias's murder.

Chapter 12

Autumn is setting in; the ships from the Nor' West return in dribs and drabs and the nights are lengthening. Even on the brightest of days, the low afternoon sun throws long shadows and dims hard edges in its mysterious golden gleam. The final day of October and not yet three, but already the light is dwindling. The gloom suits Birdie; she's been lying low, avoiding the detective. Staying away from Morag, still smarting from the sharpness of her words. And she's heard nothing from Solomon. No news is good news, she tells herself, and anyway, she is safe here in Stromness, beyond the reach of the Filth. The ghosts still haunt her dreams – the spectre of Tobias's pleading corpse regularly disrupts her sleep – but she has had no more daytime apparitions since she saw the burning woman in the storm. Indeed, these last few weeks she has begun to feel almost settled; she has a position, a wage, a clean lodging and a good employer. She flicks her eyes over the page in front of her, checks the numbers tally and closes the ledger.

Margaret asks her to go to the harbour to wait for the tramp steamer – the cargo carrier left Gravesend five days ago and the weather has been fair, so it should arrive as scheduled. She has commissioned the local shipbuilder to construct another vessel to add to her fleet, and wants Birdie to confirm that her consignment of timber is in the steamer's hold.

'A fine evening for a dander,' Margaret says as Birdie leaves the office. And then she adds, 'Pay no heed to the bairns with their neepy lanterns asking for a penny to burn the pope.' Despite Birdie's attempts to disguise her Irish origins, her avoidance of the local churches has led Margaret to suppose she is Catholic.

'They mean no harm,' Margaret adds.

Birdie smiles, and says nothing. She is used to the violence of London's anti-popery mobs. A few children with carved turnip heads are hardly going to worry her.

She reaches the creels and herring barrels of the pier head as the vast steamer hoves into view across Hoy Sound. Bang on time. Black smoke belches from the stack as it edges closer – the tide is high and the water deep enough for the ship to dock at the pier. Steamships blend in with the factories, wharves and railway tracks lining the River Thames. Here the vessel seems like a fire-breathing monster bearing down on the defenceless town. As she waits for it to dock, she watches the skiffs of local fishermen being swept into the harbour by the currents of the flood tide and the scrawny boys perched along the slipway, fishing with strings tied to twigs. A rank of girls stands behind, goading the poor lads and criticizing their efforts; they breed tough women in these islands, she notes with bemused admiration.

The steamer shudders; it barely fits alongside the pier. She heads toward the vessel, caught up with the rush of locals hurrying to meet friends and loved ones; the steamer has carried passengers north along with the cargo. Sailors secure mooring ropes to capstans. Gangplanks are fixed. A uniformed officer descends – and is immediately surrounded by people pressing for information about their cargo. It must be the master of the ship, she supposes, as it's his duty to supervise the loading and unloading of the hold. She joins the cluster. The officer's bushy eyebrows knot, his bearded mouth draws a thin line of irritation.

'Hang on a mo.' He removes his cap, wipes his forehead with the back of his hand. 'If you all badger me at once, I can't help anybody.' He mutters under his breath, 'I can't even understand a bloody word of what anybody's saying.'

There is a moment's breathing space in the hubbub. Birdie seizes the opportunity. 'Excuse me, Sir.'

He glances her way, relieved to hear an accent he can decipher. 'Yes, Ma'am. How can I help?'

'Do you have a consignment of timber for Margaret Skaill?'

'Name rings a bell, and there's certainly a lot of planks in the hold. But we won't be unloading the heavier cargo now, Ma'am. There's not enough time before the ebb tide. It'll have to wait – first thing tomorrow.'

'Thank you. I'll return then.'

As she turns to leave, she is struck by the creeping feeling she is being watched. She lifts the hood of her cape and surveys the pier warily from behind its deep hem. A grande dame in furs waves a kid-gloved hand expectantly at a porter. A besuited gentleman lopes toward the main street, swinging a leather portmanteau. Lawyer, she supposes. Or bank manager. And there is Peter Gibson, leaning on a wall, chewing the cud with one of the ship's crew. His golden curls are unmistakable – but he has his back to her so it cannot have been his eyes she felt. Her neck twinges again. She looks up and sees a figure recede from the steamer's rail. Her pulse quickens. She's been complacent. Margaret told her the steamer sailed from Gravesend. She should have foreseen it might have been carrying a consignment of trouble for her. What if there are officers from the Thames Division on board?

She lifts her skirt and strides along the pier, head down, weaving between grumpy passengers with too much luggage and shawled fisherwomen who give her sly glances as she passes. At the end of the pier, she turns north instead of south and stomps along the bay, furious with herself for being careless. She is afraid to return directly to Narwhal House; if somebody is following her, she should leave a false trail. She glances over her shoulder and catches a movement among the knots of people on the pier. She waits, but there is nothing. An uneasy sensation, that is all. She walks a few paces, still glancing over her shoulder, and almost bumps into the beefy figure leaning against one of the wooden huts used by the fishermen for sorting and selling their catches. Her heart sinks; it's Detective Thompson. His top hat is tilted at such a slant, the brim covers one eye. The uncovered pupil stares in her direction. He licks his lips, straightens himself, tips his hat with a shovel-shaped hand, and reveals his eye patch.

'Evening, Ma'am.'

His manner is less threatening than the last time she bumped into him – perhaps he's had less to drink – but she doesn't like the way his eye roves up and down her dress.

'Good evening, Sir.'

'Pleasant evening for a stroll.'

'Indeed, Sir.'

He is not after her, she reassures herself; he's on the look-out for riff-raff disembarking from the steamer.

She hurries on, past the huts, and reaches a stationary cart, piled high with sacks and packages, 'Miller's' painted in red letters along its side. Two harnessed shire horses wait patiently for their owner to return, nosebags looped around their ears. She sidesteps the vast beasts, sidles along the cart and observes the pier from behind its rear wheel: Detective Thompson is bearing down on the lads with their twig fishing rods. The girls run, shrieking with laughter. No sign of anybody following her.

She dashes to the far side of the road and clambers up a flight of narrow steps behind a dour stone house and finds herself on what she assumes is the far northern end of the main street. Although, it would be pushing it to call it a street now as it has dwindled to little more than a rutted track. To her right, she sees Gunnie's Inn; a couple of sailors lounge against the granite walls, frothing glasses in hands, pipes in mouths, too busy with their refreshments to notice her. To her left, she can make out the tall archway of the Mason's Arms, the inn from which the coach to Kirkwall and other hired gigs depart. Almost directly opposite, a narrow alleyway runs between two buildings before curving toward the rear end of the town and leading, she reckons, to the hill end of the row of hovels. If she follows this route, hopefully she will lose anybody who might be on her trail.

She darts across the road, takes a few steps along the alley and is relieved to be engulfed by the shadows. A restraining hand falls on her shoulder. She recoils and twists, alarmed, heart thumping, ready to kick and scream at whoever has cornered her, be it Detective Thompson or, worse, the Filth.

'Birdie, it's me.'

Her throat constricts, her eyes close, her whole body caught between fear and relief. She places her hand on her chest, presses to calm the thumping. She opens her eyes. It is Solomon, overcoat flapping loose, bowler a little askew and decorated with a rook's feather. Though her relief is tempered with disappointment; she has thought about meeting him again many times over the last few months but had not anticipated it would be like this. She has a fleeting recollection of another time she bumped into him unexpectedly in a dark alley a few weeks before she ended their relationship: she'd just left Frank's house, took a short cut and was perturbed to see him whispering to a swarthy man in a greasy jacket. She watched unnoticed as the stranger dug in his pocket and passed Solomon some coins. She coughed and, alerted to her presence, the stranger walked away, leaving her with the unsettling impression Solomon was being paid by somebody for information – about what or whom she didn't like to speculate. Solomon explained the man was an old mate who wanted to repay some money he'd borrowed; Solomon had tried to convince him it wasn't necessary but he'd insisted. She'd taken him at his word and forgotten about the incident, until now. The recollection adds to her urease.

'You scared me,' she says.

'That wasn't my intention.'

'You arrived on the steamer?'

'Yes. It's quite some way from London.'

'I know,' she snaps. 'Why did you sneak up on me like that?'

'I didn't want anybody to see us together.'

He reaches for her hands.

'You're trembling.'

'Are you surprised?'

She tugs her fingers from his, overcome with a sudden awkwardness and confusion. He retreats to the wall, leans against the damp stone.

She searches his shadowed face; there's a moodiness to his countenance which she finds hard to fathom. He has travelled all this way to find her, but he does not appear to be particularly overjoyed now he has located her.

'You've shaved your beard,' she observes.

He strokes his chin. 'It was irritating.'

'You look better without.'

'And you, you're still wearing mourning?'

His critical tone takes her aback. He's never questioned her habitual black before; her husband's death is an event she chose not to discuss with Solomon, and one he himself did not raise out of respect for her own avoidance of the subject, she assumed.

She finds herself answering defensively. 'I left Southwark quickly, as you advised. I took little more than I was wearing, and I've not had much opportunity to purchase new clothes. Anyway, all the women of Stromness wear dark colours. It's not my attire that makes me stand out here.'

He tips his head at the glass canary just visible beneath the folds of her cape. 'But you're still wearing that brooch.'

'I like it,' she says and shrugs.

He steps forward. His familiar smell washes over her.

'I came to warn you,' he says.

Her limbs tighten. She moves away and retreats to the far side of the alley. She'd briefly hoped he'd made this journey to tell her she was safe, that the river police had dropped their charges against her, that she can return to London. But instead she finds they are repeating the conversation they had in Crossbones Graveyard, when he instructed her to flee.

'Warn me?'

Three pale befuddled faces appear in the entrance of the alley – sheep that have strayed from their flock. They bleat and are quickly found by a collie dog, which snaps at their hooves and nags until they join the rest of the woolly creatures being herded out of town. A farmer strolls behind and raises his cap as he passes. Solomon returns the gesture, waits until the man is out of earshot.

'I have some information I must give you.'

She is sweating, despite the coolness of the hour and the dankness of the alley.

'We should find somewhere else to talk,' she says. 'There are too many gossips in this town. I cannot take you back to the house where I'm lodging.' She does not want to admit that she is boarding with the cousin of Tobias Skaill; he might think she was being reckless. 'And there is a detective.'

'Detective?'

'Thompson. A plain-clothes officer – he's been employed to keep the town safe from drunkards coming off the ferries. He wears an eye patch.'

'The stout fellow in the surtout near the pier?'

She nods. 'He makes me nervous.'

'We could walk out of town, along this road.'

His suggestion is interrupted by the squeal of carriage wheels coming from the yard of the Mason's Arms and the shout of a driver.

'Woah, woah. Steady on.'

'Or we could see if we could pay for seats in that carriage,' she says. 'Perhaps the driver could drop us at the next village.'

Solomon steps from the alley. She follows behind, across the road through the wide brick arch. A Clarence carriage harnessed to a pair of sturdy black horses fills the yard.

'Excuse me, Sir.'

The driver fiddles with his whip and eyes Solomon cagily; he is somewhat dishevelled after his long journey from London and the rook's feather in his bowler only adds to his already rakish appearance.

Solomon continues, undeterred by the driver's suspicious glances. 'Could you tell me where you are heading?'

'Kirkwall.'

'Do you stop along the way?'

'We'll take a breather at Stenness.'

Birdie's heard of the stones at Stenness – a mysterious place, according to Margaret, where couples once declared their love and made marriage vows, hands clasped through a hole in the largest Odin stone, until it was removed by an ignorant ferry-louper of a farmer. Young couples still use it as a trysting spot apparently, but Birdie reckons there are unlikely to be many romancers out on this cold, autumnal night.

'Could you take us to Stenness?' Birdie asks, as she steps toward the carriage, hoping the driver might respond more favourably to her than Solomon. The driver leers at her through bloodshot eyes.

'Ah, the Standing Stones. Where dark men sacrifice young maidens.' He winks. 'I can take you there. It'll cost you, though.'

'How much?'

'Shilling each if you want to sit inside.'

The fare is steep, but Birdie readily agrees. They can return on foot after dark; Margaret told her Stenness was no more than an hour's walk from Stromness and, for once, there are no rain clouds looming on the horizon. Solomon digs in his pocket, offers the fare and a little extra to the driver and asks him if he could kindly wait while he secures himself a room at the Mason's Arms for the night.

The sky is red and dusky by the time they clamber into the carriage. An elderly couple is already seated, a plaid spread across their laps. Birdie and Solomon take the opposite bench. The lady smiles sweetly. Birdie offers a nod and a 'good evening' in return. The driver cracks his whip and the carriage lurches through the archway and heads north along the deeply pitted road, a mist of dirt forming around its wheels as it leaves the town. They pass the farmer with his flock of sheep and the carriage veers precariously. Barefoot children playing with hoops and sticks scatter and stare. The bone rattling is almost enough to make her wish they had walked, but at least, this way, they are less likely to be seen. They pass along the bay and reach the bleak patchwork of the local Laird's land; furrows and earth-banks marking the windswept runrig strips rented to local crofters. Beyond the flatness of the fields, the tawny slopes of moorland loom.

'Woah.'

The horses halt. The driver bangs the side of the carriage. 'Stenness.'

They dismount and find themselves beside a lake, burnished and still. The driver leans down from his high seat.

'Beware the Maiden's Mound. It's where the enchantress Lodbrok performs her sorcery.' He cracks his whip against the horses' sweating flanks – the poor creatures whinny as they are steered toward a desolate inn – and leaves them standing between road and water.

The silver stones are along a muddy track and hard to miss; caught in the rays of the setting sun, their shadows purple. Solomon hangs back. Birdie finds herself drawn by the strange circle. The farmer has abandoned his attempts to tame the land, and the megaliths rear like giant sentinels from the heathery peat. Skeletal ferns catch her skirt as she slips between the stones. At the centre, she rests on what appears to be an altar, warty with lichen, cold even through her petticoats.

Solomon loiters beyond the boundary.

'Sit here with me,' she calls.

He hunches his shoulders, edges between the giants with his hands in his coat pockets. She has not seen him like this before, a bleakness evident in his bearing. He reaches the altar stone and slumps on its far end.

'What is this place?'

'It's where lovers plight their troth.' She intends to sound playful and flirtatious, but the words slip out too heavily.

He shudders. 'It feels like a land of the dead and ghosts to me.'

He is right; she can sense the unsettled wraiths and spirits waiting in the shadows. Solomon stares at the track along which they came.

'At least it will be easy to see if there are any other living beings nearby.'

She surveys the stones warily. They dance in the moonlight, the steward of the *Dog Star* said; witches gather there and perform their evil acts. She looks beyond the circle, stares at the shimmering surface of the lake, and tries to summon images of more joyous assignations with Solomon in hidden corners of the city: Greenwich Park at dusk as the nightingales sing, the cosy warmth of the coffee house on a cold spring afternoon, the first kiss under the stars on a winter's night by the Thames. Their trysts began as occasional outings and had only gradually become more frequent, but the secret rendezvous lost none of their magic as their regularity increased. Indeed, the intensity of those precious hours together seemed only to grow with the passing of the weeks and months. Now, as she conjures up memories of those days, she cannot hold them steady, and she wonders whether her relationship with Solomon was always flimsier than she thought.

Two white swans land gracefully on the water, carving a line of glistening ripples in their wake. The sun rolls down the side of a distant hill and the light splinters into misty rays. The slopes darken as the long twilight ends; the moorland shifts and billows in the gloom. She shivers; the temperature is falling. The loch takes on a leaden hue.

'We shouldn't stay here long,' he says.

'Tell me your news, and then we can leave.'

'I'm afraid it's not good.' He tips his head back; focuses on Venus glinting steadily. 'The river police are still searching for you.'

'I'm safe in Stromness.' She says it with certainty; she wants it to be true.

'You have to be careful, even here.'

He digs his hand into his jacket and produces a folded newspaper page. '*The Times*.' He rests it on his knee, flattens it with his free hand. 'You're on the front page.'

She sits bolt upright, glances around the stones nervously. She is certain the grim sentinels are closer than before, trapping her in their tightening grip. She shakes her head; she is letting her imagination get the better of her. She concentrates on the newspaper and reads the headline. *Esquimaux killer's accomplice identified.* The paragraph below is brief. Irish, of a recognizable type, short of leg and squat in stature, low jutting brow, long upper lip. She is indignant at first – how dare they misdescribe her so? Then she feels the urge to laugh. Beside the report there is a picture, an artist's impression, which is nothing like her; it is an image of what the linesman – she does not care to dignify him with the title *artist* – thinks an Irish woman looks like, a visual insult to match the words. A prejudice in a picture.

'Nobody could recognize me on the basis of that.'

'I wouldn't be so sure.'

'You're saying it's a fair depiction?'

'No, no. I'm not saying that at all. Look.' He points at the paragraph below the image. Her name. Printed on the first page of *The Times*. Or at least, her maiden name. Bridget Quinn, daughter of Gerald Quinn, hanged for killing a policeman. She panics, raises her hand to her brow, and tries to remember whether anybody here knows her by the name of Quinn. No. Margaret saw her testimonial in the name of Bridget Quinn, but Margaret cannot read. Only Morag knows she was named Bridget by her school, and Morag will not say a word. Everybody here calls her Birdie. Though there may be some in Stromness who suspect it is a shortened version of Bridget. Peter Gibson for a start.

She clenches her fists.

'Why are they doing this?'

He shakes his head. 'I thought they might forget it – Skaill was only a sailor after all – but there's too much pressure from the wharfingers, especially on the Surrey side. There's been a lot of noise about this Esquimaux killer,' he adds. 'The shilling shockers are still churning out their lurid stories of flesh-eating savages. The newspapers won't let it drop. The wharfingers say all the chatter about murderous foreigners is bad for business. The Port of London bigwigs are too powerful for the Thames Division to ignore.'

'But why are they still after me?'

'The canoe hasn't been found or seen again. The Thames police say he must have returned to his native land on one of the ships that sailed west in the summer. So now they are concentrating on their other lead.' He picks at his fraying cuffs.

'Me.'

'I'm afraid so, yes.'

'There is no evidence, all they have is a story and their malice.'

'You're misinterpreting their actions.'

'Misinterpreting? How can I misinterpret a false accusation of murder?'

'They have to eliminate the possibilities.'

'I'm not a possibility. I never was. Isn't it enough they hanged my father? Now they want me too.'

'Believe me, Birdie, they're just plodding and incompetent. Clueless about modern policing methods. They take time to investigate.'

'That's what you said in May. And now we've reached the end of October. Do you still believe what you're saying?'

She bites her tongue. She always avoided this argument

with Solomon because she knew it had no resolution. Her hatred of the Filth flows through her veins. Tastes bitter in her mouth. She resolves her attraction to Solomon by telling herself that, though he is a copper, he is different; Solomon is an outsider in the Met. Although now she is beginning to wonder. Are he and she on irrevocably opposing sides? Has he more in common with the Filth than he has with her?

He removes his bowler, places it on the stone beside him.

'We can sort this out together.'

Her spirits lift. 'Have you discovered some new information?'

He grimaces. 'Nothing definite.'

She searches the lines of his face. He looks away and leaves her with the feeling he is holding something back; there is some vital piece of information he is not prepared to share. He stares at the swans as they drift across the mercurial lake. She feels deflated; she'd placed her hopes in his detective skills and his affection for her.

'And what about you?' He looks at her askance. 'Have you discovered anything about Tobias Skaill?'

'He worked for the Company.'

'Which explains the tokens you found by his body?'

'I believe so.'

Solomon's forehead furrows, as if he does not agree with her. She ploughs on, determined to finish her explanation.

'He set himself up as a free trader after he was kicked out of York Factory, and I believe he headed north, found the place where Franklin's remains lie, and was intending to report his discovery to the Admiralty so he could claim the reward. But he was murdered by a rival for the money.'

Solomon's frown deepens. 'That's not—'

'You yourself said money was most often the motive for murder.'

'I know, but there has to be some evidence linking the money to the murder. What evidence do you have?'

'Well...' She silently lists the leads she has followed: the toggles on the sledge carved with the initials HMST, her vision of the frozen corpse, the twins' tale of the Kabloona monster. If she had to repeat any of this in Wapping Station, the cops would laugh. It's a ghost story. Solomon might take her seriously, but she does not want to bring the twins into a murder investigation, scare them back into muteness. Betray Margaret's trust. She closes her eyes, and tries to decide what to do.

'Birdie, I'm not saying you're wrong, but it's quite a fantastical story.' Solomon's voice chips away. 'My Commander at the Yard would welcome a chance to put the Thames Division in their place and point out their deficiencies when it comes to investigations. The Wapping Station is something of a thorn in the side of the Met; as you know, they resist being part of a larger force and continue to act as if they're independent. But I can't persuade my bosses to take the case away from them without some firm evidence they're pursuing the wrong line.'

She regards him through blurred eyes; she is so weary.

'Is my story any more fantastical than this story that I persuaded a savage Esquimaux to murder a man?' She waves her hand dismissively at the copy of *The Times*. 'I didn't even know his name 'til you told me.'

He shakes his head glumly. 'I agree it's an unlikely tale. I'm not sure that any part of the account is true. I'm not at all convinced by the reports of cannibalism. I can't believe the man who dumped the body intended to eat part of the poor sod's face. I have my doubts the killer was even an Esquimaux, let alone a cannibal.'

'But flesh was taken from the corpse.'

'Most likely because the murderer needed some gruesome proof he'd carried out his orders.'

'What kind of madman would demand a slice of flesh?'

'The same kind of madman that would order a killing in the first place. Unfortunately, the report that the body was brought ashore in a canoe has convinced the Thames Division there is an Esquimaux involved.' He retrieves his bowler from its resting place on the altar stone and twists its rim in his hands. 'And that he has a young Irish woman for an accomplice.'

Solomon smiles ruefully. She instinctively draws a little closer, searching for comfort; her skirt almost touches his trousers.

'Birdie, we should be careful.'

There is a cold edge to his voice that confuses her and makes her ashamed of her forwardness. She shifts away and clasps her hands in her lap. She doesn't understand why he is so frosty toward her. Does he know she is doomed? Is he distancing himself to spare his feelings – or his career? Does he still feel slighted because she ended their courtship? The doubts plague her mind and she wishes she had never suggested coming to this place. It's full of demons and bad spirits.

'I travelled to Orkney because I wanted to help you,' he says.

She wonders whether she would be better off without his assistance.

'What do you think I should do then?'

'Well…' He ponders. 'I suppose you could return with me and make a statement declaring your innocence to the Met.'

'A statement? How would that work? I have no alibi. I was out walking in the early hours when I spotted the dead body.'

The only people who saw what happened were that peculiar old woman and the mudlarker – and who would believe them?

'It was just a suggestion.' His voice is gruff.

An owl hoots and some poor creature squeals. The stars dance and fashion strange constellations above her head. Nothing they say to each other this evening is right. It's as if the dismal spirits of the stones are mangling their words as they issue from their mouths, distorting their true meaning.

'We should leave.' He stands, glances over his shoulder before setting off across the circle in the direction of the track.

She follows Solomon's receding figure. As she nears the far stones, a curlew calls. Its mournful song makes her cry, her eyes so teary she can no longer see the back of Solomon; he has vanished in the darkness. There is another figure there, though, blurry in the gloaming yet unmistakable: Da, swinging from a rope.

Chapter 13

Frost swirls across the window pane. The clearness of the night has brought freezing temperatures. The local blacksmith – a good friend of Margaret's – has made two pairs of skates for Grace and Hope, ingeniously constructed from blocks of wood with iron runners nailed below and string for tying the contraptions to their boots. They are eager to test them. Be careful on the ice, Margaret orders as they disappear through the door, wrapped in their deerskin parkas. She does not usually allow them to wear their old coats but today she is more concerned about the cold than the comments of the townsfolk. Margaret chuckles as she returns to the office and says they probably know more about ice than any soul in Stromness.

Birdie examines the papers for the timber consignment with barely open eyes; after her long evening at Stenness she was awake early to claim the planks from the steamer and organize their delivery to the boat builder. Margaret spreads the plan of the ship she has commissioned across the table. She leans over the sheet, examining it with evident glee.

'Come and look.' She smooths the cartridge paper with her palm. 'A cutter. I need one ship in my fleet that is built for speed not capacity. Something to compete with steam.'

Birdie is not convinced any sailing ship can compete with the reliability of the steamers, but Margaret is in a buoyant mood. She has even lit a small peat fire, and the room is warm despite the frost outside. Birdie joins Margaret at the table, though she stares at the mesmeric copper flames in the hearth, rather than the drawings of the ship, her mind preoccupied with Solomon. They had trudged back to Stromness in the icy starlight, slipping on the frozen puddles in the deeply rutted track, hunting owls and nervous rabbits their only companions along the way. He gave her his overcoat to wear, but she was conscious of a coldness between them. There was a saturnine edge to him she hadn't encountered before; perhaps he had changed in the years they hadn't seen each other. Or perhaps she'd never known him well at all. Whatever the source of this gloom, when they reached the Mason's Arms, she told him he should return to London as soon as possible and he said he hadn't intended to stay more than one night anyway; the steamer was returning south as soon as all the cargo had been sorted. She turned on her heel with barely a farewell.

'Birdie,' he called after her. Were his eyes teary, or was it the biting cold that made them water? 'If you need me, you know where you'll find me.'

She nodded and continued briskly along the road to Narwhal House. Fortunately, Margaret had been kind enough not to bolt the doors. She tiptoed up the stairs, lay on the bed, smelled the scent from his overcoat still clinging to her skin.

'You were out late last night,' Margaret says.

'I didn't visit Morag.'

'Did I suggest you had?' Margaret drags her gaze away from the plans for the ship and surveys Birdie's face. 'Your eyes are puffy. And you have a dismal air about you, as if somebody has snuffed your flame and left nothing but a smouldering wick.'

Birdie smiles wanly and returns to her desk and the ledgers that are her refuge from turmoil. The steamship's whistle makes her gasp; Solomon will be aboard the vessel now, preparing to return to Gravesend.

'Birdie, what ails you today?'

Margaret rarely asks her personal questions; not that she is uncaring, more that she likes to keep a respectful distance.

'It's nothing.' Birdie shuffles the papers.

Margaret places her hands on her hips. 'Tell me. Go on.'

Birdie looks up, pauses and then asks, 'Did you ever consider remarrying after the death of your husband?'

'No. The scarlet fever took him and my lasses so suddenly. I spent many years grieving their deaths. By the time I emerged from that dark place, I was already forty. Too old for bairns. What was the point of looking for another husband?'

'Companionship. Love?'

'Ah. Love. So that's what's bothering you.'

Birdie reddens. 'That's not what I meant...'

'Why be so shy? You're a bonny young woman, Birdie. And surely, you'd like bairns of your own?'

Margaret's words catch Birdie by surprise. She'd considered it fortunate that she had no children to care for when Patrick died, but perhaps spending time with the twins has shifted her feelings, for the question provokes an unexpected pang.

'You should be looking for another man while you can,' Margaret persists. 'How many years is it since your husband died?'

'Four.'

'And you're still wearing mourning?' She flicks her hand dismissively. 'Remind me, what was his name?'

'Patrick.'

'I've no heard your parrot mention him.'

Birdie's flush deepens; her cheeks burn crimson.

'Do you think I'm daft, young lady?' Margaret's tone is gently mocking rather than severe. 'Do you think I didn't realize that Solly is the name of the man who plays on your mind?'

Birdie rolls her lips together, too embarrassed to reply, surprised to find her thoughts are so obvious; half the time she's barely conscious of them herself. She wonders how many of her other secrets Margaret has discerned.

'You know, my grandfather Albert always regretted leaving his wife in Rupert's Land. He loved her deeply. But he was scared of what folk would say if he brought a Cree woman home with him. So he left her behind and took the lads.'

'Did she mind being parted from her children?'

'He persuaded her they'd have a better life in Orkney, and she was better off staying put in Rupert's Land. By the time he realized he missed her sorely, it was too late.'

'What happened?'

'He sent word with one of the Company's ships asking her to sail on the return journey to Stromness, but she'd passed away the previous winter. He regretted not bringing her here 'til his dying day.'

She folds the plan neatly, stands, plants herself squarely in front of the desk. 'Take my advice. If you've found a man you trust and love, have no care for the whisperers and the critics.'

Birdie wishes it was that simple. 'Thank you for the advice.'

'I hope you take it. Now stop moping please, and get on with my papers. I have to visit this boat builder.'

Margaret pulls the door behind her, leaves Birdie alone in the house, thoughts of Solomon churning.

The steamer's whistle shrieks; it's about to depart. She runs to the icy window, attempts to open it, realizes it is frozen tight, bangs and bangs to loosen the ice, finally manages to shift the frame. The urge to see Solomon again is suddenly overwhelming. It was the Stenness stones, she decides, that cast a glum spell over him; the restless spirits of the place and the melancholic wraiths of All Hallows' Eve. She hurries from the office, through the hall, heaves the door and tumbles into the street.

The steamer is heading into the Sound as she reaches the pier, its smoking funnel dark against the sheer cliffs of Hoy. She groans with frustration, pivots heavily on her heel and is alarmed to see Detective Thompson at the end of the pier, leaning against the wall and reading a newspaper. A quick glance is enough to confirm it is a copy of *The Times* with the artist's impression of her face on the front page. How did he get hold of that? For a fraction of a second, she considers the possibility that Solomon found him, gave him the paper and warned him about her presence in Stromness. She dismisses the idea; Solomon might be a copper but he's always kept his word. He said nothing when Hugh O'Brien denied stealing the revolver from the Colt stand at the Great Exhibition Hall. It's true he was always secretive about his business and she'd had some questions about his work. But these were fleeting concerns, she reassures herself. She cannot believe he would betray her, whatever her doubts about his current feelings for her. She pulls the hood of her cloak over her head and marches briskly back to the main street, thankful for the grip on the soles of Patrick's sturdy boots which keep her from slipping on the ice.

She is, for once, comforted as she passes beneath the whalebone arch, and is swallowed by the entrance of Margaret's premises. She spies the toy sledge lying at the bottom of the stairs.

'Hope. Grace.'

There is no answer. No ghostly giggles. The house is silent. The twins are still away testing their ice skates on a frozen burn. She removes her cape, and catches her reflection in the blotched mirror that is partially obscured by the coat stand in a dark recess of the hall; it makes her wonder whether the description in *The Times* bears any resemblance to her appearance. Short of leg and squat, she definitely isn't. Low of brow? No. Though the nose in the picture was beaky; they'd got that right. Last night, when she was with Solomon, she assumed that nobody would recognize her from the artist's impression. This morning, alone and with Solomon heading back to London, she no longer feels quite so confident.

She returns to her desk, but it's hard to concentrate on invoices. Her thoughts slip from Solomon, to the picture in *The Times*, back to the detective lurking near the pier. A shy rap at the door rouses her. She crosses the hall and is surprised to find Peter Gibson standing there, shivering. She laughs. 'The knock was so timid I was expecting a mouse.'

He rubs his hands and attempts a smile, exhaling puffs of breath in the chilly air.

'Good morning, Birdie. I have a quick question.' He peers over her shoulder.

'Were you waiting for Mrs Skaill to leave before you called?'

'Yes.'

'You're afraid of her?'

'Mrs Skaill is somewhat suspicious of reporters.'

His cherubic face takes on such a long, sheepish expression, she cannot help feeling sorry for him; she's suspicious of reporters too but, whatever Margaret might say, she reasons it's best to keep Peter Gibson on her side. She has a sudden thought; has he seen the drawing in *The Times*? Has he recognized her face? There is only one way to find out.

'You'd better come in before you freeze to death.'

He warms himself in front of the fire.

'What can I do for you?'

'I'd heard Mrs Skaill has commissioned a new ship.'

'Does anything pass unnoticed in Stromness?'

He smiles. 'I thought she might wish some details to be included in this month's report of the shipping news from Stromness harbour.'

'Well, I'm afraid you'll have to come back and ask her yourself when she's returned.'

His face falls.

'Is that the only news in Stromness this month – the shipping?'

'No.'

He grins conspiratorially. Her heart thumps, fearful he is about to reveal he has discovered that one of those accused of murdering Tobias Skaill is standing in this very room.

'The editor has given me permission to write a small account of Dr Rae's application to the Admiralty for the reward for discovering the fate of Franklin.'

'It's a huge sum, isn't it?' She hopes she doesn't sound too relieved. 'Twenty thousand pounds.'

'And an additional three thousand pounds from Lady Franklin. Though, I doubt whether Dr Rae stands a chance of being awarded any of it. Lady Franklin will certainly refuse to offer her share of the reward to him. And I've been told she's lobbying hard to dissuade the Admiralty from handing him their money too.'

'Why?'

'Because she's furious with him for reporting that Franklin is dead and his men resorted to cannibalism.'

'Of course. She must have been greatly pained to see Dr Rae's account in the newspaper.'

'Indeed.'

She watches Peter's gaze flitting around the office, seeking out anything that might furnish a story for his newspaper. His eyes alight on Margaret's cabinet of aide-mémoires. Birdie coughs politely. Peter flushes.

'And the fact that Lady Franklin knows Dr Rae surely made the injury worse,' he offers quickly, to cover his embarrassment.

'They are acquainted?'

Birdie steps closer, intrigued by this revelation.

He leans in. 'She visited Stromness several times after Sir John's disappearance, and courted the favours of Dr Rae's family as she was keen for him to search for her husband.'

'How did Lady Franklin become acquainted with the Rae family?'

'I should imagine she made herself known when she heard about his Arctic explorations for the Company.'

The fire hisses; she glances at the red flames and is struck again by the extent to which the trade of the Hudson's Bay Company is entwined with the life of Stromness. She thinks of the Company coins she found by Tobias's body, etched with a pelt.

'Dr Rae was a fur trader?'

'Well, he was employed as a surgeon originally. But the Company has a commercial interest, of course, in sending explorers to discover new trade routes. Which was what Dr Rae was doing when he bumped into the party of Esquimaux who told him about the remains of Franklin's crew.'

Peter pauses. The house is silent apart from the tick of the clock and the crackle from the hearth. He glances over his shoulder. 'I heard it was Lady Franklin who persuaded Dickens to write those pieces in *Household Words* claiming Dr Rae was naïve and the Esquimaux were savages.'

Birdie gasps. 'Surely, if Lady Franklin is known to have asked Dickens to write that article, it's unlikely she'll ever be able to show her face in Stromness again.'

'I doubt she'll return here. Folk are, of course, sympathetic to her plight. Though I've heard some here say that her efforts to discredit Dr Rae are driven as much by the fact that she stands to lose her husband's salary and inheritance if he is found to be dead as by her love for him.'

Birdie is about to encourage Peter to reveal more details of Lady Franklin's financial affairs, then feels a stab of shame for gossiping. Not to mention a certain empathy for any widow's efforts to secure her own living, no matter how underhand her methods. And anyway, she finds it hard to doubt the anguish Lady Franklin must have suffered after the disappearance of her husband in the icy wastes of the Arctic.

'Lady Franklin certainly has some influential friends,' she says. 'Dickens' opinions are read and debated in every London coffee house.'

'You're not swayed by his views?'

'I admire his concern for the poor but, in my opinion, he's not always so fair on people who are not of the English race.'

Peter nods. 'I noticed he also took a somewhat condescending view of the Scots in the article he wrote about Franklin.'

Birdie gives Peter an encouraging smile. 'And what do folk in Stromness make of Dickens' claim that the Esquimaux are savage killers?'

'Well, I've heard some claim the Esquimaux are like the Finmen. Wild sorcerers of the seas.' He shrugs. 'But these are tales told in Stromness taverns when the nights are long and there is little else to do but drink. Most sensible folk are inclined to side with Dr Rae's view that the Esquimaux are the same as any other people; they react well if treated favourably and respond in kind if threatened.'

He tilts his head to one side and grins, his curls flopping over one eye; a posture that emphasizes his boyish charm though also reminds Birdie that he is not without cunning.

'But, to play the devil's advocate,' he says, 'there is the story in *The Times* of the Esquimaux canoe paddler who brutally murdered Tobias Skaill.'

She keeps her nerves steady; it was her, after all, who raised the subject of the Esquimaux. 'Indeed, but London is a place of many stories that turn out to be untrue,' she says. 'While Orkney folk tell tales of witches and Finmen, we Londoners entertain ourselves with tales of murderers like Spring Heeled

Jack who has horns and blazing eyes and vaults across rooftops in pursuit of his victims.'

She gazes sideways at the window, the frost so thick it gleams like polished metal; it makes her think of the tin canoe and she wonders whether she can risk mentioning it to Peter. She hesitates, then pictures Detective Thompson with a newspaper under his arm; time is running out.

'Though, now you speak of Tobias Skaill, it reminds me that a friend from home wrote and told me that one of the many stories about the killer being told in the coffee houses...' she picks her words carefully, '... is that his canoe was made from some shiny material – metal apparently. Not sealskin or bark like most native canoes.'

'I'd not heard that.' The detail catches his attention; she can sense him examining it from different angles, considering whether there is something useful here.

'Apparently, people say it might have been made from tin.'

'Tin.' He strokes his chin, which has the barest trace of blonde stubble. 'Now that is interesting; I remember seeing a tin canoe in Stromness harbour once.'

'Is that so?' She can barely disguise her surprise, or her interest.

'In point of fact, it may have had something to do with one of Lady Franklin's visits.'

Birdie's eyes widen as Peter continues.

'I distinctly remember walking along the warehouse pier and seeing her standing there, looking down at this strange canoe floating around the harbour.'

Birdie clasps her hands in front of her skirt and squeezes her fingers to keep herself from overreacting.

'You must have been born with a reporter's eye for detail.'

He flushes. She silently congratulates herself on correctly identifying the best way to win him over.

'I've a very good memory for details. And, now I come to think about it, Lady Franklin must have been in Stromness to wave off one of the many expeditions to search for her husband. He stares at the frozen window, as if he can see Lady Franklin still standing on the pier beyond. 'It was 1851. The name of the ship was, I think, the *Prince Albert*. The Captain's name was William Kennedy – another Company man. He was a half-breed, his father was from Orkney and his mother Indian. Kennedy grew up among the Indians, some say, and learned their ways. Some also say he is as good an explorer as Dr Rae, but his skills were never much appreciated by the Company because he was too keen on advocating the rights of the Indian voyageurs and trappers. He thought it was wrong to trade furs for liquor.'

'I'd agree with him on that point. But why,' Birdie muses, 'would Mr Kennedy take a tin canoe with him if he knew the ways of the Indians and could use a native vessel?' Morag's fiddle provides her with the answer to her own question. 'Because a tin canoe is less likely to be crushed in the hold of a ship on rough seas.'

'Ah,' Peter says. 'That must be it.'

'I wonder where he found such an unusual vessel.'

'I should imagine it would have been made by one of the tinsmiths in the town. The *Prince Albert*, as I recall, was trapped in Stromness harbour by unfavourable winds for several days. The tin canoe would have been something Kennedy commissioned and tested in the harbour to occupy what would have otherwise been wasted time.' He strokes his chin again. 'Of course, he might have asked the gypsies...'

'The camp beyond the town?'

'They've quartered there on and off for many years, and while folk sometimes question their honesty, few would doubt their skill with tin.'

The creaking of hinges heralds Margaret's return. Peter jumps, almost to attention. Margaret enters the office, her face wreathed in friendly lines until she glimpses the reporter, shifting nervously from foot to foot. Her features take on a surly cast. Birdie is moved to intervene.

'Peter came to ask whether you might like to include a few lines in *The Orcadian* about the ship you've commissioned. I suggested he put the idea to you himself.'

Margaret still looks grim.

'Some advance publicity might encourage merchants to enquire about its future availability,' Birdie adds.

The smile returns to Margaret's face.

'Good idea.'

Peter mouths a thank you in Birdie's direction.

'I could dictate a few lines,' Margaret suggests.

Peter readily agrees and fumbles for his pencil and dog-eared notebook.

'It'll be an extremely fast cutter,' Margaret says. 'Launched and ready for merchants to contract in the New Year.'

'Is New Year a little optimistic?' Peter asks.

'No.'

Peter smiles meekly and notes the details as instructed. Birdie watches the end of his pencil bobbing and thinks about the tin canoe. Is this the key that's been eluding her? As Morag vociferously argued, the murderer of Tobias Skaill is not an Esquimaux at all, but perhaps he may be a crew member from William Kennedy's expedition to discover

Franklin's remains. A possible rival for the reward. A murkier thought crosses her mind; could Lady Franklin herself have encouraged the crime, determined to deny her husband's fate and maintain his salary?

'Birdie, what do you think?'

Margaret's question startles her. 'I'm afraid I didn't hear what you said.'

'Still mooning I see.'

Peter raises a quizzical brow.

'I was asking for your opinion of the notice.' She nods at Peter's notebook. 'Take a look.'

Birdie reaches for Peter's scribbled page, realizing she needs to cover for Margaret's illiteracy. 'Excellent. I'm sure it will attract enquiries.'

'Does the ship have a name yet?' Peter asks.

'It's bad luck to announce the name before it's launched,' Margaret says sharply.

'Of course. Well then... I'd better be going.'

Peter tweaks his mouth politely and edges toward the door, eager to disappear before he says anything else to irritate Margaret.

The moon is full and its pale beams transform the hoar-frosted window into a miniature Arctic of crystal ice floes and ridges. The house is quiet; Margaret and the twins asleep in their rooms. Birdie reaches for her cape and the parrot stirs. She lifts the shawl covering the birdcage.

'I'm going out,' she says.

The parrot tilts his head and regards her as if to say she's mad.

On the hill behind the town, she pauses to get her bearings. To the north, beyond the kirkyard her eye is caught by a greenish shimmer on the horizon; an unearthly flickering which swells and shifts. Captivated, she stands and stares at the ethereal glow until it seems as if it is all around and, despite the urgency of her mission, she finds her mind drawn back to Solomon: their last dance together, bathed in the enchanting gleam of a thousand lamps that dangled from the trees of Vauxhall Pleasure Gardens. The orchestra played and they whirled around the ballroom floor. He held her in his arms so she could feel his body against hers and sense his breath on her cheek and when she looked down she saw his hand had slipped from her waist to the curve of her hip but she said nothing and let it linger there. Her heart was pounding. He drew her closer, and when he kissed her longingly, she knew she was in danger of forgetting herself in this seductive dreamland where London's secret lovers came to dally. The next evening as she was leaving the office, Frank's wife would whisper that she'd been spotted walking with a dark stranger, and it would almost be a relief. She wasn't sure she would otherwise have had the strength to end their courtship.

She wipes her blurry eyes. The green rays still glow and wave and she realizes they must be what the townsfolk call the Merry Dancers. She watches them awhile – the mysterious light filling her with a melancholic yearning for lost times and places – before she turns south and sees the scarlet flames of the gypsy campfire searing the windless night sky. An accordion plays a plaintive melody. She heads toward the music, across the slope, around the far end of the town, past the upended half-boat hulls the fishermen use as storerooms.

The gypsy camp is separated from the last of the huts by a stretch of open, rough ground. The frozen turf creaks beneath her feet. She reaches the fire, the flames still ablaze, and, beyond, a cart rests next to a brightly painted caravan and a tent with a chimney protruding. There is nobody in sight – the accordion player has vanished. A large grey-hackled dog is tethered to a peg in front of the cart. She steps toward it. The dog snarls and bears its sharp fangs. She retreats, hears a cackle behind and turns to find herself being assessed by a tiny woman with a walnut-wrinkled face.

'You're the widow with the talking parrot.'

Even the gypsies have heard about her.

'What can I do for you at this late hour?' the woman asks. 'Have you come to have your fortune read, or do you have a question about affairs of the heart? Is there a young man on your mind?'

Birdie flashes a nervous smile, wary of the gypsy's clairvoyance.

'I've come to ask you about something more practical.'

'If you help me in a practical way, then perhaps I can return the favour.'

She holds out her creased hand. Birdie digs in her purse, her fingers fumbling in the cold, retrieves a handful of coins and places them on her own palm for the woman to see; she does not know how much she is expected to give. The gypsy's eyes narrow; she jabs the token Birdie found by Tobias's body which she has inadvertently removed along with her pennies and shillings.

'That's not a proper coin.'

'Oh. No. It's a Company coin, I believe.'

'I know what it is and I know its worth, which is why I don't want it. You won't catch me paying their price.' She spits on the ground. 'Skin for a skin.'

The gypsy's words send a sharp jolt down Birdie's spine. 'Skin for a skin?'

'That's what I said.'

'But what does it...'

Birdie curtails her questions as she catches the woman's fierce glare.

'Give me another coin,' she demands.

Birdie selects a shilling and drops it in the gypsy's palm.

'What is it you want to know?'

'Have you ever made a tin canoe?'

'A tin canoe?' She calls over her shoulder. 'Johnny, did you hear that? There's a widow here asking about a tin canoe.'

A face appears between the tent flaps, grimy with soot, cap perched on black hair. Johnny heaves himself into the open air. He eyes her mourning dress.

'Has it sunk? I told him he'd need to get it lined.'

'I'm not here to complain about it,' Birdie says. 'I'm interested in the person who came and asked for it to be made. Was he from a ship – the *Prince Albert*?'

Johnny folds his arms, glances at the old woman. 'It was a few years back. He said Captain Kennedy wanted the canoe.'

Birdie's pulse races; she's struck lucky.

'Do you know this man's name?'

'Nope.'

'Was he an Esquimaux?'

'An Esquimaux? I wouldn't know.' He knits his brow and then he laughs. 'Though he had a Cockney accent.'

'He was from London?'

'Definitely.'

'What did he look like?'

Johnny shrugs. 'Ugly mug. Broken nose – like a boxer.'

She tries to recall how the mudlarker described the man who dumped Tobias's body on the Thames.

'Did he have peculiar ears?'

'He might have done, I didn't pay him much regard. I couldn't wait to be rid of him. He was breathing down my neck while I was trying to work. He kept eyeing the canoe as I was making it and muttering about how useful it could be.' Johnny turns to the old woman. 'Do you remember, he said we should go into business together?'

The woman tuts.

'What kind of business?' Birdie demands.

'I didn't ask – folk always assume we're dishonest and on the look-out for a quick way to make a shilling, so I supposed he was talking about smuggling of some kind or another.'

The woman snorts. 'We're not interested in other people's business.'

'Do you think the canoe could have lasted four years?'

'It was well made.'

'And this man, you said he was very interested in the canoe. Do you think he might have stolen it from the *Prince Albert* when the ship returned from the Arctic?'

Johnny glowers. The dog howls. Birdie twists and watches it tip its head, snout to the full moon; just like a wolf, she thinks. She turns back to ask the woman another question, but she and Johnny have vanished. She's outstayed her welcome. Asked one too many questions. The fire is dead.

Chapter 14

Birdie sits at the desk and blows on her hands, numb despite the flames of the peat fire. Fishermen loiter on the pier, muttering that such cold weather so early in the winter is not a good sign. Only the twins appear to be enjoying themselves. While other children sit in the freezing school house learning their alphabet and times tables, Hope and Grace set off in their deerskin parkas carrying their ice skates, searching for frozen burns to explore. Margaret allows them to roam; she says their hunger will bring them back in time for tea.

The sound of cannon shot echoes across the Sound, and marks the late return of another Company ship from the Nor' West. Margaret pokes her head around the office door and says she's heading to the harbour. The ships bring with them orders for the following spring and Margaret is keen to hear what news there is of business, and whether any commissions are likely to come their way.

The front door scrapes and shuts. Birdie stokes the fire, spies the toy canoe nestling beside the hearth, picks it up and brushes its skin-covered frame. It's three days since she discovered that the owner of the tin canoe is not an Inuit but, most likely, a Cockney who sailed in 1851 on the *Prince Albert* under the captaincy of William Kennedy in search of Franklin's remains. This discovery has been a cause of both hope and frustration. The revelations of the gypsies have given her, at last, something solid to support her view that Tobias Skaill was murdered in a battle over the reward for information about Franklin. Yet the fact that she made this discovery after Solomon had departed has left her despondent and restless. She cannot decide the best course of action; should she return to London and hand Solomon this information, so he can report to his superiors and the detective branch can take over the investigation from the Thames Division? Or does she stand to lose more than she might gain from putting herself within the grasp of the river police? She shivers, heaves herself back onto her stool, fumbles with the quill, dips it in the ink pot, and holds its nib above a blank sheet of paper.

The black-backed gull taps at the window; she can hear its beak against the glass but only its outline is visible through the thick ice. The kirk bell tolls. Margaret opens the front door, clunks across the hall to the parlour. A moment of silence is followed by her fraught call.

'Hope. Grace?'

There is no answer. Heavy footsteps, faster this time, pound the stairs. A door slams upstairs. Margaret shouts again. 'Hope. Grace. If you're hiding, come out now.'

Still no reply. Birdie's pulse quickens. A stab of guilt pricks her; she's been so busy thinking about her own predicament she hasn't noticed their absence. Margaret clatters down the stairs and enters the office in a flurry, her cheeks flushed.

'Have you heard the twins return? The cook tells me she made them tea but they haven't been to the kitchen to eat it yet.'

'I haven't heard anything. I wasn't listening for them, though.'

Margaret wipes her forehead with the back of her hand; her chest is heaving as if she's about to cry. Birdie leaps from her stool and places an arm around her shoulder.

'I'm sure they're fine. Have you checked all the rooms?'

'Yes. Yes. I looked upstairs. They're not there.'

'Let me try my room. Perhaps they're with the parrot.'

She hitches her skirt and runs.

The parrot huddles on his perch, ruffling his feathers to keep warm.

'Where are the twins?'

The parrot senses her alarm, bobs and squawks, 'Skin for a skin. Skin for a skin.'

The imitation of her brother's voice chills her marrow.

She hastens back to the office, where Margaret is sitting at the table, staring blankly at the gloom. Birdie attempts to allay her fears.

'They'll come home soon, I'm sure.'

Margaret is not assuaged. She quits the office, climbs the stairs. Birdie can hear her tipping chairs and baskets over, calling the girls' names fretfully. She returns to the office, checks in unlikely places – the cabinet, behind the door. She wrings her hands.

'They'll catch their death,' Margaret says.

'They were wearing their parkas. They'll stay warm.'

'Something terrible has happened.'

'Did they say where they were going?'

'They were going skating, that's all I know. They've fallen through the ice, I'm sure.'

The last light of day has abandoned the room. The fire has died. Margaret reaches for a candle, lights the wick with a trembling hand, places it on the mantelpiece where it casts a feeble glow. 'I've no idea what to do.'

'I'll go and search for them.'

'You? I should go.'

'Stay here in case they return. Let me search.'

'You're hardly familiar with this island.'

'Maybe that's an advantage, I'm a stranger to this place. Like the twins.' She hesitates. 'And I have an idea which paths they follow.'

Margaret folds her arms and her shadow grows and looms behind her. 'How so?'

'I was followed by Hope and Grace on one occasion.'

'The bairns followed you?'

'When I first arrived. I went for a stroll in the late evening and realized they were behind me, so I brought them home.'

'At night? After I put them to bed?'

Birdie nods; her intention was to reassure Margaret that the twins had done this kind of thing before and had come to no harm. She is alarmed to find she is having the opposite effect.

'Why did you no tell me?'

Birdie grimaces and wishes she had kept her mouth shut.

Margaret wails. 'I'm no good. I lost my own bairns and now I've lost Tobias's lasses.'

'You haven't lost them.'

'I've failed them. God knows I'm useless. I was never meant to be a mother.'

'You're a good mother. You've provided Hope and Grace with a safe home and loving care.'

Margaret sinks onto the nearest chair.

'Let me go and search, please. I doubt they're harmed. They know how to look after themselves. Perhaps something or someone has scared them and they're hiding.'

Margaret shakes her head in disbelief. 'A freezing night. And they've gone missing.'

'I'll try along the coast path, beyond the graveyard.'

'The path to Morag's?'

'That's where I was heading when they followed me. There's a burn beyond the croft where Morag draws her water. Perhaps it's where they went to skate.'

Margaret catches her eye and Birdie thinks she is going to warn her again about heading to Morag's place. She doesn't. She nods. 'Morag might be of some help. She sees things other people miss. Make sure you wrap yourself up warm. I've kept my husband's old overcoat. You can use that.'

Margaret rises, collects herself, fiddles with a strand of hair that has worked its way loose from her plait.

'Right,' Margaret says. 'Right. Let's fetch this coat.' She still sounds distraught, though now she is at least focusing on what can be done, rather than giving in to despair, and marches to the hall.

Margaret stands below the whalebone arch, candle in hand, and watches her leave. The flame barely flickers, the night is so windless. The moon is waning, but in the clear sky it casts a pale light on the road, icy beneath her feet; even her sturdy docker's boots are not sufficient to prevent her slipping. She jams her hands in the pockets of the overcoat to keep them warm; she forgot to bring gloves. It's hard to imagine how anybody lives in the Arctic. She thinks of Tobias who survived the frozen wilderness of the Nor' West yet ended up dead on the Thames. Killed, she is sure, because he was about to deliver evidence of Franklin's fate to the Admiralty and claim the reward. And she will die for it too unless she can prove her innocence.

The coldness of the night has leached the land of life. Grey slopes are draped with frosty shrouds and lined with ice-embalmed dead nettles.

'Hope. Grace.'

The names fall like stray snowflakes, vanishing as they touch the earth. Yet she is certain they came this way, she can sense it in her bones. Her eyes sweep left and right, hoping for a tell-tale sign of movement. She hears a noise; was that the twins giggling? She twists around and suddenly her head spins, her limbs go numb. Her skin prickles. The fields and stone walls around her dissolve and everything is engulfed in darkness. She catches her breath, peers into the gloom, thinking perhaps this is an apparition of the place the twins are hiding, but the land she sees now is too barren to be Orkney, nothing but bare soil, jagged rocks and pockets of blue ice. No sign of Hope and Grace. Though there is something there – she hears a moan. She stumbles through the greyness toward the sound and spies a flash of coppery hair in the shadows. It is Tobias. He is squatting beside a body; a woman in a blood-stained sealskin parka. A corpse. He strokes her cheek before he turns in Birdie's direction, his face tormented. He holds up his hands imploringly and wails.

'Tobias?' Birdie shouts, though she knows he cannot be here because he is dead. There is no reply. The ghostly apparition has vanished. She calls across the fields again and finds herself panting, gripped by fear for the twins; moved by Tobias's anguish for the dead woman. Was it his wife, the mother of the twins? Could she have been murdered too? She quickens her pace and hears waves rasping the shore. The blackness of the ocean fills her with despair; if the girls tumbled in the sea they wouldn't survive long. Searching for the twins is beginning to feel like a hopeless task, though it's less painful than returning to Stromness and telling Margaret she has been unsuccessful in her efforts.

The glow falling from the window of Morag's croft offers the only warm sight in this bleakness. She heads to the door and knocks loudly.

'It's me, Birdie.'

The raven on the turf roof caws. Morag heaves the door.

'You choose some strange nights to come visiting. Last time you appeared in a storm. This time you pick an Arctic frost.'

'I need your help. It's the twins.'

Morag's eyes gleam fiercely.

'You'd better come in-aboot.'

Birdie steps into the fug of the peat fire. She does not bother with niceties.

'The girls are missing.'

'Since when?'

'They left Narwhal House this morning with their skates. They failed to return. Margaret is beside herself with worry. I said I'd search for them. They've followed me this way before, and I was sure I would find them in the fields along the path. But I've called, and looked and there's been no answer. I thought they might have been heading to the burn beyond your croft.'

Morag nods but her eyes are focused far away. She stands motionless and silent by the fire. The raven croaks and sweeps past the window, its diamond tail clear in the moonlight as it flies over the headland. The flames wane; the croft falls dark and cold. Morag remains unmoving, her face ashen. Birdie fears her companion has crossed the border between the living and the dead and cannot retreat.

'Morag.'

She doesn't reply. Scrabbling echoes down the chimney. The raven calls as it returns to its rooftop roost. A flame bursts into life in the hearth, licks the peats with its green tongue. Morag stirs abruptly.

'We have to hurry.'

She grabs her coat, and a coil of rope hanging from a beam and strides to the door. Birdie follows her into the frigid night.

'Where are we going?'

'To the cove, below Black Craig.' She points north beyond the ness to the cliffs; the direction in which the raven flew.

'How can you be certain they went there?'

Morag shoots her a withering look, and Birdie decides to ask no more questions. The townsfolk are right: Morag is a witch, she reckons. Birdie might have sensed the presence of the girls along the path, but Morag can see their location.

They cross the outrun behind the croft, the hoar-frost thick as snow on the turf.

Morag says, 'We must hurry for the tide is coming in and I'm afraid they may be trapped somewhere.'

They reach the frozen burn, a white scar gashing the blackness of the fields, and follow its course to the lip of the cliff edge, where the water escapes the ice and falls to the boulders below. The rocky descent gleams treacherously.

'They're down there?'

Morag nods.

At the base of the cliff, there is a slither of shingle, the contours of the tide marked by blackened kelp, driftwood and the debris of passing ships. The cove's sides are fringed with shards of sandstone, sliding into the sea and cracked with deep fissures; wide enough to shelter two small girls. And deep enough to create a deadly trap. Morag says nothing, stands with her hands in her jacket pockets, her mouth grim, scanning the bay. Birdie cups her hands around her mouth.

'Hope.'

The cove is still, apart from the relentless waves of the incoming tide.

'Grace. Are you here? It's me. Birdie.' Her voice is devoured by the darkness.

Morag nudges her. 'Listen.'

The rush of the sea, the drip of the burn. And then a quiet mew.

'Did you hear it?'

Birdie nods, though she thinks it could have been a seabird.

'There it is again.'

This time the mew is more of a whimper. Human. Birdie turns her head, attempting to locate the source of the cry.

'Over there.'

Morag clambers down the cliff, moving with enviable ease in her trousers. Birdie follows gingerly, edging her way, hands and boots searching for a safe grip on frozen ledges. She slides the last few feet, lands with a bump and is glad, then, of the protection her petticoats afford her coccyx. She trails Morag around the cove, over slanting stone. Morag halts at the edge of a crevice. Birdie reaches her and peers into the barnacle-spangled chasm. The twins are cowering below, looking up and clutching each other tight, the tide lapping at their feet. Birdie almost cries with relief – at least they are alive, even though they appear terrified, unable to speak or move.

'Are you hurt?'

Hope shakes her head. Grace does not react. Morag secures one end of the rope around a rocky outcrop, throws the other into the chasm and uses it as a guide as she clambers down. She secures the rope around Hope's waist. Birdie pulls, Morag pushes and between them they help the distressed girl climb the sheer wall. Birdie reaches for her hand and hauls her the last few feet. Morag returns for Grace, but is unable to persuade her to move; in the end, she carries her over one shoulder like a sack as she ascends. At the top, Morag lowers Grace gently onto the flat ridge next to her sister. Birdie squats and embraces them, feels their bodies trembling through the thickness of their parkas, their faces smudged and snotty.

'You're safe now.'

Morag produces sugary biscuits and two rosy apples from her coat pocket. The girls take Morag's offerings gladly and munch without saying a word, though all the while Grace is anxiously watching the bay.

'We should take them to Margaret now,' Morag says.

'Wait a minute.' Birdie catches Grace's scared black eyes. 'What happened?'

'It's no time for asking questions—'

Grace interrupts. 'Monster. We saw him. We hid.'

'The monster that skins and eats people?' Birdie asks. 'Kabloona?'

Grace nods. 'Very big,' she adds.

'How did you know it was him?'

Grace turns to Hope. They stare at each other and communicate silently while the waves rasp and suck the shore.

'He had a man,' Hope says. Grace sniffs and Hope cuddles her tight.

'A dead man?'

Hope nods this time.

'Where did he take him?'

Grace points. Birdie follows the line of her finger. The boulders at the head of the bay gleam in the moonlight.

'How did he arrive?'

'Boat.'

'What kind of boat?' she asks, though she knows the answer.

Hope frowns. 'Canoe.'

'Shiny,' Grace says.

'A shiny canoe?' Birdie repeats, wanting to be sure.

Grace screws her face as if she's searching for the right word.

Birdie points at Hope's parka. 'Skin?'

Grace shakes her head. 'Metal.'

Birdie gasps; she can't stop herself. The icy air hits the back of her throat; she wheezes. Morag pats her back. She closes her eyes, regains her breath and pictures the tin canoe.

Morag says, 'Enough questions. They're freezing and scared. They need to get in the warmth.'

'Will you take the twins back to Margaret? I'll look around the bay.'

'You're being foolish – staying out here by yourself with what sounds like a madman on the loose.'

'He's gone. There's no sign of him. I need to find...'

Morag sighs with frustration. 'Well, that's your look-out. I'm going to take these bairns home before they catch their death.'

Morag grasps a hand of each of the girls and sets off across the rocks.

'Morag.'

She turns.

'Please don't tell anyone what the twins said.' She means, not even Margaret.

'What do you take me for, Birdie?'

Morag sets off again, Hope and Grace at her side. Birdie watches their backs recede. Now she has to find the body.

She skids across the sloping outcrop, drops to the diminishing shingle crescent at the head of the bay and lands with a grating crunch on her hands and knees. She rights herself and sees indents in the pebbles beside her own: an uneven-edged channel that looks like the trail of something heavy being dragged. She follows the track across the shore and sniffs; the sulphurous reek of rotting seaweed fills the air, but there is something else – a faint metallic tang. Blood. The corpse, whoever it is, has been dumped on the far side of the bay. Fear grips her. Could it be Solomon? Was he followed aboard the steamer, killed and discarded? She steels herself and clambers over the slippery rocks.

And then she halts in her tracks. The body is there, grimacing at her from the bottom of a crevice, lying half-submerged in the frozen water of a rockpool. She covers her mouth and nose with her hand. It's not the sight of the body that shocks her – it's the fact that she's seen this corpse lying in the ice before; the dead man in the apparition she had when she held the toy sledge. She feels faint, her legs buckle. She teeters, her mind overcome with blackness, the spirits of the dead beckoning. A raven appears from nowhere, shrieking, its wing tip almost brushing her face as it banks. She lifts her arm to protect herself and shouts. The bird caws again and flaps clumsily away; whether it is a message from Morag or simply the raven returning for its carrion she cannot tell. Either way, it's stopped her from falling. She edges back from the rim and allows herself to breathe a sigh of relief; at least it isn't Solomon lying dead in the water.

Common sense tells her she should leave, now she has discovered this corpse, murdered and dumped. But she is desperate to discover more about the dead man. The crack is narrow; she is forced to lower herself carefully to prevent the heel of her boot landing on rigid limbs. There's barely enough space for her to crouch beside the body. It smells, though not as badly as it might have done if the night wasn't so cold. She can't stop herself from gazing at his grotesque face; the freezing water has tightened his skin and exaggerated his grimace, the grey lips retracted from his yellowing teeth. One of his eyes has gone – pecked by ravens, she supposes, from the look of the bloody socket. Below this, a circle of flesh is missing; the wound has the clean edge of a knife cut. The look of it makes her shudder – the lesion is the same as that on Tobias's cheek. And his neck is rope-marked in the same way as well.

The man's navy jacket is undone. She leans forward, and sees a bone toggle underneath the upper flap. She searches for a hanky in the pocket of the overcoat she wears, finds one, wraps it around her hand and gingerly lifts the stiff jacket material. She peers at the toggle. It's smooth, no marks at all. She lets the collar drop, disappointed not to find the letters HMST. She sits back on her heels and notices the tip of his left ring finger is missing. It's not a recent wound – the skin is entirely healed. A man who got himself into fights? An accident at sea? Other than these guesses, she has no idea of his character or identity. She adjusts the hanky, and dips her wrapped hand in the jacket pocket exposed above the jagged lines of the thin new ice. A hard, flat object is lodged in the bottom seam. She eases it out and holds it up in the moonlight. A brass token with HB etched on one face and on the flip side – the stretched pelt. *Skin for a skin.*

She holds the coin in her hand a while, wondering whether to replace it in his pocket or take it. The cold and anxiety are making it hard for her to think straight. She lifts her head and peers along the fissure to the sea. The tide has crept up the shore and within ten minutes or so it will breach the lip forming the far end of the rockpool grave and touch the dead man's boots. And there, the black line and barnacles on the rock indicate, the sea will have reached its highest point before it recedes. The body has been left above high tide mark, just as Tobias's corpse was discarded above the dirty rim of the Thames. She glances back at the frozen face, the flesh gouged out by the knife. And yet, frustratingly, there is nothing to suggest the corpse in front of her has anything to do with the fate of Franklin.

The caw of the raven circling overhead makes her look up. Morag was right, she sees suddenly – she is being reckless. This is the work of a ruthless killer and he might still be hiding among the rocks. And even if he isn't, she's already a suspect in Tobias Skaill's murder; she doesn't want to be found near another man's corpse. She has to leave. She drops the coin in her coat pocket, hauls herself across and up the rocks to the grassy lip of the cliff, then turns and inspects the scene below. Her boot tracks across the bay will be erased by the tide. She turns and finds the Stromness path. The moon coats the slopes with an eerie opaline gleam that reminds Birdie of the dead man's frozen skin. She shakes her head; she's beginning to doubt her own conclusion that Tobias was killed in a fight for Franklin's reward. The discovery of this second mutilated body makes her fear he was involved in some far more sinister business. She hears Frank's voice in her head. *Skin for a skin*, he says and laughs.

Chapter 15

Candlelight refracts through the frost-crackled glass; Margaret has not yet retired to her room. Birdie steps under the whalebone arch. Margaret heaves the door open before she has time to find the key and crushes her against her chest. Margaret has always been kind to Birdie, but this is the first time she has demonstrated such warmth. Birdie is overwhelmed, engulfed by Margaret's embrace.

'Thank you for finding the lasses.'

Margaret's tears dampen Birdie's cheek.

Birdie peers over Margaret's shoulder, searching for Morag. Margaret releases her from her arms. 'Come in. Out of the cold. Morag's gone home.'

Morag must have followed a different path back to her croft.

'The kettle is on the range. You'll want a cup of tea to warm yourself.'

Birdie sits in the parlour. Margaret fetches her a tin mug of steaming tea.

'The bairns went straight to bed. They were cold and hungry, but nothing that a good night's sleep won't cure.'

'I'm glad to hear it.'

'I canna tell you how overjoyed I was to see them.'

Birdie sips the tea, grateful for its warmth, and wonders how much Morag told her about the events of the evening. Perhaps it is better to leave the details 'til the morning; she's too tired and cold to think straight. Margaret, though, wants answers.

'Morag said they were trapped over at Black Craig.'

Birdie is conscious of Margaret's questioning gaze. 'They were too scared to move,' she answers.

'What scared them then?'

The candle flame splutters and dies with a hiss; the room lit only by the hearth fire.

'They saw a man bring a body ashore in a canoe.'

'A corpse?'

'Yes. They were so afraid, they hid in a crevice and didn't move all evening. Their fear saved them, though. Heaven knows what might have happened if the boatman had realized they were watching.'

Margaret shakes her head, unwilling to contemplate the possibilities.

'You found the body?'

'On the far side of the cove, hidden in a rockpool. He looked as…' She bites her tongue, stops herself from saying he looked as Tobias had looked when she found him: strangled, and dumped.

'He looked as what?'

Birdie moves her lips, but does not speak. She has shied away from this confession once before. She glances at Margaret. In the gloom, her eyes are black, her skin dark. Margaret is an outsider here, even though she has lived in Stromness all her life. She will not misjudge her or hand her over to the local magistrate, especially if the twins' safety is bound up with her own.

'What is it you have to tell me, Birdie?'

The hearth flames spiral and blaze in an unexpected draught. Birdie cannot find the words.

'We all have our secrets and our reasons for keeping them.' Margaret's eyes slip to the fire and back. 'But something evil has happened on this island, and now is not the time for keeping quiet.'

Birdie watches the restless shadows on the wall; she takes a deep breath. 'I found Tobias's body on the Thames foreshore. Below London Bridge.'

Margaret does not appear surprised; she knew all along there was more to Birdie's story than a chance journey north in search of a vacant situation.

'You knew Tobias, then?'

Birdie avoids mention of their meeting in the street; she doesn't want to distress Margaret with stories of her cousin's drunkenness.

'No, I didn't know him. I was walking early, and came across his body.'

Margaret searches for a handkerchief in the sleeve of her shirt, removes a neat white cotton square, wipes her eyes and nose. And then she looks sharply at Birdie. 'But why did discovering his body make you keen to find out more about him?'

It is hard to fool Margaret. Birdie has no choice now, she has to tell the whole truth. 'The police named me as a suspect in his murder.'

Margaret scrutinizes her face. 'A friend told me about the report in *The Times*. He mentioned the female accomplice.' Her brow knots. 'That is you?'

'It's what they claim.'

She awaits the angry reaction. Margaret guffaws. 'Lord, if that's the best the great Metropolitan Police force of London can do then we're better off without them. Look at you.' She waves her hand at Birdie. 'Anybody could see there's not a murderous bone in your body.'

Birdie glances at her palms; there's been many a time when she desired to kill a copper and avenge her father's death.

'I had nothing to do with the murder of Tobias.'

Her assertion sounds more defensive than she intended.

'Though why should the police invent such a thing?' Margaret asks, dubious now.

'I don't know.'

'Have you been accused of any crime before?'

Birdie squirms under Margaret's stare; she feels like one of the black stag beetles pinned in the display case of the taxidermist's shop window on the Borough.

'Never.' She pauses. 'Though my father was wrongly hanged for murdering a policeman.'

Margaret nods. 'Ah. Now I see. I'm sorry to hear that.'

'If the police find me here, I doubt I'll escape the noose myself.'

'For shame on them. It seems to me they are no better than the criminals they are supposed to capture. Scaring and torturing innocent young women.'

Birdie smiles wearily, relieved Margaret seems ready to believe her tale of false accusations, but exhausted from the exertions of the night.

'I see now why you travelled all this way from London – you were hoping to find information that might help clear your name.'

'Though I'm afraid I've discovered more than I bargained for; I wasn't expecting to trip over another corpse like Tobias's.'

A look of alarm crosses Margaret's face. 'Are you saying this corpse at Black Craig is the work of the same man who killed Tobias?'

Birdie nods.

'How do you know?'

Birdie has no wish to reveal the gruesome detail of the flesh carved from the corpse's cheek.

'They were both brought ashore by canoe.' She digs her hand in the pocket of the overcoat, retrieves the token. 'And I found two Company tokens by Tobias's body, and a similar coin in the pocket of the dead man in the cove.'

Birdie holds the coin in her palm.

Margaret pokes it with her finger. 'Tobias sailed with the Company to York Factory in 1845, so maybe that's why you found their tokens by his body. Though he returned with the missionaries from Labrador aboard the *Harmony*.'

Birdie jumps. 'Tobias sailed from Labrador with the twins last autumn?'

She'd assumed Tobias had asked the missionaries to take the twins in the autumn while he himself hadn't left America until this spring and had landed on the Surrey side of the Thames in May. And there, he was killed. Now his travels seem more complicated. If he had evidence to give to the Admiralty, why didn't he travel to London and hand it over straight away?

Margaret narrows her eyes, catching the surprise in Birdie's question, a reaction which places Margaret on her guard again.

'Aye, it was Tobias who brought the twins here, about this time last year,' she says warily. 'After dark. He didn't want folk gossiping.'

'Did he mention London?'

Margaret hesitates. 'He asked me to find him a place on a ship that was sailing east. But, he told me he had to visit London first.' She pauses again, twists her fingers. 'He said he had important business to sort out there. I gave him the name of a shipping agent in London who I knew was contracting a ship and crew for a company importing timber from the Baltic. He told me he wanted nothing more to do with the fur trade.'

'And you didn't hear anything else from him?'

'I received a letter from him in January. It came from St Petersburg. He told me he was wintering in the city and would return to London again in the spring to search out some old mates and see if they could help find him a place on a regular shipping run to Hamburg.'

Birdie senses that Margaret is the one, now, who is not revealing everything she knows. 'Can you think of any reason why somebody might have wished Tobias dead?'

Margaret leans forward, brings her face closer to Birdie's.

'Tobias was always rubbing people up the wrong way – he couldn't help it. He put up with other people's scorn and accusations. Tobias had many faults, but cowardice and fearfulness were not his weaknesses.' She stands, crosses to the door and peers into the hall, as if to check for eavesdroppers, then returns. 'He was scared when he brought the bairns to me. I could see it in his eyes. Keep the bairns safe, he told me. I'll do what I can to sort things out.' She settles back in the chair, fixes her gaze on the dying embers of the hearth as if she's searching for something there. Or trying to decide how much she can reveal about Tobias. 'He told me not...'

Her sentence drifts. A sudden blast of wind sends a cloud of cinders whirling around the room.

'There's a change in the weather.' Margaret levers herself upright abruptly. 'I have to retire, I need some sleep. And I dare say you do too.'

Birdie nods, reluctant to leave the conversation but aware that pushing Margaret to talk is likely to have the opposite effect. She follows Margaret up the stairs in the darkness, one hand on the bannister, and as she regards the hunched shoulders of the figure ahead, she is convinced it's fear that keeps her from saying all she knows.

She must have slept, though not for long, disturbed by dreams of Tobias, crouching by his dead wife and keening. She is lying on the bed still fully dressed when the dull morning light filters through the frosted glass and a gust rattles the frame. The shuffling of the parrot reminds her of his presence. She removes the shawl from around his cage. The poor bird is huddled in one corner, his feathers ruffling like ash leaves in a breeze. She fetches some seeds and drops them through the bars of the cage. He flutters from his perch and pecks at them gratefully.

'Skin for a skin,' she whispers.

The bird glances at her with his beady eye and says nothing.

She hears the children laughing as she descends the stairs. Margaret is in the office, fussing with objects in her aide-mémoire cabinet. There is an edge of mania in her movements; she picks things up, fiddles and replaces them as if she is desperately searching for something.

'The twins seem none the worse for their fright,' Birdie ventures.

Margaret looks around. The sun penetrates the window, highlights the silver in her hair and the creases scoring her forehead.

'There's something missing.' She gestures at the cabinet. 'I realized it had vanished last autumn. I didn't think much of it at the time.'

'Could you replace it with something else to remind you of the contract?'

'You misunderstand. I remember what the object represented. The thing that is missing is a token of the Company. It had a pelt etched on one side, exactly the same as the one you showed me last night.'

'You think Tobias took it with him last autumn?'

'No. I spoke to Tobias only briefly when he brought the twins here. It was at night, as I said. He didn't enter the office. The person who took the coin was, I believe, the person who gave it to me in the first place to use as a reminder for a contract. And that was the man who was your predecessor, Donald Shearer.'

'Shearer?' She steps towards the cabinet. 'Why did he take the coin?'

'I assume because he wanted to erase any evidence of that contract. It was for the purchase of beaver pelts carried on a Company ship that stopped in Stromness on the return journey from Rupert's Land. The *Lynx*, the ship was called.'

Birdie starts at the name.

Margaret nods. 'The ship I mentioned when you first arrived and showed me your school testimonial. There was a lynx on one of the crests heading the paper and it reminded me of the flag.'

A coincidence perhaps, and one that concerns Birdie more than Margaret; she continues with her train of thought.

'It's an old-fashioned brig. I don't like those ships – they're difficult to sail into the wind and require a large crew. I never had much to do with its provisions – it often sails separately from the main convoy to York Factory. I doubt it's owned by the Company; most likely contracted when extra hold space is required.' The furrows marking her brow deepen. 'I know of it because of Shearer. A merchant contacted me and asked whether I could oversee the purchase and delivery of some pelts on his behalf. Shearer said he could arrange a contract for Company pelts on the incoming *Lynx* and would manage the whole thing himself. I was surprised – the skins are usually sold in London. But he told me the token came from a clerk working in Ness House, so I assumed the deal was legitimate.'

'The Company's office?'

'Exactly. I remember, Shearer seemed very pleased with the deal. But after the shipment was delivered, the Company agent came and spoke to me in private and told me he suspected Shearer was dishonest.'

'Fiddling the books?'

'Skimming furs from the consignments passing through Stromness. The agent said he'd bumped into a merchant, by chance, and they ended up discussing the furs he'd purchased via Shearer. The agent was surprised; he knew nothing of the deal. I was in danger of being implicated in his fraudulent schemes, because he was using my business as a cover.'

'You had no idea?'

'No.' She waves her hand at the ledgers on the desk. 'I told you, the words and numbers mean nothing to me. I confronted Shearer with the information the Company agent had given me, and told him he had to leave.'

'Did he go without question?'

She nods. It's hard to imagine any person defying Margaret. At least, not to her face.

'Did you report Shearer to the bailie?'

'No. The agent said he'd prefer to deal with it internally; he said he'd take the issue to the London Committee.'

'And what happened to Shearer?'

'He spent the winter skulking around the bars of Stromness, bemoaning my lack of business sense and reminding everybody that the Skaills had a dark reputation, implying I'd given him the boot because he'd discovered some terrible secret about me.'

'Did anybody believe him?'

'Folk believe what they want to believe. I was surprised to learn, though, that he'd been taken aboard one of the ships flying the Company's flag this June. Or was it the end of May?'

'Just before I arrived?'

'Aye. I believe he was taken on as a purser on the very same ship from which he was skimming pelts.'

'The *Lynx*?'

She nods.

'Have you heard from him since?'

'No. And I've not been offered any further contracts with that ship or its cargo, though I'm still on good terms with the Company's agent and get plenty of commissions for their regular supply ships.' Margaret strides across the office, bangs on the window to open it. 'The *Lynx* arrived back from the Nor' West three days ago. And I heard some commotion this morning at high tide, which means, I presume, it's just set sail again. Heading for London I would assume.'

Birdie attempts to fit the pieces together, the connection between Tobias and Shearer, the tin canoe and the coin. 'Is it possible it could have been Donald Shearer who brought the body ashore yesterday in the canoe?'

'Well, the same question came to my mind. But Shearer was never good with boats. That was always the joke: he worked for a shipping merchant because he knew no ship would take him. That's why it's odd he ended up aboard the *Lynx*. I find it difficult to imagine him paddling a canoe. Did the lasses catch a glimpse of the man?'

She tries to recall what the twins told her. 'Grace said he was big.'

'Then it wasn't Shearer. He was slight and wersy. Though he always dressed in good wool jackets and that gave him a bit of shape.'

Something about the description strikes a chord. 'Did Shearer have any other features that might mark him out?'

Margaret narrows her eyes. 'When he was a bairn, he couldn't run very fast and one day he went with the other lads stealing goose eggs from the poor old farmer over the hill. The farmer set the dog on them. The other lads got away. Shearer had the tip of his finger bitten off.'

'His left ring finger?'

'Aye.'

Birdie shivers as she recalls the corpse at Black Craig. 'Donald Shearer is the man whose body I found in the rockpool.'

'Lord.' Margaret drops heavily on the chair by the desk. 'I no liked the man, but I didn't wish him dead.'

Birdie's mind is whirring. 'The *Lynx*. How long ago did it set sail?'

Margaret glances at the clock. 'An hour or so. The wind isn't very favourable. I thought it was peculiar when I saw the ship setting sail into the headwind – especially a brig like that. It had to tack back, and I doubt whether it would be much beyond Hoy Sound even now.'

'I'll walk over the hill and see if I can spot it. Do you have a spyglass?'

Margaret stands again, walks to her shelves, grabs a short, brass tube and hands it to Birdie. 'It's not got much magnification.'

'It'll do.'

Margaret wrings her hands. 'You'll be careful not to draw attention to yourself. What if there's a murderer aboard that ship?'

Birdie nods, pulls the old overcoat on and wraps a shawl around her head.

Though the south-westerly wind is not warm, it's broken the iron grip of the ice and the street is busy; farmers driving cattle to market, handcarts piled high with merchandise, clusters of fishermen selling their catch to passers-by. Birdie ducks her head, strides briskly and takes the road to the hill. Margaret is correct, the brig has not sailed far, the south-westerly has forced it to tack close to shore. It yaws and pitches in the gusts. The sailors that swarm the rigging are too busy trimming the mainsail to notice her. She removes the spyglass from her pocket, extends it and focuses on the deck. A glint catches her eye; she swings the glass, squints, and finds the tin canoe on deck, unmistakable with its dull grey gleam, lying to one side below the bulwark. She trains the lens along the vessel's length, but is unable to make out any details. She is uncertain, now she's made her discovery, what she should do about it. One thing is clear, though; she can't report Shearer's body to the authorities. Somebody else can find it and do that duty. She doesn't want to attract the attention of Detective Thompson and be named as a suspect in another murder.

She starts back in the direction of the town, then finds herself looking north. On the far side of the headland, beyond Warbeth cemetery, the wind whips grey smoke from Morag's chimney. She has an urge to speak to Morag and ask for her advice. It's risky, following the path that takes her closer to the corpse lying in the bay, but she tells herself she cannot act as if she has something to hide and should carry on her business as if she knows nothing of the murder.

Morag is sitting outside on her bench, smoking her pipe. 'The south-westerly has stirred things up a bit.' She removes the pipe and smiles with satisfaction, as if the wind is all her doing. 'I have the kettle boiling and some bannock on the griddle. Come in-aboot.'

They perch on low stools by the hearth to eat; the warm bread is welcome nourishment for Birdie.

'The bairns are well?'

'They seem so.'

'Yourself; you look as if you haven't slept. You found the corpse?' Morag asks matter-of-factly.

Birdie nods. 'I had a conversation with Margaret.'

'And?'

'And, it's likely the dead man is Donald Shearer.'

'I thought he'd sailed to the Nor' West. I hoped he might have been eaten by bears.'

'Was he that bad?'

'He was no good. Least of all to Margaret. What makes you think it's him?'

'He had a missing fingertip.' Birdie digs in her pocket and produces the token. 'And I found this in his pocket. Margaret said it was like the one he took from her office when she gave him the boot.'

She hands the coin to Morag, who flips it with one finger. 'A Company token.' Morag scowls. 'They're handed to trappers in exchange for pelts. Factors at the trading stations sometimes make their own tokens, and the Company allows them to decide how many tokens each pelt is worth. The Factor takes a share of the station's profits, so it's in their interest to drive down the price they pay for the skins.' She lifts the token, holds it in the light. 'Originally, a trapper would get one of these tokens in exchange for one skin, but these days, he'll be lucky if he's given one token for five pelts.'

Birdie looks at the coin in Morag's hand and fumbles for a thread that she can't quite pull. 'Skin for a skin,' she says. 'Does that mean anything to you?'

Morag raises an eyebrow. 'The Company's motto. I was surprised when you told me it was a phrase your parrot repeats. Though, of course, the Bay officers prefer to use the Latin: *Pro pelle cutem.*'

'What does it mean?'

'The Book of Job. Skin for skin, Satan tells the Lord. A man will do all he can to save his life. In the Company's case, though, the servants often said it meant the Company would risk everything for the sake of the fur trade, including the skin on their backs. The Company is a harsh employer. You could say Rupert's Land is a harsh environment which demands a tough regime.' She sniffs. 'But some of the Company's men go too far. And what can one Governor do to stop them in that vast territory?'

Morag tosses the token in the air and, as Birdie watches it twist, she has the peculiar sense that her whole life and fate are bound up with the flip of this coin. It looks as if Morag will let it drop, but at the last moment she reaches out, catches it, slaps it on the back of her hand.

'Heads or tails?' Morag asks.

'Heads,' Birdie replies and grimaces. It's only a game, but she fears she's called it wrong.

Morag lifts the hand covering the coin. 'Heads it is,' she says. 'Or in this case, pelts.'

Morag stares pensively at the coin for a while before she sniffs and returns it to Birdie. 'It has a feel of darkness to it which I don't like.'

'I found two by the side of Tobias's corpse on the Thames.'

Morag gives her a sharp glance. 'Take care, Birdie. I'll help you as much as I can, but I fear you're wading in waters beyond my reach.'

Birdie is about to tell Morag she feels Margaret is scared to reveal all she knows about Tobias when she is distracted by the murmur of distant voices. She glances through the crack of the door; three men advance along the coast path, hands to their heads to prevent top hats being blown away, jackets flapping as they stride. They look as if they mean business. Birdie's heart thumps; she recognizes one of the trio.

'Who is it?' Morag asks.

'James Thompson,' Birdie whispers. 'The detective.'

'The bloody bird shooter?' Morag peers surreptitiously through the window. 'He's with the bailie and a councillor.'

'They must have found the body.'

Birdie stands and retreats into a dark corner of the croft.

Detective Thompson's stentorian voice can be clearly heard as they near the wall of Morag's garden. 'Quite fortuitous I was up early this morning. I'd heard the great northern divers come ashore near Black Craig, and I was examining the cove for signs of the bird when I almost tripped over the corpse, frozen in a rockpool.'

Birdie and Morag remain silent until the men have passed.

Morag speaks first. 'They're bound to knock on my door on the way back to find out whether I heard or saw anything unusual, which, of course, I did not.'

'It might be best if I wasn't here.'

Morag nods. 'Go now.' And then she adds, 'While you can.'

Chapter 16

Birdie hurries along the coast path. She pictures the coterie of officials – the magistrate, the councillor, the detective – peering over the corpse of Donald Shearer. It won't take long for Detective Thompson to identify the body, after which he will question Margaret Skaill, Shearer's former employer, and discover, if he does not know already, that Margaret is the cousin of another murdered man. And then he will look at his copy of *The Times* with its artist's impression of the murderer's accomplice and realize the suspect is sitting on a stool in the office, holding a quill and making notes in Margaret's ledgers.

Birdie's legs are leaden. Her head swims. She stumbles, rights herself. The wind is strengthening, clouds scud across the sun. An Arctic skua speeds by like an arrow carried on the gusts. She keeps her head down against the taunting blasts and does not see the figure bounding along the path from the town until he is almost on top of her.

'Birdie, I barely recognized you in that huge coat and shawl. What are you doing out here?'

She lifts her head. Peter. Her mouth droops. She pulls it back into a grin, though fears it's more of a rictus than a smile.

'Margaret asked me to visit the kirkyard,' she bluffs. 'She wanted to know whether the family tombstones needed tending.'

He removes his cap as if to pay his respects at the mention of the dead, and squints at her cynically.

'And you,' she adds quickly. 'What are you doing here?'

His face brightens. 'I've heard a corpse has been found in the bay beyond the ness.'

'Heavens above.' She attempts to sound surprised.

'Detective Thompson reported it to the bailie early this morning, and they've gone to investigate. Are you all right? You seem rather pale.'

'I'm fine. Thank you.' She sticks her hands in the overcoat's pockets.

He pulls his cap down firmly on his wiry hair. 'In that case, I'll be on my way to see what I can find out about the deceased.'

'Surely, the detective will not want a reporter looking over his shoulder while he's investigating?'

'I shouldn't think he'll object. After all, I gave him a good write up in *The Orcadian*.' He beams, pleased with his reporter's skills. 'By the way, my piece about Dr Rae's application for the Admiralty's reward is in the latest edition. You can buy a copy in town.'

She attempts another smile. 'I'll do that.'

'And if you hurry, you might see the *Harmony* arriving.'

'The mission ship?'

'That's the one. She was spotted to the north early this morning. It's quite a sight; the bearded missionaries in their sealskin coats.'

'I'll make sure I'm there.'

*

She sets off at a pace; perhaps the Captain has some details about Tobias's journey with the twins the previous autumn which could help shine a light on the troubles from which he was fleeing. Lord knows she needs some light right now. Though she has no idea how she might approach the Captain and ask him anything without arousing suspicion. At least Detective Thompson's gaze has been distracted by the discovery of Shearer's corpse on another part of the island.

The latest edition of *The Orcadian* is displayed outside the post office. Peter's report is on the front page, but she doesn't stop to buy it – the Admiralty's reward for news on Franklin suddenly seems less important than reaching the harbour in time to find the *Harmony*'s Captain. The pier head is bustling with farmers, traders and fishermen. Cart wheels creak, pigs squeal, barrels clang as they are dropped and rolled. Above the usual clatter, she hears another, stranger sound; a mournful chorus rises and falls like a sad breeze blowing off the water. The music comes from the deck of a two-masted ship, easing toward the harbour. The *Harmony* with the missionaries, she assumes, singing their doleful hymns.

There is a whistle and a shout and the anchor drops; the chain clatters as the weight descends. Rowing boats set out from the nearest slipway, ready to ferry passengers ashore. A rope ladder is lowered over the gunwales. Crew members descend to the waiting skiffs, though the missionaries make no move to leave the ship. She watches the boats being rowed across the harbour, conscious of the murmur from the fishermen standing behind her, talking in thick dialect.

She cannot decipher the full meaning of their conversation, but she picks out the odd word or two. *Witch*. *Parrot*. She edges away, hoping she has misheard, and heads further along the pier, unnerved. A captain's peaked cap appears at the top of the iron ladder attached to the pier-side. He hauls himself onto dry land, his weathered face a mixture of relief and regret. Morag said he was a good man. She takes her chance.

'Captain?' She bobs a polite curtsey.

He removes his cap and reveals the receding line of his silvery hair.

'Captain Forsyth. And you are...'

'Mrs White.'

'How can I help?'

She is suddenly lost for words; she wants to ask him about a journey with a murdered man and his children without revealing either that Tobias is dead or the true nature of her connection with him. The Captain glances at his pocket watch; he may well be a good man, but he is also the Captain of a ship that has just completed a six-week voyage across the Atlantic. He has a limited amount of time in Orkney before he must set sail again for London.

She asks hurriedly, 'I was wondering, Sir, whether Tobias Skaill and his two daughters sailed with you from Labrador last autumn?'

'Aye.' Wariness creeps over the Captain's face; he's not a man to gossip. 'Is there any particular reason you're asking?'

She fumbles for a credible explanation. 'I met Tobias in London this spring, and I am afraid he was in some trouble.'

The Captain smiles wryly. 'I've known Tobias since he was a bairn, and he's always been in some trouble or other.'

CLARE CARSON

He looks over her shoulder at the gaggle of fishermen behind her. She is gripped by despair; she must discover the reason for Tobias's flight from Labrador.

'I'm afraid his daughters may be affected by his troubles...'

'Are they not safe with Margaret Skaill?'

'Indeed. And I'm lodging with Margaret as well, but as I said, I met Tobias in London before I came here, and I was wondering whether—'

'You'd be wise not to involve yourself in other's troubles,' the Captain replies sharply, though not unkindly.

'It's not always possible to avoid troubles, whether they are your own or of some other person's making.'

He frowns then catches sight of her mourning dress beneath the bulky overcoat and his features soften.

'Your husband...'

'Drowned. He was an able seaman on a ship travelling to the Baltic.' She's promoted poor Patrick in her desire to keep the Captain talking; she doubts he would have objected.

'I'm sorry to hear that.' He glances over her shoulder again. 'I'm not sure I have any information that might help you.'

She sidesteps so she stands between the Captain and the fishermen. 'Did he say anything about the reason for his journey?'

Captain Forsyth sighs, realizing she is persistent and it might be quicker to tell her what little he knows. 'He told me he was delivering his children to their aunt. I was happy to give them a berth in return for any carpentry needed aboard the ship.'

'He didn't say...'

'He wanted to take them to Margaret because their mother had recently died.'

252

Birdie conjures up the apparition of Tobias, distraught and wailing over his wife's corpse; she daren't ask the Captain for details of her death.

'He must have been grief-stricken.'

'Yes, her death was still very recent. He'd been travelling for a while, and he came back to the sad news she had died, and decided then to bring his daughters here.'

'Tobias must have regretted being absent when his wife passed away,' she ventures.

'Indeed. And to make matters worse, he said it was a pointless journey anyway.'

'Where did he go?'

'Oh, he crossed Hudson's Bay and was heading north when he met a group of Esquimaux traders.'

'He was quite an expert in their languages, I believe.'

'Aye. I had the impression he felt more at home with the Esquimaux than he did among Orkneymen.' The Captain nods his head, warming to the subject. 'He turned back when the traders warned him they'd come across a place where many white men had died. They said the land was haunted and all the animals had disappeared. They even gave him some ivory toggles from the place as a warning – and a protection against further harm.'

'Oh. I saw those on a sledge he'd made for the twins.'

'Tobias always was ingenious with his carpentry.'

'I noticed they had some initials carved in them – HMST.'

Birdie no longer believes the link to the *Terror* matters, but the Captain's interest has been piqued and she wants to keep him talking; his brow wrinkles as he recalls the details. 'That's right. We speculated whether they'd come from the *Terror* and were relics from poor Franklin's expedition. And, then of course, Dr Rae's report appeared in *The Times*.'

'Did Tobias explain why he was travelling north when he met the Esquimaux traders?' she asks, desperate to squeeze more information from him.

The Captain folds his arms. 'Well, I suppose he was looking for new areas to hunt. I remember him telling me it was difficult to be a free trapper in Labrador because some of the Company's men were moving in and taking over the area.'

'The Company's men in Labrador? I thought they operated in Rupert's Land.' She speaks with more force than she intended.

The Captain scowls, taken aback at her tone. He raises his voice in reply. 'You're lodging with Margaret Skaill, you say?'

'Yes, that's right, Sir.'

'Well, Tobias went to Narwhal House with his daughters after he disembarked; surely Margaret is the person you should be asking about her cousin.'

'Yes of course.'

She is conscious of the earwigging fishermen behind her back; she hopes they haven't heard the Captain mention Tobias's name. She needs to retreat before this conversation becomes more difficult.

'Thank you for your help, Sir. I won't use up any more of your precious time.'

Birdie turns and edges past the men in oilskins, crowding the pier head, and strides briskly along the street to Narwhal House, anxious to avoid Detective Thompson and the bailie returning from Black Craig. *Skin for a skin*, she mutters to herself as she hurries under the whalebone arch. The conversation with the Captain has confirmed her growing sense that Tobias was not murdered because he had information about Franklin's death, but because he knew too much about the darker side of the fur trade. The Captain was right, she thinks, to direct her back to Margaret; she must have been the last person Tobias spoke to before he sailed for London. Birdie should ask her again for details of what he said the night he arrived with the twins.

Margaret is in the kitchen, supervising the girls' lunch. Birdie hovers impatiently in the office, waiting for Margaret to come in so they can talk. The drip, drip of ice melting in the south-westerly wind melds with the tick of the clock. A loud knock at the door makes her jump; she fears the detective has come to question her about the corpse of Donald Shearer. The door knocker drops again, this time accompanied by a call.

'Birdie. It's me. Peter Gibson.'

At least it's not the detective. Birdie dithers – she wants to know what he has discovered out at Black Craig, but is scared to find out.

'I've got some news.'

She cannot ignore him. She crosses the hall, heaves the door. 'I apologize, I was just...'

He isn't concerned about excuses, he's bursting to talk. He steps inside before he is invited.

'Have you heard?'

He hops from foot to foot in the hall like an excited schoolboy.

'Mrs Skaill is here,' Birdie says. His face drops. She ushers him into the office, just as Margaret returns from the kitchen.

'What news do you have for us today then, Master Gibson?'

The brightness of Margaret's greeting belies her unease. Birdie can read her agitation in her tightly pressed hands, fingers pointing upwards as if in silent prayer.

'The body I told Birdie about, the one the detective found in the cove beyond Morag's croft.' Peter's boisterousness is dampened in the presence of Margaret.

'What about it?' she asks.

'It's Donald Shearer.'

Margaret does a passable impression of being shocked. 'Donald Shearer? The lad who worked for me last year?'

'The very same.' Peter smirks inappropriately, unable to contain his glee at being the bearer of news, even if it is bad.

'God bless his soul,' Margaret says.

Birdie follows Margaret's lead, and crosses herself. 'May he rest in peace.'

Peter flushes, suddenly aware of his disrespectful demeanour, and removes his hat. The clock ticks as they stand in silence.

Peter is the first to crack and declares, 'The detective thinks he must have drunk too much, attempted to row back to his ship, fallen overboard, drowned and ended up washed ashore by the tide.'

Does the relief show on Birdie's face? Peter throws her a sidelong glance. She examines her boots while she regains her composure.

'I'm not sure, myself, that he's entirely correct in his judgement,' Peter says, still assessing Birdie's reactions out the tail of his eye.

'Master Gibson,' Margaret says. 'You're a very good reporter, but perhaps you should leave the investigation to the detective.'

'Of course, Mrs Skaill. Though it seems unlikely to me that the tide and the winds of the last few days would carry a body around from Stromness to the western side of the island.'

'You're an expert on the tides and winds now, are you?'

Peter laughs, in a good-natured way. 'No, indeed, I wouldn't pretend to have such knowledge. I was merely commenting, that's all. And the detective did himself say as we parted company that, while it looked as if he had fallen overboard, first impressions could be misleading.'

'Oh?'

'The corpse's face was so badly pecked by the ravens it was hard to tell—'

'We can do without the details,' Margaret cuts in.

'My apologies. The point is, Detective Thompson and the bailie agreed that it was also possible somebody could have left the corpse at Black Craig to create the impression he had been swept there by the tides. They decided to pass their preliminary findings on to the procurator fiscal, and said he would need to investigate the circumstances in which the accident occurred. So nothing is settled yet.'

Margaret retains remarkable control of her features and her temper.

'Well, I'll look forward to reading about the detective's views on the fate of poor Mr Shearer in the next edition of *The Orcadian*. Though, I have to say, Mr Shearer always did find it hard to pull himself away from the bars of Stromness, so I should imagine, in this case, the detective's first impression is probably the correct one. Is there anything else I can do for you?'

'I was wondering whether you'd any comment, Mrs Skaill,

as Donald Shearer's erstwhile employer, that you would like to add for the report? Perhaps I could mention that you'd observed the deceased had a tendency to excessive drinking?'

He is pushing his luck and he knows it.

'Master Gibson, I do not wish you to include any comment from me in your report and, if you do, the proprietor of *The Orcadian* will hear about my displeasure. Now, some of us have work to do.'

She marches across the hall, holds the door ajar.

'Good afternoon, Master Gibson.'

He departs somewhat sheepishly, though he pauses on the threshold, turns and waves a friendly hand in Birdie's direction before Margaret shoves the door on his back and catapults him into the street.

Margaret returns to the office, sinks in a chair. 'Detective Thompson indeed. I don't like the sound of him.' She is riled. 'If the council invested more resources in the harbour instead of employing detectives to poke around in people's business we'd all be better off. I certainly don't wish to be the subject of his investigations.'

Birdie agrees. 'I'm afraid he might connect the murder of Shearer with that of Tobias.'

'And then I'll be unable to protect the bairns from poisonous gossip or worse.' She glances at Birdie. 'And you'll be in...'

Margaret shakes her head. She doesn't need to explain; Birdie knows her presence here is now a risk, both to herself and the twins.

They sit in silence for a while. Clouds blot the low sun and fill the parlour with a sombre light. Birdie watches the clock pendulum swing and tries not to picture the black-hatted detective with the magistrate and councillor, striding in her direction.

'Tobias was a good father,' Margaret says eventually.

Birdie nods and spies the toy sledge Tobias carved as he crossed the Atlantic with Hope and Grace. She stoops and lifts it, examines the toggle holding the strap. She thinks of the story Tobias told the twins about the flesh-eating monster, the Kabloona. She had assumed he was telling a tale about Franklin's starving men, but now it seems unlikely, as Tobias himself did not reach the place where they died or see their corpses.

She glances at Margaret. 'Though sometimes, the twins were scared by the stories he told them.'

'What do you know of the stories Tobias told?' Margaret asks sharply.

'The girls said they were frightened by one of Tobias's stories about a monster who skinned and ate people.'

Margaret's brow knots. 'Monster?'

'That's what the twins said,' Birdie insists. 'A monster who ate people.'

'Monster.' Margaret's visage darkens. She shakes her head. 'Tobias told me something similar. But it was a true account, not a story.'

'True?' Birdie is shocked; she pictures the lump of flesh sliced from the cheeks of Tobias and Donald Shearer.

'Tobias warned me about this evil creature when he left the twins here. But he didn't say monster,' Margaret hesitates, 'even if he is one.'

'What did he say, then?'

Margaret stands, crosses the office, steps into the hall to

ascertain the twins are still playing in the parlour, returns to her seat, leans forward and whispers, 'The Master.'

'The Master?'

Margaret glowers and shakes her head. 'Tobias told me never to mention his name if I wanted to keep the bairns safe.'

Birdie remembers her conversation with the twins; how Hope started to talk, then Grace had spoken over her and said they were scared of a monster.

'Who is he?'

'I don't know. Tobias only told me it was what they called the man who had been terrorizing the trappers all along the Labrador coast. The bairns in the camp heard all the stories – how he liked to kill men and eat their flesh. Tobias was scared for his daughters; he couldn't deny the stories were true as he didn't want them to be complacent. So he warned them they must never repeat the tales they'd heard because, if they did, they would be the Master's next victims. He told them, above all else, they must never mention his name.'

Now Birdie understands; Grace interrupted her twin and said the story was about a monster, not the Master, because she was scared.

'Tobias made me promise I wouldn't mention it to anybody either. I had to forget everything he told me – which was what I tried to do.' She wipes her brow. 'He said people who talk about the Master die.'

'Is that what happened to his wife?'

Margaret looks at her with sudden alarm, her face drained of colour. 'How do you know that?'

'I...' She conjures up again the apparition of Tobias grieving. 'I guessed.'

Margaret glances over her shoulder and checks the hall again before she continues. 'The bairns don't know their mother was killed. They believe she died in a hunting accident. You must say nothing of this.'

'Of course not.' Though she suspects the twins may well know the truth; their fear of the Master is so visceral. And children always pick up more than adults think.

'She was killed while he was away from the camp. He returned and found she had been missing for several days; she'd gone to hunt for seals and hadn't come back. He searched and found her body. She'd been shot and—' Margaret breaks off, takes a deep breath before she continues. 'Tobias said it was likely some of the Master's men had followed her and demanded to know his whereabouts, and when she refused to tell them—'

'The Master doesn't work alone then?'

Margaret sniffs. 'Tobias said he commanded a ruthless mob. If the locals refused to hand his men the skins at the price they demanded, they were shot.'

Skin for a skin. Birdie pictures the tokens she found with both corpses; Tobias told the Captain of the *Harmony* it was difficult for him to hunt in Labrador because of the Company's men.

'Do you think this man – the Master – could be a Company employee?'

Margaret pulls a face, shocked by the suggestion. 'Well, if he is, he's surely not acting with the Governor's knowledge.'

Birdie recalls Morag saying the Governor was unable to control the excesses of the Company's men in such a vast and wild territory. She stares through the open door into the gloom trying to make sense of it all and, in the shadows, sees a tent pole. Lashed to it by the ankles is a corpse, barely recognizable as human because it's nothing but exposed flesh and bone. The skin has been removed. She gasps, looks again and sees only the twins' deerskin parkas hanging on the stand in the hall, but her breath still runs fast and shallow. Even though she can now distinguish the lines of the coats, the image of a flayed body stays in her mind and makes her wonder which is the true reality. Skin for a skin. She shudders.

She hears a snort and realizes Margaret is sobbing.

'He was scared,' Margaret says. 'The Master was after him because he knew too much. He had to leave. He took the children with him; he was afraid the Master's men might hurt them if they found out they were his.'

Birdie comforts her. 'It was good that Tobias brought them here to you.'

Margaret removes a hanky from her apron pocket and wipes her nose. 'Did this Master kill Tobias?'

'One of his thugs, I should think.'

'And now Donald Shearer.'

'Shearer must have been overheard saying too much in a Stromness bar.'

'He always was a blabbermouth.' Margaret sniffs again. 'Tobias said we were safe here. He said he'd travel to London to deal with the Master.'

'Deal with him? How?'

Margaret sobs again and shakes her head. 'The bairns. I thought they were safe. I thought Tobias had dealt with it. When they found his body on the Thames, I was grief-stricken but I thought, at least, that was the end of it.'

Birdie strokes her arm in an effort to calm her. 'Please don't worry. This man won't hurt the twins.'

Margaret wipes her eyes and nose with her hand. 'How can you be sure?'

Birdie isn't sure about anything.

'He's gone,' she says with more certainty than she feels. 'He must be the master of the *Lynx*, and he's taken his men and sailed south.'

She becomes more convinced her supposition is correct as she says it: the *Lynx* sails separately from the main Company convoy, the tin canoe was on its deck, and Donald Shearer was dealing with this ship. Every ship has a master, and the master of the *Lynx* is also a monster who oversees a deadly trade; the Kabloona of Tobias's tragic story.

'I hope you're right,' Margaret says as she reaches for a candle. She strikes a match and holds it to the wick; its feeble glow barely creates any light.

'I'll brew some tea,' Margaret says. 'Do you want a mug?'

'I'm tired,' Birdie replies. 'I need to take a rest.'

'I'll no stop you.'

There is relief in Margaret's response and Birdie knows then that, in Margaret's eyes, she is more of a danger than a help while she remains under the same roof as the twins. She has no choice now but to go to London and tell Solomon what she knows. And she has to leave quickly, before Detective Thompson comes knocking on the door.

She stumbles along the landing. The parrot squawks when she enters the room. She stares at the bird in the gloom.

'The Master,' she whispers.

'Skin for a skin,' the parrot replies, and cackles like her brother.

Chapter 17

She spends two days after Shearer's body is discovered dreading the knock of Detective Thompson on the door. He doesn't turn up. Too busy, Margaret hears, arranging meetings with the procurator fiscal. On the third day, Margaret manages to secure her a berth aboard the *Serpent*, a brig carrying timber from North America, destined for Surrey Docks. The ship's ancient cook died in the open waters of the Atlantic. They dropped his corpse overboard, and managed on a galley rota until they reached Stromness, where the Captain contacted Margaret for a quick replacement. She proposed Birdie, though she gave her name as Bert Green, and said he was willing to work for nothing in exchange for a passage to London.

Birdie is nervous about leaving Stromness, but she has little choice if she wants to avoid being questioned by Detective Thompson and locked in the magistrate's cell. The dangers in London – the Filth, Frank and his pals, the master of the *Lynx* – are many. She reckons, though, that if she can make it to Solomon's lodgings without being identified, she will be safe. She will give him the information she's discovered, and he'll convince his superiors she has been falsely accused of being an accomplice in the murder of Tobias Skaill. Of course, she has moments of doubt about her plan, yet what else can she do? She has to trust Solomon.

Morag provides her with navy trousers, white shirt, wool jacket and red knitted cap. She already has the heavy boots. She is naturally flat-chested. They argue about her hair. Morag says she should cut it all off, but Birdie cannot quite bear to part with her shiny black locks; her hair, she feels, is part of her character as well as her appearance. She points out that Tobias's hair was long, and Morag replies that it drew attention, which, of course, Birdie knows to be true; it was his long red hair that caught her eye as she was walking across London Bridge that fateful May morning. Eventually, they reach a compromise; Morag shortens it but leaves enough length for it to be woven into a plait which can be secured beneath her cap without looking too obvious.

'There. You look more of a boy than a man. But there are plenty of young lads that go to sea.'

Birdie stands in the darkened hall of Narwhal House and examines herself in the mottled mirror. She doesn't look like a completely different person – more a bolder version of herself. Her features are more obvious without any strands of hair or veils or shawls to disguise them; nothing to soften the beakiness of her nose. The honesty of it pleases her and fills her with a peculiar energy; unconstrained by her petticoats and dress, she is strong and free. She lifts and stretches her leg, kicks sideways and laughs at the ease with which her limbs move. No more hitching her skirts if she wants to stride. No tight bodices to restrict her lungs. She swings her arms in the air, flaps her hand; a raven ready for flight.

Morag's reflection appears, grinning over her shoulder.

'Living as a man,' she says, 'is like being the mirror's image. Everything is in reverse.'

'I'll get used to it quickly enough.'

'Aye. You'll end up enjoying being your own person.'

Birdie assesses Morag's reflection; the breeches and loose woollen shirt. It's hard to recall the shock she first felt when she realized Morag was a woman in trousers – she's become accustomed to seeing her that way. Now the idea of Morag in petticoats seems ridiculous.

She packs her kit bag slowly, making the most of her last moments in Narwhal House. Before she leaves for the harbour, there are fond farewells.

'Look after Solly,' she says to the twins. 'Teach him some more words while I'm away.'

Margaret holds her tight. 'Come back as soon as you can.'

'I'll come back when it's safe,' she replies; she knows this is the response Margaret needs to hear.

'Summon a fair wind to carry the ship to London,' she says to Morag.

Morag huffs, as if dismissing as nonsense all talk of her powers to direct the weather. The wind is behind them, though, as the *Serpent* weighs anchor and sails on the ebb tide past the Old Man of Hoy.

The northerly gives them good speed along the coast; Aberdeen, Edinburgh, Whitby Abbey and the dreary flatlands of the Wash. They leave Yarmouth far behind. As dawn breaks on the fifth day at sea, the wind shifts to the east and carries the *Serpent* through the mouth of the Thames and swiftly past Gravesend. They enter London Reach and the jam of barges, schooners and ferries slows their progress. The sounds of the city – shouting, machinery pounding, cranes clanking – permeate the hull and fill her with deep dread. She busies herself tidying the galley, damping down the stove fire.

'We'll arrive at Surrey Docks after nightfall,' the bosun says.

She is leery of the bosun. So far, no one has questioned her disguise; as Morag predicted, she isn't the only laddish-looking man aboard the ship. But the bosun watches her too closely.

'Doubt we'll be waiting midstream, though,' he says. 'The Captain will be straight into the dock and the crew turfed ashore as soon as the anchor's dropped.'

At least she'll have the cover of darkness to slip through the streets of Rotherhithe.

'The Captain knows the right people here,' the bosun adds, and arches a brow. Before Birdie has time to wonder what he's getting at, he nudges her and winks. 'I suppose you'll be off whoring with the rest of 'em.'

She squirms and says nothing.

The anchor's chain rasps. She holds back, anxious to avoid the bosun, and waits for the sailors' shouts to diminish as they traipse down the gangplank and head for the entertainments of Rotherhithe. Silence, apart from the slap of the Thames against the ship's hull. She climbs the ladder to the deck. The wind has dropped and the air is freezing. She can almost hear the creak of frost forming on the rigging. The waxing moon gleams behind a swathe of cloud, pale and ragged as an oyster. She catches sight of the Captain and the back of another bulky figure – the harbourmaster? A porter? Whoever, the Captain is deep in conversation with him, leaning in to make sure his words do not leak. She coughs to alert them to her presence.

The Captain twists around, his face irascible. 'What are you doing here?'

'I had trouble extinguishing the stove fire, Sir. I didn't want to leave it burning.'

'You've had your passage to London, now sling your hook.'

She nods and brushes past them, eyes to the ground, and is about to step onto the gangplank when the moon glints on a coin lying on the deck. She ducks, grasps it in her already freezing fingers, straightens.

'Sir, is this yours?'

The Captain snatches it from her hand and, without a word, lifts his boot and kicks her through the gangway.

She is propelled down the shaky plank at speed, hits the quayside running, nearly catches her boot in a rusty chain, rights herself, weaves between the waterside cranes, avoids the lamplight of the night watchmen guarding wooden warehouses and heads for the darkness of an alley. She sways, unaccustomed to the firm ground beneath her feet. Or perhaps the unsteadiness is caused by fear – her head is lurching; she glimpsed the face of the coin before the Captain grabbed it and saw the pelt etched on its surface. She pulls the knitted cap over her brow and assesses the *Serpent* from the safety of the shadows. The Captain and his contact are still on the main deck, engrossed in conversation, their hunched figures spectral in the moonlight. Above their heads, the black lines of the rigging merge with the shrouds and halyards of other anchored ships and, in the gloom, it seems as if the whole quay is ensnared in one giant trawler's net. The bosun said the Captain knew the right people here in the Port of London;

she's beginning to wonder whether the Master's grasp spreads much further than the *Lynx*.

And what about Frank? What is his part in all this, she ponders as she gauges how she can traverse his manor without bumping into him or one of his pals. She has to cross the river to reach Solomon's lodgings in Great Scotland Yard. The watermen who wait at the bottom of Hanover Stairs might recognize her face. It will be safer to use London Bridge.

Head down, she strides through the cramped streets of Bermondsey, London's sooty air gritty on her tongue. The sour whiff of the river turns her stomach, and the crowded, jostling streets are unnerving after six months in Stromness. Drunken sailors lurch and puke without warning. Pimps and bawds tout for business. Though it amuses her to discover, as she strides along in her trousers, that she isn't accosted by leering sailors, calling her *darlin'* as she passes, and then *whore* if she refuses to respond. Instead it is the prostitutes who eye her up and shout after her. *Can I do you for somefink, Sir?* She ignores the offers, the sniggers and the insults and hurries on; she doesn't want to linger in Frank's home territory. She pauses only to throw a penny to the ragged children sheltering in the doorways; they'll be outside all night in this freezing weather, she thinks, and it makes her want to weep.

The air is colder on the bridge, and the river's deceptive currents race below. Upstream, the shore is chock-a-block with barges, huddling against the banks. Downstream, the lamps of a thousand ships glitter and wink. She thinks of Tobias, ferried in a tin canoe that misty May morning and deposited on the foreshore right here, below the bridge. She glances over her shoulder, searching the Surrey side for any sign of the mudlarkers. The rotting barge, home to the old woman and that mouthy boy, has been lifted by the tide. Its inhabitants are inside and invisible. They will emerge later to comb the scummy banks, she supposes, after the tide has turned, all the drunks have fallen in the gutters and the pickpockets have retired to their dens. She peers at the barge, rocking in the river's flow, and has, again, the peculiar sense she'd met the old woman before, though where or when she still could not say.

'Oi, watch where you're going, mate.'

The flat of a hand shoves her in the shoulder. She is about to shout when she sees her assailant is wearing a navy reefer jacket, and has a bullseye lamp clipped to his belt. A copper. Not just any old copper, but a constable from the Thames Division. The Filth. Her legs shudder; she fears they might give way. What's he doing here, patrolling London Bridge – shouldn't he be on the water below? She fights the urge to bolt. She smiles, then retracts the corners of her mouth when she clocks the copper's prickly reaction. A momentary lapse, forgetting she is dressed as a man. Sailors don't try to charm officers with their smile, unless they fancy a kicking. She hunches her shoulders, stares at her boots.

'What's your business here, sonny?'

'I'm going to see my aunt.'

She curses herself for being inattentive.

'Where does she live?'

'St Giles.'

'Fucking paddy.'

He eyes her suspiciously and her cheeks redden.

'Well, you'd better piss off to the bloody Holy Land then. And don't let me catch you hanging around here again unless you fancy spending time in Wapping's cells.'

Her jaw clenches involuntarily. She forces herself to nod, sticks her hands in her pockets and walks off, his eyes boring into her back. She swaggers. Attempts to roll her shoulders like a man. She strides and rolls until she reaches the north bank and is mercifully engulfed by the shadows of the city's walls.

Her teeth clatter with nerves and cold as she passes St Paul's and weaves her way east to Fleet Street. Brash barristers from the nearby Inns of Court spill out of the chop houses and bars that line the pavements, and regale each other with tales of cases brilliantly won. She knows these streets; she has strolled here with Solomon on Sunday afternoons when the baying lawyers are all gone. Her hand lifts instinctively to the canary brooch pinned to her jumper, hidden underneath her jacket. She touches the smooth yellow glass with her finger; Solomon has a room in a lodging house for the single officers of Scotland Yard, but she's never visited him there before because women are not allowed. She laughs to herself as she wonders what he'll make of her disguise, and then her spirits plummet; what if he is not there? What if he is off courting some other woman?

She hurries past the rookery that marks the end of Fleet Street and the beginning of the Strand. The whinnying of horses and the clanking of wheels on cobbles grows louder and theatre-goers swarm the streets in search of Hansom cabs to whisk them back to their comfortable suburban homes. She skirts the southern edge of St Giles. Or the Holy Land as the copper called it, the refuge of so many Irish Catholics. Ma had relatives here, but her family had lost contact with them after she died, and Da moved them from the tenements of Jacob's Island to the more salubrious streets of Southwark. Birdie's family had been on the up, until Da was done for murder. And even after that, they had all managed to keep a foot on the ladder; Donal and Aidan rising through the sailor ranks, Frank the big man of the Surrey-side dockers. She had been doing very well for herself too, as Mr Wolff's attention had confirmed. At least, she had been until she found the corpse of Tobias on the Thames foreshore and her life had come crashing down around her ears.

In Trafalgar Square, the beauty of the moonlight gilding the still water of the fountain pools makes her forget, for a moment, the ugliness of London's gutters. She crosses below the lofty gaze of Nelson, past Northumberland House, along Whitehall and there, on her left, is Great Scotland Yard. Under the gloomy arch, the dim glow of the gas lamp creates a murky puddle in the wide and shadowed street. Above, a huge clock tells the hour; not quite eleven. On her right, she identifies the entrance to the Met's headquarters; the imposing Portland stone walls of Scotland Yard are pale as if even London's soot is wary of lingering in the presence of so many coppers. This is where the detective branch has their office; three chambers, according to Solomon.

She ducks into the lee of a wall. Straight ahead, light and noise spill from a public house. The Rising Sun, licensed to sell Watney's ale. By the bar door, a ruddy-cheeked pieman sporting a fustian jacket and worsted cap, loiters with his tray. She hesitates, nervous about the reception she might get from Solomon. It's too late now. She needs his help; she has to find him. She assesses the possibilities; she could try the public room first, or bluff her way past the reputedly fierce landlord of his lodging house and knock on the door of his room. She heads to the bar.

'Pie?' The pieman pushes the tray under her nose and the whiff of rancid meat catches the back of her throat.

'No thanks.'

'Half-price. I've got to get rid of them tonight.'

'Maybe later.' She nudges him aside and shoves the pub door.

'Oi. Fucking molly…'

The door swings shut behind her and cuts short the pieman's insults.

A fug of ale, sweat and smoke greets her. Men shout. Drunken women squeal. She sways, the heat and noise make her dizzy. She has been in bar rooms many times before, though only ever to retrieve a man – her father, her brothers, her husband. And it is no different this evening, she reminds herself, even though she is wearing trousers. She edges through knots of unyielding bodies, polite requests to *excuse me* ignored. She elbows, and tweed-jacketed elbows jab back. She heads in the direction of an arch, through which she can see the green baize of a billiard table, and glimpses drooping spirals of dark hair as a figure leans along the side of the table, fingers splayed. It's Solomon. Her heart pumps faster. She flushes; the sudden pulse of desire takes her by surprise. He draws his right arm slowly and takes a shot. She wipes her burning cheek, reminds herself she's here because she is in danger, not because she wants to see Solomon again.

He stands upright, rests his hand on the end of his cue, assessing his efforts. And while she is considering how to attract his attention, he glances her way. She smiles as she returns his gaze and sees the puzzlement on his face, the narrowed eyes, the concerned line of his brow. He blinks, as if he has just stepped into sunlight and is temporarily blinded. She beckons him. His face reddens. She smiles again, and this time his eyes widen; she can almost see the penny dropping. She unbuttons her jacket, briefly pulls one flap aside and flashes the canary brooch underneath before she covers her chest again. His mouth opens. She nods, indicates the door. He shakes his head as if he is still trying to figure out what is going on. She tries to convey the urgency of the situation with a raised eyebrow. He frowns, has a brief conversation with his bulbous-nosed companion, hands him the billiard cue and makes his way to her. He stands close and whispers in her ear.

'Birdie, what on earth—'

'I had to find you.'

'You're—'

'I know.'

'You don't look bad in trousers.'

He is bemused. She is irritated by his reaction. His teasing usually charms her, but at this moment she wants him to be serious.

'We need somewhere private to talk.'

'Come back to the lodging house.' He grins. 'If anybody asks, I'll say you're my brother.'

The pieman has disappeared. The windows in the lodging house are dark. Thankfully, the landlord does not appear when Solomon opens the door and steps into the narrow hall.

'He's used to officers keeping odd hours,' Solomon whispers.

He has a garret room. Two windows in the eaves allow moonlight to flood the floor. It is devoid of furniture apart from a small press, a battered palliasse with straw poking through the threadbare ticking cover, a desk and a chair.

'It's cold in the winter and hot in the summer, but it's quiet and I can see the stars.'

A pigeon coos on the windowsill.

'I have the birds for company.' He points at a fiddle leaning against the desk. 'And I can play that without anybody complaining.'

There are many things, she realizes, with a start, that she does not know about Solomon. Fiddle-playing is one of them.

He moves the instrument and offers her the chair. She sits awkwardly, uncertain where to place her legs, overcome with a sudden shyness in Solomon's presence. Unsure how to behave in her sailor's disguise. She removes her cap and her pigtail falls.

'I'm glad you didn't cut all your hair,' he says and smiles. 'And I have to say it makes a change to see you dressed in something other than mourning.'

His reaction takes her aback; she expected him to be shocked by her disguise. Instead he acts as if he finds her sailor's attire more attractive than her black dress. She cannot make sense of his behaviour; she wants him to acknowledge the danger of her situation and instead he seems light-hearted to the point of near-evasiveness. She recalls his unexpected moodiness in Orkney and her feeling that he was holding something back from her, some information he was not – is not – sharing.

'I had to disguise myself as a man,' she says, 'because I was scared somebody would recognize me. Frank, or one of his cronies. Or a cop.'

'Of course,' he says, finally acknowledging the danger of her situation. 'Tell me then, what's happened to make you risk returning to London?'

Her explanation floods out in a gabble: Margaret, the twins, the tin canoe, the corpse of Donald Shearer, the stories of the brutal violence used to force the native trappers to hand over their skins and her suspicions these men are employees of the Company.

'We need to find the Master,' she concludes.

'But every ship has a master.'

'I'm sure it's the master of the *Lynx*, a ship the Company uses. Tobias came to London in the autumn of last year to try and do something about him – confront him perhaps – and maybe he sailed to the Baltic thinking he had dealt with the man. But when he returned this spring, he was killed. Shearer was taken aboard the *Lynx* as a purser after he was caught making underhand deals. I suspect he became a liability with his drunkenness and loose tongue, so the Master ordered him to be killed too.'

'By the boatman in the tin canoe? Not the fabled savage Esquimaux again.'

There is a note of scepticism in his tone which she finds frustrating.

'You were right,' she concedes. 'He's unlikely to be an Esquimaux. I was told by the gypsy who made the tin canoe that the man who ordered it had a Cockney accent. But he took a slice of skin from the cheek of Shearer just as he cut a piece of Tobias's face, so I'm sure it's the same person. Skin for a skin.'

He frowns when she says that and his mood becomes more sombre.

'*Pro pelle cutem*,' he says. 'The motto of the Company.'

'How do you know that?'

'I did some digging around when you went to Orkney – I was puzzled by the Company coins you found by Tobias's body.'

She's encouraged to hear he has done some investigating on her behalf while she's been away.

'I wish I'd never picked up those coins,' she says, and pauses. 'I'm beginning to wonder whether Frank has something to do with him too.'

She has been determined to stay calm as she explains all this to Solomon, but at the mention of Frank, her eyes water and her voice cracks.

'I can see Frank might not be entirely on the level,' Solomon says. 'Which London docker can afford to be completely above board? But that doesn't mean to say…' His sentence trails away.

She shakes her head; it's no good Solomon trying to reassure her, she's convinced Frank is mixed up in all this somehow.

'I'm sure,' she says, 'it's not just the crew of the *Lynx* that works for this Master.'

He puffs his cheeks and grimaces as he considers Birdie's views. 'Well, it's true the Commander here has always suspected that the criminal gangs operating the docks along the Surrey side of the river are more organized than on the north. And that the Thames Division isn't doing enough to stop it.' He rubs his bristled chin. 'So where is the *Lynx* now?'

'Somewhere between here and Gravesend Reach I should imagine.'

'That's quite a—'

She interrupts. 'We could start by talking to the old woman and the boy who saw Tobias's body being dragged ashore below London Bridge. I'm sure the woman knew more than she was saying. Maybe she could help us narrow down the search. Will you come with me?'

'Of course.'

She bounds from the chair.

'Not now, though,' he says. 'Wait until the morning. Everything seems clearer in the daylight.'

She glances at him; his expression is stern. He turns away and she is suddenly aware that she has nowhere to sleep for the night other than here; she flushes at the thought of it and wonders whether this is what is preying on his mind and making his mood so mercurial. She fishes around.

'You did say if I needed your help I should find you.'

'I know.'

'Do you mind me being here?'

'No.'

'Is there something bothering—'

'No.' He glares. 'Nothing.'

They both fall into silence, although, out the corner of her eye, she can see him twiddling his fingers.

The pigeon coos and she thinks that is the end of the conversation. She is about to suggest she should take a blanket and sleep on the floor when he crosses to the press, pulls open a drawer, rummages and removes a small object. He hands it to her; a miniature ivory cribbage board etched with images of seals and polar bears.

'I found it in Tobias's trunk the morning I was sent to investigate the disturbance on the *Snow Goose*. Perhaps his children would like it.'

She turns it in her hand. 'I'm sure they would.' She attempts a smile.

He cringes. 'I...'

She waits.

'There's something else I found the same day.' He pauses. 'You should have that too.'

He returns his hand to the drawer and this time produces a folded note, though he holds it tight as if he is reluctant to relinquish it.

'It was at the bottom of Tobias's trunk. I didn't want the river police to find it so I took it. I should've given it to you earlier. I have no excuse.' He doesn't look her in the eyes. 'To be completely honest, I didn't want you to have it either. You always insisted on wearing mourning and it made me wonder whether you still missed your husband. I didn't want you to...'

He shakes his head, passes it over. The note is addressed to Birdie Collins and written in a careful hand she instantly recognizes – her husband's. She is confused; it doesn't make sense.

'Is this...' She falters, tries again. 'Is this the message Tobias said he had for me the evening before he died?'

Solomon reddens, then shrugs. 'I suppose so.'

She stares at him, unmoving, as she wonders why on earth he didn't tell when he met her in Crossbones that he'd found a letter addressed to her in the dead man's trunk.

'You should read it now,' he says.

He takes the fiddle, retreats to the far side of the room and messes with the strings as if he is tuning the instrument, though he cannot be because he isn't making a sound.

She unfolds the note with a trembling hand and reads the painstakingly rounded letters of the script that Patrick had been taught by the lay teachers in the local school.

My dear Birdie,

I hope this letter finds you well. I asked Tobias Skaill, whom I met here and trust, to deliver this to you on his way through Surrey Docks. I've given him a description and told him the place of your work on the Borough. I wanted you to know that I am alive and living in St Petersburg. Though I am currently in something of a bind. I cannot return to London because of troubles with the river cops – as you know, I was accused of some offences and they will not let my case drop, of that I am sure. I am, in effect, bound to stay here for the foreseeable future, but as I have secure employment, it is not too much of an inconvenience. I would be very pleased if you came to live with me in this city; I could look after you well and I have lodgings which you could make into a comfortable home. Forgive me for my silence. Communication has not been easy.

Your loving husband,

Patrick Collins
4th April 1855

She reads it twice because she cannot quite believe it. Pieces of her life she thought were solid are fracturing and tumbling to the ground; her husband isn't dead. She twists the paper this way and that, checking to see whether it might be a forgery, though she is certain it is not. The writing is his, as is the form of expression – cautious and kind rather than passionate. And even though he's left her to fend for herself these last few years, he still seems to think of her as nothing more than his dutiful and homely wife. She shakes her head, confused. Patrick's corpse was never recovered, she reminds herself, so it's perfectly feasible he didn't drown. But it's quite hard to accept that, all this time when she believed him dead, he has been alive and well and living in St Petersburg. She should be angry, yet she finds it hard to raise her temper; she can see there is a rationale to his decision not to contact her until four years after his supposed death. He is – like her – in trouble with the Filth. She reads the letter once more and realizes her doubts and turmoil are caused as much by Solomon's behaviour as Patrick's; whatever else she had suspected Solomon was keeping from her, it certainly wasn't this.

She folds the paper and places it in her canvas kit bag. Solomon has had this letter since May; did he withhold it from her because of his own feelings? Was he debating whether or not to inform his superiors that Patrick Collins, a man with outstanding criminal charges against him, was hiding out in St Petersburg? She glances at him but he does not return her stare. Instead, he places the fiddle under his chin, lifts the bow, draws it across the strings and plays a bitter-sweet melody that reminds her of the gypsy's campfire music. For a moment, her mind drifts with the tune and she remembers the sadness of their parting; the two of them standing awkwardly in the hazy glow of a gas lamp. She'd told him bluntly she could not see him again and he hadn't argued; perhaps he had seen it coming. Theirs always was an unlikely relationship; a Jewish copper and the daughter of an Irish docker hanged for murdering a policeman. If that was what she wished, he'd said, he had to respect her feelings, then he turned and walked away. And left her with the memories of their times together and an emptiness she had not been expecting.

Solomon bows the final note and returns to twisting the violin's tuning pegs. She wishes he would look at her. He keeps his eyes fixed firmly on the instrument. Whatever his motivations for withholding Patrick's letter, she can tell from his demeanour that he isn't going to dissuade her from returning to her husband. Anyway, it will make life easier for him if she goes to St Petersburg; he won't have to worry about the charges against her and can get on with his own life. She crosses to the attic window, gazes over the roofs and chimneys of London. The lights of lamps and candles gleam from other garrets. A pipistrelle swoops around the valleys and ridges of this hidden city; something must have disturbed its hibernation. She suddenly feels overwhelmed; nothing is as she thought it was, she has even been mistaken about her own identity. Here she is worrying about whether people will see through her disguise as a man and yet she has spent four years wearing mourning for a husband who is not dead. She is a married woman, not a widow.

Solomon looks up from his violin. 'I could help you find a ship sailing to the Baltic in the morning. The Thames Division won't follow you to St Petersburg.'

She gazes at him a moment, then thinks of the others who have helped her along the way – Morag and Margaret, desperate to protect the orphaned twins – and makes up her mind. 'Thank you, but no. It's not just my life that's at stake.' She hesitates. 'I'll return to my husband, once I've cleared my name.'

Chapter 18

They leave as St Martin-in-the-Fields strikes six, and set off eastward toward London Bridge. She has barely slept, too aware of Solomon's presence on the other side of the room to rest, and her head is heavy. Dense, icy fog has swept downstream in the early hours, oozing through the city. There is no dawn of which to speak, though the starlings and crows are chorusing and there are plenty of workers trying to go about their early morning business in the freezing cloud. Dark-suited clerks emerge, solidify and disappear. The muffled cries of costermongers and paperboys can be heard, but the street sellers and their wares remain invisible. The faint gleams of a Hansom cab's lanterns and the creak of a Growler's reluctant wheels are the only signs that keep them from straying in front of passing vehicles.

They walk in silence. If she steps too close to him, he shrinks. They have said nothing to each other about Patrick's letter. What is there to say? They make slow progress in the fog; it's gone seven when they reach the bridge and clamber down the waterman's stairs. With each step, the vapour thickens. A solitary ferryman waits at the bottom.

'Where to?' he asks hopefully.

'Sorry, Sir, we're walking,' Solomon replies.

'Good luck with that then,' he says.

The wintry fog has frozen the banks of the Thames; the mud is hard and slippery. At least the coldness has cauterized the river's stink. They head downstream, tripping over mooring ropes, skidding on icy scum. The fog closes in around them, veils the bridge and reduces the city above to a shadow. Down here by the river, it warps all objects and sounds.

'This must be where I found Tobias's body.' She gestures uncertainly at the foreshore and continues her cautious advance. A cormorant croaks; she wonders whether it's the bird that was roosting on the mudlarkers' barge, and orients herself in the direction of its cry. She is relieved to see the dark hull looming, the decaying barge slumped on the mud like a beached whale.

'This way,' she calls to Solomon, who is still gazing at the spot where Tobias's body was dumped, as if it might yield some crucial piece of information despite the many tides that have sluiced the bank since May. Here, by the river, she has more faith in her instincts than his investigative methods. She stumbles on, reaches the barge, hauls herself up; it's easier this time without any petticoats to snag on splinters. She swings a leg over, leaps and lands, narrowly missing the children sleeping under a soiled tarpaulin.

The old woman is standing there waiting, matted hair falling like river weeds around her bony face. And there it is again – that feeling she knows this woman. Birdie's disguise doesn't throw her for a second.

'You're back then,' the woman says, before Birdie has a chance to open her mouth.

She is perplexed; how did this old woman recognize her so quickly when she's dressed as a man? The crone cracks a smile, as if she's pleased Birdie has returned, and behind the mud-smeared skin and rotten teeth, Birdie sees the lines of a younger, prettier face. Perhaps it is the ghost behind the weathered mask she recognizes, though she still cannot for the life of her think why. The woman stares at her with milky eyes as if she, too, is searching for another face below the surface. They stand without speaking while the mist eddies around the gunwales and makes even the nearest objects hazy, and Birdie tries to untangle the nature of their connection.

Solomon's head appears above the side of the barge. He hauls himself over, drops and manages to raise his bowler as he lands upright on two feet.

'Good morning, Ma'am.'

Solomon generally has an easy charm and he uses it without discrimination, though his courtesies are not always reciprocated. The woman gawks at Solomon, as if she's sizing him up for some unspoken purpose.

'Morning,' she says eventually, and turns to Birdie. 'You're thinner than last time you were here; you look quite wan.'

Birdie is taken aback by the familiarity of her tone.

'I can't say I'm surprised,' she continues. 'I thought you might be heading for trouble.'

'Will you tell me your name?' Birdie asks.

'Fedelm,' she says and tilts her head to one side, expectantly.

Birdie knows that name, but she cannot think how. Her mind is as foggy as the river's air. Fedelm smiles sadly, still seemingly waiting for Birdie to acknowledge their bond.

'Fedelm,' Birdie says slowly; Fedelm is an Irish name,

bestowed on seers, she thinks. 'I was hoping you might be able to help me.'

'How?'

'I'd like to ask you some questions about the body...'

The rustling of tarpaulin alerts them to the stirring of the children underneath, woken by the voices. Five filthy ragamuffins emerge and stand quivering, their rags barely sufficient to keep them decent, let alone dry and warm. Their skeletal limbs are painful to behold. Morag's descriptions of the starvation that stalks the Nor' West are horrific, yet Birdie finds the hunger here more monstrous, for these children are starving in sight of London's larder; the warehouses overlooking their plight are bursting with wheat and rice and sugar. It's not a shortage of food that keeps these children hungry; it's the greed of London's wealthy. Solomon digs in his pocket, retrieves a couple of farthings, holds them on the flat of his hand.

'Here. Take these. Get some pies from the market.'

Bleary eyes regard him with suspicion.

'Go on, before I change my mind.'

The tallest boy grabs the coins, and leads the pack over the side of the barge. They vanish in the fog.

Birdie returns to their conversation. 'The morning I came here...'

Fedelm nods. 'You were drawn to the body, as I recall.'

Her turn of phrase is again peculiar; though it is true – she was drawn to the corpse of Tobias unfortunately.

'You told me the body was brought here by a man in a canoe. Do you remember what he looked like?'

'I didn't see his face. It was dark and he had his back to the barge. He didn't hang around. All I can tell you is he was quite tall. About his height.' She nods at Solomon. 'But meatier.'

'Didn't you say he had pointed ears? Like a bat?'

'I don't recall.'

Birdie surveys the waterlogged barge; the rocks that have been used to build a makeshift hearth, the battered pot, the tarpaulins, stiffened with flaky rime, that serve as pathetic protection. The cormorant perched on the prow. It was the boy, she remembers, who mentioned the boatman's ears.

'Is the boy still here?' Birdie asks.

'Which boy?'

'The boy who was with you. The one who said he'd seen the corpse being brought ashore.'

'I know what the lad said,' she snaps.

The cormorant flaps its wings and stretches as if about to take flight, then changes its mind, settles again, and combs its greasy feathers with its hooked beak.

'Is he here?'

'No.'

'Where's he gone?'

'He was stupid.' Fedelm's voice is edged with frustration. 'I warned him.'

'About what?'

'Selling the story.'

Solomon flashes Birdie a cautionary glance, but she is unable to restrain her anger.

'Selling it? What, to the Filth?'

'No. Reporter.'

Birdie closes her eyes; now she understands how *The Times* got hold of the story so quickly.

'All he could think about was how to make some money

from it all. I'd stopped him from going to search the body, you see. He felt cheated. He said he knew a fella who hangs out at the Dog and Duck, a reporter from a proper paper. You could tell him a story about a murder and he'd give you a shilling. Extra if the story was a bit salty. I'll tell him about the Irish girl, he said. He might give me a few more pennies for that. I said he should tell no one, unless he thought his own life worthless. But he always was a cocky little shrimp. He took no notice of me and he ran off to tell his tale.'

Birdie's fury surges. 'He sold the reporter a lie. He told them I was an accomplice in the murder.'

'It's not fair to blame the boy,' Solomon intervenes. 'You don't know what he said. And anyway, the reporter would have checked it with the coppers before he ran with it. They might have been the ones who gave *The Times* the lie that you were an accomplice.'

Birdie is surprised by Solomon's assessment. She can't tell whether he believes what he says or whether he's criticizing the police so Fedelm doesn't suspect him of being one himself. Either way, her attention has been drawn from the boy's treachery and her rage dissipates. She can't be bothered to work it up again; she sees it's pointless – the boy was trying to make a shilling, that's all.

'Anyway,' Fedelm continues. 'It was him who ended up paying the biggest price.'

Solomon rests against the rotting planks of the hull, and straightens again when they creak alarmingly.

'What happened?'

'I found him in the mouth of a sewer, by the Neckinger.'

'Dead?'

'Strangled.'

Solomon tips his bowler back from his forehead. 'Did you report it to the police?'

Fedelm throws Solomon a sidelong glance. 'You think I'm stupid?'

'The boy was murdered,' he says.

'Boys are murdered all the time around here, and nobody gives a shit. The cops only bother with a murder when it's somebody wealthy or important or when they want to cover something up. Like the other one.' She nods her head in the direction of the foreshore. 'The Filth came to pick him up quick enough. They didn't want him lying around for some waterman to find and ferry to Wapping to claim their finder's fee.'

She kicks the tarpaulin at her feet and sends a cloud of half-frozen slurry flying. Birdie sympathizes with Fedelm's rage, but she cannot let this drop.

'And the canoe?'

'What about it?'

'Could it have been made of tin?'

'Possibly.'

Birdie leans closer. 'Have you ever heard anybody talk about the master of the *Lynx*?'

The old woman scratches her ear. 'The *Lynx*? That's not the name of a ship I recognize.'

Her questions are not producing the answers she was hoping for.

'Well, just the Master then?'

Fedelm shakes her head and snorts. 'Every ship has its master, and every sailor curses him.'

The cormorant springs suddenly, and lands at Fedelm's feet.

Solomon steps sideways to avoid the flapping wings. 'Is it tame?'

'Not exactly. Though I'd say we're on good terms.'

He regards the bird warily. 'He's your familiar then?'

'Call him what you like. You wouldn't be the first to see my skills as signs of witchcraft.'

'Ma'am, I wasn't accusing you of witchcraft; there's nothing unnatural, in my view, about women who are clever.' He flicks his eyes in Birdie's direction. 'I was asking about the bird; it has a vicious beak and it's very near my hand.'

She sniffs. 'He's not interested in your hand. He's trained. I guard his roost and he brings me food he's caught from the river.'

'I didn't think there were any fish living in the Thames.'

'There are plenty of eels.'

'Ah. Eels.' He wrinkles his nose. 'I don't eat those.'

Fedelm cackles bitterly. 'I can't afford to be so picky.'

Birdie is bemused by their sparring, but thinks it's wrong that an old woman should be reduced to scavenging the shore for anything that gleams; even the smallest piece of metal has some value to a mudlarker. The sentiment jogs her memory.

'But you refused to take one of the coins I offered, even though the boy wanted it.'

The mention of the coin unnerves Fedelm. She sucks her top lip, as if she's afraid to speak.

'What do you know about those coins?' Birdie senses she's found a more fertile track to follow. 'Why didn't you want to take it?'

Fedelm clacks her rotten teeth. 'These coins. They only bring bad luck.'

'You've seen one like it before then?'

'One?'

Fedelm hesitates, sighs, jams her gnarled hand down the waistband of her skirt, fiddles, and produces two coins which she places along her filth-filled lifeline, the pelts etched clearly on their upturned face.

'I found these on the boy,' she says. 'One on each eye.'

Birdie spots her clenched jaw; there's more to tell here, she's sure.

'There's something else,' Birdie prompts, 'something that happened before you refused the coin I offered.'

The poor woman appears increasingly agitated; she glances over her shoulder and glares at Solomon.

'Who are you anyway?'

'You can trust him,' Birdie says.

'I want to help,' Solomon adds.

'The ones that say they want to help often turn out to be the worst. Charitable men.' She spits. 'Nobody gives something for nothing.'

Fedelm's comment disturbs something in Birdie's memory – though she cannot quite grasp the thought. 'What charitable men?'

'Those that say they want to help children. Orphans.' Fedelm gestures at the crumpled tarpaulins.

'What about them?'

'They're rarely what they seem. All these grand benefactors and good Christian men puffing up their chests and telling everyone how kind they are.'

'The children you shelter here, do some of them come from an orphanage?'

Fedelm nods. 'There's an orphanage along the river near

St Saviour's Docks. The Bermondsey Hospital for Foundling Girls, it's called. Hospital. That's a joke. Nobody ever gets cured of anything there. The children have to escape if they want to survive. All the lasses here, they piss themselves if they even hear its name mentioned.'

'What are they scared of?'

'Disappearing. Those that escape in time, they tell the same story. Strange men's voices in the night. Heavy footsteps. Children being called out of bed. Screams and then silence. And in the morning the matron tells them their friends are lucky cos they've gone to a good home – a decent situation. They all know that's a lie. Owners of good homes don't come calling in the dead of night looking for domestics.'

Birdie's heard the rumours about this business; it's common gossip in London. 'The matron is trading the girls?'

'So it would seem.'

'A procuress,' Solomon suggests. 'Selling them into vice.'

Fedelm pulls a face. 'Vice or dog's meat. Though I would have thought prostitution is the likelier explanation as there's more money to be made in that. They say it's the rich gentlemen of the West End who like them young. The going rate for a fresh maid is fifteen pounds in Mayfair. Down on Ratcliff Highway nobody gives a toss what they're shagging. They're all too drunk to care.' She shrugs. 'Then again, Belgium does a brisk trade in English girls, so I've heard. So perhaps they pack 'em in a ship, set sail down the Thames and sell them on the Continent. Not that it makes much difference. They'll all end up on the streets or in the gutter eventually.'

'What do you know of these men that abduct them?'

Fedelm plucks at the sleeve of her ragged dress. 'I found this girl hiding by the barge builders, beyond London Bridge.

Petrified, she was. I brought her back here and she told me all about it. There are two dormitories at the orphanage. The younger ones in one room and when they reach thirteen they are separated, then taken.'

Solomon shakes his head. 'That's a fig-leaf of legality; waiting until the girls reach the age of consent before they trade them.'

'Consent,' she snorts. 'No thirteen-year-old consents. Anyway, this girl was twelve and in the wrong dorm messing about with a mate. She hid under the bed when she heard the voices, thinking she'd be in trouble. She watched the men come in and heard them bundling her friends away. Tied them up, she said. Whipped them with a belt when they protested. One of the kidnappers dropped something. She picked it up, waited 'til the coast was clear and ran. She hid in the sewers, because she was scared they'd come after her.'

Fedelm shakes the fist which still clasps the tokens. 'The girl found one of these.'

Birdie's eyes widen.

'The coins are used by the gang of abductors?' Solomon asks.

'Gang? I don't know whether that's the name I'd give it. It's more like… it's the way things are done along here these days – the dark side of the river. Wherever there's vice or crime or murder on this foreshore, I reckon you'll find one of those tokens if you dig deep enough in the shit.' She nods and flicks the coin in Solomon's direction. 'Take it.'

He catches it in one hand.

'Those coins are evil. All this…' She waves her hand at the fog-shrouded shore behind and falls silent.

Birdie cannot let it go, she can tell they haven't reached the bottom of it yet. 'So the coin the poor girl showed you; was this the first time you'd seen such a token?'

And then she flushes, for she sees that Fedelm is staring at her chest – the kerfuffle of clambering into the barge must have pulled on Birdie's jacket; it's undone and the canary brooch on her jumper is visible.

'Perhaps it's better not to know some things,' Fedelm says.

Birdie cannot contain her agitation. 'When was the first time you saw one of these tokens?'

Fedelm gazes at her with silent consternation.

'Tell me.'

Fedelm clucks her tongue and winces. 'It was your old fella.'

Birdie thinks she has misheard. 'My da?'

Fedelm nods. 'Gerald Quinn.'

The fog is darkening and Birdie is having trouble seeing the face in front of her, the features shifting. 'You knew him?'

'I know you too. I was there the night you were born with your spectral caul still whole. Branna. That's what your ma named you as soon as she set eyes on you. My beautiful little raven, she said.'

Birdie searches the woman's eyes; green irises glinting behind cloudy cataracts.

'And I was there the night your ma died. That's when I saw the coin spinning. You were there too.'

'I don't remember,' Birdie says. Her skin prickles and her arms feel numb.

'You don't want to remember,' Fedelm says with sudden ferocity.

'That's not true,' Birdie shouts. 'I was too young to remember.'

'If you can't remember, look. You've got the sight.'

In the periphery of Birdie's vision, the sides of the barge swim in and out of focus. 'I don't know what you mean,' she says, though she understands full well.

'You're like your ma,' Fedelm says. 'And her ma before that. There's no point fighting it. It's useless trying to make like some prim lady. You can't deny yourself. Look.'

Birdie stares at Fedelm, an inexplicable knot of anger in her gut, and as she fixes on the green of the old woman's eyes she sees their gleam intensify and the dirtied wrinkles fall away revealing the youthful face below. Fedelm is standing at the door of Birdie's old Jacob's Island home with a shawl over her head and a basket on her arm.

'Branna,' she says. 'You're quite the young lady – how old are you now? Five?'

Birdie nods and gives the handywoman a shy smile.

'Though you've still got the look of a raven,' she says as she steps over the threshold.

She's here to help with Ma. The woman sniffs the fishy air of sickness in the house, and Birdie can see she's concerned.

'Ma's upstairs,' Birdie says.

The handywoman ascends the stairs without a further word.

Birdie returns to the parlour. She is alone; her brothers have been taken to stay at their aunt's house – there wasn't enough room for her. She sits on the floor and watches the brown water oozing between the floorboards; they always seep at high tides, even in the summer when the soil is parched. Eventually the handywoman enters the room and squats beside her.

'Come with me to say goodbye to your ma.'

Birdie is scared; she wants to pretend none of this is happening.

'I don't want to see her.'

The handywoman is firm.

'You must be brave. She brought you into this life and you must see her out.'

'I don't want to see her die.'

'It'll be better for both of you if you say goodbye.'

She offers her hand and Birdie takes it and feels the woman's warmth and strength.

The handywoman leads her up the stairs. The stench of rotting fish is overpowering. There is no window in the back room and no candle has been lit; she can only just see the waxy face of her mother lying on the mattress, a halo of black hair fanning all around. Da is crumpled in a corner. His head hangs, as if his neck is broken.

'Stand by her, and say what you have to say,' the woman whispers.

Birdie moves to the bed; her mind is numb. She wants to run. The woman takes her hand again and gently calls Ma's name.

'Ellen. It's me, Fedelm. I'm here with Branna.'

Ma shifts on the mattress.

'We're here to ease your journey.'

Ma twists her head a little, and though her eyes are sunken, Birdie can see that she is still Ma. The right words tumble out then. 'Ma, I don't want you to go. Please get well.'

'My sweet little Branna, I'll be fine soon enough. You must be strong when I'm gone.' Her eyes flicker. 'Fedelm knows… Fedelm will help you.' Her eyelids close.

Birdie tries to pull away and embrace Ma, but Fedelm scoops her up, and carries her downstairs.

There is a knock on the door as they reach the bottom step. Fedelm lets Uncle Dennis into the house. He's carrying a crate, which he lowers to the floor as if it's weighty.

'Is it bad?'

'Cholera,' Fedelm says.

Uncle Dennis steps back to the door. 'I thought they said there wouldn't be another outbreak.'

'They say all sorts of things. And most of it's rubbish. It's in the air, they're saying now. The miasma.'

Uncle Dennis's hand goes to cover his mouth and nose.

'Your mitt ain't going to make no difference,' she says.

Uncle Dennis drops his hand to his side, though he still looks nervous at the thought of what he might catch. 'This place. You can smell the air is bad. I've told Gerald enough times.'

'He's a good man.'

Birdie likes Fedelm for defending Da.

'Is she in a bad way?'

'She won't last much longer.'

Uncle Dennis is silent for a moment. Birdie watches him out the corner of her eye. She isn't sure what to make of Uncle Dennis; he's always bossing Da about.

He nods at Birdie. 'I brought this over to keep you entertained.'

'What is it?'

'A magic lantern.'

She's heard of those; Aidan told her he'd seen a travelling showman who made pictures of far off places like Africa and India come alive on the wall. Perhaps Uncle Dennis isn't so bad after all.

'I'll show you how to use it.'

Da appears then, pale and haunted.

'I can't stop her pain,' he says.

'I'll go to her,' Fedelm says. 'You stay here. There's nothing you can do now.'

Uncle Dennis puts his arm around Da's shoulder. 'I've put a word in for you with the foreman down at St Saviour's. He was understanding, but he says you need to be there tomorrow.'

Da nods, though he is far away.

'Here. Help me with this magic lantern.'

They crouch on the floor, and Uncle Dennis removes the contraption from the crate and lights the oil lamp. The glow burnishes the room with an enchanting shimmer. Uncle Dennis shows Birdie how to project the slides on the peeling wall, and he spins the carousel. Vivid colours flood the room and Birdie is no longer in Bermondsey; she's surrounded by sapphire sky and up ahead a scarlet sun burns and white ice gleams.

'The North Pole,' Uncle Dennis says, 'the land where the sun never sets.' He moves the carousel, and a figure appears. 'Here's an Esquimaux.'

She squeals with excitement.

Fedelm enters the room. 'She's gone.'

Dennis crosses himself; he and Da quit the room and go upstairs together. Fedelm stays with Birdie.

'Show me how the magic lantern works,' she says.

Birdie does as she is told, moving the wheel to project the pictures of the Esquimaux. When the slides are done, she looks in the crate, finds another carousel and fits it with her tiny fingers. The lamp projects a bright yellow bird in a cage.

'Canary,' the woman says.

Birdie spins the carousel. The door of the cage opens and the yellow bird flies away. She hears the canary chirping the sweetest melody, a soothing trill of birdsong.

'I can hear the canary singing.'

'Can you now?' Fedelm seems impressed. 'Well, you should think of your ma whenever you hear the birds singing. She's flown with them and she's free from the troubles of this world. But she'll always be there to guide you if you reach for her in your thoughts.'

She likes the way Fedelm explains Ma's death. It's better than the priest's threats of Hell and damnation.

She doesn't realize Da and Uncle Dennis have returned until she hears Uncle Dennis talking behind her.

'You should get the family away from here, Gerald. The air's no good.'

Da shouts, for once. 'How can I take my family away from here? I can't afford to go anywhere else.'

'You know that's not true.' Uncle Dennis is shouting too.

They seem to have forgotten that she and Fedelm are still in the room, and that Ma is lying upstairs.

'And you know why I don't want to do it,' Da argues back. 'It'll be the death of me.'

Birdie doesn't understand what they are talking about, but she can hear the anger and desperation in Da's voice.

'You think he can do you more harm than these rotten streets?'

'I'll find another way.'

'You've been saying that for years. He's seen me good, Gerald.'

'Yes, but you sit in an office. You do the books. That's not what he'd want me for, and you know it. He'd want me because

I can keep the stevedores and the warehouse watchmen in line. He'd have me down the docks overseeing...'

Da lets the sentence slide.

'Think about it.'

'I won't work for him.'

Uncle Dennis digs in his pocket, removes a coin. 'He pays good money.'

'He takes a hefty cut as well. Skin for a skin.'

'He'll look after you. And your family.' He nods at Birdie and then he flips the coin, and it spins around and around, up and up. 'Catch it.'

Da lets the coin drop on the floor. 'Keep your bloody coin. This is a respectable family.'

'You live here in this pigsty...' Uncle Dennis waves his hand around the mouldering walls, 'and you talk about being a respectable family?'

Da looks away.

Birdie decides she'll take the coin Uncle Dennis tossed and she reaches over, but Fedelm snatches it away before her fingers touch the metal, though not before she sees the etched letters on its upturned face. One she knows – it's a B, like the letter at the start of her name. The other letter she doesn't recognize.

'You won't be needing that,' Fedelm says.

She passes the coin back to Uncle Dennis and he pockets it, and heads to the door without another word.

Da stands head bowed, shoulders hunched, the weight of it all defeating him.

Fedelm says, 'I'll go and wash her.'

She leaves Birdie alone with Da.

'Da, can we get a canary?'

He looks down at her and she can see the tears in his eyes. 'That's a grand idea,' he says. 'I'll tell you what, maybe we'll take Uncle Dennis's advice and move away from here and find ourselves a place to live further from the river where the air is cleaner, and where we've got more room. Then we can keep lots of canaries.'

The cormorant croaks. Birdie feels something cold against her palm and realizes she is clutching her brooch.

'Are you feeling ill?' Solomon asks. 'I thought you were about to faint.'

'She's fine,' Fedelm says. 'She won't keel over.'

It's true, Birdie thinks; she might go into trances quite regularly, but she's never fallen or had a fit.

'It's not a malady, it's a gift,' Fedelm says. 'It's the truth she sees, and sometimes the truth is hard for others to accept.' She gives Solomon a sideways glance. 'The words of men are often lies, and they'll say you're mad or evil rather than allow you to contradict them.'

Birdie gazes at the old woman, the smooth curves of her youth still visible beneath the wrinkles.

'Don't fight your gifts. Use them to see beyond the trickery of this world.'

Birdie reaches for Fedelm's hand. 'Thank you for all your help.'

Fedelm smiles sadly. 'I've done what I can.'

Solomon looks uncertainly from Fedelm to Birdie. 'We should visit this orphanage,' he says. 'We can take a cab from outside the station.'

Chapter 19

The driver leans over from his seat at the back of the Hansom cab and shouts through the hatch in the roof. 'Which street did you say?'

'Bermondsey Wall,' she replies.

The Bermondsey Hospital for Foundling Girls. Birdie knows it well. She always ran past the forbidding building as a child, scared because Frank had told her it's where she would be sent if she gave him any lip. Orphanages, homes for fallen women or wayward children, places for the sick and destitute. All were viewed with dread by the inhabitants of the squalid alleys and tenements surrounding the docks – only marginally better than the workhouse. Nobody believed these charitable institutions cared for those that entered their stern doors. Girls in orphanages were often kicked onto the streets when they reached fourteen, or else they were farmed out as domestic maids and ended up being abused or tricked into prostitution. She considers herself to have been lucky; the regime at the school she attended was spartan, the matron spiteful and the children, including herself, regularly beaten, but she had been taught maths and learned the skills that helped her gain respectable employment. And nobody disappeared mysteriously in the night.

The Hansom cab judders to an abrupt halt.

'I ain't going no further,' the cabbie shouts. 'These streets is bad enough when you can see where you're going.'

No point in arguing. Solomon passes the fare up through the roof hatch. The driver unlocks the cab doors, lets them out and cracks his whip. The horse trots away, leaving them in the fog and already fading light.

'It's further along the street, toward the river,' she says.

Solomon steps closer. 'I'd offer to take your arm, but you're dressed as a man.'

'You've no need to explain.'

There is a prickliness between them. Whether it's coming from her or him, she cannot tell. They have not spoken much since they left the foreshore below London Bridge. She's still mulling over the conversation with Fedelm. Solomon's reaction – to the old woman's account of Birdie's history as much as the trade in girls – is difficult to read. They make their way in silence past blackened walls and rusty railings, terraces with cracked and papered window panes. The fumes of the river grow stronger.

'There it is.'

The bleak premises lours over the street, more like a prison than an orphanage with its barred windows and menacing spear-headed railings. She proposes she should find an excuse to speak to the orphanage matron. Solomon says he would be less likely to raise eyebrows than Birdie in her sailor's trousers and jacket.

'I fooled you,' she reminds him.

'Not for long,' he replies. 'I saw through your disguise.'

She fears he is talking about more than her outfit, and wonders whether he can tell she is having second thoughts about returning to her husband; it might be the right thing to do, but is it what she wants?

'You go on,' she insists. 'I'll meet you by Mill Stairs.'

'All right,' he says. 'Walk away if you sense danger.'

Their conversation is interrupted by a whistle that makes Birdie jump. A small jiggling flame glimmers through the fog. It brightens and a figure emerges from the vapour; a lamplighter. He doffs his cap as he nears. Solomon tweaks his bowler, watches him stroll toward the river before he turns back to Birdie.

'If I'm not at Mill Stairs, wait for me,' he says.

He recedes and vanishes before she has a chance to ask him where he is going.

Three stone steps lead to the dull black front door. She lifts and drops the anchor-shaped brass knocker. The clang sounds pathetic in the fog.

'Hello, is anybody there?' Her shout is shrill and nervous.

There is no answer. Her plan seems flimsy in the face of the impenetrable entrance. She lets the knocker thud again. Nothing happens. She might as well go and join Solomon by Mill Stairs. She descends the steps, and spies the bent figure of a woman in a grubby pinafore and mob cap hobbling along by the railings. The woman cranes her neck awkwardly at Birdie, her spine refusing to straighten.

'What do you want?' she asks

'I'd like to talk to the matron.'

'She ain't fond of visitors.'

That much is already obvious.

'I'm looking for my sister. I've been at sea, and while I was away my mother died and I believe she was brought here.'

The story is too neat. The woman rumples her nose, as if she can smell its fishiness.

'You don't sound like no sailor. You're too posh.'

Birdie considers bolting. She decides to stand her ground; this crippled woman can do her no harm.

'I was taken in by a school for those orphaned by the sea when my father drowned.' This is partly true; her school had indeed been intended for the orphaned children of ships' captains. 'That's why I sound educated.'

'What can you do on a ship?' She scoffs. 'You're too scrawny to haul a sail.'

'I work as a cook.'

'Cooking?' The woman perks up. 'That's what I do.'

'You cook for the orphans?'

'Broth. That's what the orphans get. And I cook proper stuff for the matron and all that... palaver.' She flaps her hand in a dismissive gesture that perturbs Birdie. What palaver?

'Are you going inside now?' Birdie asks.

'I would be if you weren't standing in me way.'

'Would you let me in?' She digs in her pocket, retrieves a shilling, offers it to the cook. 'I'm desperate to find my sister.'

The woman snatches the coin. 'All right, but it's no good asking me about your sister. I don't know none of their names. They come and they go, and they're all the same to me. You'll have to talk to the matron, and I can't promise she'll answer cos, as I said, she don't have much time for visitors.'

She removes a key from underneath her apron, fumbles with the lock, leans her hunched shoulder against the door, shoves, and hobbles inside. Birdie follows. The place reeks of boiled cabbage and sewage. Wisps of fog languish below the high ceiling. Birdie is surprised to see the fish-tail plumes of gas lights burning in their clear glass shades; it's an unusual touch of luxury for a charitable institution. Gas lamps are common enough in the city's streets, but only the wealthiest Londoners have them in their homes. Here, they throw a jaundiced glaze on the bare, tiled floor and draw attention to the grubbiness of the high ceiling and the greyness of the walls. Arched doorways lead, she supposes, to the refectory and offices for the staff. A narrow stairway cowers in a far corner. She listens for the shouts and chatter of children, but there is silence apart from the hissing of the gas lamps, and the wheezing of the cook.

'How many girls stay here?'

'Stay? None of 'em stays. Like I said, they come and they go. It's a Hospital, you see, not long term care. We move them on when they're cured.'

'Cured of what?'

She shrugs. 'Indolence. Pride. Criminal leanings.'

Criminal leanings? Birdie is incensed by the cook's description of the orphans' dispositions, but checks her indignation.

'Do you know where they go when they've been cured?'

'Eh?'

The woman cranks her head around and gives Birdie a filthy stare. She decides to change the subject.

'Where's the matron's office?'

'Over there.' She waves her gnarled hand at the door furthest from the staircase.

'And what about the girls? Where are they?'

'In the dorms, I suppose.' The gas plumes splutter and shrink. 'Useless bloody contraptions.'

'Shouldn't you switch the gas supply off?' Birdie can taste sulphur on her tongue. 'Is there a mains tap somewhere?'

The cook ignores her, fusses with a taper and a candle on a console by the front door, lifts the candle and waves the flame in the direction of the stairs. 'That's where they stay most of the time. Up there.' Birdie's gaze follows the line of the bannister. Halfway up, her eyes are arrested by a crest decorated with heraldic creatures that seem to leap and snarl in the flickering light. She stares at the shield and her head feels woozy. Her skin creeps. Perhaps it is the gas, she thinks, and then she remembers Fedelm's words and does not resist as her eyes blur and the room around her darkens and dissolves. She keeps her gaze fixed on the misting wall and when her vision clears she finds herself in a dull hallway she recognizes: she's waiting for another matron in a different time and place. The class teacher has sent her to Matron's office to account for her poor stitching – embroidery always did defeat her. But Matron isn't there so she waits outside, and notices the door is slightly ajar. Her curiosity is roused. Hearing no sound of advancing adults, she nudges the handle and steps inside. The desk has been pushed to one side and, strewn across its dull surface, she glimpses a fur stole, a peach silk petticoat and a crimson ribbon sash from which dangles a crest decorated with strange rampant beasts. Leaning against the wall is the birch rod used to beat the pupils. Birdie doesn't notice Matron returning until a sensation at the nape of her neck makes her jump. She turns. The sour-faced woman stands in the doorway, hands on hips. Birdie hardly dares breathe as she waits for her to reach for the rod. Matron doesn't move. Birdie catches a strange look of embarrassment on her face before her thin top lip cocks in a triumphant sneer. She's not going to punish Birdie, she says, because she's got the satisfaction of knowing that one day, somebody would teach her the meaning of obedience, even if he has to beat her black and blue to do it. She smiles smugly as she watches Birdie leave the office.

'Bloody nuisances, them girls,' the cook says, and Birdie's mind snaps back to her surroundings. Her head still feels heavy. She focuses on the dull shield hanging above the stairs, tries to make out the outline of its beasts and has to dig her fingernails into her palms to stop herself from reacting; the shield is identical to the crest she saw dangling from the ribbon in her apparition of Matron's office. What's more, it's the same as the letterhead Margaret noticed on her school testimonial.

'Is that a lynx?'

'A what?'

'Lynx. A big cat – like a lion.'

'Where?'

'On that shield.' She points.

'That? I thought you were talking about the ship.'

Birdie's hands feel clammy. 'The ship?'

'The ship that comes to St Saviour's.'

At the mention of the dock where Frank has an office, her stomach sinks.

'A Company ship, perhaps?'

'Wouldn't know about that. It takes messages and delivers supplies.'

'Supplies?'

'Stuff she likes,' she nods at the matron's office. 'Furs,

perfume, lace from Belgium. You know. Fancy Continental stuff. Why're you asking anyway?'

'Oh, I wasn't really interested in the ship. I was just wondering about the shield, that's all. Is it the crest of one of the orphanage's benefactors?'

'One?' She snorts. 'Only bloody benefactor. Ain't many people going to waste their money on a bunch of dirty scrubbers from Jacob's Island.'

'Who is the benefactor then?'

'One of those fancy guilds from the city.'

'A livery company?' Uncle Dennis used to attend their functions.

'Livery company. Pah. Palaver, that's what it is. All those toffs with hats and big chains and barges on the river. Worshipful this and worshipful that. Ain't I so important.'

The cook laughs bitterly.

Birdie eggs her on. 'I met some snotty gent over in Ratcliffe Highway once, and when I asked him about his profession, he said he was a member of the Worshipful Company of Butchers. I almost laughed. Butcher? All they do is chop up bits of meat, but they dress it up as something grand by saying they're a member of a livery company.'

'Exactly. Though it ain't the Butchers who give money to this place.' She cocks her head. 'Something like butchers though, I think.'

'Bakers?'

'Nah, not them. And it ain't the candlestick makers either.' She cackles at her own wit, and the candle she is holding wobbles and sends shadows scurrying around the hall like fleeing rodents. Birdie offers her a steadying hand.

'Ta.'

The woman holds the candle closer to Birdie's face. 'You've got good skin for a sailor. All white and smooth.'

Birdie steps back from the flame. 'I spend most of my days in the galley – cooking. There's so much work, I'm rarely in the sun.'

She's overegged the explanation. Fortunately the woman isn't paying attention.

'Skin,' she says. 'Skin. That's it. The Worshipful Company of Skinners.' She jabs the candle in the direction of the shield. 'That's them. The Skinners.'

'Skinners?'

The cook holds the candle nearer to Birdie's face again, alerted to the alarm in her voice.

'What about them?' she asks.

'It's not a livery company with which I'm familiar.'

'Killing animals – beavers, wolves – then skinning them. That's what they do. Though if you saw the airs and graces the Master puts on when he visits the matron, you would never think he did something so base as cutting the pelt off dead creatures.'

'The Master?' Birdie's voice rises to a dangerously high pitch; she has to stay calm.

'The Master of the Skinners.' The woman waves the candle wildly. 'He's the one that insisted on the stupid gas lamps cos they always come to collect the supplies in the dark, and he reckoned it was easier to carry things down the stairs if you didn't have to contend with dripping candles.'

'Carry what things?'

The cook coughs, as if she has swallowed something the wrong way, wheezes, and the flame of the candle almost licks the tufts of greasy hair that have escaped from her cap before she recovers and says, 'None of your bleedin' business.' She pokes a finger in Birdie's chest. 'You stay here while I find the matron.'

The cook gives her a backwards glance as she shuffles across the hall clasping her guttering candle. Birdie is left in the phosphorous glow of the failing gas plumes. The click of a latch closing against its plate is her signal to run; she darts to the entrance, drags the heavy door across the tiles, and is about to leave when her eye is caught by a gleam on the console near the entrance. She hesitates, steps toward the table and sees a knife, its blade long and sharp and forged into a finger guard above the wooden handle. Her hand hovers, about to grab it, when a creaking hinge prompts her to leap for the entrance and head for the street.

She is momentarily confused; the fog is disorienting and the darkness has thickened. The street is empty; the stevedores and porters have already departed for the night. Through the fog, she hears a croak and recognizes the tuneless song of a cormorant. She turns toward the call and heads in its direction. Her hand brushes rimed slats of clinkered warehouses as she fumbles her way along the street until, finally, she reaches the familiar rickety wooden rail of Mill Stairs. She grips the bannister firmly as she descends. The foreshore is treacherous this side of the Neckinger; creeks and sewers gush with enough sudden force to sweep a person over and carry them to the river. It was stupid telling Solomon to wait here, she realizes as she sees the black water of the Thames sucking the bottom step. The tide is rising and only a slither of the bank remains exposed. Through the swirling fog she catches glimpses of pillars and wooden planks, tethered barges bobbing on the incoming tide, but there is no sign of him. She doesn't want to call his name in case there is a ferryman hanging around. She waits. A faint glow dances on the water. Her heart pounds. The river cops? The light grows brighter, closer. The oars splash as the rowing boat approaches the stairs. She is ready to scarper.

'Birdie.'

Solomon. She jumps the last stair, wades into the water and helps drag the boat ashore.

'Where did you find the dinghy?'

'A cousin, further along Bermondsey Wall; he's what my father would have called an allrightnik – done well for himself; started off as a lighterman and now he runs his own business unloading the ships anchored mid-river.'

She is envious of his relatives who all seem to advance themselves through honest labour. Why can't her family be like his?

'I asked him if I could borrow this rowing boat for a while. He laughed and said he wouldn't miss it; he warned me it's not the most watertight of vessels, but it should get us across the river.'

'I was scared you were the Filth.'

'They don't patrol in fog like this.' He says it confidently. 'Did you manage to find the matron?'

'I spoke to the cook.' She glances over her shoulder and whispers, 'It seems that Fedelm was right about the abductions. It's likely the girls are taken to Belgium.' She pauses. 'And the ship that takes them there is the *Lynx*. It flies the Company flag in the summer when it crosses the Atlantic and collects furs. And in winter, it sails between London and Belgium with the abducted girls on board. It anchors in St Saviour's.' She flushes, ashamed to think that her own brother Frank organizes the dockers there.

He nods. 'The man behind the illegal trading on both sides of the Atlantic might well be the master of the *Lynx* then?'

'No. It seems I was wrong about that. He's not a ship's master at all.' Her pulse races strangely as she speaks. 'He's the Master of the Worshipful Company of the Skinners.'

Solomon raises an eyebrow. 'Master of a livery company? He must be well connected then. Now, that makes more...' He gazes into the fog.

'How did you discover that?' he asks eventually.

'I saw a shield on the wall.' She hesitates; she doesn't want to say the crest caught her eye because she'd seen exactly the same coat of arms on the letterhead of her own school testimonial as well as dangling from a ribbon in her old matron's office. 'The cook told me it was the crest of the Skinners, and they are the sole benefactors of the orphanage. The Master is a regular visitor.'

'You should be a detective.'

'I'll leave that job to you.'

He smiles, but the side of his mouth twitches, as if he has an aching tooth. She is afraid to ask what's bothering him; she's concerned the answer might be her.

'I suppose it shouldn't be a surprise,' he says, 'to find that the Vast Emporium of All Nations sells young girls to the Continent.'

Birdie nods. She doesn't want to say the bigger shock for her is the realization that her own family might be involved in the trade. The mimicry of Frank's parrot echoes in her mind. *The Master*, she says to the bird. *Skin for a skin*, the parrot replies.

'Let's go back to your lodgings now,' she says.

Solomon gestures at the dinghy.

'I hope this thing makes it back to Westminster.'

He stoops and pushes it toward the water. The distant croak of a cormorant makes her look upstream. A dirty yellow beam pierces the vapour. She grabs his arm and nods behind at Bermondsey Wall. They scramble up Mill Stairs.

'Bullseye lamp,' she whispers as they wait at the top. 'I thought you said the Filth didn't patrol in thick fog.'

'They must have some pressing business.' He looks into the fog, not at her, when he speaks.

They wait for the duty boat to pass before they return to the foreshore and edge the dinghy into the river. The tide is on the turn as Solomon rows into the midstream currents; the black water eddies and swirls around the hull. The serpentine figurehead of a mermaid looms above them, floating in mid-air. Half-furled sails hang, motionless as winding sheets. Lamps warning of ships' sterns blink and fade. Birdie slumps on the bench, cold and tired. Her mind wanders; the Master dogs her thoughts. Like the fog, his chilling presence seems to be everywhere along this river, and yet he remains as shadowy as vapour; impossible to grasp.

Solomon's voice wafts over her. 'This man we're after – he's the Master of the Skinners, but, surely, he must also have some position with the Company, even if he's not the master of the *Lynx*. And he obviously has a lot of connections here in London if he's managed—'

Birdie sits upright abruptly; the boat rocks.

'What is it?'

'I've remembered something; I was told that Tobias was forced to leave the Company after he reported a clerk fiddling the books at York Factory. He reported it first to the Factor, but the Factor did nothing. So he reported it to a member of the London Committee who was visiting. And then he was given the boot.'

Solomon lifts the oars clear of the water and holds them steady in mid-air; the boat drifts downstream, back the way they came.

'I wasn't aware members of the Company's London Committee were in the habit of visiting the trading posts in Rupert's Land. I thought they'd perfected the art of governing from this side of the Atlantic. Keeping their hands clean while raking off all the profit.'

'How do you know all this?'

'I told you; when you left me with one of those coins, I did some digging around. I tried to find out about the Committee. It's a very secretive institution, though I did manage to discover that they meet every Wednesday at noon. And it seems that sometimes there is a second, smaller meeting held afterwards, in the evening.'

Solomon plays his cards close to his chest when it comes to his detective work; she wonders what else he knows and isn't revealing. Perhaps he has suspected all along that her family was involved in this business. Perhaps that's why he's made no attempt to deter her from heading back to St Petersburg.

'I've watched the comings and goings a couple of times,' Solomon continues. 'All very furtive. The Company headquarters is in Fenchurch Street.'

The bloated corpse of a Friesian cow floats toward them, side-on, its legs in the air like an upturned table. Solomon jabs its flank with an oar, producing a puff of noxious gasses from the cow and a coughing fit in him. The dinghy wobbles precipitously. Birdie is about to grab the oars but Solomon recovers himself in time to steer the prow away from the looming hull of an anchored schooner, and steadies their course.

'We could head to Billingsgate Stairs instead of going back to Scotland Yard,' he suggests. 'Billingsgate is just below Fenchurch Street.'

The water at their feet is deepening, their leaky vessel sinking lower in the sullied river.

'Is it Wednesday today?' She has lost track of time since she set sail from Stromness. He nods.

'Isn't it too late?'

'Not if there's an extra Committee meeting. We should take a look.'

She raises her feet onto the bench, to stop her boots from becoming sodden, and tightly hugs her folded legs.

'Don't worry,' Solomon says. 'We're going to clear your name.'

He sculls, and shifts the direction of the dinghy. They sit in silence for a while as he concentrates on navigating strong currents and anchored vessels. Tears well in her eyes; she can't stop them falling. She's very much afraid that in order to clear her own name, she'll have to impugn her family.

Chapter 20

'We're almost at Billingsgate,' she says. 'I can smell it.'

The wharf is deserted apart from a pack of feral cats scrabbling for pickings. Trading at Billingsgate starts at five in the morning and finishes at noon. The tugs and smacks bringing the fish upstream from cleaner waters have not yet started to arrive. Solomon ties the dinghy to a strut near the stone steps, leaving plenty of slack in the rope to allow the vessel to drop with the tide. He's done this before, she can tell. She likes this side to him, the surprising skills and knowledge; the names and locations of all the watermen's stairs along the river, the best routes from the Surrey side to the streets on the northern shore. She finds herself watching the competent way he knots the rope through the strut, the dark hairs on the back of his hand, and she pictures his hand in other places. She looks away.

Billingsgate Stairs ascend from the thick water of the river, and glisten with the scales of a million fish. She leaps for the nearest step. The cats yowl and hiss, fearing she is a competitor for their leftovers. She ignores their protests, too busy securing her footing to argue with a gang of mangy felines. The alley beside the new market building is ankle deep in filth and unidentifiable piscatorial remains. She places her hand on the wall to steady herself as she slithers in the mud; even the bricks feel as if they are covered in fish skin. Birdie holds her breath and fixes her sight on the faint glow of the gas lamp ahead. The bells of St Magnus the Martyr toll six as they emerge in Lower Thames Street. A slight breeze chases the fog on this side of the river; mist wafts through the lamp-light like smoke. Solomon glances over his shoulder to check they have not been followed.

'Ten minutes' walk,' he says.

Fenchurch Street is busy with carriages, omnibuses and city workers heading for the station. Birdie and Solomon lower their heads, fall in with the flow of suited gentlemen, and walk past the four-storeyed offices of the merchants who trade in the produce unloaded from the docks. Sugar brokers, spice merchants, sellers of fine wines and rum. They idle in front of a lone ship's chandlers, not so much admiring its window, well-stocked with compasses and halyards, as peering in the glass to see the reflections of Company House on the opposite side of the street. Even in the gloaming Birdie can see it's grand and haughty. Elongated windows glare down on the pavement from below disdainful triangular pediments. Lofty columns guard the arched and forbidding double doors. A weather-vane in the shape of a golden beaver is perched above the premises, its tail raised with contempt against the north-easterly wind.

'It used to be the Lord Mayor's,' Solomon says. 'He sold it to the Committee. Do you know whether Standing and Wolff have any contracts with the Company?'

Solomon asks the question casually, but it makes Birdie feel uneasy. Silently, she itemizes the contracts she saw pass through the books, the numbers she examined and entered into ledgers, the letters she wrote to merchants to secure supplies.

'They have a contract to supply rum and bedding for the servants at York Factory. They have another contract for hunting rifles which, I should imagine, are used as trade goods with the local trappers.' They also act as a middleman, moving furs from London to a merchant in France who distributes them across the Continent, but she's not sure that it's relevant. There are plenty of merchants in London who have similar arrangements with the Company.

Solomon nods faintly as if he's not really listening and then continues. 'And the Committee, do you think Mr Standing or Mr Wolff are familiar with any of its members?'

'No,' she replies with some ferocity. 'Well, certainly not Mr Wolff – he's an old-fashioned gentleman who doesn't have much time for hobnobbing. I've never heard him mention the name of anybody on the Company Committee.'

'Nobody ever does, it seems. The Committee keeps very quiet about its activities. I managed to obtain a report of the annual meeting, and it seemed to me the Chair spent most of his time telling the shareholders they must trust the Committee.' 'So long as the value of the shares keeps going up, the shareholders are unlikely to complain.'

'And so long as people still want to buy skins, the value of the shares will keep going up. I found a couple of hand bills notifying merchants of an auction at the Hall – the list of pelts was endless. Otter, bear, seal, wolf. All those poor creatures.' He pauses. 'And your friend who told you about Tobias Skaill's run-in with the Company...'

'Morag.'

'Did she recall the name or position of the Committee member who visited York Factory?'

'No. She was travelling at the time. Though I wonder whether it was somebody who was familiar with the accounting—'

Solomon nudges her in the ribs and she leaves her thought unfinished. A well-to-do couple saunter by, too close for comfort; him in a frock coat, her in a ruby silk gown that sweeps the paving stones. Birdie thinks she wouldn't like to see what's caught up in that hem by the end of the evening.

'One other thing I discovered,' Solomon continues when they have passed, 'is that inside Company House there's a collection of curiosities taken from the countries in which it trades. And that, I believe, is open to visitors.'

'Not this late, surely.'

The bells of St Olave's chime half past the hour.

'We can ask about the opening hours.'

He pivots around and starts across the road before she can question his plan. She dodges a passing carriage and an over-eager crossing sweeper, oblivious to pedestrians' shoes as he niggles his broom to dislodge the horse shit spread across the cobbles. He must be all of ten.

'Is this wise?' she whispers as they reach the far pavement.

He shrugs. 'We don't have time to be too cautious. We need a little chutzpah.'

He squeezes her hand surreptitiously, then strides ahead, marching straight for the double-doored entrance. He mounts the steps and knocks. A costermonger sitting on the kerb, with a red neckerchief dangling over her shoulders and a basket by her side, shouts to him. 'You're wasting yer time. Nobody will answer. It's Wednesday night. They're all too busy with their meetings.'

Solomon smiles at the woman. 'I was interested in seeing the curiosities.'

'Oh the curiosities. Not much to get excited about if you ask me. A few moth-eaten Indian headdresses, one of them totem poles and an Esquimaux sledge. I've been in meself several times, know it all by heart. The main entrance is open during office hours. The collection is in a side room. I slip in when it's cold. Takes the porter a good five minutes to chase me out. Don't s'pose you want an apple or two?'

Solomon hands her a coin in exchange for two shrivelled pippins, which he drops in his coat pocket. The costermonger points at a smaller door further along the street.

'The other door's left open on Wednesday evenings for all the bigwigs to go in and out.'

'Thank you kindly, Ma'am.' He hands her another coin.

'Heaven love you, Sir.'

The side door is indeed open and leads into a vast reception hall. Brass sconces on every side throw bright light into the high white plastered ceiling and exaggerate the darkness of the mahogany panels below. At one end of the grand hall, a wide staircase sweeps skyward, its bannisters flounced with forest green velvet swagging.

'The Court Room is upstairs,' Solomon whispers. 'That's where the Committee meets.'

The hall is extravagantly empty. She tries to calculate how many Jacob's Island tenements you could fit in here alone, but is distracted by the sight of a massive pair of moose antlers hanging on one wall, below which three men in long black frock coats, stiff white shirt collars and tall beaver toppers cluster and whisper. City gents who have invested enough money in the stocks of the Company to earn a seat on the Committee. They are too engrossed in their own conversation to notice Solomon and Birdie hovering near the entrance.

'This way.' Solomon strides quickly toward a door which stands ajar. She follows and slips into a room which is smaller than the hall, yet still large enough to house all the mudlarkers of the Thames. The light from two crystal candelabras glitters on a wall of glass-doored cabinets, behind which sit shelves of leather-spined books. A wooden stand holds newspapers and periodicals. Well-stuffed leather wingback armchairs – none of them occupied – are arranged around rosewood coffee tables. A reading room, though she suspects not much reading is done here; the books are all for show. Immediately to her right is an oil painting of a dead and bloodied beast. The brass plaque below explains it is a picture of an elk, killed in the presence of Charles XI of Sweden. She shudders. *Skin for a skin*. She takes a deep breath and the smell of leather, tobacco and something queer and musty tickles the back of her throat; the aroma is familiar, though she cannot identify its source.

Solomon crosses to the newspaper stand, collects *The Times*, settles himself in an armchair wing-side to the door, and spreads the paper in front of his face as if he is deeply engrossed in the centre pages. Chutzpah. She collects the *Illustrated London News*, sinks into an armchair close to his, crosses her ankles, remembers this is not how men sit, uncrosses her legs but cannot quite bring herself to let her knees flop apart. She slumps and stretches her legs in front of her, as she remembers Da doing when he came home late from the docks and wanted to read a book. She opens her paper.

She faces forward and stares at the newsprint, but watches the entrance hall from the tail of her eye. The trio of city gents are still deep in conversation beneath the moose antlers, though they keep glancing around nervously as if they are expecting somebody important. Her heart is pounding and her palms are sweaty with anticipation. She lowers the paper and glances at Solomon. He catches her eye, and the warmth of his look soothes her racing nerves. A carriage clock on the mantelpiece chimes the quarter hour. There is a flurry in the entrance hall. She hears the large door opening but cannot see who enters from the street.

'Ah, gentlemen.' The harshness of the newcomer's voice cuts through the fuggy atmosphere. Goose-pimples form on her arm, though she is uncertain whether she is reacting to the blast of cold air from the street or to the chilling resonance of the man's tone.

'I am so glad to see you've returned for round two. I do hope you've not been waiting long. I was delayed by some irritating business.'

The speaker remains out of sight, but the effect he has on the waiting trio is visible – they separate and stand up straight, hands behind their backs like a bunch of naughty schoolboys caught truanting. Whatever the identity of this newcomer, the other Committee members are scared of him.

'Vinge,' he calls. 'Have you brought the papers?'

'Yes, Sir.'

'Take them upstairs to the Court Room then.'

A hefty factotum, lugging a portmanteau, crosses her line of sight and brushes against the city gents as he heads to the staircase. They recoil. He looks more like a thuggish boxer than a clerk. He wears a sports jacket that strains across his broad shoulders, his bull neck jutting from the collar. Beneath his cap, his hair is poker-straight and muddy brown. The ratty tails hang down below his jaw and cover the side of his face. But his hair, she notices with alarm, fails to cover the tips of his pointed ears. She gapes, skin prickling as she watches the three men ascend the imposing staircase behind Vinge. And after them strides the owner of the icy voice, his already towering frame exaggerated by a top hat and ram-rod back. His black fur-lined cape unfurls behind him like a noxious London fog.

She wills herself to wait until he is out of her sight then drops her paper, stands and heads to the reading room door, unable to think clearly but propelled by an urgent desire to escape.

'Birdie...'

She takes no notice of Solomon, and walks briskly across the oak floorboards of the reception hall, past the moose antlers to the main entrance. She must leave. She cannot stay here. She must have air.

'A minute, Sir.' The steely voice booms after her. She ignores it; she knows she must not turn around. She senses Solomon right behind, his breath hot on her neck.

She hears a sharp command. 'Vinge. Stop those men.'

Solomon reaches the door first and heaves.

'Run,' he whispers. 'Follow me.' He leaps down the steps and sprints across the street. She is relieved to find she can run almost as fast as him. He takes a side alley and another and twists and turns around the labyrinthine streets of the city. They reach a fetid courtyard, hemmed in by dilapidated houses whose upper storeys all but touch across the yard. He stops and leans against a stair-post, panting. The faint gleam of a candle can be seen through a broken pane of glass; otherwise there is only darkness and the ubiquitous whiff of sewage.

'Birdie, I know I said we didn't have time for caution—'

'I'm sorry. It was when I saw Vinge – the ears. That poor mudlarker said the man who dumped Tobias's body had pointed ears.'

'I know. I was going to wait until they had all gone to the Court Room so we could leave without being seen.'

'I couldn't stop myself. When I heard him speak, it froze my marrow.'

'The tall man? He's at all the evening meetings. Do you have any idea who he is?'

'No.' She pauses. 'I didn't see his face. Though I'm sure I've heard his voice before.'

'Perhaps he's been to Standing and Wolff.'

'No. I've told you; he's definitely not the kind of businessman Mr Wolff would entertain.'

'He's not the Governor – that's a man called Pelly and I've seen a portrait of him.'

'He's the Master,' she says with sudden certainty. 'He must be. It's him.'

'Well, it certainly seems quite likely – the bat-eared Vinge is obviously his henchman. We could go and stake out the meeting.'

'Stake out?'

'Watch the front door of Company House. Wait for Vinge or this other man to appear and see where they go. But this time,' he adds, 'it might be better if we stay hidden.'

The brass lamps are still blazing; the meeting not yet over. The costermonger is still squatting on the kerb.

'Back again?' she enquires as they pass.

Solomon smiles, hands her a coin. 'It's your apples, I can't keep away.'

She chucks him another worm-eaten pippin, which he adds to his collection as they search for a suitable vantage point. An alley runs alongside the premises, but it doesn't give them a direct view of the entrance. They return to the costermonger. Solomon offers her a shilling.

'If you see anybody leaving Company House – could you shout *apples*?'

The woman takes the coin, flips it in the air and watches it twirl in the glow of the street lamp before she catches it.

'Sure,' she says.

He tips his bowler in appreciation.

'So long as nobody offers me a higher price,' she adds.

The alley smells of piss and vomit. Birdie is reluctant to lean against the wall. She glances up; the slight breeze has strengthened and cleared the last wisps of fog. The handle of the Plough gleams in the thin indigo strip visible overhead. The temperature is dropping. Solomon stands in front of her, his body tense, ready to run.

'You won't leave me, will you?' She isn't sure whether she is asking about this specific moment, or searching for a broader promise. He twists around, forgoing his surveillance of the street for a moment, and looks as if he is about to say something, but any reassurance he might have offered is cut short by the costermonger's shout.

'Apples. Get yer apples here.'

Solomon flattens himself against the wall, tugs her sleeve and urges her into the shadows next to him. There is a clunk of hurried footsteps and they see a figure whisking past the end of the alley. Vinge. They wait ten seconds before they emerge from the alley, and catch sight of him as he takes a left into Gracechurch Street. They stride behind. He legs it toward Fish Street Hill. They follow at a pace, walking on the opposite side of the street, hugging the walls. Instead of heading to the river, he takes a right onto Lower Thames Street.

'He's cutting across the Steelyard,' Solomon says. 'Stay close to me.'

They track Vinge as he carves a path through the warren of ramshackle premises, ignoring the figures huddled in dark doorways making surreptitious deals or fucking noisily. This neighbourhood is completely lawless. There is a rumour going around the city that a railway company has recently purchased the land but, for now, the warehouses stand empty or have been taken over by sellers of weapons, opium and sex.

'He's heading to Dowgate Hill,' Solomon whispers.

They come to a halt just before they reach the end of an alley. Vinge is ahead, standing in the middle of the road, caught in a puddle of yellow light falling from a street lamp. In front of him, an iron-gated arch. The gate is embedded in a sweeping stone façade, its opulent whiteness still visible through the blanket of London's smut. Behind the arch, a tunnel is lit with blazing lamps dangling from the pale roof and the passage ends in what appears to be an expansive courtyard. London is like this; the wealthy and the powerful exist cheek by jowl with the rotten and the squalid. Here they are, sheltering in the recesses of an opium den, watching a likely murderer go about his business with whoever is wealthy and powerful enough to reside behind that gate.

'Open up.' Vinge shouts. 'I want to speak to the Beadle. I've got a message.'

Beadle? Birdie spots a coat of arms fixed to the top of the gated railings; she squints at the now only too familiar creature on its crest. A lynx. And it dawns on her that they are staring at the Hall of the Worshipful Company of Skinners, and Vinge is shouting for its steward.

'Oi. Where's the bloody Beadle?'

A pale face appears at one of the smaller windows, sitting below the upper pediment.

'Open the fucking window.'

The sash frame creaks. The tired face of a balding, middle-aged man appears. He leans out.

'How can I help you, Sir?'

The Beadle has a Cockney accent, tinged with chippy defiance.

'Are the arrangements for tomorrow in place?'

'Of course. The procession and the Blessing Ceremony at St James Garlickhythe will take about two hours.'

'And they'll be greeted in the courtyard on their return?'

'The courtyard will be open to the public from five.'

'Public?'

'There'll be guards on the door, of course, to stop the riff-raff entering.'

'And the Lord Mayor?'

'He's expected at six. The banquet for the invited guests will start at seven.'

'What about the ceremonial barge?'

'Sir?'

'Is it prepared?'

'The ceremonial barge isn't normally used in the Blessing Ceremony.' The resistance in the Beadle's voice is turning to apprehension; he doesn't like obeying Vinge, though he's nervous about defying him.

'It's been repaired.'

'Indeed, but as I said, Sir, it's not usually used in the Blessing—'

'I'm getting tired of you and your opinions.'

'They're not my opinions, they are the rules—'

'You tried to postpone the bloody ceremony.'

'I agreed to bring forward the election and the Blessing Ceremony from the usual date of the feast of Corpus Christi.'

'Then agree to use the barge. You ought to be more careful about throwing your rule book around. The Master has connections in this city.'

Birdie tries to swallow. Her throat is too parched. She glances at Solomon and he nods. They were right – they've found the Master and his running dog.

'He's the only man ever to be elected to this position for five years in a row,' Vinge continues.

'I'm aware of the exceptional nature of his tenure and I have to say it's an issue which I, in my position as the Beadle, am not entirely happy about.'

'Nobody gives a fuck about your happiness. The barge had better be ready and waiting tomorrow for the use of the Master after the banquet, or else you can forget your position as Beadle cos the only position you'll be holding is face down in the waters of the Walbrook.'

There is a moment of silence while the Beadle decides how to react.

'Very well, Sir,' he says. 'The barge will be ready.'

He forces the sash window shut.

'Oi. I haven't finished with you yet.' Vinge chucks a coin at the window. It misses and drops to the street. 'Your name is going on the Master's blacklist.'

He spins around and for a moment they fear he will retrace his steps through the Steelyard and see them cowering there, but he is too angry to be alert and he stomps away up Dowgate. Birdie waits until he disappears before dashing across the street to collect the dropped coin and retreating to the gloom of the alley. The token sits in her palm, the lines of the etched beaver pelt on its face blurring, her hand trembling too much to hold it steady.

Chapter 21

They return the way they came. The alleys of the Steelyard are bustling; dealers in sex and stolen goods brazenly advertise their wares. Birdie and Solomon keep their eyes fixed firmly forward, quick breaths freezing in the cold night air.

'You can arrest the pair of them now,' she suggests as they leave the Steelyard behind. 'The Master and Vinge.'

He tuts, throws his hands in the air. 'I wish I could, but the Commander would laugh.'

'Why?'

'I have no evidence.'

'The boy on the barge said the canoe paddler had bat-like ears. Vinge has pointed ears.'

'The boy is dead.'

'Well, you heard what Vinge said.'

He checks over his shoulder. 'I didn't hear anybody confess to murder.'

'Vinge said he was adding the Beadle's name to the Master's blacklist.'

'If the Met arrested everybody in London who made vague threats on another man's life, there'd be nobody left on the streets.'

She halts, stock-still, folds her arms, her face crestfallen. She is tired, fed up and afraid.

'Come on, Birdie, don't get down now. The men we're after are in our sights.'

'What do we do now then?'

'Follow the leads and see if they take us to some more substantial evidence.'

'The Filth didn't bother with evidence when they decided I was a suspect in a murder.'

'Birdie, if I stood up in court and declared you were innocent without any evidence, somebody would crawl out of the woodwork and tell the judge that my opinion is worthless because Birdie Quinn is Solomon Finkel's…'

Her heart thumps. He doesn't finish the sentence. She is left wondering what he thinks she is in relation to him, though she has no doubt about the other part of his argument – the accusers creeping from the woodwork. Frank is the person that springs to mind.

'And the judge,' Solomon continues, 'would look at me and think – he's a lying Jew and she's the daughter of an Irish murderer.'

He's right, of course. The courts are no more likely than the river cops to regard her with anything other than a jaundiced eye. She glances at Solomon; square-shouldered, hands in pockets. Is she in love with him? she wonders. He is not thinking about her, though. His mind is on the case.

'We should return to Company House; I assume that's where Vinge is heading. If we hurry, we might be able to catch the Committee members leaving. We can see which way they travel.'

*

Fenchurch Street is empty; the clerks and merchants have all left for the night. The apple-seller has vanished too, undoubtedly to spend the coins she's earned from supplying information to Solomon. But the brass lamps in Company House still blaze. A line of Hansom cabs waits in the street. Solomon and Birdie retreat to the squalid alleyway. Birdie sticks her hands deep in her pockets, trying to keep them warm; the beaver on the roof has shifted and shows the wind is blowing directly from the north. Thankfully, they do not have long to wait. The voice of the Master slices the chilly air.

'Sirs, we shall meet again next week.'

The door of a cab slams shut, the crack of the whip is followed by the clip of hooves. A cab speeds by, heading west. Birdie is about to step out to watch which way it turns, but Solomon pulls her back into the shadows of the alley.

'Wait.'

There are low voices coming from Fenchurch Street. A second cab departs and passes. The conspiratorial murmurs grow louder. Footsteps approach. Two frock-coated Committee members hurry past. Solomon raises an eyebrow.

'Shall we follow?'

Birdie nods; these city gents are unlikely to lead them through the back alleys of the Steelyard. They leave a safe distance and trail them along Fenchurch Street. The two are deep in conversation, top hats almost touching as they march, barely looking where they place their feet, as if it's a route they regularly follow.

Their quarry swivels left into Bell Inn Yard, right along St

Michael's Alley. Solomon drops back, Birdie slows her pace to match. They lose sight of the pair.

'They're heading to Change Alley,' he says.

She's heard of the passage; a cut-through between the Royal Exchange on Cornhill and the post office on Lombard Street. Traders gather there to exchange news and buy and sell their stocks and shares.

'Garraway's Coffee House,' he says. 'The informal office of the Company.'

His homework is thorough, she notes.

'Ready for a warm drink?' he asks.

'Am I dressed for the part?'

'Garraway's hosts all sorts – the rich guzzle champagne. The less successful hang around sipping coffee and hoping to pick up some titbit that will make their fortune.'

Garraway's occupies a corner. The room is dimly lit and the wood panelling dark. The air is fuggy with tobacco and the smell of roasting coffee. The two Committee members are easy enough to spot through the smoke, even though they have seated themselves around a table in a gloomy corner – they have been joined by a youthful dandy who is hard to miss in his carnelian cravat and emerald coat. His voice is as vibrant as his attire. He speaks in an ostentatious whisper and is enjoying the gossip he is sharing with the two older men, along with the champagne bottle that sits in a bucket on the table, from which he regularly fills his glass.

The table beside the trio is empty. Solomon crosses the floor briskly and grabs a seat. Birdie follows. She stares intently at the menu as she listens to the conversation at the neighbouring table.

'How long has Hawkes been Treasurer now?'

'Ages. The shareholders adore him.'

'Hardly surprising; since he's held the position, the value of their dividend has increased ten-fold.'

A waitress approaches Solomon. He orders two coffees.

'Anchovy toast?' he asks Birdie.

She nods, too absorbed in her neighbours' conversation to speak.

'Well, the Hudson's Bay Company does have a monopoly on the fur trade in the Nor' West, so it's hardly surprising the shares have held up well.'

'Yes, but he doesn't take anything for granted. How many other Committee members have ever ventured to Rupert's Land? He's made numerous trips.'

'Ah yes, the field visits to make sure the accounting and management practices are in good order.'

'You sound sceptical.'

'You must've heard the stories about the Company's treatment of the natives.'

'You're suggesting he goes all that way just to torture the aboriginals?'

'That's exactly what I'm suggesting. How else do you think they keep costs down over there?'

'Indeed. There are all sorts of strange rumours circulating about his activities in the Nor' West.' The taller gent glances nervously over his shoulder, then leans in to his colleagues. Birdie strains to hear the whispered conversation.

'I've heard he likes to show off his training in the trade.'

'What trade?'

'Don't you know? His family come from a long line of skinners. That's how he got his foot in the door of their guild. Though I should imagine it took some arm twisting to get himself elected Master five times.' He dabs his mouth with his napkin. 'He's rumoured to demonstrate his skills on... human subjects.'

One of the gentlemen splutters. 'Surely not.'

'I've heard he once displayed the flayed corpses of some recalcitrant native trappers like dead crows on a fence.'

The trio sit back in their chairs, arms folded, momentarily shocked into silence by the details of their own gossip. Birdie stops her face from registering disgust, but cannot prevent the image of a skinned cadaver pinned to an icy tent pole flashing before her eyes.

The dandy is the first to move. He reaches for the champagne, empties the bottle in his glass. 'Well, I doubt whether the Governor of Canada cares too much about the fate of the natives, but he's almost certainly eyeing the Company's monopoly on the fur trade in the Nor' West and wondering why some British company run from London should be allowed to continue extracting the spoils from his doorstep. If the Canadian Governor makes enough fuss, that will be the end of the good times for the Company.'

He swigs the champagne. 'And I'll tell you something else for nothing. Hawkes knows it too. I've heard he's investing heavily in Canadian rail companies. He's stripped Rupert's Land of every skin he can get his hands on. And now he's looking for more pies in which to stick his fingers.'

He drains the last drop of the bubbly.

'Well, gentlemen, thank you for the conversation. It was most illuminating. No doubt we'll meet again tomorrow.' He smirks and adds, 'At Skinners' Hall.'

He pushes his chair back, tips his top hat, swivels and leaves without waiting for his companions' farewells.

The waitress arrives with coffee and anchovy toast. Solomon nudges the plate toward Birdie.

'Eat,' he says.

She shakes her head; she's afraid that if she crunches the toast, she won't be able to eavesdrop on the continuing conversation at the next table.

'Well, it seems as if Hawkes' behaviour is even more reckless in America than it is over here.'

'But the Company's shares keep rising, despite the rumours.'

'Hawkes isn't scared of rumours. He starts them himself. I've lost count of the number of times he's boasted that he knows how to persuade the severest of school matrons to succumb to his charms.'

Birdie gasps and rapidly covers her gaping mouth with her hand.

The waitress presents the gentlemen with a bill. One of them digs in his coat pocket, hands the young girl a note. She bobs and scoots away.

'If his charms are so persuasive, why isn't he married?'

'He was until ten or fifteen years ago when his wife's body was found in the cellar – beaten and mutilated. A botched burglary, the police concluded at the time, as I recall. Maybe he's been too distressed to look for another,' he adds with a scoff.

'With that history, would any father in their right mind hand their daughter to him anyway?'

'If the price was right...'

'Perhaps he's worried that if he takes another wife, he would have to curb the amount of time he spends with prostitutes.'

The other waves his hand dismissively. 'What married gentleman doesn't spend time with prostitutes?'

'Not every gentleman insists that they are barely old enough to dress themselves.'

'I've been told he likes to hear them scream.'

The taller of the city gents stands and brushes his trousers. 'Well, I suppose I shall be attending this Master's Blessing Ceremony tomorrow. No point in getting on the wrong side of Hawkes. Or Vinge.'

'Quite so.'

Birdie watches the two men leave the coffee house and disappear down Change Alley.

Solomon whistles softly.

'So, our man's name is Hawkes, and he's the Treasurer of the Hudson's Bay Company as well as Master of the Skinners.'

She glances around the coffee house; nobody is paying them any attention.

'He is a monster,' she whispers.

He wrinkles his nose. 'I suppose he takes his pick of the young girls before they are packed off to Belgium.'

Birdie pushes the plate of untouched anchovy toast aside. She can't rid herself of the image of Matron's office in her old Rotherhithe school; the queer emblem of the Skinners

CLARE CARSON

dangling from its red ribbon. The silk petticoat. The fur stole.

'He seems to have the whole city in the palm of his hand. Everybody is in thrall to him.'

Solomon nods thoughtfully.

'The Master's Blessing Ceremony,' he says. 'I think we should attend.'

Chapter 22

Margaret shuffles the pile of papers on the office table and creates a snowstorm of dust that shimmers in the low rays of the November sun. She coughs and pats her chest. She's been suffering from a tightness in her lungs ever since Birdie departed. It's the worry; fretting about Birdie, how she'll manage without a book-keeper and, most of all, whether the twins are in danger. She believes Birdie will do her utmost to deal with this shadowy Master without increasing the risks to the bairns. But what can one woman, no matter how strong and canny, do against a powerful man and his mob who maim and kill with impunity?

The baakie lands on the office windowsill and casts a shadow across the flagstones. It stares at her with its unblinking yellow eye and taps the window with the tip of its curved beak as if it has a message for her.

'What are you after?'

She hasn't seen this bird since the day she and Morag helped Birdie escape. She can't help smiling at the memory – Birdie made a handsome young man. She coughs and the black-backed gull flies away. She is reminded then that there is another reason for concern; there is something important she forgot to tell

Birdie. Their last conversation about Tobias had been difficult for her; he had made her promise not to mention the Master to anyone and she'd been afraid that by speaking the Master's name she might immediately invoke his vengeful wrath. Later, after Birdie had sailed, she remembered something else Tobias had said, and she's been worrying about it ever since. There is one person, though, from whom she can seek advice.

Margaret hears the cook talking to the bairns in the parlour, the parrot squawking – repeating their names, making them all laugh. They'll be safe without her for a couple of hours, she decides. She crosses the hall, removes her beloved husband's overcoat from the stand and slips her arms inside. She calls to the cook and tells her she's going to the warehouse. She'll be back for tea she adds, and heads swiftly through the door before the bairns have a chance to ask if they can come with her and buy some sweeties on the way.

She hurries, head down; she has no wish to be waylaid by curious neighbours. Her feet find the path up Brinkie's Brae; she knows the route without looking, though she has not trodden this road for many years. As she reaches the edge of the town, she halts and takes in the familiar view. Slate roofs fall away to the harbour behind her, the breakers pound the plunging cliffs of Hoy ahead. To the north-west, she sees the kirkyard. She averts her eyes from its grey walls and obelisks and looks beyond to the ness, where a puff of smoke twists from Morag's chimney.

Morag sits on the bench outside her croft, as if she is expecting a visitor.

'Margaret, it's good to see you – and good of you to walk this way.'

'You're looking well, Morag.'

'The air's fresher here than in town. Do you want to step in-aboot or sit out here?'

'Here.'

'The kettle has boiled; I'll make a cup of tea.'

Morag stands, offers her the bench. Margaret surveys the garden, the dead heads of the roses, the bare apple trees, the neatly tilled soil of the vegetable patch, the raven pecking at worms. Morag returns with a steaming mug, and they sit in silence for a while, watching waves roll across the sea.

Margaret turns to Morag, observes her craggy features and thinks she is softer than she looks. 'Thank you for tending my family's tombstones.'

Morag shrugs. 'I didn't want townsfolk saying you didn't care for those bairns, when I know the truth is you cared too much.'

'For many years, I've feared that if I visited their graves, I would be so ashamed, I'd never leave.'

'We all end up in the kirkyard eventually. There's no point hastening the journey.' A shadow momentarily darkens the garden; a majestic sea eagle glides past overhead. 'And now you have two more bairns that need you; they're not returning to Labrador, are they?'

Margaret shakes her head. 'I promised Tobias I'd look after them to my dying day, for the poor mother's sake as well as theirs. I'll keep that promise.'

The amber sun touches the waves on the western horizon and carves a golden pathway across the swell.

'Why don't you send the bairns to the school?' Morag asks.

'The Skaills have never done well at school.'

'It would have helped Tobias if he'd learned to read.'

Margaret sips her tea, considers her response. 'It's never held me back.'

She stares resolutely across the headland and waits for Morag to make some scornful comment about her illiteracy, but Morag is silent. Margaret studies the coastline, its cliffs and geos, and finds herself thinking of Donald Shearer's corpse lying in the cove nearby. She tuts. It annoys her that he was able to pull the wool over her eyes. Now that Birdie has gone, she feels exposed again.

'Times have changed,' Morag says eventually. 'All the bairns go to school these days. You're their mother now. You have to overcome your own fears and do what's best for them. Send them to school.' Morag gives her a sideways glance. 'And if you like, I'll teach you how to read and write.'

Margaret feels the heat rising in her cheeks, though she doesn't know why; she was half hoping Morag would offer to help her read.

'Thank you. I'll think about it.'

Margaret observes the raven doing its funny dance; the blackness of its feathers and its pointy beak remind her of Birdie.

'Is there something else that troubles you?' Morag asks.

'Birdie.'

'Oh?'

'There's something I remembered after she left.'

'What's that, then?'

'When Tobias arrived last autumn, he told me he was sailing to London to see what he could do about this man, the Master. He said he had to stop him.'

Morag shakes her head. 'Folk often say Tobias was a bad man because he was always quick to throw a punch. But I think Tobias was a good man who got angry when he saw wrong being done. He didn't always know what to do about it, though; he was too innocent, trusted the wrong people.'

Margaret agrees sadly. 'I'm afraid that's what he did in this case. Tobias said he would find a friend he'd met a while back when he sailed one spring to London, and he'd tell him all about it because he thought he could help.'

'You're afraid this friend wasn't trustworthy?'

Margaret sighs. 'He was a policeman.'

Morag's brow wrinkles. 'A policeman?'

'I'm afraid so.'

'Did he tell you this man's name?'

'No. He said he worked for some part of the new London police force, that was all.'

'The Met?'

'Aye.'

Morag reaches into a pocket, removes a pipe and tin, stuffs the pipe with tobacco, lights it and puffs.

'Birdie is brave and clever. She...' Morag tips her head back, rests it against the wall of the croft. 'She sees things others do not see.'

'Second sight?'

Morag nods. 'She's wise enough to keep her visions to herself.' Morag raises an eyebrow. 'I've plenty of ancestors who paid a high price for having knowledge that the magistrates and ministers thought women should not possess.'

'There were many who were burned,' Margaret says, 'for the crime of being clever. I'm relieved that Birdie has learned to keep her perceptions well hidden,' she continues. 'Though

I'm afraid these gifts are not sufficient to protect against evil men with earthly powers and strong connections. I'm scared she'll walk into a trap. And even if she escapes, she might unwittingly lead this Master back here to the bairns.' She heaves a sigh. 'Sometimes she reminds me of Tobias; she fights her corner, but there's an innocence about her. She trusts the wrong people.'

Morag chews on the stem of her pipe.

'Is there nothing you can do?'

'Birdie has to determine her own path.'

'Surely you know some way to help her and protect the bairns from harm? You could summon the wind.'

Morag squints at the clouds gathering like migrating geese above the Pentland Firth. 'I met a shaman once who kept a snowy owl – it had been abandoned as a chick. He rescued it and raised it and then it refused to leave him. He told me the bird could fetch the snow.' She reaches for her tobacco tin and refills her pipe. 'I could find a way to ask him and his bird to help. Then, at least, it would be difficult for anyone to follow her.'

Margaret folds her arms, rests back against the croft wall while she considers Morag's suggestion. 'It would ease my mind somewey,' she says.

Morag nods and, as she does so, the raven caws, flaps its wings and catches a gust of wind. Margaret watches as it flies north-west across the ness. 'Sometimes the old ways are still useful,' she says.

Chapter 23

She rolls over on Solomon's straw mattress and gazes at him lying on the far side of the garret room, a thin blanket pulled up around his chin. He is already awake and watching her. She flushes, aware of the intensity of his gaze, the closeness of his presence. Being with him here these last few days has reminded her that she has more in common with him than she's ever had with any of Frank's pals. Including her husband. She came to London in search of the truth about the murder of Tobias and, to her surprise, discovered something else: she's in love with Solomon. The feeling has been there all along, she realizes now, coiled quietly in a corner like a sleeping cat. There are many things about him which she doesn't know, yet she is more attracted to his mystery than the familiar certainties of Patrick. Still, there is one question about him that bothers her: what are his feelings for her? She sees desire in his eyes, but she cannot be sure it is for her. He wants to prove her innocence, yet is that to save her, or to prove his worth to his colleagues in the Met? He's said nothing about the letter from Patrick, and she can only read his silence as affirmation of her own conclusion that the right thing to do is return to her husband.

He stands, brushes his crumpled clothes, walks across the room to the mattress, kneels beside her, their faces level, and gazes into her eyes. For a moment, she thinks he is going to say something about the letter. Her. Them. He blinks and sits back on his heels.

'So far, all we have is hearsay,' he says. 'Overheard conversations and rumours. We still need to find some evidence that connects Vinge and his Master to the murders. It shouldn't be difficult to slip into this Blessing Ceremony reception tonight – the Beadle said it was open to the public, even if there will be guards on the door. We'll see what information we can pick up there.'

She stares into the mid-distance, her eyes watering, searching for the answers to her questions. He leans over and tenderly wipes a stray tear with his thumb.

'We'll nail them, don't worry.'

She wants to say I was crying because I don't want to leave you. Instead she laughs and says she might not be admitted to the Master's reception at the Skinners' Hall in her badly fitting reefer jacket and her red knitted cap.

'You can borrow a suit and coat of mine,' he says.

Solomon spends the day in Scotland Yard, going about his usual business, whatever that may be. She spends the day alone and anxious. He returns in the late afternoon with a beef and stout pie, which they share. He dresses in his best suit, overcoat and bowler. He gives her a threadbare black wool coat, trousers, blue cravat and an old top hat. Everything is too big – she has to secure the trousers with a belt and roll the sleeves of the jacket. The hat keeps slipping over the bridge of her nose and it smells musty. Solomon insists she should wear it.

'I'll stand out in this attire,' she says.

'There'll be plenty of people. We'll be able to hide in the crowd.'

She hopes he's right.

He points at the truncheon lying in a corner. 'Though I doubt whether I could get away with taking that.' He frowns, reaches for a candle and a box of matches instead, and drops them in a jacket pocket. 'But I'll take these.'

'Why?'

'Just in case.'

'Out on the town tonight, are we?' the pieman shouts as they leave.

Solomon waves his hand at him in an ambiguous gesture that could either be interpreted as a friendly greeting or an encouragement to piss off.

'Don't stay out too late.'

They turn into Whitehall, busy with gents wearing frock coats and an air of importance. The chill wind is blowing from the north and the temperature is plummeting with the dwindling light.

'It smells like snow,' she says as they reach Trafalgar Square, weaving between the couples heading for the theatre and the cabs plying for trade.

Solomon surveys the sky from below the brim of his bowler. Starlings swoop in ribbons around Nelson's Column.

'All I can smell is soot.'

She points beyond the National Gallery; the north wind has brought with it a layer of flat, steely clouds. 'Snow.'

'In November?'

She squints; she thinks she can see a vast bird of prey hovering above the gallery's cupola. She must be mistaken. 'Do you see that bird?'

'The crow?'

'It's a white owl.'

He shakes his head. 'I can't see it. But I think you're right about the clouds.'

She looks again and the owl has vanished, though it leaves her with a peculiar feeling. Fear? Excitement? Determination?

'The Master hasn't picked the best night for a barge trip along the Thames,' she says.

'I doubt he's the kind of man to let a bit of snow get in the way of his self-congratulation.'

The bells of St Martin's toll the half hour. They head toward the Strand.

Dowgate Hill is alive with the whinny of horses, the crack of whips and drivers shouting obscenities as cabs and carriages compete for the kerbside in front of the Skinners' Hall. Vinge expected a large crowd and here it is; the street is a riot of gentlemen in fancy jackets, cravats and tall hats, accompanying ladies in silk dresses, velvet capes and ringlets. The wealthy of London are flocking to the reception, despite the coldness of the night.

A pair of guards in red coats and velvet fur-trimmed caps stand either side of the archway, each holding a silver staff in one hand. They are not asking attendees for invitations, though they give everybody the once over as they pass, to check they look the part. No paupers or street-walkers allowed. Solomon and Birdie slip behind a rotund gentleman with his arm around the waist of a pretty woman overflowing from a blue taffeta gown. The guards are too busy eyeing her to take much notice of them as they approach.

'Please wait in the courtyard to greet the Master's procession when it returns from the church.' The red-capped guard indicates the archway with his hand. The silver lynx affixed to the brim of his cap glimmers in the glow of the street lamp. They stroll through the passage and into the grand white-walled courtyard. Guests mingle and lift wine glasses from the laden salvers butlers carry as they weave around the throng. Birdie takes a glass and sips warily, afraid lest the wine goes to her head; she wants to stay alert.

She surveys the crowd, searching to see if she recognizes anybody here. It's hard to distinguish faces in the melee; the light is dim, with only the lamps from the archway glowing. She thinks she spots the two black-coated men they followed to Garraway's Coffee House the previous evening, but she can't be sure – there are so many city gents here. She finds herself wondering how many of these guests have heard the rumours about Hawkes. Most of them, she supposes, given the conversation she overheard in Garraway's; it must be common coffee house gossip. Though it doesn't stop them gathering to celebrate his re-election as Master of the Skinners. London's wealthy and on-the-make are prepared to ignore the stories, either because they are too scared to do otherwise or because they profit from his ventures. She turns her head and, in the corner of her eye, catches sight of an elderly gentleman who looks remarkably like Mr Wolff. When she looks again he has disappeared in the throng. She must have been mistaken; Mr Wolff would not be here. He is far too well established to curry favours with the likes of Hawkes.

As she peers around the shadowed faces, she detects a rustle of interest among the guests standing nearest the entrance. A name is whispered. *Mr Dickens.* She cranes her neck and spies a dainty gentleman, his top hat perched at a jaunty angle and his hair and wispy beard quite dark against the peacock blue of his coat. His face is lined – perhaps the gloom of the courtyard exaggerates the shadows – though his darting eyes radiate lively amusement. He has a lady on his arm. She gasps: surely, that's Lady Franklin. It's hardly surprising she's here, along with the rest of London society, yet Birdie finds it hard not to interpret her presence as a sign; Tobias wasn't murdered in the race to claim the reward for information about Franklin, but her own fate is still in some way entwined with the disappearance of his ship and crew. Birdie studies Franklin's ageing widow, her brown ringlets falling like the petals of an autumnal rose around her fine-boned face, and she feels a sudden stab of guilt. Lady Franklin spent years searching for her husband only to be informed he'd died in the frozen wastes. Birdie believed her husband to be dead and yet the discovery that he is alive and living in St Petersburg hasn't filled her with joy, as it should have done. As it would have done if she were like Lady Franklin. Indeed, her heart sank a little when she read Patrick's letter. Birdie glances at Solomon; his gaze is elsewhere. Lady Franklin's presence here is, Birdie feels, a sobering reminder that she made a promise to be Patrick's loyal and faithful wife. She cannot waver and simply ignore her own vows.

The heavy peal of St James Garlickhythe announces the end of the Blessing Ceremony. The Master and his procession will arrive any minute; it's a short walk from the church to the

Skinners' Hall. The atmosphere in the courtyard is expectant, almost fearful.

One of the guards shouts, 'Stand aside for the Master of the Worshipful Company of the Skinners and the members of his court.'

A ripple spreads through the crowd as guests turn toward the archway. To her surprise, she hears the clip of hooves. The first figure to emerge through the arch is a mounted constable; he has to duck under the hanging lamps. The white horse whinnies and dances, nostrils flaring, skittish in the confined space. The copper on horseback is followed by another uniformed figure; she stiffens when she sees the flat cap and navy jacket. It's an officer of the Thames Division. What's more, she realizes with creeping horror as she throws the river cop a second glance, there is something familiar about his imposing form. She glances over her shoulder at Solomon; his face registers alarm. He tilts his head almost imperceptibly, beckoning her into the shadows of the cloister to one side of the courtyard. She edges after him.

'Superintendent Lynch,' he whispers.

It's as bad as she feared: Lynch is the officer in charge of Wapping Station. The cop who removed Tobias Skaill's corpse from the foreshore of the Thames. She has an urge to run, but she stands her ground.

'What's he doing here?'

'I suppose he's here as a representative of the Met.' He says it casually, though his downturned mouth betrays concern. 'The bloke on the horse is from the City Police.'

She stands on her toes and spies a priest in red, another in black. Behind them, a towering figure enters alone. The guests fall back as he strides across the courtyard. His silver hair is visible below a black velvet hat, a fur-edged cape is draped from his square shoulders and, attached to his belt, he carries a knife in a leather sheath. His eyes sweep the courtyard and send a shiver down her spine. It is the Master. She strains to get a better view of his face, catches sight of the Skinners' crest dangling on its red ribbon around his neck and recalls the same crest dangling across the desk of Matron's office. She blanks the image and focuses on the procession; a muster of black-cloaked men enter, each of them displaying a ribbon attached to the crest of the Skinners. The Master's retinue brandish flaming torches in the air as they pour silently through the archway. The flames leap and dive in the north wind, glazing the white walls with a blood-red sheen and casting ominous shadows on the torchbearers' faces. These guards seem more like soldiers in an army than participants in a ceremonial procession and the audience can feel their menace; a wave of fear washes over the faces of the spectators, and those standing closest to the torchbearers shuffle back as the procession fills the courtyard.

Vinge appears; he weaves and dives, deterring anybody who steps out of line with an intimidating lunge. The red-caped Beadle enters the courtyard last. He raises a staff in his hand, brings its end down on the paving stones with a resounding crack. The crowd is silent. The only sound to be heard is the crackle of the torches burning.

'Ladies, gentlemen.' The Beadle speaks slowly, as if he's finding it difficult to articulate the words. 'It is my honour to introduce the recently re-elected Master of the Worshipful Company of the Skinners.'

Vinge shouts, 'A toast to the Master.' Superintendent Lynch seconds the call.

'To the Master's health and prosperity,' Vinge cries.

The guests raise their glasses obediently. Another voice interrupts and the steeliness of his pitch silences any chatter. 'Ladies and gentlemen.'

Birdie cannot see the speaker, but she recognizes the Master's voice immediately. His chilling tone is amplified in the courtyard. His words boom around the walls and echo in her head. The noise disorients her and sends her spiralling through her memories, searching for another time and place where she stands and hears him speak. Solomon nudges her, snaps her out of the turmoil and brings her back to the crowded courtyard.

'A few words,' the Master says. 'Thank you, good ladies and gentlemen, for braving the cold and coming to this celebration. Thank you to the warden, the court members and the representatives of the City and Thames Police.'

She twists and sees the constable, who has now dismounted and is attempting to calm his horse.

'Thank you, in particular, to Superintendent Lynch for leading, yet again, the Master's Blessing Ceremony and Procession.'

He's got the Filth in his pocket as well as half the city. She shudders, suddenly overwhelmed by the spread of the Master's reach.

She shuffles around as the Master continues his oration. Finally, she has a full view of his colourless face; heavy grey brows above his icy eyes, and a thin, sneering mouth.

'As you all know, this livery company began many centuries ago as a guild to protect and support those men who made their living by skinning creatures.'

A shiver runs through the crowd; the guests were expecting him to gloss over the nature of the Skinners' trade; it's really not their concern. He surveys his captive audience and she suspects he's enjoying their discomfort.

'Skinning creatures in a way that best preserves the pelt,' he continues, 'is a skill that requires years of training and experience to perfect. Particularly if the mammal to be skinned is large and the skin is...' He pauses and she feels his gaze scour her cheek. Scared, she drops her eyes and sees his hand grip the handle of his knife. 'Particularly if the skin is pale and delicate,' he continues. She daren't look up, though she can sense that his predatory glare has moved on. 'And while few of the good people assembled here today are trained in the art of skinning, many of you will have accrued wealth from companies that are dependent on the trade.'

He's warning his guests, she thinks, reminding them that rumours might well swirl around him, but none of them can afford to gloat because they all have dirty hands. Nobody looks at their neighbour.

'Of course, while some members of this Worshipful Company are expert skinners, their welfare is no longer the sole purpose of the guild. The Skinners now spread their benevolence more widely and offer charity to many individuals and institutions. It is through the benevolence, generosity and Christian virtue of the members of the guild that we are able to prevent the poor and needy of this great city of ours falling into a tragic life of vice and crime.'

Applause rumbles around the courtyard; city gents may gossip about the Master's activities behind his back, but none dares demur in his presence.

'Among the many good causes we are able to support, I would like to mention in particular our orphanage for young girls in Bermondsey and, of course, the excellent St Edward's boarding school in Rotherhithe for the children of those who have perished at sea.'

St Edward's? He gestures toward a figure at the back of the courtyard. Heads swivel. She follows the crowd's gaze and does a double-take because she is certain they are looking toward her one-time school matron. Older, of course. But still recognizable. And her smug expression reminds Birdie of the look she had on her face the day she discovered Birdie in her office. What was it Matron said? One day she'd meet somebody who would teach her the meaning of obedience, even if he had to beat her black and blue to do it.

Solomon whispers, 'St Edward's. Isn't that where…'

She shakes her head. Her mind is foggy. This ceremony is all wrong. It's dredging up her past, feeding her glimpses of people and places she half recognizes or remembers. Mr Wolff. Matron. And the Master himself. His voice. What is it about his voice? She can't tell whether she's heard it in an apparition or in real life. Is there any difference? She sways.

'Are you all right?' Solomon whispers.

She nods; she does not trust herself to speak.

The Master has finished his speech.

'Ladies and gentlemen,' the Beadle shouts from his position by the open doors. 'There are more refreshments in the reception hall where you might like to gather for half an hour or so. The Lord Mayor, I believe, intends to bless us with his company for the main banquet.'

At the mention of the Lord Mayor, there is a murmur among the guests. This is what they came here for; a chance to hob-nob with the city's big men. The gents in top hats and their lady companions drift toward the reception. Vinge follows behind, herding people in the direction of the hall.

'Should we leave now?' Birdie whispers. She's had enough, afraid she's being lured into a trap set with her own peculiar memories.

'Let's go inside for a while,' Solomon says, 'and leave when the banquet starts.'

She hesitates, then resolves to stick with Solomon, and see this through.

'Does Lynch know your face?' she asks.

Solomon rubs his lip with his hand; he is sweating despite the cold. 'I've seen him when I've been out and about around the docks. I doubt he knows I'm a detective. We'll stay away from Lynch, but keep an eye on Vinge.'

They lag behind the crowd. The Beadle is still holding the door, his staff firmly planted on the parquet inside the hall. He stares fixedly ahead, but speaks out the side of his mouth to one of the butlers, who holds a salver of empty glasses. Birdie pauses at the entrance to retrieve a handkerchief and blow her nose while she eavesdrops on their conversation.

'All that fuss about the barge. And guess what? It's been so cold today, the Thames has frozen at the banks. I had to give the oarsmen a quick nip of brandy to warm them. Unfortunately, it might have gone to their heads, cos when they tried to steer the barge under London Bridge, they managed to ram it into one of the arches.' His mouth twitches. 'So now there's a gaping hole in the hull and it can't be used.'

'Is the Master upset?'

'He's fucking livid.' His assertion is tinged with a mixture of defiance and fear. 'Him and his slimy mate Vinge.'

Birdie blows her nose; the Beadle notices her presence.

'Well, the procession went according to plan,' the Beadle continues in a loud voice, 'and I expect the reception and banquet will be a great success too.'

She replaces the handkerchief in her pocket, and searches for Solomon. Across the hall, a set of double doors leads into the banqueting chamber. Overhead, a vast chandelier hangs; the crystal drops on the upper tiers stir in the heat from the lower candles and jangle, like ghostly champagne glasses chinking. Solomon is on the far side, leaning against a cabinet, his back to a wall of mahogany panelling. She makes her way over and slouches beside him. The cabinet against which Solomon leans is full of knives of assorted shapes and sizes; thin sharp blades – like the one she spotted at the orphanage, curved and pointed cutters, serrated and half-moon scrapers. Skinners' tools. She recalls the story of the Master flaying native trappers who disobeyed his orders, and the strange lust in his gaze as he stared at her cheek and spoke about skinning large mammals. Her flesh crawls.

'The Beadle,' she whispers to Solomon, 'isn't happy.'

Solomon nods. He is listening but his eyes are on the room, watching Vinge and the Master. She looks for Lynch; he is obvious in his copper's uniform. He has a glass in his hand and seems to be primarily interested in chatting up young ladies. She notices several women eyeing Solomon coquettishly. She raps her knuckle against the panelling behind her, irritated by their glances.

'Odd. Sounds hollow.' She taps the panelling again. 'These old buildings often have a priest hole.'

Her musing is interrupted by the Beadle; he bangs his staff on the parquet. 'The Right Honourable the Lord Mayor of London.'

The Lord Mayor sweeps in, his diminutive figure swathed in black silk and gold trimmings – his Entertaining Robe. Vinge makes a beeline for him and escorts him through the crowds.

'He's the Admiral of the Port of London,' Solomon whispers. 'Docks, wharves, any new building or rule changes have to pass through him.'

'No wonder the Master is keen to bend his ear.' She straightens herself and glimpses the figure of the Master towering over the Lord Mayor, his hand firmly clasped around his shoulder. 'Or twist his arm,' she adds.

'Beadle.' The Master's voice cuts through the chatter of the guests. 'Fetch the Cockayne Cup and the cap.'

The Beadle leaves his post beside the door, makes his way through the guests clutching their wine glasses, enters the banqueting hall, and returns carrying a statuette of a silver cockerel – the Cockayne Cups she supposes – and a black cap. The Beadle hands the cockerel to the Master. He lifts its head and holds the decapitated body out to a butler, who fills the peculiar cup with red wine. The Beadle leans over the Lord Mayor and whispers in his ear. The Lord Mayor hesitates, then removes his tri-cornered hat to reveal a large freckled bald patch. The Beadle winces at the sight of it. Birdie feels a twinge of pity for the Lord Mayor, belittled by the Master's ceremony; there's nothing he can do except play along. The Beadle places the black cap he has retrieved from the banqueting hall at an ungainly angle on the exposed scalp of the Lord Mayor.

'Does the cap fit?' he bellows.

'No,' the crowd replies. Some of them titter.

This is a ritual, Birdie supposes, with which everybody is familiar apart from her and Solomon; the other guests are undoubtedly regular attendees at the guild halls of London. The Beadle removes the cap from the Lord Mayor. The Master has already removed his own hat to reveal a full mane of silver hair and the sharpness of his features. The Beadle has to stand on tiptoes to place the black cap on Hawkes' head; the Master refuses to stoop. He and Lynch, Birdie reckons, are the tallest men in the room.

'Does the cap fit?' the Beadle demands.

'Yes.' The Master's commanding voice leads the chorus. There are cheers. The Master swigs from the Cockayne Cup. 'Let the banquet commence.'

He swings his arm to indicate the way to the banqueting hall and as his eyes sweep the room, she is sure his gaze lingers on her face, the skin of her cheek. The guests edge toward the open doors, eager to find their places at the table. The Lord Mayor shuffles after them, his dignity battered.

The Master remains behind to have a quiet word with Vinge, who bobs around the Master's side and then, alarmingly, heads in their direction. Birdie swivels to face Solomon. They bow toward each other, as if deep in conversation, hoping that Vinge is not homing in on them. He isn't. But because their backs are turned to the hall, they are unable to see which way he goes. As the room empties, they look around in puzzlement. The last of the guests enter the banqueting hall. The reception hall is deserted and quiet, apart from the chink of the chandelier which gently sways as if it has been buffeted by a breeze, and the Beadle, who is ogling them from the other side of the room. He lifts a hand in greeting, and advances.

'Hold your nerve,' Solomon whispers.

'Evening, Sirs. Not attending the banquet?'

'No, no, we came for the reception, that's all. We'll be on our way now.'

'Weren't looking for somebody was you, Sir?' He sounds more nervous than threatening.

'No. No. Interested in the Master's Blessing Ceremony, that's all.'

'Oh, I thought you might be after that bloke Vinge.' The Beadle raises an eyebrow. 'I saw you eyeing him up earlier.'

'Ah.' Solomon hesitates, assessing the Beadle's face.

'Don't worry, Sir, he ain't no friend of mine.'

Birdie reckons he's scared, but straightforward. Solomon reaches the same conclusion. 'Well, actually, I was looking for him,' he says. 'Vinge owes me quite a large sum of money.'

'Does he now? Don't surprise me.'

'Are you well acquainted with him?' Solomon dips his hand in his pocket, produces a coin.

The Beadle waves his hand. 'No need, Sir.' He glances over his shoulder. 'I'm happy to tell you what I know. Shady character, I'm afraid.'

'Is he from around here?'

'Yes, Sir. Not a good family. His father was a well-known fraudster, and Vinge Junior is a chip off the old block. Ended up going to sea to get away from it all. And for a while it looked like he might have set himself on the straight and narrow – working on the whalers and the timber ships. He even managed to get himself on the crew of one of those ships that went to the Arctic to search for Franklin. But he must have done something wrong because he had trouble getting another job after he returned to London. Dragging that tin canoe of his with him.'

Birdie's eyes widen.

'What year was that?' Solomon asks.

'Must have been '52. A year or so after Hawkes was first elected to the office of the Master.'

'And now Vinge is always with Hawkes?'

'Not all the time, Sir. Vinge comes and goes. Hawkes likes to keep a close eye on trade across the Atlantic, so I've been told. He's a busy man; he's Treasurer of the Hudson's Bay Company as well,' the Beadle adds.

Solomon nods. 'He's acquainted with the fur trade in America then?'

'Indeed, Sir. Sometimes Hawkes goes over there himself, as I understand it. But usually Vinge goes and does his business for him. He sails with one of their supply ships.'

'The *Lynx*?' Birdie volunteers.

The Beadle throws her a sideways glance.

'That's the one. The *Lynx*. The ship sets off in early spring with its trading goods and supplies and returns in the autumn. Vinge is usually hanging around London for the best part of the winter, unfortunately. Give or take a few weeks here and there.'

'Well, thank you for your help, Sir. I don't suppose you have any idea where he might have gone? He seems to have vanished into thin air.'

'Ah. Not thin air at all, Sir. Let me show you.' He walks along the panelling, reaches the end, gives the mahogany a sharp shove with his shoulder and a panel swings open. A wave of stinking gas rushes into the room. The chandelier swings and clinks. 'Sorry, Sir, you'll have to be quick, else everyone will smell it.'

'Secret passage?'

'The Walbrook,' he says. 'Runs underneath Skinners' Hall. Direct route to the Thames. There's steps down to the water.'

'Is it deep?'

'Not any more. One of our lads – apprentice – fell in and was drowned, God rest his soul. They closed it in after that. It's more of a sewer these days. People chuck all sorts down there. You'll have to watch where you're putting your feet. If you're lucky, it'll be frozen.'

'Well, thank you for your help, Sir.'

'My pleasure.' He glances over his shoulder again, taps the side of his nose. 'I won't say nothing, Sir.'

The Beadle closes the panel behind them, leaving them with the darkness and foul odour. Solomon manages to light the wick of the candle he brought with him; the flame bends in the sluggish air. It is not so much a tunnel, or even a sewer. More an underworld. The ceiling is formed by the foundations, joists and slabs of the buildings and pavements that have been constructed, piece by piece, over the narrow culvert of what was once an open river. She feels a sadness for the poor Walbrook, reduced to a shit pit for the overcrowded tenements above. They descend the slimy steps cautiously. Trapped air creates eerie sighs and draughts. The thickness of the miasma increases with every step; she covers her mouth and nose with her hand to stop herself from gagging.

Solomon reaches the bottom and tests the surface of the putrid water.

'Frozen.'

He holds the candle high, and its dim light falls on a long, gently gleaming vessel resting on the bottom of the ditch; the tin canoe sits among the rubble, tethered to an iron ring in the wall.

'You said it was made by the gypsies in Stromness?' Solomon asks.

She nods.

He stoops to take a closer look.

'I can see their mark – a moon and a star.'

'What do you think it's doing here?'

'I should imagine Vinge has abandoned it; he must have decided it's too risky to take it out on the Thames. He's already used it to dump two bodies. If not more.' He stands and the light from his candle glints on the icicles hanging from the beams and flagstones above. The stalactites are different shades – white, pale green, brown and yellow. She doesn't like to think from what dripping substances the shards are formed.

'The river can't be far,' he says. 'I assume that's where he went. We'd better see if we can catch up with him.'

The broken kegs, rags, cracked chamber pots and other unidentifiable items strewn along the sewer's course turn out to be a blessing, as they provide footholds in the frozen surface of the ditch. They edge their way along, Birdie trying to maintain her balance while keeping her nose covered with one hand. A gust of cold air moans, rushes past and unsteadies them. She trips on a pewter tankard, its handle protruding from the ice.

'I'm surprised the mudlarkers haven't picked this drain clean.'

'Perhaps they're aware of its dangers.' Solomon directs the candle's light over a pile of grey bones and a skull lying in the bottom of the gutter. 'I suspect there's more than one apprentice boy drowned in these shallows.'

She is relieved to sense a stronger breeze and catch the glitter of lamps on water ahead; they are nearing the river. Solomon extinguishes the candle. They feel their way to the tunnel's end and lower themselves over the culvert's lip to the foreshore. The temperature has plummeted even in the hour they have been standing inside the Skinners' Hall. She blows on her un-gloved hands to warm them. The river's edge is frozen; the icy mud gleams against the black of the free-flowing tide. Above, the sulphuric glow of London's gas lamps is reflected in a low blanket of heavy cloud. The snow is coming. Directly ahead, the Skinners' ceremonial barge rests forlornly on the sludge, its stoved-in hull emblazoned with the livery's crest. A solitary cormorant croaks as it flies upstream and Birdie's eye is drawn beyond the barge to the skiff wheedling around the ships anchored midstream.

'Vinge.' She points. 'He's heading to the Surrey side.'

Vinge finds a path around the vessels, locates clear water and noses across the swift currents of mid-river. She can just make him out as he drags the rowing boat onto the far embankment, climbs a flight of wooden stairs and disappears inside one of the wooden warehouses that line the shore.

She tries to identify the premises. 'Horseshoe Wharf. Winchester Wharf. Clink Wharf,' she says. 'That's where he's gone. Clink Wharf. I've heard the rumours about that place

– it used to be owned by a corn merchant, but then he died and nobody knows who bought it. People say it's been left deserted and the purchaser is a speculator, waiting for the right moment to sell. It's all boarded up on the Borough side. You can't enter it from the street.'

Solomon removes his bowler, strokes the top of his head with his free hand and frowns.

'Do you think you can make your way back to my lodgings by yourself? I have a key, you can let yourself in.'

'Why, where are you going?'

'Clink Wharf.'

'I'll come with you.'

He scratches the back of his neck.

'Vinge might be armed.'

She notices a movement on the far side of the river.

'It doesn't matter. Look. He's leaving. I wonder what he was delivering.'

'A message most likely. I should imagine he'll return this way and report back to the Master at the banquet.'

'We can't follow him back there now. We were lucky to leave without attracting the attention of anyone apart from the Beadle.'

'I'm not suggesting that…'

Birdie isn't listening. She is slipping and stumbling in the direction of London Bridge.

'Where are you going?'

She stops and turns. 'I was going to see if that boat you borrowed yesterday is still tied up by Billingsgate Stairs. We can row it across and use the riverside stairs. We'd better hurry, we don't want Vinge to spot us.'

Away from the wolfish gaze of the Master, she has regained her courage and determination. Solomon hesitates for a moment, glances at Vinge heading to the north side of the river, replaces his bowler, and follows her along the frozen bank.

Chapter 24

The Thames is solidifying, the slurry mingles with the river's waters and tinges the ice dirty yellow. The river's banks are perilous in the dark and it takes them a good half hour to make their way downstream and locate the dinghy. They skid and slide as they manoeuvre the boat into the water and clamber aboard. A snowflake falls on her cheek. She tips her head back and sees the night sky is full of twirling flakes that settle and glisten on the grungy timbers of the river's boats. This is strange snow, she thinks; it has none of the grittiness of London's usual winter falls.

Solomon pulls hard on the oars to clear the lighters anchored around Billingsgate Wharf. The freezing of the Thames's banks goads the currents midstream; the water runs wild and fast, trying to escape the grip of the ice. He steers through the arches of London Bridge. Overhead, carriages rumble and cabbies shout. She checks over her shoulder, listens for the splash of oars.

'There's no sign of a duty boat.'

'So long as Lynch is busy enjoying himself at Skinners' Hall,' Solomon says, 'there won't be anybody at Wapping urging the officers to go out on the river.'

He uses his oar to push away from the bridge and the prow noses toward the Surrey side.

'The Master has the Filth in his pocket,' she says.

Solomon makes no reply. He shifts in his seat and looks past her at the receding bridge.

Nothing moves on the foreshore below Clink Wharf. The muddy bank is free of vessels as if the regular users of the river know it's wise to steer clear from this stretch of waterfront. They struggle to heave the rowing boat ashore; the snow is falling thickly now and the strengthening wind whips it into blinding flurries. She surveys the wooden warehouse, flat against the river's edge, windows boarded and clinkered timbers skimmed with white. It appears to be empty, but it's hard to tell. At least they know that whatever else is waiting for them inside, it's not Vinge.

'Birdie, please take the boat and go back to the lodging house.'

She inhales the snow-filled air. 'I'm coming with you. I want to find out what Vinge and the Master are up to.'

He looks downstream. 'It's not going to be savoury.'

'I don't care.'

The ceremony at the Skinners' Hall has left her with the unsettling feeling that her past is entwined with the Master's; it's too late to escape the unravelling memories.

He gazes at her briefly; his eyes are watering, though it could just be the cold. He checks the river once more; no sign of the Filth. They ascend the wooden steps to the warehouse door, breaking the crust of the settled snow, half an inch deep already. He twists the handle. The door gives. Perhaps Vinge forgot to lock it when he left. Or else they are expected. He glances over his shoulder at Birdie and she nods. He steps inside and she follows into the darkness. There is an overwhelming smell of mustiness; it's similar to the strange odour in Company House, though much fiercer here. And, this time, she recognizes it – skins. It's as if they are buried alive under a pile of dead animals.

'Light the candle,' she whispers.

'Don't bother.'

She freezes. It's not Solomon's voice.

'I have a lamp.'

A match is struck, the flame hovers in the air, lights a wick and reveals the outline of the hefty man holding the lamp; his tatty trousers and jacket barely cover his dark-skinned limbs. A one-time voyageur perhaps, or a trapper who has escaped the harshness of the Nor' West and ended up a servant of the Master. Behind him and all around the warehouse there are stacks of pelts of all shades – mink, sable, bear, seal, otter, beaver – compressed and corded. And piled in-between the bales are crates – some cracked open to reveal bottles of rum, armaments, the glint of gold and silver. Clink Wharf must be a holding point, a place where the Master's spoils are stored before being sold for profit. A double dividend; he loots the Company that pays his salary and fiddles the books so well he manages to keep the shareholders happy. She casts her eye over his bounty and jumps; a pair of bare feet stick out from behind a bale of fur, the ankles slender and the skin bruised and waxy. A corpse. A girl abducted from the orphanage, she fears, who didn't even make it as far as Belgium.

'I was warned I might have visitors,' the watchman says.

He rests the lamp on the nearest bale and raises the club he was holding at his side. There is a leisureliness to the way he swings it which suggests he would have no trouble knocking the pair of them for six, but has no particular desire to do so. Not yet anyway.

'Who warned you?' Solomon asks. 'Vinge?'

The watchman says nothing. Birdie's head is filled with the thump of her heart. And another sound; the crunch of footsteps on the warehouse stairs.

'Why don't you ask him yourself?' the watchman says.

The door scrapes open. She turns and sees Vinge enter; he must have followed them across the river unseen. He is not alone. As Vinge steps toward them, the Master slips in behind and leans against the warehouse door, hand on the knife at his belt. They are hemmed in now; the watchman on one side, Vinge on the other, the Master blocking the exit. They've walked into a trap.

'What do you two want?' Vinge asks.

The Master seems content to allow his henchman to deal with this. He says nothing, though his eyes sweep over Birdie, and linger on her cheek.

'I heard this wharf was on the market,' Solomon says. 'We came to have a look.'

'Oh right,' Vinge says. 'Just like you was interested in looking around Company House, and the Master's banquet in Skinners' Hall?'

Solomon raises an eyebrow, but makes no reply.

'The Beadle told you how to find me, did he?'

Still Solomon says nothing.

'I don't know why you thought he was trustworthy. It only took a couple of kicks to make him squeal. He told me you was after some money I owe you, apparently.'

As Vinge speaks he raises his hands; he is clutching a

length of rope. He yanks it tight; the snap echoes around the warehouse.

'I hope you haven't added the Beadle to your list of corpses, Mr Vinge.'

'What's it to you, Jew boy? You and your...' he glances at Birdie, 'little mate here. What is it exactly you're after?'

He advances. Birdie instinctively backs away, takes a step between two bales of fur. Solomon edges in front, so he is between her and Vinge. But before Vinge can move any closer, the Master intervenes.

'Out the way.'

He marches over to Solomon, prods him in the chest.

'I've had enough of this. I've had to leave my banquet to sort this out.'

If Solomon replies she doesn't hear him, for a fluttering has made her glance down and she's spotted something small and yellow in a cage, behind her on the floorboards. A canary, old and bedraggled. She leans over to take a closer look. It has two black feathers adorning its crest. She squints at the bird, huddled on its perch. Is it possible? She's heard stories of canaries that have lived eighteen years and, anyway, she's sure she's right. It is the Little Prince, Da's prized Harz Roller. Without thinking, she whistles the familiar melody, the tune Da taught her so the birds would recognize her presence. The little canary replies with a sweet chirping that fills her with joy.

'Lord,' the watchman says, 'in all the years I've looked after that bird I've never heard it sing.'

The canary concludes its melody with an enchanting trill. There's a moment of silence, followed by pandemonium as the

Master barges forward, shoves Solomon aside, grabs Birdie by the lapels of her jacket and drags her from her hiding place between the bales of fur.

'You,' he shouts in her face. And finally, she remembers where she's heard the Master's voice before.

'I thought I recognized your face when I saw you lurking in the shadows of the courtyard.'

She feels his steely eyes settling on her cheek again. There is something carnal about his gaze and it repulses her, as it did all those years ago the first time they met. He knocks her hat off and shakes her viciously.

'What are you doing here? I was hoping Lynch would have you dangling from a noose by now. Look at you, dressed like a boy, running around picking up any man you can find.' He flicks his hand in Solomon's direction. 'I should have known better. Even that bloody bird of your father's turned out to be useless.'

She feels dizzy. Her head spins and she's back in Southwark, ten years old, fleeing the sight of Da dangling from the gallows, returning home to find Uncle Dennis talking to a stranger; she runs upstairs and sees the Little Prince is gone. She hurtles back down to the hall. And this time, she's not too late to catch the bird-snatcher. He's the man with the chilling voice, who leaves behind the musty reek of dead creatures. The man who is shouting in her face.

'That canary never made a fucking sound.'

'You shouldn't have taken it. It was my father's.'

'And about as useless as your father it was too. Best singer in Southwark your uncle told me.'

'You can't bully canaries into singing.'

'Don't tell me what I can and cannot do.' His face is livid;

she has a moment's satisfaction knowing that the bird's refusal to sing has eaten at his soul. He couldn't bring himself to kill it, because that would be a defeat. He wanted to bend the bird to his will, so he gave it to the watchman, and told him to make it sing. 'The bird's good for nothing. Like everything from your family. I had to fix your father and now you've turned out to be as bad as him.'

She spits in his face. Solomon leaps forward, yanks her away. She lunges at the Master, but Solomon holds her back.

'Don't talk about my father like that,' she shrieks.

He wipes his cheek. 'I'll talk about your damned father however I like, you ungrateful little slut.'

'Ungrateful? Why should I be grateful to you?'

'Why should you be grateful to me? Why should you be grateful to the benefactor who helped your wretched family? Why should you be grateful to the person who paid for your schooling?'

Her insides burn with rage and shame. 'You paid for my schooling?'

'Who else?'

'If I'd known what kind of a man you were, I'd have asked you to stop.'

'Oh, you'd rather be on the streets, would you? Working as a whore? Well, if I'd known what you wanted, I could have saved myself a lot of bother and packed you off to a Belgian brothel instead of sending you to school. But I'm a man of my word. I keep my promises. Even the promises I make to feckless Irishmen like your pathetic father.'

'What did you do to my father?' she screams. She feels Solomon's restraining hand on her arm.

'He was a useless pile of shit. Unfortunately, Lynch had

to get rid of one of his fellow cops who saw more than he should have done. Somebody had to take the rap. Lynch was too useful to lose. Gerald Quinn was standing there, as usual, saying yes sir, if that's what you want sir, then doing nothing because he didn't like getting his hands dirty. So I decided it might as well be him. But I promised him that I'd look after his useless family if he pleaded guilty. And that's exactly what I've done.'

He says it as if he believes he is a man of great generosity and kindness.

'"Look after me Birdie," he said.' The Master mocks her father. '"She's got a good head on her, yer know. Give her a good education and she'll repay you." And I took him at his word. I told the matron to make sure you got a decent schooling. I thought I'd give you a chance. A girl, I thought, would do what she's told. A girl would know how to keep her place. A girl would be grateful to be given an opportunity to better herself, even if she was a Quinn. And now look at you – I offer you a helping hand and how do you repay me?'

She can't believe what she is hearing. 'How have I repaid you?'

'By being too full of yourself. Too headstrong. Too arrogant.' He pauses, glances at Solomon. 'And, somewhat stupidly – too friendly with Met detectives.'

She feels Solomon's grip on her arm tighten. 'Don't—' he starts. She is determined to have her answers.

'Did Frank tell you about Solomon?'

The Master tips his head and laughs. 'You overestimate your brother's intelligence. I doubt he worked out you were swanning around with a plain-clothes copper. And if he had, I should imagine that some misplaced notion of tribal loyalty would have stopped him from saying anything.'

She immediately feels a flicker of guilt; she was wrong to have suspected Frank.

'How did you find out?'

The Master smirks and flicks his eyes over Solomon's face and for a moment her heart leaps into her mouth and all the doubts she's ever had about him come tumbling back. Is Solomon on his payroll too? Did he court her then sell the tale to the Master? Has she lost her heart to a cheap fraudster?

'Wolff,' he says.

Her jaw drops. 'Mr Wolff?'

'You're surprised? You were at the banquet, weren't you? He was there.'

Her world is spinning.

'Did you really believe Wolff was being nice to you because he liked you? Thought you were clever? Who do you think told him to keep an eye on you? Who do you think supplied the gifts he gave you?'

She cannot contain a cry of pain. Mr Wolff, her kindly patron, is nothing but the Master's lackey. The fur stole, the tickets to the Great Exhibition, the kindly chats. None of it genuine. She is ashamed, she believed she had succeeded in the counting house on her own merit. And what's more, she was foolish enough to confide in him. She was the eejit who told Mr Wolff about Solomon.

'Why?' she demands. 'Why did you bother?'

'It was part of the bargain.'

'What bargain?'

'The deal I made with your wretched uncle. I saw you the day of your father's hanging, when you returned to the house. That pale skin...' He reaches over, brushes her cheek with his fingers. She is paralysed with disgust. 'Your uncle gave you to me, said you could be my wife. I was hoping for something unblemished. A clean palette on which I could make my mark.'

She stares at him in disbelief. Matron and her ominous words about meeting a man who would beat her black and blue suddenly make dreadful sense.

'Your brother thought he was being clever. He thought he could stop me from having you by marrying you off to his mate. But it really wasn't much effort to fix Collins with some charges and get him out the way.'

The parts of her life she thought were solid are dissolving into mist. Everything is swirling.

'The charges against Patrick...' she starts to say, but he's not interested in her concerns. He's determined to list the injuries she's caused him.

'Of course, I followed Wolff's advice on the best way to proceed. He's always good on these social niceties. It'll look better if you leave it a while, he said, and, anyway, he was keeping an eye on you, protecting my investment. I deferred any marriage plans until I felt I could no longer afford to be seen without a wife. And then, when I told Mr Wolff a few months ago that I needed to move quickly to stop more rumours circulating, he informed me you'd had some dalliance with a Jewish copper.' He swipes his hand furiously in Solomon's direction. 'Which was when I realised I'd have to change my plans because it was pointless marrying you. You're damaged goods—'

'I'm not anybody's goods.'

He reaches for the knife at his belt, whips it from its sheath and grabs her before Solomon has a chance to react, yanking her toward him.

'You were in the contract.' He sticks the sharp point against the skin of her cheek, draws the tip of the knife slowly downwards, twists the blade, places the cold, flat of the steel under her chin, and tilts it so her face is looking up into his. She hardly dares breathe. Sweat trickles down her back as his eyes sweep the length of her body, searching, making calculations in his mind.

'I always get what I am owed.' He lowers the blade and presses its tip against her sternum. 'And it'll give me great pleasure to take it.' Birdie's skin crawls, her vision clouds, her limbs feel dead. She hears Solomon talking, though it sounds as if he's far away.

'Put that knife down.'

'Keep out of this.'

'Hurt her and I'll kill you.'

The Master jeers, 'With what? Your bare...'

The warehouse stairs creak. A shadow of concern flits across the Master's face. The floorboards shudder with the thud of heavy boots ascending. He lets his hand drop and nods to the watchman. 'Over there behind the bales. I'll deal with them later.'

The watchman raises his club. Solomon lifts a protective arm. 'It's all right, we're moving.'

She is numb with fear, but as they pass between the bales of fur she stoops to take the canary's cage; a small source of comfort. They squat on the far side of the warehouse, invisible behind the contraband. The watchman looms over them, though he seems more concerned with the bird than guarding them; he keeps glancing at the cage. He might not have been able to make the Little Prince sing, but it would not have lived this long if he had not cared for it.

She places the cage on the floor and edges forward an inch until she can peer around the bales of skin. The door creaks open again; a flurry of snow is carried in with the blast of cold air.

'Lynch,' the Master says. He sounds surprised.

The Superintendent strides in, flanked by three of his men from Wapping. She recognizes one of them – the gangly cop who helped collect Tobias's corpse.

'What are you doing here?' the Master demands.

'I've been wanting a word with you all evening. I saw you slip away. I've come to collect my dues.'

'It could have waited.'

'I want the money now.'

'Tomorrow.'

'Hand it over.'

'Fuck you.' The Master fiddles with his pocket, produces a handful of coins. Lynch glares.

'That's not enough.'

'Take that or take nothing.'

Lynch is silent for a moment. Then he glances at the men behind him.

'Blackwood,' he says.

In a move that takes the Master by surprise, Blackwood charges at him, knocks the knife from his hand and brings him to the ground with a thud. The Master reacts swiftly; he grasps Blackwood's neck and squeezes.

'Vinge, get over here...'

His henchman doesn't move. He's waiting to see which way the tide is flowing. Loyalty always comes at a price, and death is far too high for Vinge. The Master, though, is not having it.

'Vinge, come here...' He's gasping with the effort of squeezing Blackwood's throat and talking. He's on top of the copper now, pinning him against the floor, one hand pressing his windpipe, the other groping for his knife.

'Vinge, you cunt...'

Vinge makes no move to help; he darts for the warehouse door. Before he has time to reach it, Lynch sticks his hand into his jacket and produces a revolver. It's a six-shooter, Birdie reckons; it looks just like the Colt Hugh pinched from the Crystal Palace. He aims it at Vinge, who freezes like a frightened rabbit, places his hands in the air. 'Don't shoot.'

Lynch squeezes the trigger. Vinge is blasted backwards by the force and slumps against the wooden warehouse wall, blood oozing from his mouth as he falls. Lynch doesn't bother to finish him off; his breath is already rattling.

Birdie looks away and sees the Master's fingers closing on his knife. The blade flashes through the air and Blackwood's throat is cut with one quick and deadly slash. The Master clambers to his feet. Lynch strides to face him. They match each other in height – but Lynch is the meatier. And he has a revolver, though whether the Master realizes it's loaded with five more rounds is another matter.

'What's this about?' the Master demands.

Birdie creeps back behind the bales of furs, squashes close to Solomon. He tips his head behind; the warehouse watchman has vanished. He's taken the canary and left. There must be another exit. Solomon nods again, and this time she sees a door half open, at the back of the warehouse. An escape route. She makes a move, desperate to get away from the Master and his sickening knife.

'What's that noise?' Lynch asks.

'Rats, I should imagine.'

'Leaving the sinking ship?'

Solomon shakes his head at Birdie, indicating it's not the right moment to run; they should wait until they can move without being heard. She sinks back against the skins; the reek of dead animals almost comforting now, creating a wall between her and the feuding men.

'I've had enough of your business,' Lynch says. 'I'm fed up of covering your back.'

'Covering my back?' The Master spits the words. 'I don't need you to cover for me. Who the fuck do you think you are?'

'I'm the chief of the river police.'

'And who put you into that job? I made you.'

'You made me? I don't think so. I made myself. I helped you establish your business on the Thames and now everyone knows you're overstepping the mark.'

'Be careful what you say to me.'

'It's not what I say that should worry you. It's what half the bloody city is saying that matters.'

'And what are people saying?'

'That you're a filthy fucking bastard. Everybody knows about your penchant for little girls. Like that one lying mangled on the floor over there.'

'Since when did you start having moral qualms?'

'Since you started making mistakes. And people started talking.'

'I don't give a shit about the coffee-house gossipers. I can silence anyone who causes trouble.'

'Tobias Skaill?'

'I stopped him talking, didn't I?'

'You? You were lucky Blackwood was the copper Skaill came to tell tales to.'

'Tobias Skaill was a nobody.'

'Vinge managed to turn a nobody into a front page bloody news story. Didn't he notice there was somebody watching him when he dumped the body on the shore?'

'And then I gave the reporter a good line. I used my connections at *The Times*. I turned it to an advantage.' The Master laughs. 'Two birds with one stone. Skaill and another useless Quinn.'

'I don't know why you're laughing, the Quinn widow isn't dead yet. Unless you know something I don't.'

There is a pause. She waits for the Master to reveal her hiding place. Her heart thumps so loudly she's sure Lynch will hear it. The Master says nothing, determined to deal with her himself, she supposes, in his own macabre way.

'Times are changing,' Lynch says. 'You might be able to get away with killing savages in the frozen wastes, but the Yard is all over the Thames. I don't want some blasted Commander on my case. You're a liability.'

'I've got contacts.'

'So have I, and they're offering me more money than you.'

'Well, now we get to the heart of the matter.'

'I'm not pretending otherwise. Your currency has no value around here these days. You can take your fucking tokens. I don't want any more to do with them.'

The coins chink on the floorboards. A solitary token rolls in front of Birdie, topples and lies with its etched pelt face down.

'I'm the master of the river now,' Lynch says.

The Master pitches into him, thrusts his blade at Lynch's jugular. Lynch raises his six-shooter and fires. The Master's eyes stare straight ahead as if he refuses to believe this is happening. A second shot cracks the air. He staggers. His breath rasps as he drops.

'Fucker. Him and his precious skinning trade.' Lynch kicks the bloodied body. 'Clear this place, and quickly,' he commands. 'Take as much of the valuable stuff that will fit in the duty boat and anything else...' He pauses, points at the body of the girl lying on the floor. 'That corpse – dump it in the river. Leave the others.'

There are shuffling and scraping noises as bales of fur are dragged around. Birdie presses close to Solomon for comfort, hardly daring to breathe. The warehouse reeks of gunpowder and death. The wharf door creaks open, bangs. Blasts of wind howl.

One of Lynch's men warns, 'The wind is strengthening. It's a bloody blizzard. It's almost impossible to see what you're doing out there.'

'We'll cut our losses and go. You come with me,' Lynch barks. 'And you, patrol this area. Make sure nobody comes near this place until we're... clear.'

'But Sir, the blizzard—'

'Are you questioning me?'

He fires two shots. The thwack and shudder of a body hitting the floor is followed by a moment's shocked silence as the remaining constable looks at his dead colleague. Birdie, though, is not surprised; Lynch has killed a cop before and Da was hanged for the murder.

'Oi,' Lynch shouts. 'What did I tell you about that lantern?'

'Sorry, Sir.'

Boots clump on floorboards. Light and shadows shift and sway. The door slams and a key turns in the lock. The wooden steps clatter with the weight of Lynch and the constable descending.

There is no sound, apart from the whining wind and a faint ticking. She inhales – gunpowder, flesh, fur and something else catches her throat. She coughs.

Solomon leaps up. 'Smoke.'

Birdie stands and sees the lamp has been tipped on its side. The skins are smouldering. Even as they take in their situation, a finger of flame licks the fur. The wall of bales that was protecting them from Lynch is now a burning barrier blocking their exit. The densely packed, dried-out pelts make ideal kindling. The flames blaze red as they engulf the skins; they've been locked inside a funeral pyre.

'We'll choke before we reach the door and force it open,' Birdie says.

'Then we must find the exit the watchman used.'

They charge to the rear of the warehouse. Already the smoke is thickening. Hands over their mouths, acrid plumes filling their lungs, they reach the door, and find themselves in a darkened hallway. There is only one way to go: a rickety ladder reaches to an opening in the ceiling. Birdie clambers the rungs, hands clutching splintered wood. She hauls herself through the hatch, hears Solomon behind, and stumbles in the darkness, unsure where they are heading. The timbers of the warehouse groan and whine in the heat of the fire below. The wind whips and rages through the narrow street outside, but she can find no way to reach the air. She bangs on the recess of what must be a window.

'The windows are boarded. There's no way out.'

'There must be. The watchman escaped.'

They stop, breathless and confused, the crackle of burning pelts chasing them from below. Smoke twists through the floorboards. The reek of scorched skin is suffocating. In a far corner, flames sear wood. And then, from somewhere in the darkness, Birdie hears the faint trilling of a canary.

'This way.' She edges in the direction of the melody, eyes streaming, lungs tight and painful. She feels Solomon's hand reach for hers; its warmth gives her determination. She has to find the bird. The twittering grows stronger then fades as she fumbles up another ladder. She's about to give up hope when she sees a yellow glint; the bird is sitting on its perch, its feathers gilded by a faint slither of white. She dives for the light – a board covering one window is loose. The watchman must have left the bird by his exit, intending to come back for it later. She shoves the planks, sticks her head outside to breathe, and finds her face whipped by freezing air.

Everything is a blur of whiteness. The snow races in horizontal sheets. She feels Solomon beside her, squeezing his head and shoulders between her body and the frame. He gasps. They laugh, caught for a moment in the magic of the snowstorm, before her laugh becomes a cough and she smells the fire advancing. She grabs the canary's cage, lifts it to the window. The bedraggled Little Prince sits limply on his perch. He's an old bird and the smoke has been too much for him. She opens the cage door, tips him out, and sees a flash of yellow as he falls through the twisting snowflakes. She thinks he must be dead, but she hears the sweetest trill as the Little Prince vanishes in the whiteness.

She drops the cage on the warehouse floor, lifts her leg over the sill, and struggles through the gap. She has no idea how high she is; the blizzard is too thick to see the ground. Solomon is coughing behind her. She edges as far out as she dares, and sees the dark outline of a gallows arm. She stiffens, petrified for a second before she realizes it's a winch, though she has no idea how long the rope is or whether it is securely fastened. The cable is so cold it burns her hands as she grabs it and swings. Hold fast, her hands tell her, though her gut knows sometimes you must let go. She releases her grip and finds herself flying blindly through the snow, the wind howling in her ears. The exhilaration of the release thrills her for a second, until she remembers she has to land.

She thuds and rolls and everything blackens and she cannot breathe. She splutters, lifts her head; her fall has been broken by a soft bed of fresh, loose snow. The rope hangs slack and for an unbearable moment she fears Solomon has been overcome by smoke. And then the rope is pulled and she sees a figure swinging through the falling flakes. He rolls and lies breathless a few feet from her in the snowdrift. He reaches for her hand, touches her fingertips.

She looks back and sees crimson and emerald flames blazing through the falling snow.

'Will it spread?'

'The snow should contain it.'

'What about the wind?'

'It's dropping.'

Solomon is right; the snow is falling vertically in clumps. The wind has eased.

'We can shelter in my cousin's bargehouse,' Solomon says. 'It's not far from here.'

They head east along the river, and the falling snow hides their footprints.

Chapter 25

Gravesend Reach looks better with a covering of snow. The mudflats of Kent and Essex are gleaming white, marked only by the tracks of birds and foxes. The snowfall has defied normal patterns – it was heavier in the city than out here at the mouth of the Thames. Birdie and Solomon sheltered in the bargehouse for a day and waited for the worst of the storm to pass before Solomon's cousin ferried them downstream in one of his covered vessels. Solomon's cousin gave Birdie some of his wife's old clothes to wear. She's back in a dress and a thick woollen cape. Solomon is in his bowler, suit and a borrowed herringbone coat. They stand on the quayside by the steamer's gangplank; it's heading north at noon. Birdie intends to return to Stromness and tell her friends that the Master is dead and they are safe.

'I'm sorry,' he says.

'For what?'

'I was wrong about the river police; it wasn't sheer incompetence. I didn't want to believe that the Met had rot in its core. Though I'm sure Lynch won't give you any more trouble,' he adds. His face isn't quite as confident as his voice.

'I'll report him to my superiors at Scotland Yard, and they'll be keen to deal with him and his mob at Wapping.'

She gazes at the cold black water of the Thames; maybe Solomon is right and the Commanders at Scotland Yard will root Lynch out of his den, but she knows it'll never be completely clean along these shores. Crime and vice are as much part of the river as the fogs that shroud its waters. There'll always be bent coppers, predatory city gents and cut-throat traders here, as well as those, like Fedelm, who perceive it all.

'I was wrong about many things too,' she says.

'Such as?'

'The death of my husband. My brother. Mr Wolff. Deluded, in fact, as Frank would say.'

'Well then, Frank would be wrong. You weren't deluded at all. You were manipulated. That's different.' He gives her a sideways glance. 'You see some things more clearly than most.'

She shrugs. The ship's whistle blows.

She wants to leave quickly, she doesn't want to say goodbye. She puts a foot on the gangplank.

'Sir, sir.'

An emaciated boy is tripping across the quay toward them with a canvas bag slung across his ragged jacket.

'Copy of the *Terrific Register*?' he offers. 'Story of a murderer discovered by a cat?'

'No thanks,' Solomon says.

'Last Friday's copy of *The Times*?'

Solomon shakes his head. Birdie can't help pitying the poor mite – all he has to sell are the papers and shilling shockers that others have abandoned.

'Broadsheet song?'

'I'll take one.' She hands him a penny in exchange for the folded paper and he scampers off across the snow.

The steamer's funnel belches a puff of black smoke.

'Birdie, it was wrong of me not to give you the letter from your husband,' Solomon says.

'It doesn't matter now,' she replies; she wishes to avoid an emotional exchange.

Solomon, though, is determined to speak. 'It was manipulative and you've had too many people trying to deceive you.'

She shakes her head sadly.

'It's not for me to tell you what to do.' Solomon's eyes are wet. 'But Birdie, please remember, your husband is the only person, apart from you and me, who knows that letter exists, and he's officially dead. Anyway, he's not leaving St Petersburg. You could ignore the letter if you wished. In the eyes of the authorities here, you're a widow. And if you returned to London we could...' He's been preparing his words carefully, Birdie senses, though now he falters. He tries again. 'I've always admired your cleverness and your bravery. I've had strong feelings for you ever since...' he smiles, 'ever since I saw you shoot a stuffed elephant in Hyde Park.'

She can't help smiling at the memory too.

'Birdie, I would happily marry you if you told me that's what you wanted. I don't care about...' he waves his hand, 'anything that other people might say or think.'

Her mouth opens; no words emerge. His open declaration of his feelings leaves her too surprised to speak.

'I would quit the Met,' he says, 'if it would make you happier. We don't have to live in London. Maybe it would be better if we went somewhere else; we could live near the sea. Anywhere you want to be, I'll go.'

Her heart feels as if it's been ripped in two. She's spent the last few days tormented by desires, wishing she could stay with Solomon but hardly daring to hope he reciprocated her feelings. Yet now he has said exactly what she longed to hear, she can see more clearly that it doesn't change the fact that she's a married woman. She looks away from his eyes – brimming with sadness rather than their usual fire – and glances down at the broadsheet in her hand; the page is headed with a woodcut of a three-masted ship and below the words of a ballad she recognizes. 'Lady Franklin's Lament'. *And now my burden it gives me pain. For my long-lost Franklin I would cross the main.* She pictures Lady Franklin's haunted face and a tear trickles down her cheek. She stands there for a moment, her damp skin tingling in the freezing cold. She doesn't know what to say or do.

'I'll think about it.'

'Of course. You must do what your heart desires.'

He tips his bowler, turns and walks away.

Chapter 26

Birdie stands at the stern of the clipper in her new blue velvet gown and cape, which she purchased from a local merchant in Stromness. She's been at Narwhal House a week, and would have liked to stay longer, but if she doesn't leave now she'll be unable to reach St Petersburg until the spring. She waves at the small knot of people gathered on the pier. Peter Gibson has sent his apologies. He got his story; Donald Shearer murdered as a result of his involvement in illegal fur trading. And he is now on Papa Westray on the trail of another scoop; Detective Thompson has injured himself with his own shotgun while hunting what was rumoured to be the last great auk in Orkney.

Hope and Grace dance and wave. They have not brought Solly with them, though it's not for want of asking. Margaret told them firmly no; the bird stays in the house – she's already given in to their requests to allow the creature out of its cage to fly free around the parlour. Margaret's also bowed to Morag's advice about the twins; she's spoken to the headmaster, and he has agreed that the girls can join the school in the new year. Margaret waves and wipes her eye. She was reluctant to lose her companion, though she helped to arrange the passage, as Birdie requested. Morag is there too, arms folded, and shaking her head glumly. Birdie told her pressing family concerns meant she had to travel to St Petersburg; Morag said she was an idiot to leave.

The ship's whistle blows, the anchor is weighed, a breeze fills the vast sails and the grey piers and slipways of Stromness recede. Did she really think this safe harbour was a miserable little place the first time she set eyes on it? She waves farewell and walks away across the deck; it makes her too sad to watch her friends disappear. They have their own lives, and she has hers. She has made up her mind and she must see her decision through; she pictures Lady Franklin and tells herself she's doing the right thing. It's her way of making peace with her family; she still feels guilty for having suspected Frank of betraying her when, all along, he was trying to protect her from the Master. She remains overwhelmed by the discovery that her father sacrificed his life for her advancement. Much of her past, it transpires, has been a charade. A manipulation. She was nurtured, coaxed and rewarded by the unseen hand of Hawkes. She was an object of his perverted obsession. Everyone around her was bullied or blackmailed into submission if they refused to collude in his deplorable trade. From now on, there will be no deception. She does not want to live with any more lies. She wants the security of the familiar, not the danger of desire.

She stands at the port rail as the ship sails across Hoy Sound, the red cliffs looming. She removes Patrick's letter from her pocket and her eyes fill with tears. It seemed straightforward when she was in Stromness, but now she is here alone she can feel the pull of her feelings more strongly. She is heading for St Petersburg because her head says it is the right thing to do, yet her heart is telling her to return to London and find Solomon. She reads the letter again, and keeps it gripped in her hand.

She can't pretend her husband is dead, because that would be a lie, and yet, she realizes now, neither can she pretend she is in love with him or is happy to be his wife. For that would be a greater lie. She thinks of her conversations with Margaret about love and regrets, and glances up; a vast bird is flying overhead. Is she seeing things or is it the snowy owl again? She glances around for somebody else to ask; she wants confirmation. A sailor crouches nearby, coiling a rope.

'Excuse me, Sir.'

'Ma'am, how can I help?'

'Do you see that bird?'

He follows her finger. The bird is diving lower, the length of its white wingspan visible.

'Good Lord. It's a snowy owl.'

'That's what I thought.'

'I've seen them in Baffin Bay, but not in these parts before. It must have flown right across the Atlantic.'

The owl veers north and, as it banks, the wind loses some of its cold bite and she thinks of Morag, windseller of Stromness, sitting outside her croft in her britches, puffing on her pipe. Morag doesn't care if folk say she doesn't behave as a woman should. She doesn't care if people think she's a witch. She's comfortable with her power. Birdie watches the white owl recede and is reminded of the snowstorm in London, the pretences and lies falling to the ground around her and, in the middle of the blizzard, the one person who lifted her heart when he appeared. The man who likes her for who she is and has never wanted her to be anything else. As the white of the bird's wings merges with the clouds gathering on the far horizon, she finds her free hand searching for the canary brooch, which she pinned to the bodice of her velvet dress.

She turns to the sailor again. 'One last question, Sir, if you please.'

'Of course, Ma'am.'

'Where does the pilot leave the ship?'

'He'll row himself back to the mainland at Wick. Why do you ask?'

She smiles. 'I was wondering whether I could go ashore with him.'

'You're not heading to St Petersburg then?'

'I've changed my mind,' she says.

She stands at the port rail. They are passing the Old Man of Hoy. She takes the letter, folds it, tears it in half and in half again, throws the pieces into the air. The low winter sun catches the fragments in its rays and they glitter like a trail of golden stars falling from a firework, before they sink to the sea and are carried away by the waves.

Author's Note

A huge thank you to Maddy for her enthusiasm and editorial help. Thank you also to Laura for her invaluable advice, Mark Swan for the lovely cover, and Oli at A.M. Heath for his very much appreciated support and guidance. My daughters, Eva and Rosa, both provided excellent assistance with background historical research. Thanks to Jo and Danny, who gave me useful advice about names. And biggest thanks to Andy for being interested, helpful and encouraging throughout.

This is a work of fiction, but I have drawn on a number of historical records. The wonderful Stromness Museum was a rich source for everyday period detail, and many of the objects in its collections provided me with inspiration, including the lovely toy Inuit kayak and sledge. Morag's croft was inspired by the croft at the Corrigall Farm Museum, where a pair of homemade skates (known locally as *clogs*) can be found.

I also drew on the wealth of records and photographs from the Archive at Orkney Library. In particular, newspaper articles about Dr John Rae's application for Franklin's reward, Detective Thompson, and the near-dead chicken miraculously revived by a swig of whisky were all found in the Archive's record of early editions of *The Orcadian*. The articles about

Dr Rae (November 1854) and Detective Thompson (August 2, 1856) are quoted verbatim, though I have changed the dates of their publication.

There are many accounts of Franklin's expedition and the subsequent search for his ship. *The Arctic Journals of John Rae*, published by Touchwood in 2012, was one of my primary sources; this contains Dr Rae's report to the Admiralty on the fate of Franklin's crew, which was then published in *The Times* on October 23, 1854. It also includes the articles written by Charles Dickens, attempting to rebut Dr Rae's claims, and published in *Household Words* on December 2 and December 9, 1854.

William Kennedy's tin canoe is described in his account of the search for Franklin; *A Short Narrative of the Second Voyage of the Prince Albert, in search of Sir John Franklin*, originally published in 1853, and republished in 2010 by Cambridge University Press.

Bryce Wilson's *Stromness, a history*, published by The Orcadian (Kirkwall Press) in 2013 proved to be an indispensable guide to the town. It includes an account of Isabel Gunn, the inspiration for Morag, who disguised herself as a man and sailed to Rupert's Land with the Hudson's Bay Company.

A number of musicians have recorded versions of the broadside ballad *Lady Franklin's Lament*. My favourite is by Míchaél Ó Domhnaill and Kevin Burke.

Any historical errors are entirely my own.

About the Author

Clare Carson grew up in the suburbs of London. She studied anthropology at university, and lived for a while in villages in Tanzania and Zimbabwe doing ethnographic research. She has worked as an adviser on human rights and international development for nearly twenty years and has written three novels, all published by Head of Zeus. She lives by the sea in Sussex with her partner, two daughters and a couple of very large cats.